THE NOVELS AND TALES OF
HENRY JAMES

New York Edition

VOLUME XVI

The New England Street

THE
AUTHOR OF BELTRAFFIO
THE MIDDLE YEARS
GREVILLE FANE
AND OTHER TALES

BY

HENRY JAMES

NEW YORK
CHARLES SCRIBNER'S SONS
1909

PREFACE

WHAT I had lately and most particularly to say of "The Coxon Fund" is no less true of "The Middle Years," first published in *Scribner's Magazine* (1893) — that recollection mainly and most promptly associates with it the number of times I had to do it over to make sure of it. To get it right was to squeeze my subject into the five or six thousand words I had been invited to make it consist of — it consists, in fact, should the curious care to know, of some 5550 — and I scarce perhaps recall another case, with the exception I shall presently name, in which my struggle to keep compression rich, if not, better still, to keep accretions compressed, betrayed for me such community with the anxious effort of some warden of the insane engaged at a critical moment in making fast a victim's straitjacket. The form of "The Middle Years" is not that of the *nouvelle*, but that of the concise anecdote; whereas the subject treated would perhaps seem one comparatively demanding "developments" — if indeed, amid these mysteries, distinctions were so absolute. (There is of course neither close nor fixed measure of the reach of a development, which in some connexions seems almost superfluous and then in others to represent the whole sense of the matter; and we should doubtless speak more thoroughly by book had we some secret for exactly tracing deflexions and returns.) However this may be, it was as an anecdote, an anecdote only, that I was determined my little situation here should figure; to which end my effort was of course to follow it as much as possible from its outer edge in, rather than from its centre outward. That fond formula, I had alas already discovered, may set as many traps in the garden as its opposite may set in the wood; so that after boilings and reboilings of the contents of my small cauldron, after added

v

pounds of salutary sugar, as numerous as those prescribed in the choicest recipe for the thickest jam, I well remember finding the whole process and act (which, to the exclusion of everything else, dragged itself out for a month) one of the most expensive of its sort in which I had ever engaged.

But I recall, by good luck, no less vividly how much finer a sweetness than any mere spooned-out saccharine dwelt in the fascination of the questions involved. Treating a theme that "gave" much in a form that, at the best, would give little, might indeed represent a peck of troubles; yet who, none the less, beforehand, was to pronounce with authority such and such an idea anecdotic and such and such another developmental? One had, for the vanity of *a priori* wisdom here, only to be so constituted that to see any form of beauty, for a particular application, proscribed or even questioned, was forthwith to covet that form more than any other and to desire the benefit of it exactly there. One had only to be reminded that for the effect of quick roundness the small smooth situation, though as intense as one will, is prudently indicated, and that for a fine compli-cated entangled air nothing will serve that does n't naturally swell and bristle — one had only, I say, to be so warned off or warned on, to see forthwith no beauty for the simple thing that should n't, and even to perversity, enrich it, and none for the other, the comparatively intricate, that should n't press it out as a mosaic. After which fashion the careful craftsman would have prepared himself the special inviting treat of scarce being able to say, at his highest infatuation, before any series, which might be the light thing weighted and which the dense thing clarified. The very attempt so to discriminate leaves him in fact at moments even a little ashamed; whereby let him shirk here frankly certain of the issues presented by the remainder of our company — there being, independently of these mystic matters, other remarks to make. Blankness overtakes me, I confess, in connexion with the brief but concentrated "Greville Fane" — *that* emerges, how concentrated I tried to make it — which must have appeared in a London weekly journal at the

beginning of the " nineties "; but as to which I further re-
tain only a dim warm pleasantness as of old Kensington
summer hours. I re-read, ever so kindly, to the promotion
of a mild aftertaste — that of a certain feverish pressure, in
a cool north room resorted to in heavy London Augusts,
with stray, rare echoes of the town, beyond near roofs and
chimneys, making harmless detonations, and with the perception, over my page, as I felt poor Greville grow, that
her scant record, to be anything at all, would have to be
a minor miracle of foreshortening. For here is exactly an
illustrative case : the subject, in this little composition, is
" developmental " enough, while the form has to make the
anecdotic concession ; and yet who shall say that for the
right effect of a small harmony the fusion has failed ? We
desire doubtless a more detailed notation of the behaviour of
the son and daughter, and yet had I believed the right effect
missed " Greville Fane " would n't have figured here.

Nothing, by the same stroke, could well have been condemned to struggle more for that harmony than " The Abasement of the Northmores " and " The Tree of Knowledge " :
the idea in these examples (1900) being developmental
with a vengeance and the need of an apparent ease and a
general congruity having to enforce none the less — as on
behalf of some victim of the income-tax who would minimise
his " return " — an almost heroic dissimulation of capital.
These things, especially the former, are novels intensely
compressed, and with that character in them yet keeping at
bay, under stress of their failing else to be good short stories,
any air of mutilation. They had had to be good short stories
in order to earn, however precariously, their possible wage
and "appear " — so certain was it that there would be no
appearance, and consequently no wage, for them as frank
and brave *nouvelles*. They could but conceal the fact that
they *were* "nouvelles"; they could but masquerade as little
anecdotes. I include them here by reason of that successful,
that achieved and consummate — as it strikes me — duplicity :
which, however, I may add, was in the event to avail them
little — since they were to find nowhere, the unfortunates,

PREFACE

hospitality and the reward of their effort. It is to " The Tree of Knowledge " I referred just above, I may further mention, as the production that had cost me, for keeping it "down," even a greater number of full revolutions of the merciless screw than " The Middle Years." On behalf also of this member of the group, as well as for " The Author of Beltraffio," I recover exceptionally the sense of the grain of suggestion, the tiny air-blown particle. In presence of a small interesting example of a young artist long dead, and whom I had yet briefly seen and was to remember with kindness, a friend had made, thanks to a still greater personal knowledge of him and of his quasi-conspicuous father, likewise an artist, one of those brief remarks that the dramatist feels as fertilising. " And then," the lady I quote had said in allusion to certain troubled first steps of the young man's career, to complications of consciousness that had made his early death perhaps less strange and less lamentable, even though superficially more tragic ; " and then he had found his father out, artistically : having grown up in so happy a personal relation with him only to feel, at last, quite awfully, that he did n't and could n't believe in him." That fell on one's ear of course only to prompt the inward cry : " How can there possibly *not* be all sorts of good things in it ? " Just so for " The Author of Beltraffio " — long before this and some time before the first appearance of the tale in *The English Illustrated Magazine* (1884): it had been said to me of an eminent author, these several years dead and on some of the embarrassments of whose life and character a common friend was enlarging : "Add to them all, moreover, that his wife objects intensely to what he writes. She can't bear it (as you can for that matter rather easily conceive) and that naturally creates a tension — ! " *There* had come the air-blown grain which, lodged in a handful of kindly earth, was to produce the story of Mark Ambient.

Elliptic, I allow, and much of a skipping of stages, so bare an account of such performances ; yet with the constitutive process for each idea quite sufficiently noted by my having had, always, only to say to myself sharply enough :

PREFACE

" Dramatise it, dramatise it!" That answered, in the connexion, always, all my questions — that provided for all my
" fun." The two tales I have named but represent therefore
their respective grains of seed dramatically handled. In the
case of " Broken Wings " (1900), however, I but see to-
day the produced result — I fail to disinter again the buried
germ. Little matters it, no doubt, that I recall as operative
here the brush of no winged word; for when had I been, as
a fellow scribbler, closed to the general admonition of such
adventures as poor Mrs. Harvey's, the elegant representative
of literature at Mundham ? — to such predicaments as Stuart Straith's, gallant victim of the same hospitality and with
the same confirmed ache beneath his white waistcoat? The
appeal of mature purveyors obliged, in the very interest of
their presumed, their marketable, freshness, to dissimulate
the grim realities of shrunken " custom," the felt chill of a
lower professional temperature — any old note-book would
show *that* laid away as a tragic " value " not much less
tenderly than some small plucked flower of association left
between the leaves for pressing. What had happened here,
visibly, was that the value had had to wait long to become
active. " Dramatise, dramatise, dramatise ! " had been just
there more of an easy admonition than of a ready feat;
the case for dramatisation was somehow not whole. Under
some forgotten touch, however, at its right hour, it was to
round itself. What the single situation lacked the *pair* of
situations would supply — there was drama enough, with
economy, from the moment sad companions, looking each
other, with their identities of pluck and despair, a little hard
in the face, should confess each to the other, relievingly,
what they kept from every one else. With the right encounter and the right surprise, that is with the right persons,
postulated, the relief, if in the right degree exquisite, might
be the drama — and the right persons, in fine, to make it exquisite, were Stuart Straith and Mrs. Harvey. There remains
" The Great Good Place " (1900) — to the spirit of which,
however, it strikes me, any gloss or comment would be a
tactless challenge. It embodies a calculated effect, and to

PREFACE

plunge into it, I find, even for a beguiled glance — a course I indeed recommend — is to have left all else outside. There then my indications must wait.

The origin of "Paste" is rather more expressible, since it was to consist but of the ingenious thought of transposing the terms of one of Guy de Maupassant's admirable *contes*. In "La Parure" a poor young woman, under "social" stress, the need of making an appearance on an important occasion, borrows from an old school friend, now much richer than herself, a pearl necklace which she has the appalling misfortune to lose by some mischance never afterwards cleared up. Her life and her pride, as well as her husband's with them, become subject, from the hour of the awful accident, to the redemption of their debt; which, effort by effort, sacrifice by sacrifice, franc by franc, with specious pretexts, excuses, a rage of desperate explanation of their failure to restore the missing object, they finally obliterate — all to find that their whole consciousness and life have been convulsed and deformed in vain, that the pearls were but highly artful "imitation" and that their passionate penance has ruined them for nothing. It seemed harmless sport simply to turn that situation round — to shift, in other words, the ground of the horrid mistake, making this a matter not of a false treasure supposed to be true and precious, but of a real treasure supposed to be false and hollow : though a new little "drama," a new setting for *my* pearls — and as different as possible from the other — had of course withal to be found.

"Europe," which is of 1899, when it appeared in *Scribner's Magazine*, conspicuously fails, on the other hand, to disown its parentage; so distinct has its "genesis" remained to me. I had preserved for long years an impression of an early time, a visit, in a sedate American city — for there *were* such cities then — to an ancient lady whose talk, whose allusions and relics and spoils and mementoes and credentials, so to call them, bore upon a triumphant sojourn in Europe, long years before, in the hey-day of the high scholarly reputation of her husband, a dim displaced superseded celebrity at the time of my own observation. They

PREFACE

had been " much made of," he and she, at various foreign centres of polite learning, and above all in the England of early Victorian days; and my hostess had lived ever since on the name and fame of it; a treasure of legend and anecdote laid up against the comparatively lean half-century, or whatever, that was to follow. For myself even, after this, a good slice of such a period had elapsed; yet with my continuing to believe that fond memory would still somehow be justified of this scrap too, along with so many others: the unextinguished sense of the temperature of the January morning on which the little Sunday breakfast-party, at half-past nine across the snow, had met to the music of a chilly ghostly kindly tinkle; that of the roomful of cherished echoes and of framed and glazed, presented and autographed and thumb-marked mementoes — the wealth of which was somehow explained (this was part of the legend) by the ancient, the at last almost prehistoric, glory of like matutinal hours, type and model of the emulous shrunken actual.

The justification I awaited, however, only came much later, on my catching some tender mention of certain admirable ladies, sisters and spinsters under the maternal roof, for whom the century was ebbing without remedy brought to their eminent misfortune (such a ground of sympathy always in the " good old " American days when the touching case was still possible) of not having "been to Europe." Exceptionally prepared by culture for going, they yet could n't leave their immemorial mother, the headspring, precisely, of that grace in them, who on the occasion of each proposed start announced her approaching end — only to postpone it again after the plan was dished and the flight relinquished. So the century ebbed, and so Europe altered — for the worse — and so perhaps even a little did the sisters who sat in bondage; only so did n't at all the immemorial, the inextinguishable, the eternal mother. Striking to the last degree, I thought, that obscure, or at least that muffled, tragedy, which had the further interest of giving me on the spot a setting for my own so long uninserted gem and of enabling me to bring out with maximum confidence my in-

xi

PREFACE

veterate "Dramatise!" "Make this *one* with such projection as you are free to permit yourself of the brooding parent in the other case," I duly remarked, " and the whole thing falls together; the paradise the good sisters are apparently never to attain becoming by this conversion just the social cake on which they have always been fed and that has so notoriously opened their appetite." Or something of that sort. I recognise that I so but express here the "plot" of my tale as it stands; except for so far as my formula, " something of that sort," was to make the case bristle with as many vivid values, with as thick and yet as clear a little complexity of interest, as possible. The merit of the thing is in the feat, once more, of the transfusion; the receptacle (of form) being so exiguous, the brevity imposed so great. I undertook the brevity, so often undertaken on a like scale before, and again arrived at it by the innumerable repeated chemical reductions and condensations that tend to make of the very short story, as I risk again noting, one of the costliest, even if, like the hard, shining sonnet, one of the most indestructible, forms of composition in general use. I accepted the rigour of its having, all sternly, in this case, to treat so many of its most appealing values as waste; and I now seek my comfort perforce in the mere exhibited result, the union of whatever fulness with whatever clearness.

HENRY JAMES.

CONTENTS

THE AUTHOR OF BELTRAFFIO

THE
AUTHOR OF BELTRAFFIO

I

Much as I wished to see him I had kept my letter of introduction three weeks in my pocket-book. I was nervous and timid about meeting him — conscious of youth and ignorance, convinced that he was tormented by strangers, and especially by my country-people, and not exempt from the suspicion that he had the irritability as well as the dignity of genius. Moreover, the pleasure, if it should occur — for I could scarcely believe it was near at hand — would be so great that I wished to think of it in advance, to feel it there against my breast, not to mix it with satisfactions more superficial and usual. In the little game of new sensations that I was playing with my ingenuous mind I wished to keep my visit to the author of " Beltraffio " as a trump-card. It was three years after the publication of that fascinating work, which I had read over five times and which now, with my riper judgement, I admire on the whole as much as ever. This will give you about the date of my first visit — of any duration — to England; for you will not have forgotten the commotion, I may even say the scandal, produced by Mark Ambient's masterpiece. It was the most complete presentation

3

that had yet been made of the gospel of art; it was a kind of æsthetic war-cry. People had endeavoured to sail nearer to "truth" in the cut of their sleeves and the shape of their sideboards; but there had not as yet been, among English novels, such an example of beauty of execution and "intimate" importance of theme. Nothing had been done in that line from the point of view of art for art. That served me as a fond formula, I may mention, when I was twenty-five; how much it still serves I won't take upon myself to say — especially as the discerning reader will be able to judge for himself. I had been in England, briefly, a twelve-month before the time to which I began by alluding, and had then learned that Mr. Ambient was in distant lands — was making a considerable tour in the East; so that there was nothing to do but to keep my letter till I should be in London again. It was of little use to me to hear that his wife had not left England and was, with her little boy, their only child, spending the period of her husband's absence — a good many months — at a small place they had down in Surrey. They had a house in London, but actually in the occupation of other persons. All this I had picked up, and also that Mrs. Ambient was charming — my friend the American poet, from whom I had my intro-duction, had never seen her, his relations with the great man confined to the exchange of letters; but she was n't, after all, though she had lived so near the rose, the author of "Beltraffio," and I did n't go down into Surrey to call on her. I went to the Con-tinent, spent the following winter in Italy and re-turned to London in May. My visit to Italy had opened my eyes to a good many things, but to nothing more than the beauty of certain pages in the works of Mark Ambient. I carried his productions about in my trunk — they are not, as you know, very numerous, but he had preluded to "Beltraffio" by some exquisite things — and I used to read them over in the evening at the inn. I used profoundly to reason that the man who drew those characters and wrote that style understood what he saw and knew what he was doing. This is my sole ground for mentioning my winter in Italy. He had been there much in former years — he was saturated with what painters call the "feeling" of that classic land. He expressed the charm of the old hill-cities of Tuscany, the look of certain lonely grass-grown places which, in the past, had echoed with life; he understood the great artists, he understood the spirit of the Renaissance; he understood everything. The scene of one of his earlier novels was laid in Rome, the scene of another in Florence, and I had moved through these cities in company with the figures he set so firmly on their feet. This is why I was now so much happier even than before in the prospect of making his acquaintance.

At last, when I had dallied with my privilege long enough, I dispatched to him the missive of the American poet. He had already gone out of town; he shrank from the rigour of the London "season," and it was his habit to migrate on the first of June. Moreover I had heard he was this year hard at work on a new book, into which some of his impressions of the East were to be wrought, so that he desired nothing so much as quiet days. That knowledge,' however, did n't prevent me — *cet âge est sans pitié* — from sending with my friend's letter a note of my own, in which I asked his leave to come down and see him for an hour or two on some day to be named by himself. My proposal was accompanied with a very frank expression of my sentiments, and the effect of the entire appeal was to elicit from the great man the kindest possible invitation. He would be delighted to see me, especially if I should turn up on the following Saturday and would remain till the Monday morning. We would take a walk over the Surrey commons, and I could tell him all about the other great man, the one in America. He indicated to me the best train, and it may be imagined whether on the Saturday afternoon I was punctual at Waterloo. He carried his benevolence to the point of coming to meet me at the little station at which I was to alight, and my heart beat very fast as I saw his handsome face, surmounted with a soft wide-awake and which I knew by a photograph long since enshrined on my mantel-shelf, scanning the carriage-windows as the train rolled up. He recognised me as infallibly as I had recognised himself; he appeared to know by instinct how a young American of critical pretensions, rash youth, would look when much divided between eagerness and modesty. He took me by the hand and smiled at me and said: "You must be — a — *you*, I think!" and asked if I should mind going on foot to his house, which would take but a few minutes. I remember feeling it a piece of extraordinary affability that he should give directions about the conveyance of my bag; I remember feeling altogether very happy and rosy, in fact quite transported, when he laid his hand on my shoulder as we came out of the station.

I surveyed him, askance, as we walked together; I had already, I had indeed instantly, seen him as all delightful. His face is so well known that I need n't describe it; he looked to me at once an English gentleman and a man of genius, and I thought that a happy combination. There was a brush of the Bohemian in his fineness; you would easily have guessed his belonging to the artist guild. He was addicted to velvet jackets, to cigarettes, to loose shirt-collars, to looking a little dishevelled. His features, which were firm but not perfectly regular, are fairly enough represented in his portraits; but no portrait I have seen gives any idea of his expression. There were innumerable things in it, and they chased each other in and out of his face. I have seen people who were grave and gay in quick alternation; but Mark Ambient was grave and gay at one and the same moment. There were other strange oppositions and contradictions in his slightly faded and fatigued countenance. He affected me somehow as at once fresh and stale, at once anxious and indifferent. He had evidently had an active past, which inspired one with curiosity; yet what was that compared to his obvious future? He was just enough above middle height to be spoken of as tall, and rather lean and long in the flank. He had the friendliest frankest manner possible, and yet I could see it cost him something. It cost him small spasms of the self-consciousness that is an Englishman's last and dearest treasure — the thing he pays his way through life by sacrificing small pieces of even as the gallant but moneyless adventurer in "Quentin Durward" broke off links of his brave gold chain. He had been thirty-eight years old at the time "Beltraffio" was published. He asked me about his friend in America, about the length of my stay in England, about the last news in London and the people I had seen there; and I remember looking for the signs of genius in the very form of his questions and thinking I found it. I liked his voice as if I were somehow myself having the use of it.

There was genius in his house too I thought when we got there; there was imagination in the carpets and curtains, in the pictures and books, in the garden behind it, where certain old brown walls were muffled in creepers that appeared to me to have been copied from a masterpiece of one of the pre-Raphaelites. That was the way many things struck me at that time, in England — as reproductions of something that existed primarily in art or literature. It was not the picture, the poem, the fictive page, that seemed to me a copy; these things were the originals, and the life of happy and distinguished people was fashioned in their image. Mark Ambient called his house a cottage, and I saw afterwards he was right; for if it had n't been a cottage it must have been a villa, and a villa, in England at least, was not a place in which one could fancy him at home. But it was, to my vision, a cottage glorified and translated; it was a palace of art, on a slightly reduced scale — and might besides have been the dearest haunt of the old English *genius loci*. It nestled under a cluster

of magnificent beeches, it had little creaking lattices
that opened out of, or into, pendent mats of ivy, and
gables, and old red tiles, as well as a general aspect
of being painted in water-colours and inhabited by
people whose lives would go on in chapters and volumes. The lawn seemed to me of extraordinary extent, the garden-walls of incalculable height, the
whole air of the place delightfully still, private, proper
to itself. "My wife must be somewhere about,"
Mark Ambient said as we went in. "We shall find
her perhaps — we've about an hour before dinner.
She may be in the garden. I'll show you my little
place."

We passed through the house and into the grounds,
as I should have called them, which extended into
the rear. They covered scarce three or four acres, but,
like the house, were very old and crooked and full
of traces of long habitation, with inequalities of level
and little flights of steps — mossy and cracked were
these — which connected the different parts with
each other. The limits of the place, cleverly dissimu-
lated, were muffled in the great verdurous screens.
They formed, as I remember, a thick loose curtain
at the further end, in one of the folds of which, as it
were, we presently made out from afar a little group.
"Ah there she is!" said Mark Ambient; "and she
has got the boy." He noted that last fact in a slightly
different tone from any in which he yet had spoken.
I was n't fully aware of this at the time, but it lingered
in my ear and I afterwards understood it.

"Is it your son?" I enquired, feeling the question
not to be brilliant.

"Yes, my only child. He's always in his mother's pocket. She coddles him too much." It came back to me afterwards too — the sound of these critical words. They were n't petulant; they expressed rather a sudden coldness, a mechanical submission. We went a few steps further, and then he stopped short and called the boy, beckoning to him repeatedly.

"Dolcino, come and see your daddy!" There was something in the way he stood still and waited that made me think he did it for a purpose. Mrs. Ambient had her arm round the child's waist, and he was leaning against her knee; but though he moved at his father's call she gave no sign of releasing him. A lady, apparently a neighbour, was seated near her, and before them was a garden-table on which a tea-service had been placed.

Mark Ambient called again, and Dolcino struggled in the maternal embrace; but, too tightly held, he after two or three fruitless efforts jerked about and buried his head deep in his mother's lap. There was a certain awkwardness in the scene; I thought it odd Mrs. Ambient should pay so little attention to her husband. But I would n't for the world have betrayed my thought and, to conceal it, I began loudly to rejoice in the prospect of our having tea in the garden. "Ah she won't let him come!" said my host with a sigh; and we went our way till we reached the two ladies. He mentioned my name to his wife, and I noticed that he addressed her as "My dear," very genially, without a trace of resentment at her detention of the child. The quickness of the transition made me vaguely ask myself if he were perchance henpecked — a shocking surmise which I instantly dismissed. Mrs. Ambient was quite such a wife as I should have expected him to have; slim and fair, with a long neck and pretty eyes and an air of good breeding. She shone with a certain coldness and practised in intercourse a certain bland detachment, but she was clothed in gentleness as in one of those vaporous redundant scarves that muffle the heroines of Gainsborough and Romney. She had also a vague air of race, justified by my afterwards learning that she was "connected with the aristocracy." I have seen poets married to women of whom it was difficult to conceive that they should gratify the poetic fancy — women with dull faces and glutinous minds, who were none the less, however, excellent wives. But there was no obvious disparity in Mark Ambient's union. My hostess — so far as she could be called so — delicate and quiet, in a white dress, with her beautiful child at her side, was worthy of the author of a work so distinguished as "Beltraffio." Round her neck she wore a black velvet ribbon, of which the long ends, tied behind, hung down her back, and to which, in front, was attached a miniature portrait of her little boy. Her smooth shining hair was confined in a net. She gave me an adequate greeting and Dolcino — I thought this small name of endearment delightful — took advantage of her getting up to slip away from her and go to his father, who seized him in silence and held him high for a long moment, kissing him several times.

I had lost no time in observing that the child, not more than seven years old, was extraordinarily beautiful. He had the face of an angel — the eyes, the hair, the smile of innocence, the more than mortal bloom. There was something that deeply touched, that almost alarmed, in his beauty, composed, one would have said, of elements too fine and pure for the breath of this world. When I spoke to him and he came and held out his hand and smiled at me I felt a sudden strange pity for him — quite as if he had been an orphan or a changeling or stamped with some social stigma. It was impossible to be in fact more exempt from these misfortunes, and yet, as one kissed him, it was hard to keep from murmuring all tenderly "Poor little devil!" though why one should have applied this epithet to a living cherub is more than I can say. Afterwards indeed I knew a trifle better; I grasped the truth of his being too fair to live, wondering at the same time that his parents should n't have guessed it and have been in proportionate grief and despair. For myself I had no doubt of his evanescence, having already more than once caught in the fact the particular infant charm that 's as good as a death-warrant.

The lady who had been sitting with Mrs. Ambient was a jolly ruddy personage in velveteen and limp feathers, whom I guessed to be the vicar's wife — our hostess did n't introduce me — and who immediately began to talk to Ambient about chrysanthemums. This was a safe subject, and yet there was a certain surprise for me in seeing the author of "Beltraffio" even in such superficial communion with the Church of England. His writings implied so much detachment from that institution, expressed a view of life so profane, as it were, so independent and so little likely in general to be thought edifying, that I should have expected to find him an object of horror to vicars and their ladies — of horror repaid on his own part by any amount of effortless derision. This proved how little I knew as yet of the English people and their extraordinary talent for keeping up their forms, as well as of some of the mysteries of Mark Ambient's hearth and home. I found afterwards that he had, in his study, between nervous laughs and free cigar-puffs, some wonderful comparisons for his clerical neighbours; but meanwhile the chrysanthemums were a source of harmony, as he and the vicaress were equally attached to them, and I was surprised at the knowledge they exhibited of this interesting plant. The lady's visit, however, had presumably been long, and she presently rose for departure and kissed Mrs. Ambient. Mark started to walk with her to the gate of the grounds, holding Dolcino by the hand.

"Stay with me, darling," Mrs. Ambient said to the boy, who had surrendered himself to his father.

Mark paid no attention to the summons, but Dolcino turned and looked at her in shy appeal. "Can't I go with papa?"

"Not when I ask you to stay with me."

"But please don't ask me, mamma," said the child in his small clear new voice.

"I must ask you when I want you. Come to me, dearest." And Mrs. Ambient, who had seated herself again, held out her long slender slightly too osseous hands.

Her husband stopped, his back turned to her, but without releasing the child. He was still talking to the vicaress, but this good lady, I think, had lost the thread of her attention. She looked at Mrs. Ambient and at Dolcino, and then looked at me, smiling in a highly amused cheerful manner and almost to a grimace.

"Papa," said the child, "mamma wants me not to go with you."

"He's very tired — he has run about all day. He ought to be quiet till he goes to bed. Otherwise he won't sleep." These declarations fell successively and very distinctly from Mrs. Ambient's lips.

Her husband, still without turning round, bent over the boy and looked at him in silence. The vicaress gave a genial irrelevant laugh and observed that he was a precious little pet. "Let him choose," said Mark Ambient. "My dear little boy, will you go with me or will you stay with your mother?"

"Oh it's a shame!" cried the vicar's lady with increased hilarity.

"Papa, I don't think I can choose," the child answered, making his voice very low and confidential. "But I've been a great deal with mamma to-day," he then added.

"And very little with papa! My dear fellow, I think you *have* chosen!" On which Mark Ambient walked off with his son, accompanied by re-echoing but inarticulate comments from my fellow visitor.

His wife had seated herself again, and her fixed eyes, bent on the ground, expressed for a few moments so much mute agitation that anything I could think of to say would be but a false note. Yet she none the less quickly recovered herself, to express the sufficiently civil hope that I did n't mind having had to walk from the station. I reassured her on this point, and she went on : "We've got a thing that might have gone for you, but my husband would n't order it." After which and another longish pause, broken only by my plea that the pleasure of a walk with our friend would have been quite what I would have chosen, she found for reply : "I believe the Americans walk very little."

"Yes, we always run," I laughingly allowed.

She looked at me seriously, yet with an absence in her pretty eyes. "I suppose your distances are so great."

"Yes, but we break our marches! I can't tell you the pleasure to me of finding myself here," I added. "I've the greatest admiration for Mr. Ambient."

"He'll like that. He likes being admired."

"He must have a very happy life then. He has many worshippers."

"Oh yes, I've seen some of them," she dropped, looking away, very far from me, rather as if such a vision were before her at the moment. It seemed to indicate, her tone, that the sight was scarcely edifying, and I guessed her quickly enough to be in no great intellectual sympathy with the author of "Beltraffio." I thought the fact strange, but somehow, in the glow of my own enthusiasm, did n't think it important : it only made me wish rather to emphasise that homage.

"For me, you know," I returned — doubtless with

a due *suffisance* — "he's quite the greatest of living writers."

"Of course I can't judge. Of course he's very clever," she said with a patient cheer.

"He's nothing less than supreme, Mrs. Ambient! There are pages in each of his books of a perfection classing them with the greatest things. Accordingly for me to see him in this familiar way, in his habit as he lives, and apparently to find the man as delightful as the artist — well, I can't tell you how much too good to be true it seems and how great a privilege I think it." I knew I was gushing, but I couldn't help it, and what I said was a good deal less than what I felt. I was by no means sure I should dare to say even so much as this to the master himself, and there was a kind of rapture in speaking it out to his wife which was not affected by the fact that, as a wife, she appeared peculiar. She listened to me with her face grave again and her lips a little compressed, listened as if in no doubt, of course, that her husband was remarkable, but as if at the same time she had heard it frequently enough and couldn't treat it as stirring news. There was even in her manner a suggestion that I was so young as to expose myself to being called forward — an imputation and a word I had always loathed; as well as a hinted reminder that people usually got over their early extravagance. "I assure you that for me this is a red-letter day," I added.

She didn't take this up, but after a pause, looking round her, said abruptly and a trifle dryly: "We're very much afraid about the fruit this year."

My eyes wandered to the mossy mottled garden-walls, where plum-trees and pears, flattened and fastened upon the rusty bricks, looked like crucified figures with many arms. "Does n't it promise well?"

"No, the trees look very dull. We had such late frosts."

Then there was another pause. She addressed her attention to the opposite end of the grounds, kept it for her husband's return with the child. "Is Mr. Ambient fond of gardening?" it occurred to me to ask, irresistibly impelled as I felt myself, moreover, to bring the conversation constantly back to him.

"He's very fond of plums," said his wife.

"Ah well then I hope your crop will be better than you fear. It's a lovely old place," I continued. "The whole impression's that of certain places he has described. Your house is like one of his pictures."

She seemed a bit frigidly amused at my glow. "It's a pleasant little place. There are hundreds like it."

"Oh it has his *tone*," I laughed, but sounding my epithet and insisting on my point the more sharply that my companion appeared to see in my appreciation of her simple establishment a mark of mean experience.

It was clear I insisted too much. "His tone?" she repeated with a harder look at me and a slightly heightened colour.

"Surely he has a tone, Mrs. Ambient."

"Oh yes, he has indeed! But I don't in the least consider that I'm living in one of his books at all. I should n't care for that in the least," she went on with a smile that had in some degree the effect of converting her really sharp protest into an insincere joke. "I'm afraid I'm not very literary. And I'm not artistic," she stated.

"I'm very sure you're not ignorant, not stupid," I ventured to reply, with the accompaniment of feeling immediately afterwards that I had been both familiar and patronising. My only consolation was in the sense that she had begun it, had fairly dragged me into it. She had thrust forward her limitations.

"Well, whatever I am I'm very different from my husband. If you like him you won't like me. You needn't say anything. Your liking me isn't in the least necessary!"

"Don't defy me!" I could but honourably make answer.

She looked as if she hadn't heard me, which was the best thing she could do; and we sat some time without further speech. Mrs. Ambient had evidently the enviable English quality of being able to be mute without unrest. But at last she spoke — she asked me if there seemed many people in town. I gave her what satisfaction I could on this point, and we talked a little of London and of some of its characteristics at that time of the year. At the end of this I came back irrepressibly to Mark.

"Doesn't he like to be there now? I suppose he doesn't find the proper quiet for his work. I should think his things had been written for the most part in a very still place. They suggest a great stillness following on a kind of tumult. Don't you think so?" I laboured on. "I suppose London's a tremendous place to collect impressions, but a refuge like this, in the country, must be better for working them up. Does he get many of his impressions in London, should you say?" I proceeded from point to point in this malign enquiry simply because my hostess, who probably thought me an odious chattering person, gave me time; for when I paused — I've not represented my pauses — she simply continued to let her eyes wander while her long fair fingers played with the medallion on her neck. When I stopped altogether, however, she was obliged to say something, and what she said was that she had n't the least idea where her husband got his impressions. This made me think her, for a moment, positively disagreeable; delicate and proper and rather aristocratically fine as she sat there. But I must either have lost that view a moment later or been goaded by it to further aggression, for I remember asking her if our great man were in a good vein of work and when we might look for the appearance of the book on which he was engaged. I've every reason now to know that she found me insufferable.

She gave a strange small laugh as she said: "I'm afraid you think I know much more about my husband's work than I do. I have n't the least idea what he's doing," she then added in a slightly different, that is a more explanatory, tone and as if from a glimpse of the enormity of her confession. "I don't read what he writes."

She did n't succeed, and would n't even had she tried much harder, in making this seem to me anything less than monstrous. I stared at her and I think

I blushed. "Don't you admire his genius? Don't you admire 'Beltraffio'?

She waited, and I wondered what she could possibly say. She did n't speak, I could see, the first words that rose to her lips; she repeated what she had said a few minutes before. "Oh of course he 's very clever!" And with this she got up; our two absentees had reappeared.

II

Mrs. Ambient left me and went to meet them; she stopped and had a few words with her husband that I didn't hear and that ended in her taking the child by the hand and returning with him to the house. Her husband joined me in a moment, looking, I thought, the least bit conscious and constrained, and said that if I would come in with him he would show me my room. In looking back upon these first moments of my visit I find it important to avoid the error of appearing to have at all fully measured his situation from the first or made out the signs of things mastered only afterwards. This later knowledge throws a backward light and makes me forget that, at least on the occasion of my present reference — I mean that first afternoon — Mark Ambient struck me as only enviable. Allowing for this he must yet have failed of much expression as we walked back to the house, though I remember well the answer he made to a remark of mine on his small son.

"That's an extraordinary little boy of yours. I've never seen such a child."

"Why," he asked while we went, "do you call him extraordinary?"

"He's so beautiful, so fascinating. He's like some perfect little work of art."

He turned quickly in the passage, grasping my arm. "Oh don't call him that, or you'll — you'll —!"

But in his hesitation he broke off suddenly, laughing at my surprise. Immediately afterwards, however, he added: "You'll make his little future very difficult."

I declared that I wouldn't for the world take any liberties with his little future — it seemed to me to hang by threads of such delicacy. I should only be highly interested in watching it.

"You Americans are very keen," he commented on this. "You notice more things than we do."

"Ah if you want visitors who aren't struck with you," I cried, "you shouldn't have asked me down here!"

He showed me my room, a little bower of chintz, with open windows where the light was green, and before he left me said irrelevantly: "As for my small son, you know, we shall probably kill him between us before we've done with him!" And he made this assertion as if he really believed it, without any appearance of jest, his fine near-sighted expressive eyes looking straight into mine.

"Do you mean by spoiling him?"

"No, by fighting for him!"

"You had better give him to me to keep for you," I said. "Let me remove the apple of discord!"

It was my extravagance of course, but he had the air of being perfectly serious. "It would be quite the best thing we could do. I should be all ready to do it."

"I'm greatly obliged to you for your confidence."

But he lingered with his hands in his pockets. I felt as if within a few moments I had, morally speaking, taken several steps nearer to him. He looked weary, just as he faced me then, looked preoccupied and as if there were something one might do for him. I was terribly conscious of the limits of my young ability, but I wondered what such a service might be, feeling at bottom nevertheless that the only thing I could do for him was to like him. I suppose he guessed this and was grateful for what was in my mind, since he went on presently: "I have n't the advantage of being an American, but I also notice a little, and I 've an idea that" — here he smiled and laid his hand on my shoulder — "even counting out your nationality you 're not destitute of intelligence. I 've only known you half an hour, but —!" For which again he pulled up. "You 're very young after all."

"But you may treat me as if I could understand you!" I said; and before he left me to dress for dinner he had virtually given me a promise that he would.

When I went down into the drawing-room — I was very punctual — I found that neither my hostess nor my host had appeared. A lady rose from a sofa, however, and inclined her head as I rather surprisedly gazed at her. "I dare say you don't know me," she said with the modern laugh. "I 'm Mark Ambient's sister." Whereupon I shook hands with her, saluting her very low. Her laugh was modern — by which I mean that it consisted of the vocal agitation serving between people who meet in drawing-rooms as the solvent of social disparities, the medium of transitions; but her appearance was — what shall I call it ? — mediæval. She was pale and angular, her long thin face was inhabited by sad dark eyes and her black hair intertwined with golden fillets and curious clasps. She wore a faded velvet robe which clung to her when she moved and was "cut," as to the neck and sleeves, like the garments of old Italians. She suggested a symbolic picture, something akin even to Dürer's Melancholia, and was so perfect an image of a type which I, in my ignorance, supposed to be extinct, that while she rose before me I was almost as much startled as if I had seen a ghost. I afterwards concluded that Miss Ambient was n't incapable of deriving pleasure from this weird effect, and I now believe that reflexion concerned in her having sunk again to her seat with her long lean but not ungraceful arms locked together in an archaic manner on her knees and her mournful eyes addressing me a message of intentness which foreshadowed what I was subsequently to suffer. She was a singular fatuous artificial creature, and I was never more than half to penetrate her motives and mysteries. Of one thing I'm sure at least: that they were considerably less insuperable than her appearance announced. Miss Ambient was a restless romantic disappointed spinster, consumed with the love of Michael-Angel-esque attitudes and mystical robes; but I'm now convinced she had n't in her nature those depths of unutterable thought which, when you first knew her, seemed to look out from her eyes and to prompt her complicated gestures. Those features in especial had a misleading eloquence; they lingered on you with a far-off dimness, an air of obstructed sympathy, which was certainly not always a key to the spirit of their owner; so that, of a truth, a young lady could scarce have been so dejected and disillusioned without having committed a crime for which she was consumed with remorse, or having parted with a hope that she could n't sanely have entertained. She had, I believe, the usual allowance of rather vain motives : she wished to be looked at, she wished to be married, she wished to be thought original.

It costs me a pang to speak in this irreverent manner of one of Ambient's name, but I shall have still less gracious things to say before I 've finished my anecdote, and moreover — I confess it — I owe the young lady a bit of a grudge. Putting aside the curious cast of her face she had no natural aptitude for an artistic development, had little real intelligence. But her affectations rubbed off on her brother's renown, and as there were plenty of people who darkly disapproved of him they could easily point to his sister as a person formed by his influence. It was quite possible to regard her as a warning, and she had almost compromised him with the world at large. He was the original and she the inevitable imitation. I suppose him scarce aware of the impression she mainly produced, beyond having a general idea that she made up very well as a Rossetti; he was used to her and was sorry for her, wishing she would marry and observing how she did n't. Doubtless I take her too seriously, for she did me no harm, though I 'm bound to allow that I can only half-account for her. She was n't so mystical as she looked, but was a strange indirect uncomfortable embarrassing woman.

25

My story gives the reader at best so very small a knot to untie that I need n't hope to excite his curiosity by delaying to remark that Mrs. Ambient hated her sister-in-law. This I learned but later on, when other matters came to my knowledge. I mention it, however, at once, for I shall perhaps not seem to count too much on having beguiled him if I say he must promptly have guessed it. Mrs. Ambient, a person of conscience, put the best face on her kinswoman, who spent a month with her twice a year; but it took no great insight to recognise the very different personal paste of the two ladies, and that the usual feminine hypocrisies would cost them on either side much more than the usual effort. Mrs. Ambient, smooth-haired, thin-lipped, perpetually fresh, must have regarded her crumpled and dishevelled visitor as an equivocal joke; she herself so the opposite of a Rossetti, she herself a Reynolds or a Lawrence, with no more far-fetched note in her composition than a cold ladylike candour and a well-starched muslin dress.

It was in a garment and with an expression of this kind that she made her entrance after I had exchanged a few words with Miss Ambient. Her husband presently followed her and, there being no other company, we went to dinner. The impressions I received at that repast are present to me still. The elements of oddity in the air hovered, as it were, without descending — to any immediate check of my delight. This came mainly of course from Ambient's talk, the easiest and richest I had ever heard. I may n't say to-day whether he laid himself out to dazzle a rather juvenile pilgrim from over the sea; but that matters little — it seemed so natural to him to shine. His spoken wit or wisdom, or whatever, had thus a charm almost beyond his written; that is if the high finish of his printed prose be really, as some people have maintained, a fault. There was such a kindness in him, however, that I've no doubt it gave him ideas for me, or about me, to see me sit as open-mouthed as I now figure myself. Not so the two ladies, who not only were very nearly dumb from beginning to end of the meal, but who had n't even the air of being struck with such an exhibition of fancy and taste. Mrs. Ambient, detached, and inscrutable, met neither my eye nor her husband's: she attended to her dinner, watched her servants, arranged the puckers in her dress, exchanged at wide intervals a remark with her sister-in-law and, while she slowly rubbed her lean white hands between the courses, looked out of the window at the first signs of evening — the long June day allowing us to dine without candles. Miss Ambient appeared to give little direct heed to anything said by her brother; but on the other hand she was much engaged in watching its effect upon me. Her "die-away" pupils continued to attach themselves to my countenance, and it was only her air of belonging to another century that kept them from being importunate. She seemed to look at me across the ages, and the interval of time diminished for me the inconvenience. It was as if she knew in a general way that he must be talking very well, but she herself was so at home among such allusions that she had no need to pick them up and was at liberty to see what would become of the exposure of a candid young American to a high æsthetic temperature.

The temperature was æsthetic certainly, but it was less so than I could have desired, for I failed of any great success in making our friend abound about himself. I tried to put him on the ground of his own genius, but he slipped through my fingers every time and shifted the saddle to one or other of his contemporaries. He talked about Balzac and Browning, about what was being done in foreign countries, about his recent tour in the East and the extraordinary forms of life to be observed in that part of the world. I felt he had reasons for holding off from a direct profession of literary faith, a full consistency or sincerity, and therefore dealt instead with certain social topics, treating them with extraordinary humour and with a due play of that power of ironic evocation in which his books abound. He had a deal to say about London as London appears to the observer who has the courage of some of his conclusions during the high-pressure time — from April to July — of its gregarious life. He flashed his faculty of playing with the caught image and liberating the wistful idea over the whole scheme of manners or conception of intercourse of his compatriots, among whom there were evidently not a few types for which he had little love. London in short was grotesque to him, and he made capital sport of it; his only allusion that I can remember to his own work was his saying that he meant some day to do an immense and general, a kind of epic, social satire. Miss Ambient's perpetual gaze seemed to put to me: "Do you perceive how artistic, how very strange and interesting, we are? Frankly now is it possible to be *more* artistic, *more* strange and interesting, than this? You surely won't deny that we're remarkable." I was irritated by her use of the plural pronoun, for she had no right to pair herself with her brother; and moreover of course I could n't see my way to — at all genially — include Mrs. Ambient. Yet there was no doubt they were, taken together, unprecedented enough, and, with all allowances, I had never been left, or condemned, to draw so many rich inferences.

After the ladies had retired my host took me into his study to smoke, where I appealingly brought him round, or so tried, to some disclosure of fond ideals. I was bent on proving I was worthy to listen to him, on repaying him for what he had said to me before dinner, by showing him how perfectly I understood. He liked to talk; he liked to defend his convictions and his honour (not that I attacked them); he liked a little perhaps — it was a pardonable weakness — to bewilder the youthful mind even while wishing to win it over. My ingenuous sympathy received at any rate a shock from three or four of his professions — he made me occasionally gasp and stare. He could n't help forgetting, or rather could n't know, how little, in another and dryer clime, I had ever sat in the school in which he was master; and he promoted me as at a jump to a sense of its penetralia. My trepidations, however, were delightful; they were just what I had hoped for, and their only fault was that they passed away too quickly; since I found that for the main points I was essentially, I was quite constitutionally, on Mark Ambient's "side." This was the taken stand of the artist to whom every manifestation of human energy was a thrilling spectacle and who felt for ever the desire to resolve his experience of life into a literary form. On that high head of the passion for form — the attempt at perfection, the quest for which was to his mind the real search for the holy grail — he said the most interesting, the most inspiring things. He mixed with them a thousand illustrations from his own life, from other lives he had known, from history and fiction, and above all from the annals of the time that was dear to him beyond all periods, the Italian cinque-cento. It came to me thus that in his books he had uttered but half his thought, and that what he had kept back — from motives I deplored when I made them out later — was the finer, and braver part. It was his fate to make a great many still more "prepared" people than me not inconsiderably wince; but there was no grain of bravado in his ripest things (I've always maintained it, though often contradicted), and at bottom the poor fellow, disinterested to his finger-tips and regarding imperfection not only as an æsthetic but quite also as a social crime, had an extreme dread of scandal. There are critics who regret that having gone so far he did n't go further; but I regret nothing — putting aside two or three of the motives I just mentioned — since he arrived at a noble rarity and I don't see how you can go beyond that. The hours I spent in his study — this first one and the few that followed it; they were not after all so numerous — seem to glow, as I look back on them, with a tone that is partly that of the brown old room, rich, under the shaded candle-light where we sat and smoked, with the dusky delicate bindings of valuable books; partly that of his voice, of which I still catch the echo, charged with the fancies and figures that came at his command. When we went back to the drawing-room we found Miss Ambient alone in possession and prompt to mention that her sister-in-law had a quarter of an hour before been called by the nurse to see the child, who appeared rather unwell — a little feverish.

"Feverish! how in the world comes he to be feverish?" Ambient asked. "He was perfectly right this afternoon."

"Beatrice says you walked him about too much — you almost killed him."

"Beatrice must be very happy — she has an opportunity to triumph!" said my friend with a bright bitterness which was all I could have wished it.

"Surely not if the child's ill," I ventured to remark by way of pleading for Mrs. Ambient.

"My dear fellow, you are n't married — you don't know the nature of wives!" my host returned with spirit.

I tried to match it. "Possibly not; but I know the nature of mothers."

"Beatrice is perfect as a mother," sighed Miss Ambient quite tremendously and with her fingers interlaced on her embroidered knees.

"I shall go up and see my boy," her brother went on. "Do you suppose he's asleep?"

"Beatrice won't let you see him, dear" — as to

which our young lady looked at me, though addressing our companion.

"Do you call that being perfect as a mother?" Ambient asked.

"Yes, from her point of view."

"Damn her point of view!" cried the author of "Beltraffio." And he left the room; after which we heard him ascend the stairs.

I sat there for some ten minutes with Miss Ambient, and we naturally had some exchange of remarks, which began, I think, by my asking her what the point of view of her sister-in-law could be.

"Oh it's so very odd. But we're so very odd altogether. Don't you find us awfully unlike others of our class? — which indeed mostly, in England, is awful. We've lived so much abroad. I adore 'abroad.' Have you people like us in America?"

"You're not all alike, you interesting three — or, counting Dolcino, four — surely, surely; so that I don't think I understand your question. We've no one like your brother — I may go so far as that."

"You've probably more persons like his wife," Miss Ambient desolately smiled.

"I can tell you that better when you've told me about her point of view."

"Oh yes — oh yes. Well," said my entertainer, "she does n't like his ideas. She does n't like them for the child. She thinks them undesirable."

Being quite fresh from the contemplation of some of Mark Ambient's *arcana* I was particularly in a position to appreciate this announcement. But the effect of it was to make me, after staring a moment, burst into laughter which I instantly checked when I remembered the indisposed child above and the possibility of parents nervously or fussily anxious.

"What has that infant to do with ideas?" I asked. "Surely he can't tell one from another. Has he read his father's novels?"

"He's very precocious and very sensitive, and his mother thinks she can't begin to guard him too early." Miss Ambient's head drooped a little to one side and her eyes fixed themselves on futurity. Then of a sudden came a strange alteration; her face lighted to an effect more joyless than any gloom, to that indeed of a conscious insincere grimace, and she added: "When one has children what one writes becomes a great responsibility."

"Children are terrible critics," I prosaically answered. "I'm really glad I haven't any."

"Do you also write then? And in the same style as my brother? And do you like that style? And do people appreciate it in America? I don't write, but I think I feel." To these and various other enquiries and observations my young lady treated me till we heard her brother's step in the hall again and Mark Ambient reappeared. He was so flushed and grave that I supposed he had seen something symptomatic in the condition of his child. His sister apparently had another idea; she gazed at him from afar — as if he had been a burning ship on the horizon — and simply murmured "Poor old Mark!"

"I hope you're not anxious," I as promptly pronounced.

"No, but I'm disappointed. She won't let me in.

She has locked the door, and I'm afraid to make a noise." I dare say there might have been a touch of the ridiculous in such a confession, but I liked my new friend so much that it took nothing for me from his dignity. "She tells me — from behind the door — that she'll let me know if he's worse."

"It's very good of her," said Miss Ambient with a hollow sound.

I had exchanged a glance with Mark in which it's possible he read that my pity for him was untinged with contempt, though I scarce know why he should have cared; and as his sister soon afterward got up and took her bedroom candlestick he proposed we should go back to his study. We sat there till after midnight; he put himself into his slippers and an old velvet jacket, he lighted an ancient pipe, but he talked considerably less than before. There were longish pauses in our communion, but they only made me feel we had advanced in intimacy. They helped me further to understand my friend's personal situation and to imagine it by no means the happiest possible. When his face was quiet it was vaguely troubled, showing, to my increase of interest — if that was all that was wanted! — that for him too life was the same struggle it had been for so many another man of genius. At last I prepared to leave him, and then, to my ineffable joy, he gave me some of the sheets of his forthcoming book — which, though unfinished, he had indulged in the luxury, so dear to writers of delibera-tion, of having "set up," from chapter to chapter, as he advanced. These early pages, the *prémices*, in the language of letters, of that new fruit of his imagination, I should take to my room and look over at my leisure. I was in the act of leaving him when the door of the study noiselessly opened and Mrs. Ambient stood before us. She observed us a moment, her candle in her hand, and then said to her husband that as she supposed he had n't gone to bed she had come down to let him know Dolcino was more quiet and would probably be better in the morning. Mark Ambient made no reply; he simply slipped past her in the doorway, as if for fear she might seize him in his passage, and bounded upstairs to judge for himself of his child's condition. She looked so frankly discomfited that I for a moment believed her about to give him chase. But she resigned herself with a sigh and her eyes turned, ruefully and without a ray, to the lamplit room where various books at which I had been looking were pulled out of their places on the shelves and the fumes of tobacco hung in mid-air. I bade her good-night and then, without intention, by a kind of fatality, a perversity that had already made me address her overmuch on that question of her husband's powers, I alluded to the precious proof-sheets with which Ambient had entrusted me and which I nursed there under my arm. "They 're the opening chapters of his new book," I said. "Fancy my satisfaction at being allowed to carry them to my room!"

She turned away, leaving me to take my candle-stick from the table in the hall; but before we separated, thinking it apparently a good occasion to let me know once for all — since I was beginning, it would seem, to be quite "thick" with my host — that there was no fitness in my appealing to her for sympathy in such a case; before we separated, I say, she remarked to me with her quick fine well-bred inveterate curtness: "I dare say you attribute to me ideas I have n't got. I don't take that sort of interest in my husband's proof-sheets. I consider his writings most objectionable!"

III

I HAD an odd colloquy the next morning with Miss Ambient, whom I found strolling in the garden before breakfast. The whole place looked as fresh and trim, amid the twitter of the birds, as if, an hour before, the housemaids had been turned into it with their dust-pans and feather-brushes. I almost hesitated to light a cigarette and was doubly startled when, in the act of doing so, I suddenly saw the sister of my host, who had, at the best, something of the weirdness of an apparition, stand before me. She might have been posing for her photograph. Her sad-coloured robe arranged itself in serpentine folds at her feet; her hands locked themselves listlessly together in front; her chin rested on a cinque-cento ruff. The first thing I did after bidding her good-morning was to ask her for news of her little nephew — to express the hope she had heard he was better. She was able to gratify this trust — she spoke as if we might expect to see him during the day. We walked through the shrubberies together and she gave me further light on her brother's household, which offered me an opportunity to repeat to her what his wife had so startled and distressed me with the night before. *Was* it the sorry truth that she thought his productions objectionable?

"She does n't usually come out with that so soon!" Miss Ambient returned in answer to my breathlessness.

"Poor lady," I pleaded, "she saw I'm a fanatic."

"Yes, she won't like you for that. But you must n't mind, if the rest of us like you! Beatrice thinks a work of art ought to have a 'purpose.' But she's a charming woman — don't you think her charming? I find in her quite the grand air."

"She's very beautiful," I produced with an effort; while I reflected that though it was apparently true that Mark Ambient was mismated it was also perceptible that his sister was perfidious. She assured me her brother and his wife had no other difference but this one — that she thought his writings immoral and his influence pernicious. It was a fixed idea; she was afraid of these things for the child. I answered that it was in all conscience enough, the trifle of a woman's regarding her husband's mind as a well of corruption, and she seemed much struck with the novelty of my remark. "But there has n't been any of the sort of trouble that there so often is among married people," she said. "I suppose you can judge for yourself that Beatrice is n't at all — well, whatever they call it when a woman kicks over! And poor Mark does n't make love to other people either. You might think he would, but I assure you he does n't. All the same of course, from her point of view, you know, she has a dread of my brother's influence on the child — on the formation of his character, his 'ideals,' poor little brat, his principles. It's as if it were a subtle poison or a contagion — something that would rub off on his tender sensibility when his father kisses him or holds him on his knee. If she could she'd prevent Mark from even so much as

touching him. Every one knows it — visitors see it
for themselves; so there's no harm in my telling you.
Isn't it excessively odd? It comes from Beatrice's
being so religious and so tremendously moral — so *à
cheval* on fifty thousand *riguardi*. And then of course
we mustn't forget," my companion added, a little
unexpectedly, to this polyglot proposition, "that some
of Mark's ideas are — well, really — rather impossible,
don't you know?"

I reflected as we went into the house, where we
found Ambient unfolding *The Observer* at the break-
fast-table, that none of them were probably quite so
"impossible, don't you know?" as his sister. Mrs.
Ambient, a little "the worse," as was mentioned, for
her ministrations, during the night to Dolcino, didn't
appear at breakfast. Her husband described her however as hoping to go to church. I afterwards learnt
that she did go, but nothing naturally was less on
the cards than that we should accompany her. It
was while the church-bell droned near at hand that
the author of "Beltraffio" led me forth for the ramble
he had spoken of in his note. I shall attempt here no
record of where we went or of what we saw. We kept
to the fields and copses and commons, and breathed
the same sweet air as the nibbling donkeys and the
browsing sheep, whose woolliness seemed to me, in
those early days of acquaintance with English objects,
but part of the general texture of the small dense
landscape, which looked as if the harvest were gathered by the shears and with all nature bleating and
braying for the violence. Everything was full of expression for Mark Ambient's visitor — from the big

39

bandy-legged geese whose whiteness was a "note" amid all the tones of green as they wandered beside a neat little oval pool, the foreground of a thatched and whitewashed inn, with a grassy approach and a pictorial sign — from these humble wayside animals to the crests of high woods which let a gable or a pinnacle peep here and there and looked even at a distance like trees of good company, conscious of an individual profile. I admired the hedge-rows, I plucked the faint-hued heather, and I was for ever stopping to say how charming I thought the thread-like footpaths across the fields, which wandered in a diagonal of finer grain from one smooth stile to another. Mark Ambient was abundantly good-natured and was as much struck, dear man, with some of my observations as I was with the literary allusions of the landscape. We sat and smoked on stiles, broaching paradoxes in the decent English air; we took short cuts across a park or two where the bracken was deep and my companion nodded to the old woman at the gate; we skirted rank coverts which rustled here and there as we passed, and we stretched ourselves at last on a heathery hillside where if the sun was n't too hot neither was the earth too cold, and where the country lay beneath us in a rich blue mist. Of course I had already told him what I thought of his new novel, having the previous night read every word of the opening chapters before I went to bed.

"I'm not without hope of being able to make it decent enough," he said as I went back to the subject while we turned up our heels to the sky. "At least the people who dislike my stuff — and there are plenty of them, I believe — will dislike this thing (if it does turn out well) most." This was the first time I had heard him allude to the people who could n't read him — a class so generally conceived to sit heavy on the consciousness of the man of letters. A being organised for literature as Mark Ambient was must certainly have had the normal proportion of sensitiveness, of irritability; the artistic *ego*, capable in some cases of such monstrous development, must have been in his composition sufficiently erect and active. I won't therefore go so far as to say that he never thought of his detractors or that he had any illusions with regard to the number of his admirers — he could never so far have deceived himself as to believe he was popular, but I at least then judged (and had occasion to be sure later on) that stupidity ruffled him visibly but little, that he had an air of thinking it quite natural he should leave many simple folk, tasting of him, as simple as ever he found them, and that he very seldom talked about the newspapers, which, by the way, were always even abnormally vulgar about him. Of course he may have thought them over — the newspapers — night and day; the only point I make is that he did n't show it; while at the same time he did n't strike one as a man actively on his guard. I may add that, touching his hope of making the work on which he was then engaged the best of his books, it was only partly carried out. That place belongs incontestably to "Beltraffio," in spite of the beauty of certain parts of its successor. I quite believe, however, that he had at the moment of which I speak no sense of having declined; he was in love with his idea, which was indeed magnificent, and though for him, as I suppose for every sane artist, the act of execution had in it as much torment as joy, he saw his result grow like the crescent of the young moon and promise to fill the disk. "I want to be truer than I've ever been," he said, settling himself on his back with his hands clasped behind his head; "I want to give the impression of life itself. No, you may say what you will, I've always arranged things too much, always smoothed them down and rounded them off and tucked them in — done everything to them that life does n't do. I've been a slave to the old superstitions."

"You a slave, my dear Mark Ambient? You've the freest imagination of our day!"

"All the more shame to me to have done some of the things I have! The reconciliation of the two women in 'Natalina,' for instance, which could never really have taken place. That sort of thing's ignoble — I blush when I think of it! This new affair must be a golden vessel, filled with the purest distillation of the actual; and oh how it worries me, the shaping of the vase, the hammering of the metal! I have to hammer it so fine, so smooth; I don't do more than an inch or two a day. And all the while I have to be so careful not to let a drop of the liquor escape! When I see the kind of things Life herself, the brazen hussy, does, I despair of ever catching her peculiar trick. She has an impudence, Life! If one risked a fiftieth part of the effects she risks! It takes ever so long to believe it. You don't know yet, my dear youth. It is n't till one has been watching her

some forty years that one finds out half of what she's
up to! Therefore one's earlier things must inevitably
contain a mass of rot. And with what one sees, on one
side, with its tongue in its cheek, defying one to be real
enough, and on the other the *bonnes gens* rolling up
their eyes at one's cynicism, the situation has elements of the ludicrous which the poor reproducer
himself is doubtless in a position to appreciate better
than any one else. Of course one must n't worry
about the *bonnes gens*," Mark Ambient went on while
my thoughts reverted to his ladylike wife as interpreted by his remarkable sister.

"To sink your shaft deep and polish the plate
through which people look into it — that's what your
work consists of," I remember ingeniously observing.

"Ah polishing one's plate — that's the torment
of execution!" he exclaimed, jerking himself up and
sitting forward. "The effort to arrive at a surface,
if you think anything of that decent sort necessary —
some people don't, happily for them! My dear fellow,
if you could see the surface I dream of as compared
with the one with which I've to content myself.
Life's really too short for art — one has n't time to
make one's shell ideally hard. Firm and bright, firm
and bright is very well to say — the devilish thing
has a way sometimes of being bright, and even of being
hard, as mere tough frozen pudding is hard, without
being firm. When I rap it with my knuckles it does n't
give the right sound. There are horrible sandy
stretches where I've taken the wrong turn because
I could n't for the life of me find the right. If you
knew what a dunce I am sometimes! Such things

figure to me now base pimples and ulcers on the brow of beauty!"

"They're very bad, very bad," I said as gravely as I could.

"Very bad? They're the highest social offence I know; it ought — it absolutely ought; I'm quite serious — to be capital. If I knew I should be publicly thrashed else I'd manage to find the true word. The people who can't — some of them don't so much as know it when they see it — would shut their inkstands, and we should n't be deluged by this flood of rubbish!"

I shall not attempt to repeat everything that passed between us, nor to explain just how it was that, every moment I spent in his company, Mark Ambient revealed to me more and more the consistency of his creative spirit, the spirit in him that felt all life as plastic material. I could but envy him the force of that passion, and it was at any rate through the receipt of this impression that by the time we returned I had gained the sense of intimacy with him that I have noted. Before we got up for the homeward stretch he alluded to his wife's having once — or perhaps more than once — asked him whether he should like Dolcino to read "Beltraffio." He must have been unaware at the moment of all that this conveyed to me — as well doubtless of my extreme curiosity to hear what he had replied. He had said how much he hoped Dolcino would read *all* his works — when he was twenty; he should like him to know what his father had done. Before twenty it would be useless; he would n't understand them.

"And meanwhile do you propose to hide them — to lock them up in a drawer?" Mrs. Ambient had proceeded.

"Oh no — we must simply tell him they're not intended for small boys. If you bring him up properly after that he won't touch them."

To this Mrs. Ambient had made answer that it might be very awkward when he was about fifteen, say; and I asked her husband if it were his opinion in general then that young people should n't read novels.

"Good ones — certainly not!" said my companion. I suppose I had had other views, for I remember saying that for myself I was n't sure it was bad for them if the novels were "good" to the right intensity of goodness. "Bad for *them*, I don't say so much!" my companion returned. "But very bad, I'm afraid, for the poor dear old novel itself." That oblique accidental allusion to his wife's attitude was followed by a greater breadth of reference as we walked home. "The difference between us is simply the opposition between two distinct ways of looking at the world, which have never succeeded in getting on together, or in making any kind of common household, since the beginning of time. They've borne all sorts of names, and my wife would tell you it's the difference between Christian and Pagan. I may be a pagan, but I don't like the name; it sounds sectarian. She thinks me at any rate no better than an ancient Greek. It's the difference between making the most of life and making the least, so that you'll get another better one in some other time and place. Will it be a sin to make the most of that one too, I wonder; and shall we have to be bribed off in the future state as well as in the present? Perhaps I care too much for beauty — I don't know, I doubt if a poor devil *can;* I delight in it, I adore it, I think of it continually, I try to produce it, to reproduce it. My wife holds that we should n't cultivate or enjoy it without extraordinary precautions and reserves. She 's always afraid of it, always on her guard. I don't know what it can ever have done to her, what grudge it owes her or what resentment rides. And she 's so pretty too herself! Don't you think she 's lovely? She was at any rate when we married. At that time I was n't aware of that difference I speak of — I thought it all came to the same thing: in the end, as they say. Well, perhaps it will in the end. I don't know what the end will be. Moreover I care for seeing things as they are; that 's the way I try to show them in any professed picture. But you must n't talk to Mrs. Ambient about things as they are. She has a mortal dread of things as they are."

"She 's afraid of them for Dolcino," I said: surprised a moment afterwards at being in a position — thanks to Miss Ambient — to be so explanatory; and surprised even now that Mark should n't have shown visibly that he wondered what the deuce I knew about it. But he did n't; he simply declared with a tenderness that touched me: "Ah nothing shall ever hurt *him!*"

He told me more about his wife before we arrived at the gate of home, and if he be judged to have aired overmuch his grievance I 'm afraid I must admit that he had some of the foibles as well as the gifts of the artistic temperament; adding, however, instantly that hitherto, to the best of my belief, he had rarely let this particular cat out of the bag. "She thinks me immoral — that's the long and short of it," he said as we paused outside a moment and his hand rested on one of the bars of his gate; while his conscious expressive perceptive eyes — the eyes of a foreigner, I had begun to account them, much more than of the usual Englishman — viewing me now evidently as quite a familiar friend, took part in the declaration. "It's very strange when one thinks it all over, and there's a grand comicality in it that I should like to bring out. She's a very nice woman, extraordinarily well-behaved, upright and clever and with a tremendous lot of good sense about a good many matters. Yet her conception of a novel — she has explained it to me once or twice, and she does n't do it badly as exposition — is a thing so false that it makes me blush. It's a thing so hollow, so dishonest, so lying, in which life is so blinked and blinded, so dodged and disfigured, that it makes my ears burn. It's two different ways of looking at the whole affair," he repeated, pushing open the gate. "And they're irreconcileable!" he added with a sigh. We went forward to the house, but on the walk, half-way to the door, he stopped and said to me : "If you're going into this kind of thing there's a fact you should know beforehand; it may save you some disappointment. There's a hatred of art, there's a hatred of literature — I mean of the genuine kinds. Oh the shams — *those* they'll swallow by the bucket!" I looked up at the charming house, with its genial colour and crookedness, and I answered with a smile that those evil passions might exist, but that I should never have expected to find them there. "Ah it does n't matter after all," he a bit nervously laughed; which I was glad to hear, for I was reproaching myself with having worked him up.

If I had it soon passed off, for at luncheon he was delightful; strangely delightful considering that the difference between himself and his wife was, as he had said, irreconcileable. He had the art, by his manner, by his smile, by his natural amenity, of reducing the importance of it in the common concerns of life; and Mrs. Ambient, I must add, lent herself to this trans-action with a very good grace. I watched her at table for further illustrations of that fixed idea of which Miss Ambient had spoken to me; for in the light of the united revelations of her sister-in-law and her husband she had come to seem to me almost a sinister personage. Yet the signs of a sombre fan-aticism were not more immediately striking in her than before; it was only after a while that her air of incorruptible conformity, her tapering monosyllabic correctness, began to affect me as in themselves a cold thin flame. Certainly, at first, she resembled a woman with as few passions as possible; but if she had a passion at all it would indeed be that of Philis-tinism. She might have been (for there are guardian-spirits, I suppose, of all great principles) the very angel of the pink of propriety — putting the pink for a principle, though I'd rather put some dismal cold blue. Mark Ambient, apparently, ten years be-fore, had simply and quite inevitably taken her for an angel, without asking himself of what. He had been right in calling my attention to her beauty. In looking for some explanation of his original surrender to her I saw more than before that she was, physically speaking, a wonderfully cultivated human plant — that he might well have owed her a brief poetic inspiration. It was impossible to be more propped and pencilled, more delicately tinted and petalled.

If I had had it in my heart to think my host a little of a hypocrite for appearing to forget at table everything he had said to me in our walk, I should instantly have cancelled such a judgement on reflecting that the good news his wife was able to give him about their little boy was ground enough for any optimistic reaction. It may have come partly too from a certain compunction at having breathed to me at all harshly on the cool fair lady who sat there — a desire to prove himself not after all so mismated. Dolcino continued to be much better, and it had been promised him he should come downstairs after his dinner. As soon as we had risen from our own meal Mark slipped away, evidently for the purpose of going to his child; and no sooner had I observed this than I became aware his wife had simultaneously vanished. It happened that Miss Ambient and I, both at the same moment, saw the tail of her dress whisk out of a doorway; an incident that led the young lady to smile at me as if I now knew all the secrets of the Ambients. I passed with her into the garden and we sat down on a dear old bench that rested against the west wall of the house. It was a perfect spot for the middle period of a Sunday in June, and its felicity seemed to come partly from an antique sun-dial which, rising in front of us and forming the centre of a small intricate parterre, measured the moments ever so slowly and made them safe for leisure and talk. The garden bloomed in the suffused afternoon, the tall beeches stood still for an example, and, behind and above us, a rose-tree of many seasons, clinging to the faded grain of the brick, expressed the whole character of the scene in a familiar exquisite smell. It struck me as a place to offer genius every favour and sanction — not to bristle with challenges and checks. Miss Ambient asked me if I had enjoyed my walk with her brother and whether we had talked of many things.

"Well, of most things," I freely allowed, though I remembered we had n't talked of Miss Ambient.

"And don't you think some of his theories are very peculiar?"

"Oh I guess I agree with them all." I was very particular, for Miss Ambient's entertainment, to guess.

"Do you think art's everything?" she put to me in a moment.

"In art, of course I do!"

"And do you think beauty's everything?"

"Everything's a big word, which I think we should use as little as possible. But how can we not want beauty?"

"Ah there you are!" she sighed, though I did n't quite know what she meant by it. "Of course it's difficult for a woman to judge how far to go," she went on. "I adore everything that gives a charm to life. I'm intensely sensitive to form. But sometimes

I draw back — don't you see what I mean ? — I don't quite see where I shall be landed. I only want to be quiet, after all," Miss Ambient continued as if she had long been baffled of this modest desire. "And one must be good, at any rate, must not one ?" she pursued with a dubious quaver — an intimation apparently that what I might say one way or the other would settle it for her. It was difficult for me to be very original in reply, and I'm afraid I repaid her confidence with an unblushing platitude. I remember moreover attaching to it an enquiry, equally destitute of freshness and still more wanting perhaps in tact, as to whether she did n't mean to go to church, since that was an obvious way of being good. She made answer that she had performed this duty in the morning, and that for her, of Sunday afternoons, supreme virtue consisted in answering the week's letters. Then suddenly and without transition she brought out: "It's quite a mistake about Dolcino's being better. I've seen him and he's not at all right."

I wondered, and somehow I think I scarcely believed. "Surely his mother would know, would n't she ?"

She appeared for a moment to be counting the leaves on one of the great beeches. "As regards most matters one can easily say what, in a given situation, my sister-in-law will, or would, do. But in the present case there are strange elements at work."

"Strange elements ? Do you mean in the constitution of the child ?"

"No, I mean in my sister-in-law's feelings."

"Elements of affection of course; elements of anxiety," I concurred. "But why do you call them strange?"

She repeated my words. "Elements of affection, elements of anxiety. She's very anxious."

Miss Ambient put me indescribably ill at ease; she almost scared me, and I wished she would go and write her letters. "His father will have seen him now," I said, "and if he's not satisfied he will send for the doctor."

"The doctor ought to have been here this morning," she promptly returned. "He lives only two miles away."

I reflected that all this was very possibly but a part of the general tragedy of Miss Ambient's view of things; yet I asked her why she had n't urged that view on her sister-in-law. She answered me with a smile of extraordinary significance and observed that I must have very little idea of her "peculiar" relations with Beatrice; but I must do her the justice that she re-enforced this a little by the plea that any distinguishable alarm of Mark's was ground enough for a difference of his wife's. He was always nervous about the child, and as they were predestined by nature to take opposite views, the only thing for the mother was to cultivate a false optimism. In Mark's absence and that of his betrayed fear she would have been less easy. I remembered what he had said to me about their dealings with their son — that between them they'd probably put an end to him; but I did n't repeat this to Miss Ambient: the less so that just then her brother emerged from the house, carrying the boy in his arms. Close behind him moved his wife, grave and pale; the little sick face was turned over Ambient's shoulder and toward the mother. We rose to receive the group, and as they came near us Dolcino twisted himself about. His enchanting eyes showed me a smile of recognition, in which, for the moment, I should have taken a due degree of comfort. Miss Ambient, however, received another impression, and I make haste to say that her quick sensibility, which visibly went out to the child, argues that in spite of her affectations she might have been of some human use. "It won't do at all — it won't do at all," she said to me under her breath. "I shall speak to Mark about the Doctor."

Her small nephew was rather white, but the main difference I saw in him was that he was even more beautiful than the day before. He had been dressed in his festal garments — a velvet suit and a crimson sash — and he looked like a little invalid prince too young to know condescension and smiling familiarly on his subjects.

"Put him down, Mark, he's not a bit at his ease," Mrs. Ambient said.

"Should you like to stand on your feet, my boy?" his father asked.

He made a motion that quickly responded. "Oh yes; I'm remarkably well."

Mark placed him on the ground; he had shining pointed shoes with enormous bows. "Are you happy now, Mr. Ambient?"

"Oh yes, I'm particularly happy," Dolcino replied. But the words were scarce out of his mouth when his mother caught him up and, in a moment, holding him on her knees, took her place on the bench where Miss Ambient and I had been sitting. This young lady said something to her brother, in consequence of which the two wandered away into the garden together.

IV

I REMAINED with Mrs. Ambient, but as a servant
had brought out a couple of chairs I was n't obliged
to seat myself beside her. Our conversation failed
of ease, and I, for my part, felt there would be a
shade of hypocrisy in my now trying to make myself
agreeable to the partner of my friend's existence. I
did n't dislike her — I rather admired her; but I was
aware that I differed from her inexpressibly. Then
I suspected, what I afterwards definitely knew and
have already intimated, that the poor lady felt small
taste for her husband's so undisguised disciple; and
this of course was not encouraging. She thought me
an obtrusive and designing, even perhaps a depraved,
young man whom a perverse Providence had dropped
upon their quiet lawn to flatter his worst tendencies.
She did me the honour to say to Miss Ambient, who
repeated the speech, that she did n't know when she
had seen their companion take such a fancy to a
visitor; and she measured apparently my evil influence by Mark's appreciation of my society. I had a
consciousness, not oppressive but quite sufficient, of
all this; though I must say that if it chilled my flow
of small-talk it yet did n't prevent my thinking the
beautiful mother and beautiful child, interlaced there
against their background of roses, a picture such as
I doubtless should n't soon see again. I was free,
I supposed, to go into the house and write letters, to

sit in the drawing-room, to repair to my own apartment and take a nap; but the only use I made of my freedom was to linger still in my chair and say to myself that the light hand of Sir Joshua might have painted Mark Ambient's wife and son. I found myself looking perpetually at the latter small mortal, who looked constantly back at me, and that was enough to detain me. With these vaguely-amused eyes he smiled, and I felt it an absolute impossibility to abandon a child with such an expression. His attention never strayed; it attached itself to my face as if among all the small incipient things of his nature throbbed a desire to say something to me. If I could have taken him on my own knee he perhaps would have managed to say it; but it would have been a critical matter to ask his mother to give him up, and it has remained a constant regret for me that on that strange Sunday afternoon I did n't even for a moment hold Dolcino in my arms. He had said he felt remarkably well and was especially happy; but though peace may have been with him as he pillowed his charming head on his mother's breast, dropping his little crimson silk legs from her lap, I somehow did n't think security was. He made no attempt to walk about; he was content to swing his legs softly and strike one as languid and angelic.

Mark returned to us with his sister; and Miss Ambient, repeating her mention of the claims of her correspondence, passed into the house. Mark came and stood in front of his wife, looking down at the child, who immediately took hold of his hand and kept it while he stayed. "I think Mackintosh ought

56

to see him," he said; "I think I'll walk over and fetch him."

"That's Gwendolen's idea, I suppose," Mrs. Ambient replied very sweetly.

"It's not such an out-of-the-way idea when one's child's ill," he returned.

"I'm not ill, papa; I'm much better now," sounded in the boy's silver pipe.

"Is that the truth, or are you only saying it to be agreeable? You've a great idea of being agreeable, you know."

The child seemed to meditate on this distinction, this imputation, for a moment; then his exaggerated eyes, which had wandered, caught my own as I watched him. "Do *you* think me agreeable?" he enquired with the candour of his age and with a look that made his father turn round to me laughing and ask, without saying it, "Isn't he adorable?"

"Then why don't you hop about, if you feel so lusty?" Ambient went on while his son swung his hand.

"Because mamma's holding me close!"

"Oh yes; I know how mamma holds you when I come near!" cried Mark with a grimace at his wife.

She turned her charming eyes up to him without deprecation or concession. "You can go for Mackintosh if you like. I think myself it would be better. You ought to drive."

"She says that to get me away," he put to me with a gaiety that I thought a little false; after which he started for the Doctor's.

I remained there with Mrs. Ambient, though even

our exchange of twaddle had run very thin. The boy's little fixed white face seemed, as before, to plead with me to stay, and after a while it produced still another effect, a very curious one, which I shall find it difficult to express. Of course I expose myself to the charge of an attempt to justify by a strained logic after the fact a step which may have been on my part but the fruit of a native want of discretion; and indeed the traceable consequences of that perversity were too lamentable to leave me any desire to trifle with the question. All I can say is that I acted in perfect good faith and that Dolcino's friendly little gaze gradually kindled the spark of my inspiration. What helped it to glow were the other influences — the silent suggestive garden-nook, the perfect opportunity (if it was not an opportunity for that it was an opportunity for nothing) and the plea I speak of, which issued from the child's eyes and seemed to make him say: "The mother who bore me and who presses me here to her bosom — sympathetic little organism that I am — has really the kind of sensibility she has been represented to you as lacking, if you only look for it patiently and respectfully. How is it conceivable she should n't have it? How is it possible that *I* should have so much of it — for I'm quite full of it, dear strange gentleman — if it were n't also in some degree in her? I'm my great father's child, but I'm also my beautiful mother's, and I'm sorry for the difference between them!" So it shaped itself before me, the vision of reconciling Mrs. Ambient with her husband, of putting an end to their ugly difference. The project was absurd of course, for had

I not had his word for it — spoken with all the bitterness of experience — that the gulf dividing them was well-nigh bottomless? Nevertheless, a quarter of an hour after Mark had left us, I observed to my hostess that I could n't get over what she had told me the night before about her thinking her husband's compositions "objectionable." I had been so very sorry to hear it, had thought of it constantly and wondered whether it might n't be possible to make her change her mind. She gave me a great cold stare, meant apparently as an admonition to me to mind my business. I wish I had taken this mute counsel, but I did n't take it. I went on to remark that it seemed an immense pity so much that was interesting should be lost on her.

"Nothing 's lost upon me," she said in a tone that did n't make the contradiction less. "I know they 're very interesting."

"Don't you like papa's books?" Dolcino asked, addressing his mother but still looking at me. Then he added to me: "Won't you read them to me, American gentleman?"

"I 'd rather tell you some stories of my own," I said. "I know some that are awfully good."

"When will you tell them? To-morrow?"

"To-morrow with pleasure, if that suits you."

His mother took this in silence. Her husband, during our walk, had asked me to remain another day; my promise to her son was an implication that I had consented, and it was n't possible the news could please her. This ought doubtless to have made me more careful as to what I said next, but all I can plead is that it did n't. I soon mentioned that just after leaving her the evening before, and after hearing her apply to her husband's writings the epithet already quoted, I had on going up to my room sat down to the perusal of those sheets of his new book that he had been so good as to lend me. I had sat entranced till nearly three in the morning — I had read them twice over. "You say you have n't looked at them. I think it's such a pity you should n't. Do let me beg you to take them up. They're so very remarkable. I'm sure they'll convert you. They place him in — really — such a dazzling light. All that's best in him is there. I've no doubt it's a great liberty, my saying all this; but pardon me, and *do* read them!"

"Do read them, mamma!" the boy again sweetly shrilled. "Do read them!"

She bent her head and closed his lips with a kiss. "Of course I know he has worked immensely over them," she said; after which she made no remark, but attached her eyes thoughtfully to the ground. The tone of these last words was such as to leave me no spirit for further pressure, and after hinting at a fear that her husband might n't have caught the Doctor I got up and took a turn about the grounds. When I came back ten minutes later she was still in her place watching her boy, who had fallen asleep in her lap. As I drew near she put her finger to her lips and a short time afterwards rose, holding him; it being now best, she said, that she should take him upstairs. I offered to carry him and opened my arms for the purpose; but she thanked me and turned away with the child still in her embrace, his head on her shoulder. "I'm very strong," was her last word as she passed into the house, her slim flexible figure bent backward with the filial weight. So I never laid a longing hand on Dolcino.

I betook myself to Ambient's study, delighted to have a quiet hour to look over his books by myself. The windows were open to the garden; the sunny stillness, the mild light of the English summer, filled the room without quite chasing away the rich dusky tone that was a part of its charm and that abode in the serried shelves where old morocco exhaled the fragrance of curious learning, as well as in the brighter intervals where prints and medals and miniatures were suspended on a surface of faded stuff. The place had both colour and quiet; I thought it a perfect room for work and went so far as to say to myself that, if it were mine to sit and scribble in, there was no knowing but I might learn to write as well as the author of "Beltraffio." This distinguished man still did n't reappear, and I rummaged freely among his treasures. At last I took down a book that detained me a while and seated myself in a fine old leather chair by the window to turn it over. I had been occupied in this way for half an hour — a good part of the afternoon had waned — when I became conscious of another presence in the room and, looking up from my quarto, saw that Mrs. Ambient, having pushed open the door quite again in the same noiseless way marking or disguising her entrance the night before, had advanced across the threshold. On seeing me she stopped; she had not, I think, expected to find me. But her hesitation was only of a moment; she came straight to her husband's writing-table as if she were looking for something. I got up and asked her if I could help her. She glanced about an instant and then put her hand upon a roll of papers which I recognised, as I had placed it on that spot at the early hour of my descent from my room.

"Is this the new book?" she asked, holding it up.

"The very sheets," I smiled; "with precious annotations."

"I mean to take your advice" — and she tucked the little bundle under her arm. I congratulated her cordially and ventured to make of my triumph, as I presumed to call it, a subject of pleasantry. But she was perfectly grave and turned away from me, as she had presented herself, without relaxing her rigour; after which I settled down to my quarto again with the reflexion that Mrs. Ambient was truly an eccentric. My triumph too suddenly seemed to me rather vain. A woman who could n't unbend at a moment exquisitely indicated would never understand Mark Ambient. He came back to us at last in person, having brought the Doctor with him. "He was away from home," Mark said, "and I went after him to where he was supposed to be. He had left the place, and I followed him to two or three others, which accounts for my delay." He was now with Mrs. Ambient, looking at the child, and was to see Mark again before leaving the house. My host noticed at the end of two minutes that the proof-sheets of his new book had been removed from the table; and when I told him, in reply to his question as to what I knew about them, that Mrs. Ambient had carried them off to read he turned almost pale with surprise. "What has suddenly made her so curious?" he cried; and I was obliged to tell him that I was at the bottom of the mystery. I had had it on my conscience to assure her that she really ought to know of what her husband was capable. "Of what I'm capable? Elle ne s'en doute que trop!" said Ambient with a laugh; but he took my meddling very good-naturedly and contented himself with adding that he was really much afraid she would burn up the sheets, his emendations and all, of which latter he had no duplicate. The Doctor paid a long visit in the nursery, and before he came down I retired to my own quarters, where I remained till dinner-time. On entering the drawing-room at this hour I found Miss Ambient in possession, as she had been the evening before.

"I was right about Dolcino," she said, as soon as she saw me, with an air of triumph that struck me as the climax of perversity. "He's really very ill."

"Very ill! Why when I last saw him, at four o'clock, he was in fairly good form."

"There has been a change for the worse, very sudden and rapid, and when the Doctor got here he found diphtheritic symptoms. He ought to have been called, as I knew, in the morning, and the child ought n't to have been brought into the garden."

"My dear lady, he was very happy there," I protested with horror.

"He would be very happy anywhere. I've no doubt he's very happy now, with his poor little temperature —!" She dropped her voice as her brother came in, and Mark let us know that as a matter of course Mrs. Ambient would n't appear. It was true the boy had developed diphtheritic symptoms, but he was quiet for the present and his mother earnestly watching him. She was a perfect nurse, Mark said, and Mackintosh would come back at ten. Our dinner was n't very gay — with my host worried and absent; and his sister annoyed me by her constant tacit assumption, conveyed in the very way she nibbled her bread and sipped her wine, of having "told me so." I had had no disposition to deny anything she might have told me, and I could n't see that her satisfaction in being justified by the event relieved her little nephew's condition. The truth is that, as the sequel was to prove, Miss Ambient had some of the qualities of the sibyl and had therefore perhaps a right to the sibylline contortions. Her brother was so preoccupied that I felt my presence an indiscretion and was sorry I had promised to remain over the morrow. I put it to Mark that clearly I had best leave them in the morning; to which he replied that, on the contrary, if he was to pass the next days in the fidgets my company would distract his attention. The fidgets had already begun for him, poor fellow; and as we sat in his study with our cigars after dinner he wandered to the door whenever he heard the sound of the Doctor's wheels. Miss Ambient, who shared this apartment with us, gave me at such moments significant glances; she had before rejoining us gone upstairs to ask about the child. His mother and his nurse gave a fair report, but Miss Ambient found his fever high and his symptoms very grave. The Doctor came at ten o'clock, and I went to bed after hearing from Mark that he saw no present cause for alarm. He had made every provision for the night and was to return early in the morning.

I quitted my room as eight struck the next day and when I came downstairs saw, through the open door of the house, Mrs. Ambient standing at the front gate of the grounds in colloquy with Mackintosh. She wore a white dressing-gown, but her shining hair was carefully tucked away in its net, and in the morning freshness, after a night of watching, she looked as much "the type of the lady" as her sister-in-law had described her. Her appearance, I suppose, ought to have reassured me; but I was still nervous and uneasy, so that I shrank from meeting her with the necessary challenge. None the less, however, was I impatient to learn how the new day found him; and as Mrs. Ambient had n't seen me I passed into the grounds by a roundabout way and, stopping at a further gate, hailed the Doctor just as he was driving off. Mrs. Ambient had returned to the house before he got into his cart.

"Pardon me, but as a friend of the family I should like very much to hear about the little boy."

The stout sharp circumspect man looked at me from head to foot and then said: "I'm sorry to say I have n't seen him."

"Have n't seen him?"

"Mrs. Ambient came down to meet me as I alighted, and told me he was sleeping so soundly, after a restless night, that she did n't wish him disturbed. I assured her I would n't disturb him, but she said he was quite safe now and she could look after him herself."

"Thank you very much. Are you coming back?"

"No sir; I'll be hanged if I come back!" cried the honest practitioner in high resentment. And the horse started as he settled beside his man.

I wandered back into the garden, and five minutes later Miss Ambient came forth from the house to greet me. She explained that breakfast would n't be served for some time and that she desired a moment herself with the Doctor. I let her know that the good vexed man had come and departed, and I repeated to her what he had told me about his dismissal. This made Miss Ambient very serious, very serious indeed, and she sank into a bench, with dilated eyes, hugging her elbows with crossed arms. She indulged in many strange signs, she confessed herself immensely distressed, and she finally told me what her own last news of her nephew had been. She had sat up very late — after me, after Mark — and before going to bed had knocked at the door of the child's room, opened to her by the nurse. This good woman had admitted her and she had found him quiet, but flushed and "unnatural," with his mother sitting by his bed. "She held his hand in one of hers," said Miss Ambient, "and in the other —, what do you think? — the proof-sheets of Mark's new book! She was reading them there intently: did you ever hear of anything so extraordinary? Such a very odd time to be reading an author whom she never could abide!" In her agitation Miss Ambient was guilty of this vulgarism of speech, and I was so impressed by her narrative that only in recalling her words later did I notice the lapse. Mrs. Ambient had looked up from her reading with her finger on her lips — I recognised the gesture she had addressed me in the afternoon — and, though the nurse was about to go to rest, had not encouraged her sister-in-law to relieve her of any part of her vigil. But certainly at that time the boy's state was far from reassuring — his poor little breathing so painful; and what change could have taken place in him in those few hours that would justify Beatrice in denying Mackintosh access? This was the moral of Miss Ambient's anecdote, the moral for herself at least. The moral for me, rather, was that it *was* a very singular time for Mrs. Ambient to be going into a novelist she had never appreciated and who had simply happened to be recommended to her by a young American she disliked. I thought of her sitting there in the sick-chamber in the still hours of the night and after the nurse had left her, turning and turning those pages of genius and wrestling with their magical influence.

I must be sparing of the minor facts and the later emotions of this sojourn — it lasted but a few hours longer — and devote but three words to my subsequent relations with Ambient. They lasted five years — till his death — and were full of interest, of satisfaction and, I may add, of sadness. The main thing to be said of these years is that I had a secret from him which I guarded to the end. I believe he never suspected it, though of this I'm not absolutely sure. If he had so much as an inkling the line he had taken, the line of absolute negation of the matter to himself, shows an immense effort of the will. I may at last lay bare my secret, giving it for what it is worth; now that the main sufferer has gone, that he has begun to be alluded to as one of the famous early dead and that his wife has ceased to survive him; now too that Miss Ambient, whom I also saw at intervals during the time that followed, has, with her embroideries and her attitudes, her necromantic glances and strange intuitions, retired to a Sisterhood, where, as I am told, she is deeply immured and quite lost to the world.

Mark came in to breakfast after this lady and I had for some time been seated there. He shook hands with me in silence, kissed my companion, opened his letters and newspapers and pretended to drink his coffee. But I took these movements for mechanical and was little surprised when he suddenly pushed away everything that was before him and, with his head in his hands and his elbows on the table, sat staring strangely at the cloth.

"What's the matter, *caro fratello mio?*" Miss Ambient quavered, peeping from behind the urn.

He answered nothing, but got up with a certain violence and strode to the window. We rose to our feet, his relative and I, by a common impulse, exchanging a glance of some alarm; and he continued to stare into the garden. "In heaven's name what has got possession of Beatrice?" he cried at last, turning round on us a ravaged face. He looked from one of us to the other—the appeal was addressed to us alike.

Miss Ambient gave a shrug. "My poor Mark, Beatrice is always — Beatrice!"

"She has locked herself up with the boy — bolted and barred the door. She refuses to let me come near him!" he went on.

"She refused to let Mackintosh see him an hour ago!" Miss Ambient promptly returned.

"Refused to let Mackintosh see him? By heaven I'll smash in the door!" And Mark brought his fist down upon the sideboard, which he had now approached, so that all the breakfast-service rang.

I begged Miss Ambient to go up and try to have speech of her sister-in-law, and I drew Mark out into the garden. "You're exceedingly nervous, and Mrs. Ambient's probably right," I there undertook to plead. "Women know; women should be supreme in such a situation. Trust a mother — a devoted mother, my dear friend!" With such words as these I tried to soothe and comfort him, and, marvellous to relate, I succeeded, with the help of many cigarettes, in making him walk about the garden and talk, or suffer me at least to do so for near an hour. When about that time had elapsed his sister reappeared, reaching us rapidly and with a convulsed face while she held her hand to her heart.

"Go for the Doctor, Mark — go for the Doctor this moment!"

"Is he dying? Has she killed him?" my poor friend cried, flinging away his cigarette.

"I don't know what she has done! But she's frightened, and now she wants the Doctor."

"He told me he'd be hanged if he came back!" I felt myself obliged to mention.

"Precisely — therefore Mark himself must go for

him, and not a messenger. You must see him and
tell him it's to save your child. The trap has been
ordered — it's ready."

"To save him? I'll save him, please God!" Ambient cried, bounding with his great strides across
the lawn.

As soon as he had gone I felt I ought to have
volunteered in his place, and I said as much to Miss
Ambient; but she checked me by grasping my arm
while we heard the wheels of the dog-cart rattle away
from the gate. "He's off — he's off — and now I
can think! To get him away — while I think —
while I think!"

"While you think of what, Miss Ambient?"

"Of the unspeakable thing that has happened
under this roof!"

Her manner was habitually that of such a prophet-
ess of ill that I at first allowed for some great extravagance. But I looked at her hard, and the next thing
felt myself turn white. "Dolcino *is* dying then —
he's dead?"

"It's too late to save him. His mother has let
him die! I tell you that because you're sympathetic,
because you've imagination," Miss Ambient was good
enough to add, interrupting my expression of horror.
"That's why you had the idea of making her read
Mark's new book!"

"What has that to do with it? I don't understand
you. Your accusation's monstrous."

"I see it all — I'm not stupid," she went on, heedless of my emphasis. "It was the book that finished
her — it was that decided her!"

"Decided her? Do you mean she has murdered her child?" I demanded, trembling at my own words.

"She sacrificed him; she determined to do nothing to make him live. Why else did she lock herself in, why else did she turn away the Doctor? The book gave her a horror; she determined to rescue him — to prevent him from ever being touched. He had a crisis at two o'clock in the morning. I know that from the nurse, who had left her then, but whom, for a short time, she called back. The darling got much worse, but she insisted on the nurse's going back to bed, and after that she was alone with him for hours."

I listened with a dread that stayed my credence, while she stood there with her tearless glare. "Do you pretend then she has no pity, that she's cruel and insane?"

"She held him in her arms, she pressed him to her breast, not to see him; but she gave him no remedies; she did nothing the Doctor ordered. Everything's there untouched. She has had the honesty not even to throw the drugs away!"

I dropped upon the nearest bench, overcome with my dismay — quite as much at Miss Ambient's horrible insistence and distinctness as at the monstrous meaning of her words. Yet they came amazingly straight, and if they did have a sense I saw myself too woefully figure in it. Had I been then a proximate cause —? "You're a very strange woman and you say incredible things," I could only reply.

She had one of her tragic headshakes. "You think it necessary to protest, but you're really quite ready

71

to believe me. You 've received an impression of my sister-in-law—you 've guessed of what she 's capable."

I don't feel bound to say what concession on this score I made to Miss Ambient, who went on to relate to me that within the last half-hour Beatrice had had a revulsion, that she was tremendously frightened at what she had done; that her fright itself betrayed her; and that she would now give heaven and earth to save the child. "Let us hope she will!" I said, looking at my watch and trying to time poor Ambient; whereupon my companion repeated all portentously "Let us hope so!" When I asked her if she herself could do nothing, and whether she ought n't to be with her sister-in-law, she replied: "You had better go and judge! She 's like a wounded tigress!"

I never saw Mrs. Ambient till six months after this, and therefore can't pretend to have verified the comparison. At the latter period she was again the type of the perfect lady. "She 'll treat him better after this," I remember her sister-in-law's saying in response to some quick outburst, on my part, of compassion for her brother. Though I had been in the house but thirty-six hours this young lady had treated me with extraordinary confidence, and there was therefore a certain demand I might, as such an intimate, make of her. I extracted from her a pledge that she 'd never say to her brother what she had just said to me, that she 'd let him form his own theory of his wife's conduct. She agreed with me that there was misery enough in the house without her contributing a new anguish, and that Mrs. Ambient's proceedings might be explained, to her husband's mind, by the extravagance of a jealous devotion. Poor Mark came back with the Doctor much sooner than we could have hoped, but we knew five minutes afterwards that it was all too late. His sole, his adored little son was more exquisitely beautiful in death than he had been in life. Mrs. Ambient's grief was frantic; she lost her head and said strange things. As for Mark's — but I won't speak of that. *Basta, basta,* as he used to say. Miss Ambient kept her secret — I've already had occasion to say that she had her good points — but it rankled in her conscience like a guilty participation and, I imagine, had something to do with her ultimately retiring from the world. And, apropos of consciences, the reader is now in a position to judge of my compunction for my effort to convert my cold hostess. I ought to mention that the death of her child in some degree converted her. When the new book came out (it was long delayed) she read it over as a whole, and her husband told me that during the few supreme weeks before her death — she failed rapidly after losing her son, sank into a consumption and faded away at Mentone — she even dipped into the black "Beltraffio."

THE MIDDLE YEARS

THE MIDDLE YEARS

I

THE April day was soft and bright, and poor Dencombe, happy in the conceit of reasserted strength, stood in the garden of the hotel, comparing, with a deliberation in which however there was still something of languor, the attractions of easy strolls. He liked the feeling of the south so far as you could have it in the north, he liked the sandy cliffs and the clustered pines, he liked even the colourless sea. "Bournemouth as a health-resort" had sounded like a mere advertisement, but he was thankful now for the commonest conveniences. The sociable country postman, passing through the garden, had just given him a small parcel which he took out with him, leaving the hotel to the right and creeping to a bench he had already haunted, a safe recess in the cliff. It looked to the south, to the tinted walls of the Island, and was protected behind by the sloping shoulder of the down. He was tired enough when he reached it, and for a moment was disappointed; he was better of course, but better, after all, than what? He should never again, as at one or two great moments of the past, be better than himself. The infinite of life was gone, and what remained of the dose a small glass scored like a thermometer by the apothecary. He sat and stared at the sea, which appeared all surface and twinkle, far shallower than the spirit of man. It was the abyss of human illusion that was the real, the tideless deep. He held his packet, which had come by book-post, unopened on his knee, liking, in the lapse of so many joys — his illness had made him feel his age — to know it was there, but taking for granted there could be no complete renewal of the pleasure, dear to young experience, of seeing one's self "just out." Dencombe, who had a reputation, had come out too often and knew too well in advance how he should look.

His postponement associated itself vaguely, after a little, with a group of three persons, two ladies and a young man, whom, beneath him, straggling and seemingly silent, he could see move slowly together along the sands. The gentleman had his head bent over a book and was occasionally brought to a stop by the charm of this volume, which, as Dencombe could perceive even at a distance, had a cover alluringly red. Then his companions, going a little further, waited for him to come up, poking their parasols into the beach, looking around them at the sea and sky and clearly sensible of the beauty of the day. To these things the young man with the book was still more clearly indifferent; lingering, credulous, absorbed, he was an object of envy to an observer from whose connexion with literature all such artlessness had faded. One of the ladies was large and mature; the other had the spareness of comparative youth and of a social situation possibly inferior. The large lady carried back Dencombe's imagination to the age of crinoline; she wore a hat of the shape of a mushroom, decorated with a blue veil, and had the air, in her aggressive amplitude, of clinging to a vanished fashion or even a lost cause. Presently her companion produced from under the folds of a mantle a limp portable chair which she stiffened out and of which the large lady took possession. This act, and something in the movement of either party, at once characterised the performers — they performed for Dencombe's recreation — as opulent matron and humble dependent. Where moreover was the virtue of an approved novelist if one could n't establish a relation between such figures? the clever theory for instance that the young man was the son of the opulent matron and that the humble dependent, the daughter of a clergyman or an officer, nourished a secret passion for him. Was that not visible from the way she stole behind her protectress to look back at him? — back to where he had let himself come to a full stop when his mother sat down to rest. His book was a novel, it had the catchpenny binding; so that while the romance of life stood neglected at his side he lost himself in that of the circulating library. He moved mechanically to where the sand was softer and ended by plumping down in it to finish his chapter at his ease. The humble dependent, discouraged by his remoteness, wandered with a martyred droop of the head in another direction, and the exorbitant lady, watching the waves, offered a confused resemblance to a flying-machine that had broken down.

When his drama began to fail Dencombe remembered that he had after all another pastime. Though such promptitude on the part of the publisher was

rare he was already able to draw from its wrapper
his "latest," perhaps his last. The cover of "The
Middle Years" was duly meretricious, the smell of
the fresh pages the very odour of sanctity; but for the
moment he went no further — he had become conscious of a strange alienation. He had forgotten what
his book was about. Had the assault of his old ailment, which he had so fallaciously come to Bournemouth to ward off, interposed utter blankness as to
what had preceded it? He had finished the revision
of proof before quitting London, but his subsequent
fortnight in bed had passed the sponge over colour.
He could n't have chanted to himself a single sentence, could n't have turned with curiosity or confidence to any particular page. His subject had already
gone from him, leaving scarce a superstition behind.
He uttered a low moan as he breathed the chill of this
dark void, so desperately it seemed to represent the
completion of a sinister process. The tears filled his
mild eyes; something precious had passed away.
This was the pang that had been sharpest during the
last few years — the sense of ebbing time, of shrinking
opportunity; and now he felt not so much that his
last chance was going as that it was gone indeed.
He had done all he should ever do, and yet had n't
done what he wanted. This was the laceration —
that practically his career was over: it was as violent
as a grip at his throat. He rose from his seat nervously
— a creature hunted by a dread; then he fell back in
his weakness and nervously opened his book. It was
a single volume; he preferred single volumes and
aimed at a rare compression. He began to read and,

little by little, in this occupation, was pacified and reassured. Everything came back to him, but came back with a wonder, came back above all with a high and magnificent beauty. He read his own prose, he turned his own leaves, and had as he sat there with the spring sunshine on the page an emotion peculiar and intense. His career was over, no doubt, but it was over, when all was said, with *that*.

He had forgotten during his illness the work of the previous year; but what he had chiefly forgotten was that it was extraordinarily good. He dived once more into his story and was drawn down, as by a siren's hand, to where, in the dim underworld of fiction, the great glazed tank of art, strange silent subjects float. He recognised his motive and surrendered to his talent. Never probably had that talent, such as it was, been so fine. His difficulties were still there, but what was also there, to his perception, though probably, alas! to nobody's else, was the art that in most cases had surmounted them. In his surprised enjoyment of this ability he had a glimpse of a possible reprieve. Surely its force was n't spent — there was life and service in it yet. It had n't come to him easily, it had been backward and roundabout. It was the child of time, the nursling of delay; he had struggled and suffered for it, making sacrifices not to be counted, and now that it was really mature was it to cease to yield, to confess itself brutally beaten? There was an infinite charm for Dencombe in feeling as he had never felt before that diligence *vincit omnia*. The result produced in his little book was somehow a result beyond his conscious intention: it was as if he had planted his genius, had trusted his method, and they had grown up and flowered with this sweetness. If the achievement had been real, however, the process had been painful enough. What he saw so intensely to-day, what he felt as a nail driven in, was that only now, at the very last, had he come into possession. His development had been abnormally slow, almost grotesquely gradual. He had been hindered and retarded by experience, he had for long periods only groped his way. It had taken too much of his life to produce too little of his art. The art had come, but it had come after everything else. At such a rate a first existence was too short — long enough only to collect material; so that to fructify, to use the material, one should have a second age, an extension. This extension was what poor Dencombe sighed for. As he turned the last leaves of his volume he murmured "Ah for another go, ah for a better chance!"

The three persons drawing his attention to the sands had vanished and then reappeared; they had now wandered up a path, an artificial and easy ascent, which led to the top of the cliff. Dencombe's bench was halfway down, on a sheltered ledge, and the large lady, a massive heterogeneous person with bold black eyes and kind red cheeks, now took a few moments to rest. She wore dirty gauntlets and immense diamond ear-rings; at first she looked vulgar, but she contradicted this announcement in an agreeable off-hand tone. While her companions stood waiting for her she spread her skirts on the end of Dencombe's seat. The young man had gold spectacles, through which, with his finger still in his red-covered book, he glanced at the volume, bound in the same shade of the same colour, lying on the lap of the original occupant of the bench. After an instant Dencombe felt him struck with a resemblance; he had recognised the gilt stamp on the crimson cloth, was reading "The Middle Years" and now noted that somebody else had kept pace with him. The stranger was startled, possibly even a little ruffled, to find himself not the only person favoured with an early copy. The eyes of the two proprietors met a moment, and Dencombe borrowed amusement from the expression of those of his competitor, those, it might even be inferred, of his admirer. They confessed to some resentment — they seemed to say: "Hang it, has he got it *already?* Of course he's a brute of a reviewer!" Dencombe shuffled his copy out of sight while the opulent matron, rising from her repose, broke out: "I feel already the good of this air!"

"I can't say I do," said the angular lady. "I find myself quite let down."

"I find myself horribly hungry. At what time did you order luncheon?" her protectress pursued.

The young person put the question by. "Doctor Hugh always orders it."

"I ordered nothing to-day — I'm going to make you diet," said their comrade.

"Then I shall go home and sleep. *Qui dort dine!*"

"Can I trust you to Miss Vernham?" asked Doctor Hugh of his elder companion.

"Don't I trust *you?*" she archly enquired.

"Not too much!" Miss Vernham, with her eyes

on the ground, permitted herself to declare. "You must come with us at least to the house," she went on while the personage on whom they appeared to be in attendance began to mount higher. She had got a little out of ear-shot; nevertheless Miss Vernham became, so far as Dencombe was concerned, less distinctly audible to murmur to the young man: "I don't think you realise all you owe the Countess!"

Absently, a moment, Doctor Hugh caused his gold-rimmed spectacles to shine at her. "Is that the way I strike you? I see — I see!"

"She's awfully good to us," continued Miss Vernham, compelled by the lapse of the other's motion to stand there in spite of his discussion of private matters. Of what use would it have been that Dencombe should be sensitive to shades had n't he detected in that arrest a strange influence from the quiet old convalescent in the great tweed cape? Miss Vernham appeared suddenly to become aware of some such connexion, for she added in a moment: "If you want to sun yourself here you can come back after you 've seen us home."

Doctor Hugh, at this, hesitated, and Dencombe, in spite of a desire to pass for unconscious, risked a covert glance at him. What his eyes met this time, as happened, was, on the part of the young lady, a queer stare, naturally vitreous, which made her remind him of some figure — he could n't name it — in a play or a novel, some sinister governess or tragic old maid. She seemed to scan him, to challenge him, to say out of general spite: "What have you got to do with us?" At the same instant the rich humour of the Countess reached them from above: "Come, come, my little lambs; you should follow your old *bergère!*" Miss Vernham turned away for it, pursuing the ascent, and Doctor Hugh, after another mute appeal to Dencombe and a minute's evident demur, deposited his book on the bench as if to keep his place, or even as a gage of earnest return, and bounded without difficulty up the rougher part of the cliff.

Equally innocent and infinite are the pleasures of observation and the resources engendered by the trick of analysing life. It amused poor Dencombe, as he dawdled in his tepid air-bath, to believe himself awaiting a revelation of something at the back of a fine young mind. He looked hard at the book on the end of the bench, but would n't have touched it for the world. It served his purpose to have a theory that should n't be exposed to refutation. He already felt better of his melancholy; he had, according to his old formula, put his head at the window. A passing Countess could draw off the fancy when, like the elder of the ladies who had just retreated, she was as obvious as the giantess of a caravan. It was indeed general views that were terrible; short ones, contrary to an opinion sometimes expressed, were the refuge, were the remedy. Doctor Hugh could n't possibly be anything but a reviewer who had understandings for early copies with publishers or with newspapers. He reappeared in a quarter of an hour with visible relief at finding Dencombe on the spot and the gleam of white teeth in an embarrassed but generous smile. He was perceptibly disappointed at the eclipse of the other copy of the book; it made a pretext the less for speaking to the quiet gentleman. But he spoke notwithstanding; he held up his own copy and broke out pleadingly: "*Do* say, if you have occasion to speak of it, that it's the best thing he has done yet!"

Dencombe responded with a laugh: "Done yet" was so amusing to him, made such a grand avenue of the future. Better still, the young man took *him* for a reviewer. He pulled out "The Middle Years" from under his cape, but instinctively concealed any telltale look of fatherhood. This was partly because a person was always a fool for insisting to others on his work. "Is that what you're going to say yourself?" he put to his visitor.

"I'm not quite sure I shall write anything. I don't, as a regular thing — I enjoy in peace. But it's awfully fine."

Dencombe just debated. If the young man had begun to abuse him he would have confessed on the spot to his identity, but there was no harm in drawing out any impulse to praise. He drew it out with such success that in a few moments his new acquaintance, seated by his side, was confessing candidly that the works of the author of the volumes before them were the only ones he could read a second time. He had come the day before from London, where a friend of his, a journalist, had lent him his copy of the last, the copy sent to the office of the journal and already the subject of a "notice" which, as was pretended there — but one had to allow for "swagger" — it had taken a full quarter of an hour to prepare. He intimated that he was ashamed for his friend, and in the case of a work demanding and repaying study, of such inferior manners; and, with his fresh appreciation and his so irregular wish to express it, he speedily became for poor Dencombe a remarkable, a delightful apparition. Chance had brought the weary man of letters face to face with the greatest admirer in the new generation of whom it was supposable he might boast. The admirer in truth was mystifying, so rare a case was it to find a bristling young doctor — he looked like a German physiologist — enamoured of literary form. It was an accident, but happier than most accidents, so that Dencombe, exhilarated as well as confounded, spent half an hour in making his visitor talk while he kept himself quiet. He explained his premature possession of "The Middle Years" by an allusion to the friendship of the publisher, who, knowing he was at Bournemouth for his health, had paid him this graceful attention. He allowed he had been ill, for Doctor Hugh would infallibly have guessed it; he even went so far as to wonder if he might n't look for some hygienic "tip" from a personage combining so bright an enthusiasm with a presumable knowledge of the remedies now in vogue. It would shake his faith a little perhaps to have to take a doctor seriously who could take *him* so seriously, but he enjoyed this gushing modern youth and felt with an acute pang that there would still be work to do in a world in which such odd combinations were presented. It was n't true, what he had tried for renunciation's sake to believe, that all the combinations were exhausted. They were n't by any means

— they were infinite : the exhaustion was in the miserable artist.

Doctor Hugh, an ardent physiologist, was saturated with the spirit of the age — in other words he had just taken his degree; but he was independent and various, he talked like a man who would have preferred to love literature best. He would fain have made fine phrases, but nature had denied him the trick. Some of the finest in "The Middle Years" had struck him inordinately, and he took the liberty of reading them to Dencombe in support of his plea. He grew vivid, in the balmy air, to his companion, for whose deep refreshment he seemed to have been sent; and was particularly ingenuous in describing how recently he had become acquainted, and how instantly infatuated, with the only man who had put flesh between the ribs of an art that was starving on superstitions. He had n't yet written to him — he was deterred by a strain of respect. Dencombe at this moment rejoiced more inwardly than ever that he had never answered the photographers. His visitor's attitude promised him a luxury of intercourse, though he was sure a due freedom for Doctor Hugh would depend not a little on the Countess. He learned without delay what type of Countess was involved, mastering as well the nature of the tie that united the curious trio. The large lady, an Englishwoman by birth and the daughter of a celebrated baritone, whose taste *minus* his talent she had inherited, was the widow of a French nobleman and mistress of all that remained of the handsome fortune, the fruit of her father's earnings, that had constituted her dower.

Miss Vernham, an odd creature but an accomplished pianist, was attached to her person at a salary. The Countess was generous, independent, eccentric; she travelled with her minstrel and her medical man. Ignorant and passionate she had nevertheless moments in which she was almost irresistible. Dencombe saw her sit for her portrait in Doctor Hugh's free sketch, and felt the picture of his young friend's relation to her frame itself in his mind. This young friend, for a representative of the new psychology, was himself easily hypnotised, and if he became abnormally communicative it was only a sign of his real subjection. Dencombe did accordingly what he wanted with him, even without being known as Dencombe.

Taken ill on a journey in Switzerland the Countess had picked him up at an hotel, and the accident of his happening to please her had made her offer him, with her imperious liberality, terms that could n't fail to dazzle a practitioner without patients and whose resources had been drained dry by his studies. It was n't the way he would have proposed to spend his time, but it was time that would pass quickly, and meanwhile she was wonderfully kind. She exacted perpetual attention, but it was impossible not to like her. He gave details about his queer patient, a "type" if there ever was one, who had in connexion with her flushed obesity, and in addition to the morbid strain of a violent and aimless will, a grave organic disorder; but he came back to his loved novelist, whom he was so good as to pronounce more essentially a poet than many of those who went in for verse, with a zeal ex-

cited, as all his indiscretion had been excited, by the
happy chance of Dencombe's sympathy and the
coincidence of their occupation. Dencombe had confessed to a slight personal acquaintance with the
author of "The Middle Years," but had not felt
himself as ready as he could have wished when his
companion, who had never yet encountered a being
so privileged, began to be eager for particulars. He
even divined in Doctor Hugh's eye at that moment
a glimmer of suspicion. But the young man was too
inflamed to be shrewd and repeatedly caught up the
book to exclaim: "Did you notice this?" or "Weren't
you immensely struck with that?" "There's a beautiful passage toward the end," he broke out; and
again he laid his hand on the volume. As he turned
the pages he came upon something else, while Dencombe saw him suddenly change colour. He had
taken up as it lay on the bench Dencombe's copy
instead of his own, and his neighbour at once guessed
the reason of his start. Doctor Hugh looked grave
an instant; then he said: "I see you've been altering
the text!" Dencombe was a passionate corrector, a
fingerer of style; the last thing he ever arrived at was
a form final for himself. His ideal would have been
to publish secretly, and then, on the published text,
treat himself to the terrified revise, sacrificing always
a first edition and beginning for posterity and even
for the collectors, poor dears, with a second. This
morning, in "The Middle Years," his pencil had
pricked a dozen lights. He was amused at the effect
of the young man's reproach; for an instant it made
him change colour. He stammered at any rate

ambiguously, then through a blur of ebbing consciousness saw Doctor Hugh's mystified eyes. He only had time to feel he was about to be ill again — that emotion, excitement, fatigue, the heat of the sun, the solicitation of the air, had combined to play him a trick, before, stretching out a hand to his visitor with a plaintive cry, he lost his senses altogether.

Later he knew he had fainted and that Doctor Hugh had got him home in a Bath-chair, the conductor of which, prowling within hail for custom, had happened to remember seeing him in the garden of the hotel. He had recovered his perception on the way, and had, in bed that afternoon, a vague recollection of Doctor Hugh's young face, as they went together, bent over him in a comforting laugh and expressive of something more than a suspicion of his identity. That identity was ineffaceable now, and all the more that he was rueful and sore. He had been rash, been stupid, had gone out too soon, stayed out too long. He ought n't to have exposed himself to strangers, he ought to have taken his servant. He felt as if he had fallen into a hole too deep to descry any little patch of heaven. He was confused about the time that had passed — he pieced the fragments together. He had seen his doctor, the real one, the one who had treated him from the first and who had again been very kind. His servant was in and out on tiptoe, looking very wise after the fact. He said more than once something about the sharp young gentleman. The rest was vagueness in so far as it was n't despair. The vagueness, however, justified itself by dreams, dozing anxieties from which he finally emerged to the consciousness of a dark room and a shaded candle.

"You'll be all right again — I know all about you now," said a voice near him that he felt to be young. Then his meeting with Doctor Hugh came back. He was too discouraged to joke about it yet, but made out after a little that the interest was intense for his visitor. "Of course I can't attend you professionally — you've got your own man, with whom I've talked and who's excellent," Doctor Hugh went on. "But you must let me come to see you as a good friend. I've just looked in before going to bed. You're doing beautifully, but it's a good job I was with you on the cliff. I shall come in early to-morrow. I want to do something for you. I want to do everything. You've done a tremendous lot for me." The young man held his hand, hanging over him, and poor Dencombe, weakly aware of this living pressure, simply lay there and accepted his devotion. He couldn't do anything less — he needed help too much.

The idea of the help he needed was very present to him that night, which he spent in a lucid stillness, an intensity of thought that constituted a reaction from his hours of stupor. He was lost, he was lost — he was lost if he couldn't be saved. He wasn't afraid of suffering, of death, wasn't even in love with life; but he had had a deep demonstration of desire. It came over him in the long quiet hours that only with "The Middle Years" had he taken his flight; only on that day, visited by soundless processions, had he recognised his kingdom. He had had a revelation of his range. What he dreaded was the idea that his reputation should stand on the unfinished. It wasn't with his past but with his future that it should properly be concerned. Illness and age rose before him like spectres with pitiless eyes: how was he to bribe such fates to give him the second chance? He had had the one chance that all men have—he had had the chance of life. He went to sleep again very late, and when he awoke Doctor Hugh was sitting at hand. There was already by this time something beautifully familiar in him.

"Don't think I've turned out your physician," he said; "I'm acting with his consent. He has been here and seen you. Somehow he seems to trust me. I told him how we happened to come together yesterday, and he recognises that I've a peculiar right."

Dencombe felt his own face pressing. "How have you squared the Countess?"

The young man blushed a little, but turned it off. "Oh never mind the Countess!"

"You told me she was very exacting."

Doctor Hugh had a wait. "So she is."

"And Miss Vernham's an *intrigante*."

"How do you know that?"

"I know everything. One *has* to, to write decently!'

"I think she's mad," said limpid Doctor Hugh.

"Well, don't quarrel with the Countess — she's a present help to you."

"I don't quarrel," Doctor Hugh returned. "But I don't get on with silly women." Presently he added: "You seem very much alone."

"That often happens at my age. I've outlived, I've lost by the way."

Doctor Hugh faltered; then surmounting a soft scruple: "Whom have you lost?"

"Every one."

"Ah no," the young man breathed, laying a hand on his arm.

"I once had a wife — I once had a son. My wife died when my child was born, and my boy, at school, was carried off by typhoid."

"I wish I'd been there!" cried Doctor Hugh.

"Well — if you're here!" Dencombe answered with a smile that, in spite of dimness, showed how he valued being sure of his companions's whereabouts.

"You talk strangely of your age. You're not old."

"Hypocrite — so early!"

"I speak physiologically."

"That's the way I've been speaking for the last five years, and it's exactly what I've been saying to myself. It isn't till we *are* old that we begin to tell ourselves we're not."

"Yet I know I myself am young," Doctor Hugh returned.

"Not so well as I!" laughed his patient, whose visitor indeed would have established the truth in question by the honesty with which he changed the point of view, remarking that it must be one of the charms of age — at any rate in the case of high distinction — to feel that one has laboured and achieved. Doctor Hugh employed the common phrase about earning one's rest, and it made poor Dencombe for

94

an instant almost angry. He recovered himself, however, to explain, lucidly enough, that if, ungraciously, he knew nothing of such a balm, it was doubtless because he had wasted inestimable years. He had followed literature from the first, but he had taken a lifetime to get abreast of her. Only to-day at last had he begun to *see*, so that all he had hitherto shown was a movement without a direction. He had ripened too late and was so clumsily constituted that he had had to teach himself by mistakes.

"I prefer your flowers then to other people's fruit, and your mistakes to other people's successes," said gallant Doctor Hugh. "It's for your mistakes I admire you."

"You're happy — you don't know," Dencombe answered.

Looking at his watch the young man had got up; he named the hour of the afternoon at which he would return. Dencombe warned him against committing himself too deeply, and expressed again all his dread of making him neglect the Countess — perhaps incur her displeasure.

"I want to be like you — I want to learn by mistakes!" Doctor Hugh laughed.

"Take care you don't make too grave a one! But do come back," Dencombe added with the glimmer of a new idea.

"You should have had more vanity!" His friend spoke as if he knew the exact amount required to make a man of letters normal.

"No, no — I only should have had more time. I want another go."

"Another go?"

"I want an extension."

"An extension?" Again Doctor Hugh repeated Dencombe's words, with which he seemed to have been struck.

"Don't you know? — I want to what they call 'live.'"

The young man, for good-bye, had taken his hand, which closed with a certain force. They looked at each other hard. "You *will* live," said Doctor Hugh.

"Don't be superficial. It's too serious!"

"You *shall* live!" Dencombe's visitor declared, turning pale.

"Ah that's better!" And as he retired the invalid, with a troubled laugh, sank gratefully back.

All that day and all the following night he wondered if it might n't be arranged. His doctor came again, his servant was attentive, but it was to his confident young friend that he felt himself mentally appeal. His collapse on the cliff was plausibly explained and his liberation, on a better basis, promised for the morrow; meanwhile, however, the intensity of his meditations kept him tranquil and made him indifferent. The idea that occupied him was none the less absorbing because it was a morbid fancy. Here was a clever son of the age, ingenious and ardent, who happened to have set him up for connoisseurs to worship. This servant of his altar had all the new learning in science and all the old reverence in faith; would n't he therefore put his knowledge at the disposal of his sympathy, his craft at the disposal of his love? Could n't he be trusted to invent a remedy

for a poor artist to whose art he had paid a tribute ?
If he could n't the alternative was hard : Dencombe
would have to surrender to silence unvindicated and
undivined. The rest of the day and all the next he
toyed in secret with this sweet futility. Who would
work the miracle for him but the young man who
could combine such lucidity with such passion ? He
thought of the fairy-tales of science and charmed himself into forgetting that he looked for a magic that was
not of this world. Doctor Hugh was an apparition,
and that placed him above the law. He came and
went while his patient, who now sat up, followed him
with supplicating eyes. The interest of knowing the
great author had made the young man begin "The
Middle Years" afresh and would help him to find a
richer sense between its covers. Dencombe had told
him what he "tried for"; with all his intelligence, on
a first perusal, Doctor Hugh had failed to guess it.
The baffled celebrity wondered then who in the world
would guess it: he was amused once more at the
diffused massive weight that could be thrown into the
missing of an intention. Yet he would n't rail at the
general mind to-day — consoling as that ever had
been : the revelation of his own slowness had seemed
to make all stupidity sacred.

Doctor Hugh, after a little, was visibly worried,
confessing, on enquiry, to a source of embarrassment
at home. "Stick to the Countess — don't mind me,"
Dencombe said repeatedly; for his companion was
frank enough about the large lady's attitude. She
was so jealous that she had fallen ill — she resented
such a breach of allegiance. She paid so much for

his fidelity that she must have it all : she refused him the right to other sympathies, charged him with scheming to make her die alone, for it was needless to point out how little Miss Vernham was a resource in trouble. When Doctor Hugh mentioned that the Countess would already have left Bournemouth if he had n't kept her in bed, poor Dencombe held his arm tighter and said with decision : "Take her straight away." They had gone out together, walking back to the sheltered nook in which, the other day, they had met. The young man, who had given his companion a personal support, declared with emphasis that his conscience was clear — he could ride two horses at once. Did n't he dream for his future of a time when he should have to ride five hundred ? Longing equally for virtue, Dencombe replied that in that golden age no patient would pretend to have contracted with him for his whole attention. On the part of the Countess was n't such an avidity lawful ? Doctor Hugh denied it, said there was no contract, but only a free understanding, and that a sordid servitude was impossible to a generous spirit; he liked moreover to talk about art, and that was the subject on which, this time, as they sat together on the sunny bench, he tried most to engage the author of "The Middle Years." Dencombe, soaring again a little on the weak wings of convalescence and still haunted by that happy notion of an organised rescue, found another strain of eloquence to plead the cause of a certain splendid "last manner," the very citadel, as it would prove, of his reputation, the stronghold into which his real treasure would be gathered. While

his listener gave up the morning and the great still
sea ostensibly waited he had a wondrous explanatory
hour. Even for himself he was inspired as he told
what his treasure would consist of; the precious metals
he would dig from the mine, the jewels rare, strings
of pearls, he would hang between the columns of his
temple. He was wondrous for himself, so thick his
convictions crowded, but still more wondrous for
Doctor Hugh, who assured him none the less that
the very pages he had just published were already
encrusted with gems. This admirer, however, panted
for the combinations to come and, before the face of
the beautiful day, renewed to Dencombe his guarantee
that his profession would hold itself responsible for
such a life. Then he suddenly clapped his hand upon
his watch-pocket and asked leave to absent himself
for half an hour. Dencombe waited there for his
return, but was at last recalled to the actual by the
fall of a shadow across the ground. The shadow
darkened into that of Miss Vernham, the young lady
in attendance on the Countess; whom Dencombe,
recognising her, perceived so clearly to have come
to speak to him that he rose from his bench to acknowledge the civility. Miss Vernham indeed proved not
particularly civil; she looked strangely agitated, and
her type was now unmistakeable.

"Excuse me if I do ask," she said, "whether it's
too much to hope that you may be induced to leave
Doctor Hugh alone." Then before our poor friend,
greatly disconcerted, could protest: "You ought to
be informed that you stand in his light — that you
may do him a terrible injury."

"Do you mean by causing the Countess to dispense with his services?"

"By causing her to disinherit him." Dencombe stared at this, and Miss Vernham pursued, in the gratification of seeing she could produce an impression: "It has depended on himself to come into something very handsome. He has had a grand prospect, but I think you've succeeded in spoiling it."

"Not intentionally, I assure you. Is there no hope the accident may be repaired?" Dencombe asked.

"She was ready to do anything for him. She takes great fancies, she lets herself go — it's her way. She has no relations, she's free to dispose of her money, and she's very ill," said Miss Vernham for a climax.

"I'm very sorry to hear it," Dencombe stammered.

"Would n't it be possible for you to leave Bournemouth? That's what I've come to see about."

He sank to his bench. "I'm very ill myself, but I'll try!"

Miss Vernham still stood there with her colourless eyes and the brutality of her good conscience. "Before it's too late, please!" she said; and with this she turned her back, in order, quickly, as if it had been a business to which she could spare but a precious moment, to pass out of his sight.

Oh yes, after this Dencombe was certainly very ill. Miss Vernham had upset him with her rough fierce news; it was the sharpest shock to him to discover what was at stake for a penniless young man of fine parts. He sat trembling on his bench, staring at the waste of waters, feeling sick with the directness of the blow. He was indeed too weak, too unsteady, too alarmed; but he would make the effort to get away, for he could n't accept the guilt of interference and his honour was really involved. He would hobble home, at any rate, and then think what was to be done. He made his way back to the hotel and, as he went, had a characteristic vision of Miss Vernham's great motive. The Countess hated women of course — Dencombe was lucid about that; so the hungry pianist had no personal hopes and could only console herself with the bold conception of helping Doctor Hugh in order to marry him after he should get his money or else induce him to recognise her claim for compensation and buy her off. If she had befriended him at a fruitful crisis he would really, as a man of delicacy — and she knew what to think of that point — have to reckon with her.

At the hotel Dencombe's servant insisted on his going back to bed. The invalid had talked about catching a train and had begun with orders to pack; after which his racked nerves had yielded to a sense of sickness. He consented to see his physician, who immediately was sent for, but he wished it to be understood that his door was irrevocably closed to Doctor Hugh. He had his plan, which was so fine that he rejoiced in it after getting back to bed. Doctor Hugh, suddenly finding himself snubbed without mercy, would, in natural disgust and to the joy of Miss Vernham, renew his allegiance to the Countess. When his physician arrived Dencombe learned that he was feverish and that this was very wrong: he was to cultivate calmness and try, if possible, not to think. For the rest of the day he wooed stupidity; but there

was an ache that kept him sentient, the probable
sacrifice of his "extension," the limit of his course.
His medical adviser was anything but pleased; his
successive relapses were ominous. He charged this
personage to put out a strong hand and take Doctor
Hugh off his mind — it would contribute so much to
his being quiet. The agitating name, in his room,
was not mentioned again, but his security was a
smothered fear, and it was not confirmed by the
receipt, at ten o'clock that evening, of a telegram
which his servant opened and read him and to which,
with an address in London, the signature of Miss
Vernham was attached. "Beseech you to use all influence to make our friend join us here in the morning.
Countess much the worse for dreadful journey, but
everything may still be saved." The two ladies had
gathered themselves up and had been capable in the
afternoon of a spiteful revolution. They had started
for the capital, and if the elder one, as Miss Vernham had announced, was very ill, she had wished to
make it clear that she was proportionately reckless.
Poor Dencombe, who was not reckless and who only
desired that everything should indeed be "saved,"
sent this missive straight off to the young man's lodg-
ing and had on the morrow the pleasure of knowing
that he had quitted Bournemouth by an early train.

Two days later he pressed in with a copy of a literary journal in his hand. He had returned because
he was anxious and for the pleasure of flourishing the
great review of "The Middle Years." Here at least
was something adequate — it rose to the occasion;
it was an acclamation, a reparation, a critical attempt

to place the author in the niche he had fairly won.
Dencombe accepted and submitted; he made neither
objection nor enquiry, for old complications had
returned and he had had two dismal days. He was
convinced not only that he should never again leave
his bed, so that his young friend might pardonably
remain, but that the demand he should make on the
patience of beholders would be of the most moderate. Doctor Hugh had been to town, and he tried to
find in his eyes some confession that the Countess
was pacified and his legacy clinched; but all he
could see there was the light of [his juvenile joy in
two or three of the phrases of the newspaper. Dencombe could n't read them, but when his visitor had
insisted on repeating them more than once he was
able to shake an unintoxicated head. "Ah no —
but they would have been true of what I *could* have
done!"

"What people 'could have done' is mainly what
they 've in fact done," Doctor Hugh contended.

"Mainly, yes; but I 've been an idiot!" Dencombe
said.

Doctor Hugh did remain; the end was coming fast.
Two days later his patient observed to him, by way
of the feeblest of jokes, that there would now be no
question whatever of a second chance. At this the
young man stared; then he exclaimed: "Why it has
come to pass — it has come to pass! The second
chance has been the public's — the chance to find
the point of view, to pick up the pearl!"

"Oh the pearl!" poor Dencombe uneasily sighed.
A smile as cold as a winter sunset flickered on his

drawn lips as he added: "The pearl is the unwritten — the pearl is the unalloyed, the *rest*, the lost!"

From that hour he was less and less present, heedless to all appearance of what went on round him. His disease was definitely mortal, of an action as relentless, after the short arrest that had enabled him to fall in with Doctor Hugh, as a leak in a great ship. Sinking steadily, though this visitor, a man of rare resources, now cordially approved by his physician, showed endless art in guarding him from pain, poor Dencombe kept no reckoning of favour or neglect, betrayed no symptom of regret or speculation. Yet toward the last he gave a sign of having noticed how for two days Doctor Hugh had n't been in his room, a sign that consisted of his suddenly opening his eyes to put a question. Had he spent those days with the Countess?

"The Countess is dead," said Doctor Hugh. "I knew that in a particular contingency she would n't resist. I went to her grave."

Dencombe's eyes opened wider. "She left you 'something handsome'?"

The young man gave a laugh almost too light for a chamber of woe. "Never a penny. She roundly cursed me."

"Cursed you?" Dencombe wailed.

"For giving her up. I gave her up for *you*. I had to choose," his companion explained.

"You chose to let a fortune go?"

"I chose to accept, whatever they might be, the consequences of my infatuation," smiled Doctor Hugh. Then as a larger pleasantry: "The fortune be hanged! It's your own fault if I can't get your things out of my head."

The immediate tribute to his humour was a long bewildered moan; after which, for many hours, many days, Dencombe lay motionless and absent. A response so absolute, such a glimpse of a definite result and such a sense of credit, worked together in his mind and, producing a strange commotion, slowly altered and transfigured his despair. The sense of cold submersion left him — he seemed to float without an effort. The incident was extraordinary as evidence, and it shed an intenser light. At the last he signed to Doctor Hugh to listen and, when he was down on his knees by the pillow, brought him very near. "You've made me think it all a delusion."

"Not your glory, my dear friend," stammered the young man.

"Not my glory — what there is of it! It *is* glory — to have been tested, to have had our little quality and cast our little spell. The thing is to have made somebody care. You happen to be crazy of course, but that does n't affect the law."

"You're a great success!" said Doctor Hugh, putting into his young voice the ring of a marriage-bell.

Dencombe lay taking this in; then he gathered strength to speak once more. "A second chance— *that's* the delusion. There never was to be but one. We work in the dark — we do what we can — we give what we have. Our doubt is our passion and our passion is our task. The rest is the madness of art."

"If you 've doubted, if you 've despaired, you 've always 'done' it," his visitor subtly argued.

"We 've done something or other," Dencombe conceded.

"Something or other is everything. It 's the feasible. It 's *you!*"

"Comforter!" poor Dencombe ironically sighed.

"But it 's true," insisted his friend.

"It 's true. It 's frustration that does n't count."

"Frustration 's only life," said Doctor Hugh.

"Yes, it 's what passes." Poor Dencombe was barely audible, but he had marked with the words the virtual end of his first and only chance.

GREVILLE FANE

GREVILLE FANE

Coming in to dress for dinner I found a telegram: "Mrs. Stormer dying; can you give us half a column for to-morrow evening? Let her down easily, but not too easily." I was late; I was in a hurry; I had very little time to think; but at a venture I dispatched a reply: "Will do what I can." It was not till I had dressed and was rolling away to dinner that, in the hansom, I bethought myself of the difficulty of the condition attached. The difficulty was not of course in letting her down easily but in qualifying that indulgence. "So I simply won't qualify it," I said. I didn't admire but liked her, and had known her so long that I almost felt heartless in sitting down at such an hour to a feast of indifference. I must have seemed abstracted, for the early years of my acquaintance with her came back to me. I spoke of her to the lady I had taken down, but the lady I had taken down had never heard of Greville Fane. I tried my other neighbour, who pronounced her books "too vile." I had never thought them very good, but I should let her down more easily than that.

I came away early, for the express purpose of driving to ask about her. The journey took time, for she lived in the northwest district, in the neighbourhood of Primrose Hill. My apprehension that I should be too late was justified in a fuller sense than I had attached to it — I had only feared that the house would be shut up. There were lights in the windows, and the temperate tinkle of my bell brought a servant immediately to the door; but poor Mrs. Stormer had passed into a state in which the resonance of no earthly knocker was to be feared. A lady hovering behind the servant came forward into the hall when she heard my voice. I recognised Lady Luard, but she had mistaken me for the doctor.

"Pardon my appearing at such an hour," I said; "it was the first possible moment after I heard."

"It's all over," Lady Luard replied. "Dearest mamma!"

She stood there under the lamp with her eyes on me; she was very tall, very stiff, very cold, and always looked as if these things, and some others beside, in her dress, in her manner and even in her name, were an implication that she was very admirable. I had never been able to follow the argument, but that's a detail. I expressed briefly and frankly what I felt, while the little mottled maidservant flattened herself against the wall of the narrow passage and tried to look detached without looking indifferent. It was not a moment to make a visit, and I was on the point of retreating when Lady Luard arrested me with a queer casual drawling "Would you — a — would you perhaps be *writing* something?" I felt for the instant like an infamous interviewer, which I was n't. But I pleaded guilty to this intention, on which she returned: "I'm so very glad — but I think my brother would like to see you." I detested her brother, but it was n't an occasion to act this out; so I suffered myself to be inducted, to my surprise, into a small back room which I immediately recognised as the scene, during the later years, of Mrs. Stormer's imperturbable industry. Her table was there, the battered and blotted accessory to innumerable literary lapses, with its contracted space for the arms (she wrote only from the elbow down) and the confusion of scrappy scribbled sheets which had already become literary remains. Leolin was also there, smoking a cigarette before the fire and looking impudent even in his grief, sincere as it well might have been.

To meet him, to greet him, I had to make a sharp effort; for the air he wore to me as he stood before me was quite that of his mother's murderer. She lay silent for ever upstairs — as dead as an unsuccessful book, and his swaggering erectness was a kind of symbol of his having killed her. I wondered if he had already, with his sister, been calculating what they could get for the poor papers on the table; but I hadn't long to wait to learn, since in reply to the few words of sympathy I addressed him he puffed out: "It's miserable, miserable, yes; but she has left three books complete." His words had the oddest effect; they converted the cramped little room into a seat of trade and made the "book" wonderfully feasible. He would certainly get all that could be got for the three. Lady Luard explained to me that her husband had been with them, but had had to go down to the House. To her brother she mentioned that I was going to write something, and to me again made it clear that she hoped I would "do mamma justice." She added that she did n't think this had ever been done. She said to her brother: "Don't you think there are some things he ought thoroughly to understand?" and on his instantly exclaiming "Oh thoroughly, thoroughly!" went on rather austerely: "I mean about mamma's birth."

"Yes and her connexions," Leolin added.

I professed every willingness, and for five minutes I listened; but it would be too much to say I clearly understood. I don't even now, but it's not important. My vision was of other matters than those they put before me, and while they desired there should be no mistake about their ancestors I became keener and keener about themselves. I got away as soon as possible and walked home through the great dusky empty London — the best of all conditions for thought. By the time I reached my door my little article was practically composed — ready to be transferred on the morrow from the polished plate of fancy. I believe it attracted some notice, was thought "graceful" and was said to be by some one else. I had to be pointed without being lively, and it took some doing. But what I said was much less interesting than what I thought — especially during the half-hour I spent in my armchair by the fire, smoking the cigar I always light before going to bed. I went to sleep there, I believe; but I continued to moralise about Greville Fane. I'm reluctant to lose that retrospect altogether, and this is a dim little memory of it, a document not to "serve." The dear woman had written a hundred stories, but none so curious as her own.

When first I knew her she had published half a dozen fictions, and I believe I had also perpetrated

a novel. She was more than a dozen years my elder,
but a person who always acknowledged her comparative state. It was n't so very long ago, but in
London, amid the big waves of the present, even a
near horizon gets hidden. I met her at some dinner
and took her down, rather flattered at offering my
arm to a celebrity. She did n't look like one, with her
matronly mild inanimate face, but I supposed her
greatness would come out in her conversation. I gave
it all the opportunities I could, but was nevertheless
not disappointed when I found her only a dull kind
woman. This was why I liked her — she rested me
so from literature. To myself literature was an irritation, a torment; but Greville Fane slumbered in
the intellectual part of it even as a cat on a hearth-
rug or a Creole in a hammock. She was n't a woman
of genius, but her faculty was so special, so much
a gift out of hand, that I 've often wondered why
she fell below that distinction. This was doubtless
because the transaction, in her case, had remained
incomplete; genius always pays for the gift, feels the
debt, and she was placidly unconscious of a call.
She could invent stories by the yard, but could n't
write a page of English. She went down to her grave
without suspecting that though she had contributed
volumes to the diversion of her contemporaries she
had n't contributed a sentence to the language. This
had n't prevented bushels of criticism from being
heaped on her head; she was worth a couple of
columns any day to the weekly papers, in which it
was shown that her pictures of life were dreadful but
her style superior. She asked me to come and see

her and I complied. She lived then in Montpellier Square; which helped me to see how dissociated her imagination was from her character.

An industrious widow, devoted to her daily stint, to meeting the butcher and baker and making a home for her son and daughter, from the moment she took her pen in her hand she became a creature of passion. She thought the English novel deplorably wanting in that element, and the task she had cut out for herself was to supply the deficiency. Passion in high life was the general formula of this work, for her imagination was at home only in the most exalted circles. She adored in truth the aristocracy, and they constituted for her the romance of the world or, what is more to the point, the prime material of fiction. Their beauty and luxury, their loves and revenges, their temptations and surrenders, their immoralities and diamonds were as familiar to her as the blots on her writing-table. She was not a belated producer of the old fashionable novel, but, with a cleverness and a modernness of her own, had freshened up the fly-blown tinsel. She turned off plots by the hundred and — so far as her flying quill could convey her — was perpetually going abroad. Her types, her illustrations, her tone were nothing if not cosmopolitan. She recognised nothing less provincial than European society, and her fine folk knew each other and made love to each other from Doncaster to Bucharest. She had an idea that she resembled Balzac, and her favourite historical characters were Lucien de Rubempré and the Vidame de Pamiers. I must add that when I once asked her who the latter personage was she was unable to tell me. She was very brave and healthy and cheerful, very abundant and innocent and wicked. She was expert and vulgar and snobbish, and never so intensely British as when she was particularly foreign.

This combination of qualities had brought her early success, and I remember having heard with wonder and envy of what she "got," in those days, for a novel. The revelation gave me a pang: it was such a proof that, practising a totally different style, I should never make my fortune. And yet when, as I knew her better she told me her real tariff and I saw how rumour had quadrupled it, I liked her enough to be sorry. After a while I discovered too that if she got less it was not that *I* was to get any more. My failure never had what Mrs. Stormer would have called the banality of being relative — it was always admirably absolute. She lived at ease however in those days — ease is exactly the word, though she produced three novels a year. She scorned me when I spoke of difficulty — it was the only thing that made her angry. If I hinted at the grand licking into shape that a work of art required she thought it a pretension and a *pose*. She never recognised the "torment of form"; the furthest she went was to introduce into one of her books (in satire her hand was heavy) a young poet who was always talking about it. I could n't quite understand her irritation on this score, for she had nothing at stake in the matter. She had a shrewd perception that form, in prose at least, never recommended any one to the public we were condemned to address; according to which she lost nothing (her private humiliation not counted) by having none to show. She made no pretence of producing works of art, but had comfortable tea-drinking hours in which she freely confessed herself a common pastrycook, dealing in such tarts and puddings as would bring customers to the shop. She put in plenty of sugar and of cochineal, or whatever it is that gives these articles a rich and attractive colour. She had a calm independence of observation and opportunity which constituted an inexpugnable strength and would enable her to go on indefinitely. It's only real success that wanes, it's only solid things that melt. Greville Fane's ignorance of life was a resource still more unfailing than the most approved receipt. On her saying once that the day would come when she should have written herself out I answered: "Ah you open straight into fairyland, and the fairies love you and *they* never change. Fairyland's always there; it always was from the beginning of time and always will be to the end. They've given you the key and you can always open the door. With me it's different; I try, in my clumsy way, to be in some direct relation to life." "Oh bother your direct relation to life!" she used to reply, for she was always annoyed by the phrase — which would n't in the least prevent her using it as a note of elegance. With no more prejudices than an old sausage-mill, she would give forth again with patient punctuality any poor verbal scrap that had been dropped into her. I cheered her with saying that the dark day, at the end, would be for the 'likes' of *me;* since, proceeding in our small way by experience and study — priggish we! —

we depended not on a revelation but on a little tiresome process. Attention depended on occasion, and where should we be when occasion failed?

One day she told me that as the novelist's life was so delightful and, during the good years at least, such a comfortable support — she had these staggering optimisms — she meant to train up her boy to follow it. She took the ingenious view that it was a profession like another and that therefore everything was to be gained by beginning young and serving an apprenticeship. Moreover the education would be less expensive than any other special course, inasmuch as she could herself administer it. She did n't profess to keep a school, but she could at least teach her own child. It was n't that she had such a gift, but — she confessed to me as if she were afraid I should laugh at her — that *he* had. I did n't laugh at her for that, because I thought the boy sharp — I had seen him sundry times. He was well-grown and good-looking and unabashed, and both he and his sister made me wonder about their defunct papa, concerning whom the little I knew was that he had been a country vicar and brother to a small squire. I explained them to myself by suppositions and imputations possibly unjust to the departed; so little were they — superficially at least — the children of their mother. There used to be on an easel in her drawing-room an enlarged photograph of her husband, done by some horrible posthumous "process" and draped, as to its florid frame, with a silken scarf which testified to the candour of Greville Fane's bad taste. It made him look like an unsuccessful tragedian, but it was n't a thing

to trust. He may have been a successful comedian.
Of the two children the girl was the elder, and struck
me in all her younger years as singularly colourless.
She was only long, very long, like an undecipherable
letter. It was n't till Mrs. Stormer came back from
a protracted residence abroad that Ethel (which was
this young lady's name) began to produce the effect,
large and stiff and afterwards eminent in her, of
a certain kind of resolution, something as public and
important as if a meeting and a chairman had passed
it. She gave one to understand she meant to do
all she could for herself. She was long-necked and
near-sighted and striking, and I thought I had never
seen sweet seventeen in a form so hard and high and
dry. She was cold and affected and ambitious, and
she carried an eyeglass with a long handle, which she
put up whenever she wanted not to see. She had
come out, as the phrase is, immensely; and yet I felt
as if she were surrounded with a spiked iron railing.
What she meant to do for herself was to marry, and
it was the only thing, I think, that she meant to do for
any one else; yet who would be inspired to clamber
over that bristling barrier? What flower of tenderness
or of intimacy would such an adventurer conceive as
his reward?

This was for Sir Baldwin Luard to say; but he
naturally never confided me the secret. He was a
joyless jokeless young man, with the air of having
other secrets as well, and a determination to get on
politically that was indicated by his never having been
known to commit himself—as regards any proposition whatever—beyond an unchallengeable "Oh!"

His wife and he must have conversed mainly in prim
ejaculations, but they understood sufficiently that
they were kindred spirits. I remember being angry
with Greville Fane when she announced these nuptials to me as magnificent; I remember asking her
what splendour there was in the union of the daughter
of a woman of genius with an irredeemable mediocrity. "Oh he has immense ability," she said; but she
blushed for the maternal fib. What she meant was
that though Sir Baldwin's estates were not vast — he
had a dreary house in South Kensington and a still
drearier "Hall" somewhere in Essex, which was let
— the connexion was a "smarter" one than a child
of hers could have aspired to form. In spite of the
social bravery of her novels she took a very humble
and dingy view of herself, so that of all her productions "my daughter Lady Luard" was quite the one
she was proudest of. That personage thought our
authoress vulgar and was distressed and perplexed
by the frequent freedoms of her pen, but had a
complicated attitude for this indirect connexion with
literature. So far as it was lucrative her ladyship
approved of it and could compound with the inferi-
ority of the pursuit by practical justice to some of its
advantages. I had reason to know — my reason was
simply that poor Mrs. Stormer told me — how she
suffered the inky fingers to press an occasional bank-
note into her palm. On the other hand she deplored
the "peculiar style" to which Greville Fane had devoted herself, and wondered where a spectator with
the advantage of so ladylike a daughter could have
picked up such views about the best society. "She

might know better, with Leolin and me," Lady Luard
had been heard to remark; but it appeared that some
of Greville Fane's superstitions were incurable. She
did n't live in Lady Luard's society, and the best
was n't good enough for her — she must improve on
it so prodigiously.

I could see this necessity increase in her during
the years she spent abroad, when I had glimpses of
her in the shifting sojourns that lay in the path of my
annual ramble. She betook herself from Germany
to Switzerland and from Switzerland to Italy; she
favoured cheap places and set up her desk in the
smaller capitals. I took a look at her whenever I
could, and I always asked how Leolin was getting
on. She gave me beautiful accounts of him, and,
occasion favouring, the boy was produced for my
advantage. I had entered from the first into the joke
of his career — I pretended to regard him as a conse-
crated child. It had been a joke for Mrs. Stormer at
first, but the youth himself had been shrewd enough
to make the matter serious. If his parent accepted
the principle that the intending novelist can't begin
too early to see life, Leolin was n't interested in hanging back from the application of it. He was eager
to qualify himself and took to cigarettes at ten on the
highest literary grounds. His fond mother gazed at
him with extravagant envy and, like Desdemona,
wished heaven had made *her* such a man. She explained to me more than once that in her profession
she had found her sex a dreadful drawback. She
loved the story of Madame George Sand's early rebellion against this hindrance, and believed that if she

had worn trousers she could have written as well as
that lady. Leolin had for the career at least the
qualification of trousers, and as he grew older he
recognised its importance by laying in ever so many
pair. He grew up thus in gorgeous apparel, which
was his way of interpreting his mother's system.
Whenever I met her, accordingly, I found her still
under the impression that she was carrying this system
out and that the sacrifices made him were bearing
heavy fruit. She was giving him experience, she was
giving him impressions, she was putting a *gagne-pain*
into his hand. It was another name for spoiling him
with the best conscience in the world. The queerest
pictures come back to me of this period of the good
lady's life and of the extraordinarily virtuous muddled
bewildering tenor of it. She had an idea she was
seeing foreign manners as well as her petticoats
would allow; but in reality she was n't seeing anything, least of all, fortunately, how much she was
laughed at. She drove her whimsical pen at Dresden
and at Florence — she produced in all places and at
all times the same romantic and ridiculous fictions.
She carried about her box of properties, tumbling
out promptly the familiar tarnished old puppets. She
believed in them when others could n't, and as they
were like nothing that was to be seen under the sun
it was impossible to prove by comparison that they
were wrong. You can't compare birds and fishes; you
could only feel that, as Greville Fane's characters
had the fine plumage of the former species, human
beings must be of the latter.

It would have been droll if it had n't been so

exemplary to see her tracing the loves of the duchesses beside the innocent cribs of her children. The
immoral and the maternal lived together, in her dilig-
ent days, on the most comfortable terms, and she
stopped curling the moustaches of her Guardsmen to
pat the heads of her babes. She was haunted by
solemn spinsters who came to tea from Continental
pensions, and by unsophisticated Americans who told
her she was just loved in *their* country. "I had
rather be just paid there," she usually replied; for
this tribute of transatlantic opinion was the only
thing that galled her. The Americans went away
thinking her coarse; though as the author of so
many beautiful love-stories she was disappointing to
most of these pilgrims, who had n't expected to find
a shy stout ruddy lady in a cap like a crumbled pyramid. She wrote about the affections and the impossibility of controlling them, but she talked of the price
of pension and the convenience of an English chemist.
She devoted much thought and many thousands of
francs to the education of her daughter, who spent
three years at a very superior school at Dresden,
receiving wonderful instruction in sciences, arts and
tongues, and who, taking a different line from Leolin,
was to be brought up wholly as a *femme du monde*.
The girl was musical and philological; she went in
for several languages and learned enough about
them to be inspired with a great contempt for her
mother's artless accents. Greville Fane's French
and Italian were droll; the imitative faculty had been
denied her, and she had an unequalled gift, especially
pen in hand, of squeezing big mistakes into small

opportunities. She knew it but did n't care; correctness was the virtue in the world that, like her heroes and heroines, she valued least. Ethel, who had noted in her pages some remarkable lapses, undertook at one time to revise her proofs; but I remember her telling me a year after the girl had left school that this function had been very briefly exercised. "She can't read me," said Mrs. Stormer; "I offend her taste. She tells me that at Dresden — at school — I was never allowed." The good lady seemed surprised at this, having the best conscience in the world about her lucubrations. She had never meant to fly in the face of anything, and considered that she grovelled before the Rhadamanthus of the English literary tribunal, the celebrated and awful Young Person. I assured her, as a joke, that she was frightfully indecent — she had in fact that element of truth as little as any other — my purpose being solely to prevent her guessing that her daughter had dropped her not because she was immoral but because she was vulgar. I used to figure her children closeted together and putting it to each other with a gaze of dismay: "Why should she *be* so — and so *fearfully* so — when she has the advantage of our society? Should n't *we* have taught her better?" Then I imagined their recognising with a blush and a shrug that she was unteachable, irreformable. Indeed she was, poor lady, but it's never fair to read by the light of taste things essentially not written in it. Greville Fane kept through all her riot of absurdity a witless confidence that should have been as safe from criticism as a stutter or a squint.

She did n't make her son ashamed of the profession to which he was destined, however; she only made him ashamed of the way she herself exercised it. But he bore his humiliation much better than his sister, being ready to assume he should one day restore the balance. A canny and far-seeing youth, with appetites and aspirations, he had n't a scruple in his composition. His mother's theory of the happy knack he could pick up deprived him of the wholesome discipline required to prevent young idlers from becoming cads. He enjoyed on foreign soil a casual tutor and the common snatch or two of a Swiss school, but addressed himself to no consecutive study nor to any prospect of a university or a degree. It may be imagined with what zeal, as the years went on, he entered into the pleasantry of there being no manual so important to him as the massive book of life. It was an expensive volume to peruse, but Mrs. Stormer was willing to lay out a sum in what she would have called her *premiers frais*. Ethel disapproved — she found this education irregular for an English gentleman. Her voice was for Eton and Oxford or for any public school — she would have resigned herself to one of the scrubbier — with the army to follow. But Leolin never was afraid of his sister, and they visibly disliked, though they sometimes agreed to assist, each other. They could combine to work the oracle — to keep their mother at her desk.

When she reappeared in England, telling me she had "secured" all the Continent could give her, Leolin was a broad-shouldered red-faced young man with an immense wardrobe and an extraordinary

assurance of manner. She was fondly, quite aggress-
ively certain she had taken the right course with
him, and addicted to boasting of all he knew and had
seen. He was now quite ready to embark on the
family profession, to commence author, as they used
to say, and a little while later she told me he had
started. He had written something tremendously
clever which was coming out in the *Cheapside*. I
believe it came out; I had no time to look for it; I
never heard anything about it. I took for granted that
if this contribution had passed through his mother's
hands it would virtually rather illustrate *her* fine
facility, and it was interesting to consider the poor
lady's future in the light of her having to write her
son's novels as well as her own. This was n't the
way she looked at it herself — she took the charming
ground that he 'd help her to write hers. She used
to assure me he supplied passages of the greatest
value to these last — all sorts of telling technical
things, happy touches about hunting and yachting
and cigars and wine, about City slang and the way
men talk at clubs — that she could n't be expected
to get very straight. It was all so much practice for
him and so much alleviation for herself. I was unable
to identify such pages, for I had long since ceased to
"keep up" with Greville Fane; but I could quite believe at least that the wine-question had been put by
Leolin's good offices on a better footing, for the dear
woman used to mix her drinks — she was perpetually
serving the most splendid suppers — in the queerest
fashion. I could see him quite ripe to embrace regularly that care. It occurred to me indeed, when she

settled in England again, that she might by a shrewd use of both her children be able to rejuvenate her style. Ethel had come back to wreak her native, her social yearning, and if she could n't take her mother into company would at least go into it herself. Silently, stiffly, almost grimly, this young lady reared her head, clenched her long teeth, squared her lean elbows and found her way up the staircases she had marked. The only communication she ever made, the only effusion of confidence with which she ever honoured me, was when she said "I don't want to know the people mamma knows, I mean to know others." I took due note of the remark, for I was n't one of the "others." I could n't trace therefore the steps and stages of her climb; I could only admire it at a distance and congratulate her mother in due course on the results. The results, the gradual, the final, the wonderful, were that Ethel went to "big" parties and got people to take her. Some of them were people she had met abroad, and others people the people she had met abroad had met. They ministered alike to Miss Ethel's convenience, and I wondered how she extracted so many favours without the expenditure of a smile. Her smile was the dimmest thing in nature, diluted, unsweetened, inexpensive lemonade, and she had arrived precociously at social wisdom, recognising that if she was neither pretty enough nor rich enough nor clever enough, she could at least, in her muscular youth, be rude enough. Therefore, so placed to give her parent tips, to let her know what really occurred in the mansions of the great, to supply her with local colour, with

data to work from, she promoted the driving of the
well-worn quill, over the brave old battered blot-
ting book, to a still lustier measure and precisely
at the moment when most was to depend on this
labour. But if she became a great critic it appeared
that the labourer herself was constitutionally inapt
for the lesson. It was late in the day for Greville
Fane to learn, and I heard nothing of her having
developed a new manner. She was to have had only
one manner, as Leolin would have said, from start
to finish.

She was weary and spent at last, but confided to
me that she could n't afford to pause. She continued
to speak of her son's work as the great hope of their
future — she had saved no money — though the
young man wore to my sense an air more and more
professional if you like, but less and less literary.
There was at the end of a couple of years something
rare in the impudence of his playing of his part in
the comedy. When I wondered how she could play
hers it was to feel afresh the fatuity of her fondness,
which was proof, I believed — I indeed saw to the end
— against any interference of reason. She loved the
young impostor with a simple blind benighted love,
and of all the heroes of romance who had passed before her eyes he was by far the brightest. He was at
any rate the most real — she could touch him, pay
for him, suffer for him, worship him. He made her
think of her princes and dukes, and when she wished
to fix these figures in her mind's eye she thought of
her boy. She had often told me she was herself carried
away by her creations, and she was certainly carried

away by Leolin. He vivified — by what romantically might have been at least — the whole question of youth and passion. She held, not unjustly, that the sincere novelist should feel the whole flood of life; she acknowledged with regret that she had n't had time to feel it herself, and the lapse in her history was in a manner made up by the sight of its rush through this magnificent young man. She exhorted him, I suppose, to encourage the rush; she wrung her own flaccid little sponge into the torrent. What passed between them in her pedagogic hours was naturally a blank to me, but I gathered that she mainly impressed on him that the great thing was to live, because that gave you material. He asked nothing better; he collected material, and the recipe served as a universal pretext. You had only to look at him to see that, with his rings and breastpins, his cross-barred jackets, his early *embonpoint*, his eyes that looked like imitation jewels, his various indications of a dense full-blown temperament, his idea of life was singularly vulgar; but he was so far auspicious as that his response to his mother's expectations was in a high degree practical. If she had imposed a profession on him from his tenderest years it was exactly a profession that he followed. The two were not quite the same, inasmuch as the one he had adopted was simply to live at her expense; but at least she could n't say he had n't taken a line. If she insisted on believing in him he offered himself to the sacrifice. My impression is that her secret dream was that he should have a *liaison* with a countess, and he persuaded her without difficulty that he had one. I don't know what countesses are capable of, but I've a clear notion of what Leolin was.

He did n't persuade his sister, who despised him — she wished to work her mother in her own way; so that I asked myself why the girl's judgement of him did n't make me like her better. It was because it did n't save her after all from the mute agreement with him to go halves. There were moments when I could n't help looking hard into his atrocious young eyes, challenging him to confess his fantastic fraud and give it up. Not a little tacit conversation passed between us in this way, but he had always the best of the business. If I said: "Oh come now, with *me* you need n't keep it up; plead guilty and I'll let you off," he wore the most ingenuous, the most candid expression, in the depths of which I could read: "Ah yes, I know it exasperates you — that's just why I do it." He took the line of earnest enquiry, talked about Balzac and Flaubert, asked me if I thought Dickens *did* exaggerate and Thackeray *ought* to be called a pessimist. Once he came to see me, at his mother's suggestion he declared, on purpose to ask me how far, in my opinion, in the English novel, one really might venture to "go." He was n't resigned to the usual pruderies, the worship of childish twaddle; he suffered already from too much bread and butter. He struck out the brilliant idea that nobody knew how far we might go, since nobody had ever tried. Did I think *he* might safely try — would it injure his mother if he did? He would rather disgrace himslf by his timidities than injure his mother, but certainly some one ought to try. Would n't *I* try — could n't I be prevailed upon to look at it as a duty? Surely the ultimate point ought to be fixed — he was worried, haunted by the question. He patronised me unblushingly, made me feel a foolish amateur, a helpless novice, enquired into my habits of work and conveyed to me that I was utterly *vieux jeu* and had n't had the advantage of an early training. I had n't been brought up from the egg, I knew nothing of life — did n't go at it on *his* system. He had dipped into French feuilletons and picked up plenty of phrases, and he made a much better show in talk than his poor mother, who never had time to read anything and could only be showy with her pen. If I did n't kick him down-stairs it was because he would have landed on her at the bottom.

When she went to live at Primrose Hill I called there and found her wasted and wan. It had visibly dropped, the elation caused the year before by Ethel's marriage; the foam on the cup had subsided and there was bitterness in the draught. She had had to take a cheaper house—and now had to work still harder to pay even for that. Sir Baldwin was obliged to be close; his charges were fearful, and the dream of her living with her daughter — a vision she had never mentioned to me — must be renounced. "I 'd have helped them with things, and could have lived per-fectly in one room," she said; "I 'd have paid for everything, and — after all— I 'm some one, ain't I? But I don't fit in, and Ethel tells me there are tire-some people she *must* receive. I can help them from here, no doubt, better than from there. She told me once, you know, what she thinks of my picture of life. 'Mamma, your picture of life's preposterous!' No doubt it is, but she's vexed with me for letting my prices go down; and I had to write three novels to pay for all her marriage cost me. I did it very well — I mean the outfit and the wedding; but that's why I'm here. At any rate she doesn't want a dingy old woman at Blicket. I should give the place an atmosphere of literary prestige, but literary prestige is only the eminence of nobodies. Besides, she knows what to think of my glory — she knows I'm glorious only at Peckham and Hackney. She doesn't want her friends to ask if I've never known nice people. She can't tell them I've never been in society. She tried to teach me better once, but I couldn't catch on. It would seem too as if Peckham and Hackney had had enough of me; for (don't tell any one!) I've had to take less for my last than I ever took for anything." I asked her how little this had been, not from curiosity, but in order to upbraid her, more disinterestedly than Lady Luard had done, for such concessions. She answered "I'm ashamed to tell you" and then began to cry.

I had never seen her break down and I was proportionately moved; she sobbed like a frightened child over the extinction of her vogue and the exhaustion of her vein. Her little workroom seemed indeed a barren place to grow flowers for the market, and I wondered in the after years (for she continued to produce and publish) by what desperate and heroic process she dragged them out of the soil. I remember asking her on that occasion what had become of

Leolin and how much longer she intended to allow him to amuse himself at her cost. She retorted with spirit, wiping her eyes, that he was down at Brighton hard at work — he was in the midst of a novel — and that he *felt* life so, in all its misery and mystery, that it was cruel to speak of such experiences as a pleasure. "He goes beneath the surface," she said, "and he *forces* himself to look at things from which he'd rather turn away. Do you call that amusing yourself? You should see his face sometimes! And he does it for me as much as for himself. He tells me everything — he comes home to me with his *trouvailles*. We're artists together, and to the artist all things are pure. I've often heard you say so yourself." The novel Leolin was engaged in at Brighton never saw the light, but a friend of mine and of Mrs. Stormer's who was staying there happened to mention to me later that he had seen the young apprentice to fiction driving, in a dog-cart, a young lady with a very pink face. When I suggested that she was perhaps a woman of title with whom he was conscientiously flirting my informant replied: "She is indeed, but do you know what her title is?" He pronounced it — it was familiar and descriptive — but I won't reproduce it here. I don't know whether Leolin mentioned it to his mother: she would have needed all the purity of the artist to forgive him. I hated so to come across him that in the very last years I went rarely to see her, though I knew she had come pretty well to the end of her rope. I didn't want her to tell me she had fairly to give her books away; I didn't want to see her old and abandoned and derided; I didn't want, in a word, to see her terribly cry. She still, however, kept it up amazingly, and every few months, at my club, I saw three new volumes, in green, in crimson, in blue, on the book-table that groaned with light literature. Once I met her at the Academy soirée, where you meet people you thought were dead, and she vouchsafed the information, as if she owed it to me in candour, that Leolin had been obliged to recognise the insuperable difficulties of the question of *form* — he was so fastidious; but that she had now arrived at a definite understanding with him (it was such a comfort!) that *she* would do the form if he would bring home the substance. That was now his employ — he foraged for her in the great world at a salary. "He's my 'devil,' don't you see? as if I were a great lawyer: he gets up the case and I argue it." She mentioned further that in addition to his salary he was paid by the piece: he got so much for a striking character, so much for a pretty name, so much for a plot, so much for an incident, and had so much promised him if he would invent a new crime.

"He *has* invented one," I said, "and he's paid every day of his life."

"What is it?" she asked, looking hard at the picture of the year, "Baby's Tub," near which we happened to be standing.

I hesitated a moment. "I myself will write a little story about it, and then you'll see."

But she never saw; she had never seen anything, and she passed away with her fine blindness unimpaired. Her son published every scrap of scribbled paper that could be extracted from her table-drawers, and his sister quarrelled with him mortally about the proceeds, which showed her only to have wanted a pretext, for they can't have been great. I don't know what Leolin lives on unless on a queer lady many years older than himself, whom he lately married. The last time I met him he said to me with his infuriating smile: "Don't you think we can go a little further still — just a little?" *He* really — with me at least — goes too far.

BROKEN WINGS

BROKEN WINGS

I

CONSCIOUS as he was of what was between them,
though perhaps less conscious than ever of why there
should at that time of day be anything, he would yet
scarce have supposed they could be so long in a house
together without some word or some look. It had
been since the Saturday afternoon, and that made
twenty-four hours. The party — five-and-thirty people and some of them great — was one in which words
and looks might more or less have gone astray. The
effect, none the less, he judged, would have been, for
her quite as for himself, that no sound and no sign
from the other had been picked up by either. They
had happened both at dinner and at luncheon to be
so placed as not to have to glare — or to grin —
across; and for the rest they could each, in such a
crowd, as freely help the general ease to keep them
apart as assist it to bring them together. One chance
there was, of course, that might be beyond their control. He had been the night before half-surprised at
not finding her his "fate" when the long procession
to the dining-room solemnly hooked itself together.
He would have said in advance — recognising it as
one of the sharp "notes" of Mundham — that,
should the gathering contain a literary lady, the literary lady would, for congruity, be apportioned to the

arm, when there was a question of arms, of the gentleman present who represented the nearest thing to
literature. Poor Straith represented "art," and that,
no doubt, would have been near enough had not the
party offered for choice a slight excess of men. The
representative of art had been of the two or three who
went in alone, whereas Mrs. Harvey had gone in with
one of the representatives of banking.

It was certain, however, that she would n't again
be consigned to Lord Belgrove, and it was just possible that he himself should not be again alone. She
would be on the whole the most probable remedy to
that state, on his part, of disgrace; and this precisely
was the great interest of their situation — they were
the only persons present without some advantage over
somebody else. They had n't a single advantage; they
could be named for nothing but their cleverness; they
were at the bottom of the social ladder. The social
ladder had even at Mundham — as they might properly have been told, as indeed practically they *were*
told — to end somewhere; which is no more than to
say that as he strolled about and thought of many
things Stuart Straith had after all a good deal the
sense of helping to hold it up. Another of the things
he thought of was the special oddity — for it was nothing else — of his being there at all, being there in
particular so out of his order and turn. He could n't
answer for Mrs. Harvey's turn and order. It might
well be that she was *in* hers; but these Saturday-to-
Monday occasions had hitherto mostly struck him
as great gilded cages as to which care was taken that
the birds should be birds of a feather.

BROKEN WINGS

There had been a wonderful walk in the afternoon, within the limits of the place, to a far-away tea-house; and in spite of the combinations and changes of this episode he had still escaped the necessity of putting either his old friend or himself to the test. Also it had been all, he flattered himself, without the pusillanimity of his avoiding her. Life was indeed well understood in these great conditions; the conditions constituted in their greatness a kind of fundamental facility, provided a general exemption, bathed the hour, whatever it was, in a universal blandness, that were all a happy solvent for awkward relations. It was for instance beautiful that if their failure to meet amid so much meeting had been of Mrs. Harvey's own contrivance he could n't be in the least vulgarly sure of it. There were places in which he would have had no doubt, places different enough from Mundham. He felt all the same and without anguish that these were much more *his* places—even if she did n't feel that they were much more hers. The day had been warm and splendid, and this moment of its wane —with dinner in sight, but as across a field of polished pink marble which seemed to say that wherever in such a house there was space there was also, benignantly, time — formed, of the whole procession of the hours, the one dearest to our friend, who on such occasions interposed it, whenever he could, between the set of impressions that ended and the set that began with "dressing." The great terraces and gardens were almost void; people had scattered, though not altogether even yet to dress. The air of the place, with the immense house all seated aloft in strength,

139

robed with summer and crowned with success, was such as to contribute something of its own to the poetry of early evening. This visitor at any rate saw and felt it all through one of those fine hazes of August that remind you — at least they reminded *him* — of the artful gauze stretched across the stage of a theatre when an effect of mystery or some particular pantomimic ravishment is desired.

Should he in fact have to pair with Mrs. Harvey for dinner it would be a shame to him not to have addressed her sooner; and should she on the contrary be put with some one else the loss of so much of the time would have but the greater ugliness. Did n't he meanwhile make out that there were ladies in the lower garden, from which the sound of voices, faint but, as always in the upper air of Mundham, exceedingly sweet, was just now borne to him? She might be among them, and if he should find her he 'd let her know he had sought her. He 'd treat it frankly as an occasion for declaring that what had happened between them — or rather what had *not* happened — was too absurd. What at present occurred, however, was that in his quest of her he suddenly, at the turn of an alley, perceived her, not far off, seated in a sort of bower with the Ambassador. With this he pulled up, going another way and pretending not to see them. Three times already that afternoon he had observed her in different situations with the Ambassador. He was the more struck accordingly when, upwards of an hour later, again alone and with his state unremedied, he saw her placed for dinner next his Excellency. It was n't at all what would have been at

Mundham her right seat, so that it could only be explained by his Excellency's direct request. She *was* a success! This time Straith was well in her view and could see that in the candle-light of the wonderful room, where the lustres were, like the table, all crystal and silver, she was as handsome as any one, taking the women of her age, and also as "smart" as the evening before, and as true as any of the others to the law of a marked difference in her smartness. If the beautiful way she held herself — for decidedly it *was* beautiful — came in a great measure from the good thing she professionally made of it all, our observer could reflect that the poor thing *he* professionally made of it probably affected his attitude in just the opposite way; but they communicated neither in the glare nor in the grin he had dreaded. Still, their eyes did now meet, and then it struck him her own were strange.

II

SHE, on her side, had her private consciousness, and quite as full a one, doubtless, as he, but with the advantage that when the company separated for the night she was not, like her friend, reduced to a vigil unalloyed. Lady Claude, at the top of the stairs, had said "May I look in — in five minutes — if you don't mind?" and then had arrived in due course and in a wonderful new beribboned gown, the thing just launched for such occasions. Lady Claude was young and earnest and delightfully bewildered and bewildering, and however interesting she might, through certain elements in her situation, have seemed to a literary lady, her own admirations and curiosities were such as from the first promised to rule the hour. She had already expressed to Mrs. Harvey a really informed enthusiasm. She not only delighted in her numerous books, which was a tribute the author had not infrequently met, but she even appeared to have read them — an appearance with which our authoress was much less acquainted. The great thing was that she also yearned to write, and that she had turned up in her fresh furbelows not only to reveal this secret and to ask for direction and comfort, but literally to make a stranger confidence, for which the mystery of midnight seemed propitious. Midnight was indeed, as the situation developed, well over before her confidence was spent, for it had ended by gathering such a current as floated forth, with everything in Lady Claude's own life, many things more in that of her adviser. Mrs. Harvey was at all events amused, touched and effectually kept awake; so by the end of half an hour they had quite got what might have been called their second wind of frankness and were using it for a discussion of the people in the house. Their primary communion had been simply on the question of the pecuniary profits of literature as the producer of so many admired volumes was prepared to present them to an aspirant. Lady Claude was in financial difficulties and desired the literary issue. This was the breathless revelation she had rustled over a mile of crimson velvet corridor to make.

"Nothing?" she had three minutes later incredulously gasped. "I can make nothing at all?" But the gasp was slight compared with the stupefaction communicated by a brief further parley, in the course of which Mrs. Harvey had, after an hesitation, taken her own plunge. "*You* make so little — wonderful *you?*" And then as the producer of the admired volumes simply sat there in her dressing-gown, with the saddest of slow headshakes, looking suddenly too wan even to care that it was at last all out: "What in that case is the use of success and celebrity and genius? You *have* no success?" She had looked almost awestruck at this further confession of her friend. They were face to face in a poor human crudity, which transformed itself quickly into an effusive embrace. "You've had it and lost it? Then when it has been as great as yours one *can* lose it?"

"More easily than one can get it."

Lady Claude continued to marvel. "But you do so much — and it's so beautiful!" On which Mrs. Harvey simply smiled again in her handsome despair, and after a moment found herself again in the arms of her visitor. The younger woman had remained for a time a good deal arrested and hushed, and had at any rate, sensitive and charming, immediately dropped, in the presence of this almost august unveiling, the question of her own thin troubles. But there are short cuts at that hour of night that morning scarce knows, and it took but little more of the breath of the real to suggest to Lady Claude more questions in such a connexion than she could answer for herself. "How then, if you have n't private means, do you get on?"

"Ah I don't get on!"

Lady Claude looked about. There were objects scattered in the fine old French room. "You 've lovely things."

"Two."

"Two?"

"Two frocks. I could n't stay another day."

"Ah what's *that?* I could n't either," said Lady Claude soothingly. "And you have," she continued, in the same spirit, "your nice maid —"

"Who's indeed a charming woman, but my cook in disguise!" Mrs. Harvey dropped.

"Ah you *are* clever!" her friend cried with a laugh that was as a climax of reassurance.

"Extraordinarily. But don't think," Mrs. Harvey hastened to add, "that I mean that that's why I'm here."

Her companion candidly thought. "Then why are you?"

"I have n't the least idea. I 've been wondering all the while, as I 've wondered so often before on such occasions, and without arriving at any other reason than that London's so wild."

Lady Claude wondered. "Wild?"

"Wild!" said her friend with some impatience. "That's the way London strikes."

"But do you call such an invitation a blow?"

"Yes — crushing. No one else, at all events, either," Mrs. Harvey added, "could tell you why I 'm here."

Lady Claude's power to drink in (and it was perhaps her most attaching quality) was greater still, when she felt strongly, than her power to reject. "Why how can you say that when you 've only to see how every one likes and admires you? Just look at the Ambassador," she had earnestly insisted. And this was what had precisely, as I have mentioned, carried the stream of their talk a good deal away from its source. It had therefore not much further to go before setting in motion the name of Stuart Straith, as to whom Lady Claude confessed to an interest — good-looking, distinguished, "sympathetic" as he was — that she could really almost hate him for having done nothing whatever to encourage. He had n't spoken to her once.

"But, my dear, if he has n't spoken to *me* —!"

Lady Claude appeared to regret this not too much for a hint that after all there might be a difference. "Oh but *could* he?"

"Without my having spoken to him first?" Mrs. Harvey turned it over. "Perhaps not; but I could n't have done that." Then to explain, and not only because Lady Claude was naturally vague, but because what was still visibly most vivid to her was her independent right to have been "made up" to: "And yet not because we 're not acquainted."

"You know him then?"

"But too well."

"You mean you don't like him?"

"On the contrary I like him to distraction."

"Then what 's the matter?" Lady Claude asked with some impatience.

Her friend hung fire but a moment. "Well, he would n't have me."

"'Have' you?"

"Ten years ago, after Mr. Harvey's death, when if he had lifted a finger I 'd have married him."

"But he did n't lift it?"

"He was too grand. I was too small — by *his* measure. He wanted to keep himself. He saw his future."

Lady Claude earnestly followed. "His present position?"

"Yes — everything that was to come to him; his steady rise in value."

"Has it been so great?"

"Surely — his situation and name. Don't you know his lovely work and what 's thought of it?"

"Oh yes, I know. That 's why —" But Lady Claude stopped. After which: "But if he 's still keeping himself?"

BROKEN WINGS

"Oh it's not for me," said Mrs. Harvey.

"And evidently not for *me*. Whom then," her visitor asked, "does he think good enough?"

"Oh these great people!" Mrs. Harvey smiled.

"But *we're* great people — you and I!" And Lady Claude kissed her good-night.

"You mustn't, all the same," the elder woman said, "betray the secret of *my* greatness, which I've told you, please remember, only in the deepest confidence."

Her tone had a quiet purity of bitterness that for a moment longer held her friend, after which Lady Claude had the happy inspiration of meeting it with graceful gaiety. "It's quite for the best, I'm sure, that Mr. Straith wouldn't have you. You've kept yourself too; you'll marry yet — an ambassador!" And with another good-night she reached the door. "You say you don't get on, but you do."

"Ah!" said Mrs. Harvey with vague attenuation.

"Oh yes, you do," Lady Claude insisted, while the door emphasised it with a little clap that sounded through the still house.

III

THE first night of "The New Girl" occurred, as every one remembers, three years ago, and the play is running yet, a fact that may render strange the failure to be deeply conscious of which two persons in the audience were guilty. It was not till afterwards present either to Mrs. Harvey or to Stuart Straith that "The New Girl" was one of the greatest successes of modern times. Indeed if the question had been put to them on the spot they might have appeared much at sea. But this, I may as well immediately say, was the result of their having found themselves side by side in the stalls and thereby given most of their attention to their own predicament. Straith showed he felt the importance of meeting it promptly, for he turned to his neighbour, who was already in her place, as soon as her identity had flushed well through his own arrival and subsidence. "I don't quite see how you can help speaking to me now."

Her face could only show him how long she had been aware of his approach. "The sound of your voice, coming to me straight, makes it indeed as easy for me as I could possibly desire."

He looked about at the serried rows, the loaded galleries and the stuffed boxes, with recognitions and nods; and this made between them another pause, during which, while the music seemed perfunctory and the bustle that in a London audience represents concentration increased, they felt how effectually, in the thick preoccupied medium, how extraordinarily, they were together.

"Well, that second afternoon at Mundham, just before dinner, I was very near forcing your hand. But something put me off. You're really too grand."

"Oh!" she murmured.

"Ambassadors," said Stuart Straith.

"Oh!" she again sounded. And before anything more could pass the curtain was up. It came down in due course and achieved, after various intervals, the rest of its motions without interrupting for our friends the sense of an evening of talk. They said when it was down almost nothing about the play, and when one of them toward the end put to the other, vaguely, "Is — a — this thing going?" the question had scarce the effect of being even relevant. What was clearest to them was that the people about were somehow enough taken up to leave them at their ease — but what taken up with they but half made out. Mrs. Harvey had none the less mentioned early that her presence had a reason and that she ought to attend, and her companion had asked her what she thought of a certain picture made at a given moment by the stage, in the reception of which he was so interested that it was really what had brought him. These were glances, however, that quickly strayed — strayed, for instance (as this could carry them far), in its coming to one of them to say that, whatever the piece might be, the real thing, as they had seen it at Mundham, was more than a match for any piece. For Mundham *was*, theatrically, the real thing; better for scenery, dresses,

music, pretty women, bare shoulders, everything —
even coherent dialogue; a much bigger and braver
show, and got up, as it were, infinitely more "re-
gardless." By Mundham they were held long enough
to find themselves, though with an equal surprise,
quite at one as to the special oddity of their having
caught each other in such a plight. Straith said that
he supposed what his friend meant was that it was
odd *he* should have been there; to which she returned
that she had been imputing to him exactly that judgement of her own presence.

"But why should n't *you* be?" he asked. "Is n't
that just what you *are*? Are n't you in your way —
like those people — a child of fortune and fashion?"

He got no more answer to this for some time than
if he had fairly wounded her. He indeed that evening
got no answer at all that was direct. But in the next
interval she brought out with abruptness, taking no
account of some other matter he had just touched:
"Don't you really know — ?"

She had paused. "Know what?"

Again she went on without heeding. "A place like
Mundham is, for me, a survival, though poor Mundham in particular won't, for me, have survived that
visit — on which it's to be pitied, is n't it? It was
a glittering ghost — since laid! — of my old time."

Straith, at this, almost gave a start. "Have *you* got
a new time?"

"Do you mean you yourself have?"

"Well," said Straith, "mine may now be called
middle-aged. It seems so long, I mean, since I set my
watch to it."

"Oh I have n't even a watch!" she returned with a laugh. "I'm beyond watches." After which she added: "We *might* have met more — or, I should say perhaps, have got more out of it when we *have* met."

"Yes, it has been too little. But I've always explained it by our living in such different worlds."

Mrs. Harvey could risk an abruptness. "Are you unhappy?"

He gave her a mild glare. "You said just now that you're beyond watches. I'm beyond unhappiness."

She turned from him and presently brought out: "I ought absolutely to take away *something* of the play."

"By all means. There's certainly something *I* shall take."

"Ah then you must help me — give it me."

"With all my heart," said Straith, "if it *can* help you. It's my feeling of our renewal."

She had one of the sad slow headshakes that at Mundham had been impressive to Lady Claude. "That won't help me."

"Then you must let me put to you now what I should have tried to get near enough to you there to put if I had n't been so afraid of the Ambassador. What has it been so long — our impossibility?"

"Well, I can only answer for my own vision of it, which is — which always was — that you were sorry for me, but felt a sort of scruple of showing me you had nothing better than pity to give."

"May I come to see you?" Straith asked some minutes after this.

Her words, for which he had also a while to wait, had in truth as little as his own the appearance of a reply. "*Are* you unhappy—really? Have n't you everything?"

"You're beautiful!" he said for all answer. "May n't I come?"

She demurred. "Where's your studio?"

"Oh not too far for me to go to places. Don't be anxious; I can walk, or even take the bus."

Mrs. Harvey once more delayed. Then she said: "May n't I rather come there?"

"I shall be but too delighted."

It was spoken promptly, even eagerly; yet the understanding appeared shortly after to have left between them a certain awkwardness, and it was almost as if to change the subject and relieve them equally that she suddenly reminded him of something he had spoken earlier. "You were to tell me why in particular you had to be here."

"Oh yes. To see my dresses."

"Yours!" She wondered.

"The second act. I made them out for them — designed them."

Before she could check it her tone escaped. "You?"

"I." He looked straight before him. "For the fee. And we did n't even notice them."

"*I* did n't," she confessed. But it offered the fact as a sign of her kindness for him, and this kindness was traceably what inspired something she said in the draughty porch, after the performance, while the footman of the friend, a fat rich immensely pleased lady who had given her a lift and then rejoined her from a seat in the balcony, went off to make sure of the brougham. "May I do something about your things?"

"'Do something'?"

"When I 've paid you my visit. Write something — about your pictures. I do a correspondence," said Mrs. Harvey.

He wondered as she had done in the stalls. "For a paper?"

"*The Blackport Banner*. A 'London Letter.' The new books, the new plays, the new twaddle of any sort — a little music, a little gossip, a little 'art.' You 'll help me — I need it awfully — with the art. I do three a month."

"*You* — wonderful you?" He spoke as Lady Claude had done, and could no more help it again than Mrs. Harvey had been able to help it in the stalls.

"Oh as you say, for the fee!" On which, as the footman signalled, her old lady began to plunge through the crowd.

IV

At the studio, where she came to him within the week, her first movement had been to exclaim on the splendid abundance of his work. She had looked round charmed — so struck as to be, as she called it, crushed. "You've such a wonderful lot to show."

"Indeed I have!" said Stuart Straith.

"That's where you beat *us*."

"I think it may very well be," he went on, "where I beat almost every one."

"And is much of it new?"

He looked about with her. "Some of it's pretty old. But my things have a way, I admit, of growing old extraordinarily fast. They seem to me in fact nowadays quite 'born old.'"

She had after a little the manner of coming back to something. "You *are* unhappy. You're *not* beyond it. You're just nicely, just fairly and squarely, in the middle of it."

"Well," said Straith, "if it surrounds me like a desert, so that I'm lost in it, that comes to the same thing. But I want you to tell me about yourself."

She had continued at first to move about and had taken out a pocket-book, which she held up at him. "This time I shall insist on notes. You made my mind a blank about that play, which is the sort of thing we can't afford. If it hadn't been for my fat old lady and the next day's papers!" She kept looking, going up to things, saying "How wonderful!" and "Oh your *way!*" and then stopping for a general impression, something in the whole charm. The place, high, handsome, neat, with two or three pale tapestries and several rare old pieces of furniture, showed a perfection of order, an absence of loose objects, as if it had been swept and squared for the occasion and made almost too immaculate. It was polished and cold — rather cold for the season and the weather; and Stuart Straith himself, buttoned and brushed, as fine and as clean as his room, might at her arrival have reminded her of the master of a neat bare ship on his deck and awaiting a cargo. "May I see everything? May I 'use' everything?"

"Oh no; you may n't by any means use everything. You may n't use half. *Did* I spoil your 'London Letter'?" he continued after a moment.

"No one can spoil them as I spoil them myself. I can't do them — I don't know how, and don't want to. I do them wrong, and the people want such trash. Of course they 'll 'sack' me."

She was in the centre, and he had the effect of going round her, restless and vague, in large slow circles. "Have you done them long?"

"Two or three months — this lot. But I 've done others and I know what happens. Oh, my dear, I 've done strange things!"

"And is it a good job?"

She hesitated, then puffed prettily enough an indifferent sigh. "Three and ninepence. Is that good?" He had stopped before her, looking at her up and down. "What do you get?" she went on, "for what you do for a play?"

"A little more, it would seem, than you. Four and sixpence. But I've only done as yet that one. Nothing else has offered."

"I see. But something *will*, eh?"

Poor Straith took a turn again. "Did you like them — for colour?" But again he pulled up. "Oh I forgot; we didn't notice them!"

For a moment they could laugh about it. "I noticed them, I assure you, in the *Banner*. 'The costumes in the second act are of the most marvellous beauty.' That's what I said."

"Oh that'll fetch the managers!" But before her again he seemed to take her in from head to foot. "You speak of 'using' things. If you'd only use yourself — for my enlightenment. Tell me all."

"You look at me," said Mrs. Harvey, "as with the wonder of who designs *my* costumes. How I dress on it, how I do even what I still do on it — on the three and ninepence — is *that* what you want to know?"

"What has happened to you?" Straith asked.

"How do I keep it up?" she continued as if she hadn't heard him. "But I *don't* keep it up. *You* do," she declared as she again looked round her.

Once more it set him off, but for a pause again almost as quick. "How long have you been — ?"

"Been what?" she asked as he faltered.

"Unhappy."

She smiled at him from a depth of indulgence. "As long as you've been ignorant — that what I've been *wanting* is your pity. Ah to have to know, as I believed I did, that you supposed it would wound me, and not to have been able to make you see it was the one thing left to me that would help me! Give me your pity now. It's all I want. I don't care for anything else. But give me that."

He had, as it happened at the moment, to do a smaller and a usual thing before he could do one so great and so strange. The youth whom he kept for service arrived with a tea-tray, in arranging a place for which, with the sequel of serving Mrs. Harvey, seating her and seeing the youth again out of the room, some minutes passed. "What pity could I dream of for you," he demanded as he at last dropped near her, "when I was myself so miserably sore?"

"Sore?" she wondered. "But you were happy — then."

"Happy not to have struck you as good enough? For I did n't, you know," he insisted. "You had your success, which was so immense. You had your high value, your future, your big possibilities; and I perfectly understood that, given those things, and given also my very much smaller situation, you should wish to keep yourself."

"Oh, oh!" She gasped as if hurt.

"I understand it; but how could it really make me 'happy'?" he asked.

She turned at him as with her hand on the old scar she could now carry. "You mean that all these years you 've really not known — ?"

"But not known what?"

His voice was so blank that at the sound of it, and at something that looked out from him, she only found another "Oh, oh!" which became the next instant a burst of tears.

V

SHE had appeared at first unwilling to receive him at home; but he understood it after she had left him, turning over more and more everything their meeting had shaken to the surface and piecing together memories that at last, however darkly, made a sense. He was to call on her, it was finally agreed, but not till the end of the week, when she should have finished "moving" — she had but just changed quarters; and meanwhile, as he came and went, mainly in the cold chamber of his own past endeavour, which looked even to himself as studios look when artists are dead and the public, in the arranged place, are admitted to stare, he had plenty to think about. What had come out — he could see it now — was that each, ten years before, had miserably misunderstood and then had turned for relief from pain to a perversity of pride. But it was himself above all he now sharply judged, since women, he felt, have to get on as they can, and for the mistake of this woman there were reasons he had to acknowledge with a sore heart. She had really found in the pomp of his early success, at the time they used to meet, and to care to, exactly the ground for her sense of failure with him that he had found in the vision of her gross popularity for his conviction that she judged him as comparatively small. Each had blundered, as sensitive souls of the "artistic temperament" blunder, into a conception

not only of the other's attitude, but of the other's
material situation at the moment, that had thrown
them back on stupid secrecy, where their estrange-
ment had grown like an evil plant in the shade. He
had positively believed her to have gone on all the
while making the five thousand a year that the first
eight or ten of her so supremely happy novels had
brought her in, just as she on her side had read into
the felicity of his first new hits, his pictures "of the
year" at three or four Academies, the absurdest
theory of the sort of career that, thanks to big dealers
and intelligent buyers, his gains would have built up
for him. It looked vulgar enough now, but it had
been grave enough then. His long detached delusion
about her "prices," at any rate, appeared to have
been more than matched by the strange stories occasionally floated to her — and all to make her but
draw more closely in — on the subject of his own.

It was with each equally that everything had
changed — everything but the stiff consciousness in
either of the need to conceal changes from the other.
If she had cherished for long years the soreness of her
not being "good" enough, so this was what had
counted most in her sustained effort to appear at least
as good as he. London meanwhile was big, London
was blind and benighted; and nothing had ever
occurred to undermine for him the fiction of her prosperity. Before his eyes there while she sat with him
she had pulled off one by one those vain coverings of
her state that she confessed she had hitherto done her
best — and so always with an eye on himself — de-
ceptively to draw about it. He had felt frozen, as he

listened, by such likenesses to things he knew. He recognised as she talked, he groaned as he understood. He understood — oh at last, whatever he had n't done before! And yet he could well have smiled, out of their common abyss, at such odd identities and recurrences. Truly the arts were sisters, as was so often said; for what apparently could be more like the experience of one than the experience of another? And she spared him things with it all. He felt this too, just as, even while showing her how he followed, he had bethought himself of closing his lips for the hour, none too soon, on his own stale story. There had been a beautiful intelligence for that matter in her having asked him nothing more. She had overflowed because shaken by not finding him happy, and her surrender had somehow offered itself to him as her way — the first that sprang up — of considering his trouble. She had left him at all events in full possession of all the phases through which in "literary circles" acclaimed states may pass on their regular march to eclipse and extinction. One had but one's hour, and if one had it soon — it was really almost a case of choice — one did n't have it late. It might also never even remotely have approached, at its best, things ridiculously rumoured. Straith felt on the whole how little he had known of literary circles, or of any mystery but his own indeed; on which, up to actual impending collapse, he had mounted such anxious guard.

It was when he went on the Friday to see her that he took in the latest of the phases in question, which might very well be almost the final one; there was at least that comfort in it. She had just settled in a small flat, where he recognised in the steady disposal, for the best, of various objects she had not yet parted with, her reason for having made him wait. Here they had together — these two worn and baffled workers — a wonderful hour of gladness in their lost battle and of freshness in their lost youth; for it was not till Stuart Straith had also raised the heavy mask and laid it beside her own on the table that they began really to feel themselves recover something of that possibility of each other they had so wearily wasted. Only she could n't get over it that he was like herself and that what she had shrunken to in her three or four simplified rooms had its perfect image in the specious show of his ordered studio and his accumulated work. He told everything now, kept no more back than she had kept at their previous meeting, while she repeated over and over "You — wonderful you?" as if the knowledge made a deeper darkness of fate, as if the pain of his having come down at all almost quenched the joy of his having come so much nearer. When she learned that he had n't for three years sold a picture — "You, beautiful you?" — it seemed a new cold breath out of the dusk of her own outlook. Disappointment and despair were in such relations contagious, and there was clearly as much less again left to her as the little that was left to him. He showed her, laughing at the long queerness of it, how awfully little, as they called it, this was. He let it all come, but with more mirth than misery, and with a final abandonment of pride that was like changing at the end of a dreadful day from tight shoes to loose ones.

There were moments when they might have resembled a couple united by some misdeed and meeting to decide on some desperate course; they gave themselves so to the great irony — the vision of the comic in contrasts — that precedes surrenders and extinctions.

They went over the whole thing, remounted the dwindling stream, reconstructed, explained, understood — recognised in short the particular example they gave and how without mutual suspicion they had been giving it side by side. "We're simply the case," Straith familiarly put it, "of having been had enough of. No case is perhaps more common, save that for you and for me, each in our line, it did look in the good time — did n't it? — as if nobody *could* have enough." With which they counted backward, gruesome as it was, the symptoms of satiety up to the first dawn, and lived again together the unforgettable hours — distant now — out of which it had begun to glimmer that the truth had to be faced and the right names given to the wrong facts. They laughed at their original explanations and the minor scale even of their early fears; compared notes on the fallibility of remedies and hopes and, more and more united in the identity of their lesson, made out perfectly that, though there appeared to be many kinds of success, there was only one kind of failure. And yet what had been hardest had not been to have to shrink, but in the long game of bluff as Straith called it, to have to keep up. It fairly swept them away at present, however, the hugeness of the relief of no longer keeping up as against each other. This gave them all the measure of the motive their courage, on either side, in silence and gloom, had forced into its service.

"Only what shall we do now for a motive?" Straith went on.

She thought. "A motive for courage?"

"Yes — to keep up."

"And go again for instance, do you mean, to Mundham? We shall, thank heaven, never go again to Mundham. The Mundhams are over."

> "Nous n'irons plus au bois;
> Les lauriers sont coupés,"

sang Straith. "It does cost."

"As everything costs that one does for the rich. It's not our poor relations who make us pay."

"No; one must have means to acknowledge the others. We can't afford the opulent. But it is n't only the money they take."

"It's the imagination," said Mrs. Harvey. "As they have none themselves —"

"It's an article we have to supply? We've certainly to use a lot to protect ourselves," Straith agreed. "And the strange thing is they like us."

She thought again. "That's what makes it easy to cut them. They forgive."

"Yes," her companion laughed; "once they really don't know you enough —!"

"They treat you as old friends. But what do we want now of courage?" she went on.

He wondered. "Yes, after all, what?"

"To keep up, I mean. Why *should* we keep up?"

It seemed to strike him. "I see. After all, why? The courage *not* to keep up —!"

"We have *that* at least," she declared, "have n't we?" United there at her little high-perched window overhanging grey house-tops they let the consideration of this pass between them in a deep look as well as in a hush of which the intensity had something commensurate. "If we 're beaten —!" she then continued.

"Let us at least be beaten together!" He took her in his arms, she let herself go, and he held her long and close for the compact. But when they had recovered themselves enough to handle their agreement more responsibly the words in which they confirmed it broke in sweetness as well as sadness from both together: "And now to work!"

THE TREE OF KNOWLEDGE

THE TREE OF KNOWLEDGE

I

IT was one of the secret opinions, such as we all have, of Peter Brench that his main success in life would have consisted in his never having committed himself about the work, as it was called, of his friend Morgan Mallow. This was a subject on which it was, to the best of his belief, impossible with veracity to quote him, and it was nowhere on record that he had, in the connexion, on any occasion and in any embarrassment, either lied or spoken the truth. Such a triumph had its honour even for a man of other triumphs — a man who had reached fifty, who had escaped marriage, who had lived within his means, who had been in love with Mrs. Mallow for years without breathing it, and who, last not least, had judged himself once for all. He had so judged himself in fact that he felt an extreme and general humility to be his proper portion; yet there was nothing that made him think so well of his parts as the course he had steered so often through the shallows just mentioned. It became thus a real wonder that the friends in whom he had most confidence were just those with whom he had most reserves. He could n't tell Mrs. Mallow — or at least he supposed, excellent man, he could n't — that she was the one beautiful reason he had never married; any more than he could tell her

167

husband that the sight of the multiplied marbles in that gentleman's studio was an affliction of which even time had never blunted the edge. His victory, however, as I have intimated, in regard to these productions, was not simply in his not having let it out that he deplored them; it was, remarkably, in his not having kept it in by anything else.

The whole situation, among these good people, was verily a marvel, and there was probably not such another for a long way from the spot that engages us — the point at which the soft declivity of Hampstead began at that time to confess in broken accents to Saint John's Wood. He despised Mallow's statues and adored Mallow's wife, and yet was distinctly fond of Mallow, to whom, in turn, he was equally dear. Mrs. Mallow rejoiced in the statues — though she preferred, when pressed, the busts; and if she was visibly attached to Peter Brench it was because of his affection for Morgan. Each loved the other moreover for the love borne in each case to Lancelot, whom the Mallows respectively cherished as their only child and whom the friend of their fireside identified as the third — but decidedly the handsomest — of his godsons. Already in the old years it had come to that — that no one, for such a relation, could possibly have occurred to any of them, even to the baby itself, but Peter. There was luckily a certain independence, of the pecuniary sort, all round: the Master could never otherwise have spent his solemn *Wanderjahre* in Florence and Rome, and continued by the Thames as well as by the Arno and the Tiber to add unpurchased group to group and model, for what was too apt to prove in the event mere love, fancy-heads of celebrities either too busy or too buried — too much of the age or too little of it — to sit. Neither could Peter, lounging in almost daily, have found time to keep the whole complicated tradition so alive by his presence. He was massive but mild, the depositary of these mysteries — large and loose and ruddy and curly, with deep tones, deep eyes, deep pockets, to say nothing of the habit of long pipes, soft hats and brownish greyish weather-faded clothes, apparently always the same.

He had "written," it was known, but had never spoken, never spoken in particular of that; and he had the air (since, as was believed, he continued to write) of keeping it up in order to have something more — as if he had n't at the worst enough — to be silent about. Whatever his air, at any rate, Peter's occasional unmentioned prose and verse were quite truly the result of an impulse to maintain the purity of his taste by establishing still more firmly the right relation of fame to feebleness. The little green door of his domain was in a garden-wall on which the discoloured stucco made patches, and in the small detached villa behind it everything was old, the furniture, the servants, the books, the prints, the immemorial habits and the new improvements. The Mallows, at Carrara Lodge, were within ten minutes, and the studio there was on their little land, to which they had added, in their happy faith, for building it. This was the good fortune, if it was not the ill, of her having brought him in marriage a portion that put them in a manner at their ease and enabled them thus, on their side, to keep it up. And they did keep it up — they always had — the infatuated sculptor and his wife, for whom nature had refined on the impossible by relieving them of the sense of the difficult. Morgan had at all events everything of the sculptor but the spirit of Phidias — the brown velvet, the becoming *beretto*, the "plastic" presence, the fine fingers, the beautiful accent in Italian and the old Italian factotum. He seemed to make up for everything when he addressed Egidio with the "tu" and waved him to turn one of the rotary pedestals of which the place was full. They were tremendous Italians at Carrara Lodge, and the secret of the part played by this fact in Peter's life was in a large degree that it gave him, sturdy Briton as he was, just the amount of "going abroad" he could bear. The Mallows were all his Italy, but it was in a measure for Italy he liked them. His one worry was that Lance — to which they had shortened his godson — was, in spite of a public school, perhaps a shade too Italian. Morgan meanwhile looked like somebody's flattering idea of somebody's own person as expressed in the great room provided at the Uffizzi Museum for the general illustration of that idea by eminent hands. The Master's sole regret that he had n't been born rather to the brush than to the chisel sprang from his wish that he might have contributed to that collection.

It appeared with time at any rate to be to the brush that Lance had been born; for Mrs. Mallow, one day when the boy was turning twenty, broke it to their friend, who shared, to the last delicate morsel, their problems and pains, that it seemed as if nothing would really do but that he should embrace the career. It had been impossible longer to remain blind to the fact that he was gaining no glory at Cambridge, where Brench's own college had for a year tempered its tone to him as for Brench's own sake. Therefore why renew the vain form of preparing him for the impossible? The impossible — it had become clear — was that he should be anything but an artist.

"Oh dear, dear!" said poor Peter.

"Don't you believe in it?" asked Mrs. Mallow, who still, at more than forty, had her violet velvet eyes, her creamy satin skin and her silken chestnut hair.

"Believe in what?"

"Why in Lance's passion."

"I don't know what you mean by 'believing in it.' I've never been unaware, certainly, of his disposition, from his earliest time, to daub and draw; but I confess I've hoped it would burn out."

"But why should it," she sweetly smiled, "with his wonderful heredity? Passion is passion — though of course indeed *you*, dear Peter, know nothing of that. Has the Master's ever burned out?"

Peter looked off a little and, in his familiar formless way, kept up for a moment a sound between a smothered whistle and a subdued hum. "Do you think he's going to be another Master?"

She seemed scarce prepared to go that length, yet she had on the whole a marvellous trust. "I know what you mean by that. Will it be a career to incur the jealousies and provoke the machinations that have

been at times almost too much for his father? Well—
say it may be, since nothing but clap-trap, in these
dreadful days, *can*, it would seem, make its way, and
since, with the curse of refinement and distinction,
one may easily find one's self begging one's bread.
Put it at the worst — say he *has* the misfortune to
wing his flight further than the vulgar taste of his
stupid countrymen can follow. Think, all the same,
of the happiness — the same the Master has had.
He'll *know*."

Peter looked rueful. "Ah but *what* will he know?"

"Quiet joy!" cried Mrs. Mallow, quite impatient
and turning away.

II

HE had of course before long to meet the boy himself on it and to hear that practically everything was settled. Lance was not to go up again, but to go instead to Paris where, since the die was cast, he would find the best advantages. Peter had always felt he must be taken as he was, but had never perhaps found him so much of that pattern as on this occasion. "You chuck Cambridge then altogether? Does n't that seem rather a pity?"

Lance would have been like his father, to his friend's sense, had he had less humour, and like his mother had he had more beauty. Yet it was a good middle way for Peter that, in the modern manner, he was, to the eye, rather the young stockbroker than the young artist. The youth reasoned that it was a question of time — there was such a mill to go through, such an awful lot to learn. He had talked with fellows and had judged. "One has got, to-day," he said, "don't you see? to know."

His interlocutor, at this, gave a groan. "Oh hang it, *don't* know!"

Lance wondered. "'Don't'? Then what's the use —?"

"The use of what?"

"Why of anything. Don't you think I 've talent?"

Peter smoked away for a little in silence; then went on: "It is n't knowledge, it 's ignorance that — as we 've been beautifully told — is bliss."

"Don't you think I've talent?" Lance repeated.

Peter, with his trick of queer kind demonstrations, passed his arm round his godson and held him a moment. "How do I know?"

"Oh," said the boy, "if it's your own ignorance you're defending —!"

Again, for a pause, on the sofa, his godfather smoked. "It isn't. I've the misfortune to be omniscient."

"Oh well," Lance laughed again, "if you know *too* much —!"

"That's what I do, and it's why I'm so wretched."

Lance's gaiety grew. "Wretched? Come, I say!"

"But I forgot," his companion went on — "you're not to know about that. It would indeed for you too make the too much. Only I'll tell you what I'll do." And Peter got up from the sofa. "If you'll go up again I'll pay your way at Cambridge."

Lance stared, a little rueful in spite of being still more amused. "Oh Peter! You disapprove so of Paris?"

"Well, I'm afraid of it."

"Ah I see!"

"No, you don't see — yet. But you will — that is you would. And you must n't."

The young man thought more gravely. "But one's innocence, already —!"

"Is considerably damaged? Ah that won't matter," Peter persisted — "we'll patch it up here."

"Here? Then you want me to stay at home?"

Peter almost confessed to it. "Well, we're so

right — we four together — just as we are. We're so safe. Come, don't spoil it."

The boy, who had turned to gravity, turned from this, on the real pressure in his friend's tone, to consternation. "Then what's a fellow to be?"

"My particular care. Come, old man" — and Peter now fairly pleaded — "*I'll* look out for you."

Lance, who had remained on the sofa with his legs out and his hands in his pockets, watched him with eyes that showed suspicion. Then he got up. "You think there's something the matter with me — that I can't make a success."

"Well, what do you call a success?"

Lance thought again. "Why the best sort, I suppose, is to please one's self. Isn't that the sort that, in spite of cabals and things, is — in his own peculiar line — the Master's?"

There were so much too many things in this question to be answered at once that they practically checked the discussion, which became particularly difficult in the light of such renewed proof that, though the young man's innocence might, in the course of his studies, as he contended, somewhat have shrunken, the finer essence of it still remained. That was indeed exactly what Peter had assumed and what above all he desired; yet perversely enough it gave him a chill. The boy believed in the cabals and things, believed in the peculiar line, believed, to be brief, in the Master. What happened a month or two later wasn't that he went up again at the expense of his godfather, but that a fortnight after he had got settled in Paris this personage sent him fifty pounds.

He had meanwhile at home, this personage, made up his mind to the worst; and what that might be had never yet grown quite so vivid to him as when, on his presenting himself one Sunday night, as he never failed to do, for supper, the mistress of Carrara Lodge met him with an appeal as to — of all things in the world — the wealth of the Canadians. She was earnest, she was even excited. "Are many of them *really* rich?"

He had to confess he knew nothing about them, but he often thought afterwards of that evening. The room in which they sat was adorned with sundry specimens of the Master's genius, which had the merit of being, as Mrs. Mallow herself frequently suggested, of an unusually convenient size. They were indeed of dimensions not customary in the products of the chisel, and they had the singularity that, if the objects and features intended to be small looked too large, the objects and features intended to be large looked too small. The Master's idea, either in respect to this matter or to any other, had in almost any case, even after years, remained undiscoverable to Peter Brench. The creations that so failed to reveal it stood about on pedestals and brackets, on tables and shelves, a little staring white population, heroic, idyllic, allegoric, mythic, symbolic, in which "scale" had so strayed and lost itself that the public square and the chimney-piece seemed to have changed places, the monumental being all diminutive and the diminutive all monumental; branches at any rate,' markedly, of a family in which stature was rather oddly irrespective of function, age and sex. They formed, like the Mallows themselves, poor Brench's own family — having at least to such a degree the note of familiarity. The occasion was one of those he had long ago learnt to know and to name — short flickers of the faint flame, soft gusts of a kinder air. Twice a year regularly the Master believed in his fortune, in addition to believing all the year round in his genius. This time it was to be made by a bereaved couple from Toronto, who had given him the handsomest order for a tomb to three lost children, each of whom they desired to see, in the composition, emblematically and characteristically represented.

Such was naturally the moral of Mrs. Mallow's question: if their wealth was to be assumed, it was clear, from the nature of their admiration, as well as from mysterious hints thrown out (they were a little odd!) as to other possibilities of the same mortuary sort, that their further patronage might be; and not less evident that should the Master become at all known in those climes nothing would be more inevitable than a run of Canadian custom. Peter had been present before at runs of custom, colonial and domestic — present at each of those of which the aggregation had left so few gaps in the marble company round him; but it was his habit never at these junctures to prick the bubble in advance. The fond illusion, while it lasted, eased the wound of elections never won, the long ache of medals and diplomas carried off, on every chance, by every one but the Master; it moreover lighted the lamp that would glimmer through the next eclipse. They lived, however, after all — as it was always beautiful to see — at a height scarce susceptible of ups and downs. They strained a point at times charmingly, strained it to admit that the public was here and there not too bad to buy; but they would have been nowhere without their attitude that the Master was always too good to sell. They were at all events deliciously formed, Peter often said to himself, for their fate; the Master had a vanity, his wife had a loyalty, of which success, depriving these things of innocence, would have diminished the merit and the grace. Any one could be charming under a charm, and as he looked about him at a world of prosperity more void of proportion even than the Master's museum he wondered if he knew another pair that so completely escaped vulgarity.

"What a pity Lance is n't with us to rejoice!" Mrs. Mallow on this occasion sighed at supper.

"We 'll drink to the health of the absent," her husband replied, filling his friend's glass and his own and giving a drop to their companion; "but we must hope he 's preparing himself for a happiness much less like this of ours this evening — excusable as I grant it to be! — than like the comfort we have always (whatever has happened or has not happened) been able to trust ourselves to enjoy. The comfort," the Master explained, leaning back in the pleasant lamplight and firelight, holding up his glass and looking round at his marble family, quartered more or less, a monstrous brood, in every room — "the comfort of art in itself!"

Peter looked a little shyly at his wine. "Well — I don't care what you may call it when a fellow does n't — but Lance must learn to *sell*, you know. I drink to his acquisition of the secret of a base popularity!"

"Oh yes, *he* must sell," the boy's mother, who was still more, however, this seemed to give out, the Master's wife, rather artlessly allowed.

"Ah," the sculptor after a moment confidently pronounced, "Lance *will*. Don't be afraid. He'll have learnt."

"Which is exactly what Peter," Mrs. Mallow gaily returned — "why in the world were you so perverse, Peter? — would n't when he told him hear of."

Peter, when this lady looked at him with accusatory affection — a grace on her part not infrequent — could never find a word; but the Master, who was always all amenity and tact, helped him out now as he had often helped him before. "That's his old idea, you know — on which we've so often differed: his theory that the artist should be all impulse and instinct. *I* go in of course for a certain amount of school. Not too much — but a due proportion. There's where his protest came in," he continued to explain to his wife, "as against what *might*, don't you see? be in question for Lance."

"Ah well" — and Mrs. Mallow turned the violet eyes across the table at the subject of this discourse — "he's sure to have meant of course nothing but good. Only that would n't have prevented him, if Lance *had* taken his advice, from being in effect horribly cruel."

They had a sociable way of talking of him to his face as if he had been in the clay or — at most — in the plaster, and the Master was unfailingly generous. He might have been waving Egidio to make him revolve. "Ah but poor Peter was n't so wrong as to what it may after all come to that he *will* learn."

"Oh but nothing artistically bad," she urged — still, for poor Peter, arch and dewy.

"Why just the little French tricks," said the Master: on which their friend had to pretend to admit, when pressed by Mrs. Mallow, that these æsthetic vices had been the objects of his dread.

III

"I KNOW now," Lance said to him the next year, "why you were so much against it." He had come back supposedly for a mere interval and was looking about him at Carrara Lodge, where indeed he had already on two or three occasions since his expatriation briefly reappeared. This had the air of a longer holiday. "Something rather awful has happened to me. It *is n't* so very good to know."

"I 'm bound to say high spirits don't show in your face," Peter was rather ruefully forced to confess. "Still, are you very sure you do know?"

"Well, I at least know about as much as I can bear." These remarks were exchanged in Peter's den, and the young man, smoking cigarettes, stood before the fire with his back against the mantel. Something of his bloom seemed really to have left him.

Poor Peter wondered. "You 're clear then as to what in particular I wanted you not to go for?"

"In particular?" Lance thought. "It seems to me that in particular there can have been only one thing."

They stood for a little sounding each other. "Are you quite sure?"

"Quite sure I 'm a beastly duffer? Quite — by this time."

"Oh!" — and Peter turned away as if almost with relief.

"It's *that* that isn't pleasant to find out."

"Oh I don't care for 'that,'" said Peter, presently coming round again. "I mean I personally don't."

"Yet I hope you can understand a little that I myself should!"

"Well, what do you mean by it?" Peter sceptically asked.

And on this Lance had to explain — how the upshot of his studies in Paris had inexorably proved a mere deep doubt of his means. These studies had so waked him up that a new light was in his eyes; but what the new light did was really to show him too much. "Do you know what's the matter with me? I'm too horribly intelligent. Paris was really the last place for me. I've learnt what I can't do."

Poor Peter stared — it was a staggerer; but even after they had had, on the subject, a longish talk in which the boy brought out to the full the hard truth of his lesson, his friend betrayed less pleasure than usually breaks into a face to the happy tune of "I told you so!" Poor Peter himself made now indeed so little a point of having told him so that Lance broke ground in a different place a day or two after. "What was it then that — before I went — you were afraid I should find out?" This, however, Peter refused to tell him — on the ground that if he hadn't yet guessed perhaps he never would, and that in any case nothing at all for either of them was to be gained by giving the thing a name. Lance eyed him on this an instant with the bold curiosity of youth — with the air indeed of having in his mind two or three names, of which one or other would be right. Peter nevertheless, turn-

ing his back again, offered no encouragement, and
when they parted afresh it was with some show of
impatience on the side of the boy. Accordingly on
their next encounter Peter saw at a glance that he
had now, in the interval, divined and that, to sound
his note, he was only waiting till they should find
themselves alone. This he had soon arranged and
he then broke straight out. "Do you know your
conundrum has been keeping me awake? But in the
watches of the night the answer came over me — so
that, upon my honour, I quite laughed out. Had you
been supposing I had to go to Paris to learn *that?*"
Even now, to see him still so sublimely on his guard,
Peter's young friend had to laugh afresh. "You won't
give a sign till you're sure? Beautiful old Peter!"
But Lance at last produced it. "Why, hang it, the
truth about the Master."

It made between them for some minutes a lively
passage, full of wonder for each at the wonder of
the other. "Then how long have you understood —"

"The true value of his work? I understood it,"
Lance recalled, "as soon as I began to understand
anything. But I didn't begin fully to do that, I
admit, till I got *là-bas.*"

"Dear, dear!" — Peter gasped with retrospective
dread.

"But for what have you taken me? I'm a hopeless
muff — that I *had* to have rubbed in. But I'm not
such a muff as the Master!" Lance declared.

"Then why did you never tell me —?"

"That I hadn't, after all" — the boy took him up
— "remained such an idiot? Just because I never

dreamed *you* knew. But I beg your pardon. I only wanted to spare you. And what I don't now understand is how the deuce then for so long you've managed to keep bottled."

Peter produced his explanation, but only after some delay and with a gravity not void of embarrassment. "It was for your mother."

"Oh!" said Lance.

"And that's the great thing now — since the murder *is* out. I want a promise from you. I mean" — and Peter almost feverishly followed it up — "a vow from you, solemn and such as you owe me here on the spot, that you'll sacrifice anything rather than let her ever guess —"

"That *I've* guessed?" — Lance took it in. "I see." He evidently after a moment had taken in much. "But what is it you've in mind that I may have a chance to sacrifice?"

"Oh one has always something."

Lance looked at him hard. "Do you mean that *you've* had — ?" The look he received back, however, so put the question by that he found soon enough another. "Are you really sure my mother doesn't know?"

Peter, after renewed reflexion, was really sure. "If she does she's too wonderful."

"But aren't we all too wonderful?"

"Yes," Peter granted — "but in different ways. The thing's so desperately important because your father's little public consists only, as you know then," Peter developed — "well, of how many?"

"First of all," the Master's son risked, "of himself. And last of all too. I don't quite see of whom else."

Peter had an approach to impatience. "Of your mother, I say — *always.*"

Lance cast it all up. "You absolutely feel that?"

"Absolutely."

"Well then with yourself that makes three."

"Oh *me!*" — and Peter, with a wag of his kind old head, modestly excused himself. "The number's at any rate small enough for any individual dropping out to be too dreadfully missed. Therefore, to put it in a nutshell, take care, my boy — that's all — that *you're* not!"

"I've got to keep on humbugging?" Lance wailed.

"It's just to warn you of the danger of your failing of that that I've seized this opportunity."

"And what do you regard in particular," the young man asked, "as the danger?"

"Why this certainty: that the moment your mother, who feels so strongly, should suspect your secret — well," said Peter desperately, "the fat would be on the fire."

Lance for a moment seemed to stare at the blaze. "She'd throw me over?"

"She'd throw *him* over."

"And come round to us?"

Peter, before he answered, turned away. "Come round to *you.*" But he had said enough to indicate — and, as he evidently trusted, to avert — the horrid contingency.

IV

Within six months again, none the less, his fear was on more occasions than one all before him. Lance had returned to Paris for another trial; then had reappeared at home and had had, with his father, for the first time in his life, one of the scenes that strike sparks. He described it with much expression to Peter, touching whom (since they had never done so before) it was the sign of a new reserve on the part of the pair at Carrara Lodge that they at present failed, on a matter of intimate interest, to open themselves — if not in joy then in sorrow — to their good friend. This produced perhaps practically between the parties a shade of alienation and a slight intermission of commerce — marked mainly indeed by the fact that to talk at his ease with his old playmate Lance had in general to come to see him. The closest if not quite the gayest relation they had yet known together was thus ushered in. The difficulty for poor Lance was a tension at home — begotten by the fact that his father wished him to be at least the sort of success he himself had been. He had n't "chucked" Paris — though nothing appeared more vivid to him than that Paris had chucked him: he would go back again because of the fascination in trying, in seeing, in sounding the depths — in learning one's lesson, briefly, even if the lesson were simply that of one's impotence in the presence of one's larger vision. But what did the Master, all aloft in his senseless fluency, know of impotence, and what vision — to be called such — had he in all his blind life ever had? Lance, heated and indignant, frankly appealed to his godparent on this score.

His father, it appeared, had come down on him for having, after so long, nothing to show, and hoped that on his next return this deficiency would be repaired. *The* thing, the Master complacently set forth was — for any artist, however inferior to himself — at least to "do" something. "What can you do? That's all I ask!" *He* had certainly done enough, and there was no mistake about what he had to show. Lance had tears in his eyes when it came thus to letting his old friend know how great the strain might be on the "sacrifice" asked of him. It was n't so easy to continue humbugging — as from son to parent — after feeling one's self despised for not grovelling in mediocrity. Yet a noble duplicity was what, as they intimately faced the situation, Peter went on requiring; and it was still for a time what his young friend, bitter and sore, managed loyally to comfort him with. Fifty pounds more than once again, it was true, rewarded both in London and in Paris the young friend's loyalty; none the less sensibly, doubtless, at the moment, that the money was a direct advance on a decent sum for which Peter had long since privately prearranged an ultimate function. Whether by these arts or others, at all events, Lance's just resentment was kept for a season — but only for a season — at bay. The day arrived when he warned his companion that he could hold out — or hold in — no longer.

Carrara Lodge had had to listen to another lecture delivered from a great height — an infliction really heavier at last than, without striking back or in some way letting the Master have the truth, flesh and blood could bear.

"And what I don't see is," Lance observed with a certain irritated eye for what was after all, if it came to that, owing to himself too; "what I don't see is, upon my honour, how *you*, as things are going, can keep the game up."

"Oh the game for me is only to hold my tongue," said placid Peter. "And I have my reason."

"Still my mother?"

Peter showed a queer face as he had often shown it before — that is by turning it straight away. "What will you have? I have n't ceased to like her."

"She's beautiful — she's a dear of course," Lance allowed; "but what is she to you, after all, and what is it to you that, as to anything whatever, she should or she should n't?"

Peter, who had turned red, hung fire a little. "Well — it's all simply what I make of it."

There was now, however, in his young friend a strange, an adopted insistence. "What are you after all to *her*?"

"Oh nothing. But that's another matter."

"She cares only for my father," said Lance the Parisian.

"Naturally — and that's just why."

"Why you've wished to spare her?"

"Because she cares so tremendously much."

Lance took a turn about the room, but with his

eyes still on his host. "How awfully — always — you must have liked her!"

"Awfully. Always," said Peter Brench.

The young man continued for a moment to muse — then stopped again in front of him. "Do you know how much she cares?" Their eyes met on it, but Peter, as if his own found something new in Lance's, appeared to hesitate, for the first time in an age, to say he did know. "*I've* only just found out," said Lance. "She came to my room last night, after being present, in silence and only with her eyes on me, at what I had had to take from him: she came — and she was with me an extraordinary hour."

He had paused again and they had again for a while sounded each other. Then something—and it made him suddenly turn pale—came to Peter. "She *does* know?"

"She does know. She let it all out to me — so as to demand of me no more than ' that,' as she said, of which she herself had been capable. She has always, always known," said Lance without pity.

Peter was silent a long time; during which his companion might have heard him gently breathe, and on touching him might have felt within him the vibration of a long low sound suppressed. By the time he spoke at last he had taken everything in. "Then I do see how tremendously much."

"Is n't it wonderful?" Lance asked.

"Wonderful," Peter mused.

"So that if your original effort to keep me from Paris was to keep me from knowledge —!" Lance exclaimed as if with a sufficient indication of this futility.

It might have been at the futility Peter appeared for a little to gaze. "I think it must have been — without my quite at the time knowing it — to keep *me!*" he replied at last as he turned away.

THE
ABASEMENT OF THE NORTHMORES

THE ABASEMENT OF THE
NORTHMORES

I

WHEN Lord Northmore died public reference to the
event took for the most part rather a ponderous and
embarrassed form. A great political figure had passed
away. A great light of our time had been quenched
in mid-career. A great usefulness had somewhat an-
ticipated its term, though a great part, none the less,
had been signally played. The note of greatness, all
along the line, kept sounding, in short, by a force of
its own, and the image of the departed evidently lent
itself with ease to figures and flourishes, the poetry
of the daily press. The newspapers and their pur-
chasers equally did their duty by it — arranged it
neatly and impressively, though perhaps with a hand
a little violently expeditious, upon the funeral-car,
saw the conveyance properly down the avenue and
then, finding the subject suddenly quite exhausted,
proceeded to the next item on their list. His lordship
had been a person in connexion with whom — that
was it — there was almost nothing but the fine mono-
tony of his success to mention. This success had
been his profession, his means as well as his end; so
that his career admitted of no other description and
demanded, indeed suffered, no further analysis. He

had made politics, he had made literature, he had made land, he had made a bad manner and a great many mistakes, he had made a gaunt foolish wife, two extravagant sons and four awkward daughters — he had made everything, as he *could* have made almost anything, thoroughly pay. There had been something deep down in him that did it, and his old friend Warren Hope, the person knowing him earliest and probably on the whole best, had never, even to the last, for curiosity, quite made out what it was. The secret was one that this distinctly distanced competitor had in fact mastered as little for intellectual relief as for emulous use; and there was a virtual tribute to it in the way that, the night before the obsequies and addressing himself to his wife, he said after some silent thought: "Hang it, you know, I must see the old boy through. I must go to the grave."

Mrs. Hope at first looked at her husband but in anxious silence. "I've no patience with you. You're much more ill than *he* ever was."

"Ah but if that qualifies me only for the funerals of others —!"

"It qualifies you to break my heart by your exaggerated chivalry, your renewed refusal to consider your interests. You sacrificed them to him, for thirty years, again and again, and from this supreme sacrifice — possibly that of your life — you might, in your condition, I think, be absolved." She indeed lost patience. "To the grave — in this weather — after his treatment of you?"

"My dear girl," Hope replied, "his treatment of

me is a figment of your ingenious mind — your too-passionate, your beautiful loyalty. Loyalty, I mean, to *me*."

"I certainly leave it to you," she declared, "to have any to *him!*"

"Well, he was after all one's oldest, one's earliest friend. I'm not in such bad case — I do go out; and I want to do the decent thing. The fact remains that we never broke — we always kept together."

"Yes indeed," she laughed in her bitterness, "he always took care of that! He never recognised you, but he never let you go. You kept him up, and he kept you down. He used you, to the last drop he could squeeze, and left you the only one to wonder, in your incredible idealism and your incorrigible modesty, how on earth such an idiot made his way. He made his way on your back. You put it candidly to others — 'What in the world was his gift?' And others are such gaping idiots that they too have n't the least idea. *You* were his gift!"

"And you're mine, my dear!" her husband, pressing her to him, more gaily and resignedly cried. He went down the next day by "special" to the interment, which took place on the great man's own property and in the great man's own church. But he went alone — that is in a numerous and distinguished party, the flower of the unanimous gregarious demonstration; his wife had no wish to accompany him, though she was anxious while he travelled. She passed the time uneasily, watching the weather and fearing the cold; she roamed from room to room, pausing vaguely at dull windows, and before he came back she had

thought of many things. It was as if, while he saw
the great man buried, she also, by herself, in the
contracted home of their later years, stood before an
open grave. She lowered into it with her weak hands
the heavy past and all their common dead dreams and
accumulated ashes. The pomp surrounding Lord
Northmore's extinction made her feel more than ever
that it was not Warren who had made anything pay.
He had been always what he was still, the cleverest
man and the hardest worker she knew; but what was
there, at fifty-seven, as the vulgar said, to "show"
for it all but his wasted genius, his ruined health and
his paltry pension? It was the term of comparison
conveniently given her by his happy rival's now fore-
shortened splendour that set these things in her eye.
It was as happy rivals to their own flat union that she
always had thought of the Northmore pair; the two
men at least having started together, after the University, shoulder to shoulder and with — superficially
speaking — much the same outfit of preparation,
ambition and opportunity. They had begun at the
same point and wanting the same things — only wanting them in such different ways. Well, the dead man
had wanted them in the way that got them; but got
too, in his peerage for instance, those Warren had
never wanted: there was nothing else to be said.
There was nothing else, and yet, in her sombre, her
strangely apprehensive solitude at this hour, she said
much more than I can tell. It all came to this — that
there had been somewhere and somehow a wrong.
Warren was the one who should have succeeded. But
she was the one person who knew it now, the single

other person having descended, with *his* knowledge, to the tomb.

She sat there, she roamed there, in the waiting greyness of her small London house, with a deepened sense of the several odd knowledges that had flourished in their company of three. Warren had always known everything and, with his easy power — in nothing so high as for indifference — had never cared. John Northmore had known, for he had, years and years before, told her so; and thus had had a reason the more — in addition to not believing her stupid — for guessing at her view. She lived back; she lived it over; she had it all there in her hand. John Northmore had known her first, and how he had wanted to marry her the fat little bundle of his love-letters still survived to tell. He had introduced Warren Hope to her — quite by accident and because, at the time they had chambers together, he could n't help it: that was the one thing he *had* done for them. Thinking of it now she perhaps saw how much he might conscientiously have considered that it disburdened him of more. Six months later she had accepted Warren, and just for the reason the absence of which had determined her treatment of his friend. She had believed in his future. She held that John Northmore had never afterwards remitted the effort to ascertain the degree in which she felt herself "sold." But, thank God, she had never shown him.

Her husband came home with a chill and she put him straight to bed. For a week, as she hovered near him, they only looked deep things at each other;

the point was too quickly passed at which she could bearably have said "I told you so!" That his late patron should never have had difficulty in making *him* pay was certainly no marvel. But it was indeed a little too much, after all, that he should have made him pay with his life. This was what it had come to — she was now sure from the first. Congestion of the lungs declared itself that night and on the morrow, sickeningly, she was face to face with pneumonia. It was more than — with all that had gone before — they could meet. Ten days later Warren Hope succumbed. Tenderly, divinely as he loved her, she felt his surrender, through all the anguish, as an unspeakable part of the sublimity of indifference into which his hapless history had finally flowered. "His easy power, his easy power!" — her passion had never yet found such relief in that simple secret phrase for him. He was so proud, so fine and so flexible that to fail a little had been as bad for him as to fail much; therefore he had opened the flood-gates wide — had thrown, as the saying was, the helve after the hatchet. He had amused himself with seeing what the devouring world would take. Well, it had taken all.

II

But it was after he had gone that his name showed as written in water. What had he left? He had only left *her* and her grey desolation, her lonely piety and her sore unresting rebellion. When a man died it sometimes did for him what life had n't done; people after a little, on one side or the other, discovered and named him, claiming him for their party, annexing him to their flag. But the sense of having lost Warren Hope appeared not in the least to have quickened the world's wit; the sharper pang for his widow indeed sprang just from the commonplace way in which he was spoken of as known. She received letters enough, when it came to that, for personally of course he had been liked; the newspapers were fairly copious and perfectly stupid; the three or four societies, "learned" and other, to which he had belonged, passed resolutions of regret and condolence, and the three or four colleagues about whom he himself used to be most amusing stammered eulogies; but almost anything really would have been better for her than the general understanding that the occasion had been met. Two or three solemn noodles in "administrative circles" wrote her that she must have been gratified at the unanimity of regret, the implication being quite that she was else of the last absurdity. Meanwhile what she felt was that she could have borne well enough his not being noticed at all; what she could n't bear was this treatment of him as a minor celebrity. He was, in economics, in the higher politics, in philosophic history, a splendid unestimated genius or he was nothing. He was n't at any rate — heaven forbid! — a "notable figure." The waters, none the less, closed over him as over Lord Northmore; which was precisely, as time went on, the fact she found it hardest to accept. That personage, the week after his death, without an hour of reprieve, the place swept as clean of him as a hall lent for a charity, of the tables and booths of a three-days' bazaar — that personage had gone straight to the bottom, dropped like a crumpled circular into the waste-basket. Where then was the difference? — if the end *was* the end for each alike? For Warren it should have been properly the beginning.

During the first six months she wondered what she could herself do, and had much of the time the sense of walking by some swift stream on which an object dear to her was floating out to sea. All her instinct was to keep up with it, not to lose sight of it, to hurry along the bank and reach in advance some point from which she could stretch forth and catch and save it. Alas it only floated and floated; she held it in sight, for the stream was long, but no gentle promontory offered itself to the rescue. She ran, she watched, she lived with her great fear; and all the while, as the distance to the sea diminished, the current visibly increased. To do anything at the last she must hurry. She went into his papers, she ransacked his drawers; something of that sort at least she might do. But there were difficulties, the case was

special; she lost herself in the labyrinth and her com-
petence was challenged; two or three friends to whose
judgement she appealed struck her as tepid, even as
cold, and publishers, when sounded — most of all in
fact the house through which his three or four important volumes had been given to the world —
showed an absence of eagerness for a collection of
literary remains. It was only now she fully understood how remarkably little the three or four important volumes had "done." He had successfully kept
that from her, as he had kept other things she might
have ached at: to handle his notes and memoranda
was to come at every turn, amid the sands of her be-
reavement, upon the footsteps of some noble reason.
But she had at last to accept the truth that it was only
for herself, her own relief, that she must follow him.
His work, unencouraged and interrupted, failed of a
final form: there would have been nothing to offer
but fragments of fragments. She felt, all the same,
in recognising this, that she abandoned him: he died
for her at that hour over again.

The hour moreover happened to coincide with
another hour, so that the two mingled their bitterness. She received from Lady Northmore a note
announcing a desire to gather in and publish his late
lordship's letters, so numerous and so interesting,
and inviting Mrs. Hope, as a more than probable
depositary, to be so good as to enrich the scheme
with those addressed to her husband. This gave
her a start of more kinds than one. The long comedy
of his late lordship's greatness was *not* then over?
The monument was to be built to him that she had

but now schooled herself to regard as impossible for his defeated friend? Everything was to break out afresh, the comparisons, the contrasts, the conclusions so invidiously in his favour? — the business all cleverly managed to place him in the light and keep every one else in the shade? Letters? — had John Northmore indited three lines that could at that time of day be of the smallest consequence? Whose inept idea was such a publication, and what infatuated editorial patronage could the family have secured? She of course did n't know, but she should be surprised if there were material. Then it came to her, on reflexion, that editors and publishers must of course have flocked — his star would still rule. Why should n't he make his letters pay in death as he had made them pay in life? Such as they were they *had* paid. They would be a tremendous hit. She thought again of her husband's rich confused relics — thought of the loose blocks of marble that could only lie now where they had fallen; after which, with one of her deep and frequent sighs, she took up anew Lady Northmore's communication.

His letters to Warren, kept or not kept, had never so much as occurred to her. Those to herself were buried and safe — she knew where her hand would find them; but those to herself her correspondent had carefully not asked for and was probably unaware of the existence of. They belonged moreover to that phase of the great man's career that was distinctly — as it could only be called — previous: previous to the greatness, to the proper subject of the volume, previous above all to Lady Northmore. The faded fat packet lurked still where it had lurked for years; but she could no more to-day have said why she had kept it than why — though he knew of the early episode — she had never mentioned her preservation of it to Warren. This last maintained reserve certainly absolved her from mentioning it to Lady Northmore, who probably knew of the episode too. The odd part of the matter was at any rate that her retention of these documents had not been an accident. She had obeyed a dim instinct or a vague calculation. A calculation of what? She couldn't have told: it had operated, at the back of her head, simply as a sense that, not destroyed, the complete little collection made for safety. But for whose, just heaven? Perhaps she should still see; though nothing, she trusted, would occur requiring her to touch the things or to read them over. She wouldn't have touched them or read them over for the world.

She had not as yet, in any case, overhauled those receptacles in which the letters Warren kept would have accumulated; and she had her doubts of their containing any of Lord Northmore's. Why should he have kept any? Even she herself had had more reasons. Was his lordship's later epistolary manner supposed to be good, or of the kind that, on any grounds, prohibited the waste-basket or the glowing embers? Warren had lived in a deluge of documents, but these perhaps he might have regarded as contributions to contemporary history. None the less, surely, he wouldn't have stored up many. She began a search in cupboards, boxes, drawers yet unvisited, and she had her surprises both at what he had kept and at what he had n't. Every word of her own was there — every note that in occasional absence he had ever had from her. Well, that matched happily enough her knowing just where to put her finger on every note that, on such occasions, she herself had received. *Their* correspondence at least was complete. But so, in fine, on one side, it gradually appeared, was Lord Northmore's. The superabundance of these missives had n't been sacrificed by her husband, evidently, to any passing convenience; she judged more and more that he had preserved every scrap; and she was unable to conceal from herself that she was — she scarce knew why — a trifle disappointed. She had n't quite unhopefully, even though vaguely, seen herself informing Lady Northmore that, to her great regret and after a general hunt, she could find nothing at all.

She in fact, alas, found everything. She was conscientious and she rummaged to the end, by which time one of the tables quite groaned with the fruits of her quest. The letters appeared moreover to have been cared for and roughly classified — she should be able to consign them to the family in excellent order. She made sure at the last that she had overlooked nothing, and then, fatigued and distinctly irritated, she prepared to answer in a sense so different from the answer she had, as might have been said, planned. Face to face with her note, however, she found she could n't write it; and, not to be alone longer with the pile on the table, she presently went out of the room. Late in the evening — just before going to bed — she came back almost as if hoping there might have been since the afternoon some pleasant intervention in the interest of her distaste. Might n't it have magically happened that her discovery was a mistake ? — that the letters either were n't there or were after all somebody's else ? Ah they *were* there, and as she raised her lighted candle in the dusk the pile on the table squared itself with insolence. On this, poor lady, she had for an hour her temptation.

It was obscure, it was absurd; all that could be said of it was that it was for the moment extreme. She saw herself, as she circled round the table, writing with perfect impunity : "Dear Lady Northmore, I 've hunted high and low and have found nothing whatever. My husband evidently, before his death, destroyed everything. I 'm *so* sorry — I should have liked so much to help you. Yours most truly." She should have only on the morrow privately and resolutely to annihilate the heap, and those words would remain an account of the matter that nobody was in a position to challenge. What good it would do her ? — was *that* the question ? It would do her the good that it would make poor Warren seem to have been just a little less used and duped. This, in her mood, would ease her off. Well, the temptation was real; but so, she after a while felt, were other things. She sat down at midnight to her note. "Dear Lady Northmore, I 'm happy to say I 've found a great deal—my husband appears to have been so careful to keep everything. I 've a mass at your disposition if you can conveniently send. So glad to be able to help your work. Yours most truly." She stepped out as she was and dropped the letter into the nearest pillar-box. By noon the next day the table had, to her relief, been cleared. Her ladyship sent a responsible servant — her butler — in a four-wheeler and with a large japanned box.

III

AFTER this, for a twelvemonth, there were frequent announcements and allusions. They came to her from every side, and there were hours at which the air, to her imagination, contained almost nothing else. There had been, at an early stage, immediately after Lady Northmore's communication to her, an official appeal, a circular *urbi et orbi*, reproduced, applauded, commented in every newspaper, desiring all possessors of letters to remit them without delay to the family. The family, to do it justice, rewarded the sacrifice freely — so far as it was a reward to keep the world informed of the rapid progress of the work. Material had shown itself more copious than was to have been conceived. Interesting as the imminent volumes had naturally been expected to prove, those who had been favoured with a glimpse of their contents already felt warranted in promising the public an unprecedented treat. They would throw upon certain sides of the writer's mind and career lights hitherto unsuspected. Lady Northmore, deeply indebted for favours received, begged to renew her solicitation; gratifying as the response had been it was believed that, particularly in connexion with several dates now specified, a residuum of buried treasure might still be looked for.

Mrs. Hope saw, she could but recognise, fewer and fewer people; yet her circle was even now not too narrow for her to hear it blown about that Thompson and Johnson had "been asked." Conversation in the London world struck her for a time as almost confined to such questions and answers. "Have *you* been asked?" "Oh yes — rather. Months ago. And you?" With the whole place under contribution the striking thing seemed that being asked had been attended in every case by the ability to respond. The spring had but to be touched — millions of letters flew out. Ten volumes at such a rate, Mrs. Hope brooded, would n't exhaust the supply. She brooded a great deal, did nothing but brood; and, strange as this may at first appear, one of the final results of her brooding was the growth of a germ of doubt. It could only seem possible, in view of such unanimity, that she should have been stupidly mistaken. The great departed's reputation *was* then to the general sense a sound safe thing. Not he, immortal, had been at fault, but just her silly self, still burdened with the fallibility of Being. He had thus been a giant, and the letters would triumphantly show it. She had looked only at the envelopes of those she had surrendered, but she was prepared for anything. There was the fact, not to be blinked, of Warren's own marked testimony. The attitude of others was but *his* attitude; and she sighed as she found him in this case for the only time in his life on the side of the chattering crowd.

She was perfectly aware that her obsession had run away with her, but as Lady Northmore's publication really loomed into view — it was now definitely announced for March, and they were in January —

her pulses quickened so that she found herself, in the long nights, mostly lying awake. It was in one of these vigils that suddenly, in the cold darkness, she felt the brush of almost the only thought that for many a month had n't made her wince; the effect of which was that she bounded out of bed with a new felicity. Her impatience flashed on the spot up to its maximum — she could scarce wait for day to give herself to action. Her idea was neither more nor less than immediately to collect and put forth the letters of *her* hero. She would publish her husband's own — glory be to God! — and she even wasted none of her time in wondering why she had waited. She *had* waited — all too long; yet it was perhaps no more than natural that, for eyes sealed with tears and a heart heavy with injustice, there should n't have been an instant vision of where her remedy lay. She thought of it already as her remedy — though she would probably have found an awkwardness in giving a name publicly to her wrong. It was a wrong to feel, but doubtless not to talk about. And lo, straightway, the balm had begun to drop : the balance would so soon be even. She spent all that day in reading over her own old letters, too intimate and too sacred — oh unluckily! — to figure in her project, but pouring wind nevertheless into its sails and adding greatness to her presumption. She had of course, with separation, all their years, never frequent and never prolonged, known her husband as a correspondent much less than others; still, these relics constituted a property — she was surprised at their number — and testified hugely to his inimitable gift.

THE ABASEMENT OF THE NORTHMORES

He was a letter-writer if you liked — natural witty various vivid, playing with the idlest lightest hand up and down the whole scale. His easy power — his easy power: everything that brought him back brought back that. The most numerous were of course the earlier and the series of those during their engagement, witnesses of their long probation, which were rich and unbroken; so full indeed and so wonderful that she fairly groaned at having to defer to the common measure of married modesty. There was discretion, there was usage, there was taste; but she would fain have flown in their face. If many were pages too intimate to publish, most others were too rare to suppress. Perhaps after her death —! It not only pulled her up, the happy thought of that liberation alike for herself and for her treasure, making her promise herself straightway to arrange: it quite re-emphasised her impatience for the term of her mortality, which would leave a free field to the justice she invoked. Her great resource, however, clearly, would be the friends, the colleagues, the private admirers to whom he had written for years, to whom she had known him to write, and many of whose own letters, by no means remarkable, she had come upon in her recent sortings and siftings. She drew up a list of these persons and immediately wrote to them or, in cases in which they had passed away, to their widows, children, representatives; reminding herself in the process not disagreeably, in fact quite inspiringly, of Lady Northmore in person. It had struck her that Lady Northmore in person took somehow a good deal for granted; but this idea failed, oddly enough, to occur to her in regard to Mrs. Hope. It was indeed with her ladyship she began, addressing her exactly in the terms of the noble widow's own appeal, every word of which she recalled.

Then she waited, but she had not, in connexion with that quarter, to wait long. "Dear Mrs. Hope, I have hunted high and low and have found nothing whatever. My husband evidently before his death destroyed everything. I'm so sorry — I should have liked so much to help you. Yours most truly." This was all Lady Northmore wrote, without the grace of an allusion to the assistance she herself had received; though even in the first flush of amazement and resentment our friend recognised the odd identity of form between her note and another that had never been written. She was answered as she had, in the like case and in her one evil hour, dreamed of answering. But the answer was n't over with this — it had still to flow in, day after day, from every other source reached by her question. And day after day, while amazement and resentment deepened, it consisted simply of three lines of regret. Everybody had looked, and everybody had looked in vain. Everybody would have been so glad, but everybody was reduced to being, like Lady Northmore, so sorry. Nobody could find anything, and nothing, it was therefore to be gathered, had been kept. Some of these informants were more prompt than others, but all replied in time, and the business went on for a month, at the end of which the poor woman, stricken, chilled to the heart, accepted perforce her situation and turned her face to the wall. In this position, as it were, she remained for days, taking heed of nothing and only feeling and nursing her wound. It was a wound the more cruel for having found her so unguarded. From the moment her remedy had glimmered to her she had n't had an hour of doubt, and the beautiful side of it had seemed that it was just so easy. The strangeness of the issue was even greater than the pain. Truly it was a world *pour rire*, the world in which John Northmore's letters were classed and labelled for posterity and Warren Hope's helped housemaids to light fires. All sense, all measure of anything, could only leave one — leave one indifferent and dumb. There was nothing to be done — the show was upside-down. John Northmore was immortal and Warren Hope was damned. For herself, therefore, she was finished. She was beaten. She leaned thus, motionless, muffled, for a time of which, as I say, she took no account; then at last she was reached by a great sound that made her turn her veiled head. It was the report of the appearance of Lady Northmore's volumes.

IV

THIS filled the air indeed, and all the papers that day were particularly loud with it. It met the reader on the threshold and then within, the work everywhere the subject of a "leader" as well as of a review. The reviews moreover, she saw at a glance, overflowed with quotation; to look at two or three sheets was to judge fairly of the raptures. Mrs. Hope looked at the two or three that, for confirmation of the single one she habitually received, she caused, while at breakfast, to be purchased; but her attention failed to penetrate further: she could n't, she found, face the contrast between the pride of the Northmores on such a morning and her own humiliation. The papers brought it too sharply home; she pushed them away and, to get rid of them, not to feel their presence, left the house early. She found pretexts for remaining out; there had been a cup prescribed for her to drain, yet she could put off the hour of the ordeal. She filled the time as she might; bought things, in shops, for which she had no use, and called on friends for whom she had no taste. Most of her friends at present were reduced to that category, and she had to choose for visits the houses guiltless, as she might have said, of her husband's blood. She could n't speak to the people who had answered in such dreadful terms her late circular; on the other hand the people out of its range were such as would also be stolidly unconscious of Lady Northmore's publication and from whom the sop of sympathy could be but circuitously extracted. As she had lunched at a pastry-cook's so she stopped out to tea, and the March dusk had fallen when she got home. The first thing she then saw in her lighted hall was a large neat package on the table; whereupon she knew before approaching it that Lady Northmore had sent her the book. It had arrived, she learned, just after her going out; so that, had she not done this, she might have spent the day with it. She now quite understood her prompt instinct of flight. Well, flight had helped her, and the touch of the great indifferent general life. She would at last face the music.

She faced it, after dinner, in her little closed drawing-room, unwrapping the two volumes — *The Public and Private Correspondence of the Right Honourable &c., &c.* — and looking well, first, at the great escutcheon on the purple cover and at the various portraits within, so numerous that wherever she opened she came on one. It had n't been present to her before that he was so perpetually "sitting," but he figured in every phase and in every style, while the gallery was further enriched with views of his successive residences, each one a little grander than the last. She had ever, in general, found that in portraits, whether of the known or the obscure, the eyes seemed to seek and to meet her own; but John Northmore everywhere looked straight away from her, quite as if he had been in the room and were unconscious of acquaintance. The effect of this was, oddly enough, so sharp that at the end of ten minutes she felt herself sink into his text as if she had been a stranger beholden, vulgarly and accidentally, to one of the libraries. She had been afraid to plunge, but from the moment she got in she was — to do every one all round justice — thoroughly held. Sitting there late she made so many reflexions and discoveries that — as the only way to put it — she passed from mystification to stupefaction. Her own offered series figured practically entire; she had counted Warren's letters before sending them and noted now that scarce a dozen were absent — a circumstance explaining to her Lady Northmore's courtesy. It was to these pages she had turned first, and it was as she hung over them that her stupefaction dawned. It took in truth at the outset a particular form — the form of a sharpened wonder at Warren's unnatural piety. Her original surprise had been keen — when she had tried to take reasons for granted; but her original surprise was as nothing to her actual bewilderment. The letters to Warren had been virtually, she judged, for the family, the great card; yet if the great card made only that figure what on earth was one to think of the rest of the pack?

She pressed on at random and with a sense of rising fever; she trembled, almost panting, not to be sure too soon; but wherever she turned she found the prodigy spread. The letters to Warren were an abyss of inanity; the others followed suit as they could; the book was surely then a gaping void, the publication a theme for mirth. She so lost herself in uplifting visions as her perception of the scale of the mistake deepened that toward eleven o'clock, when her parlour-maid opened the door, she almost gave the start of guilt surprised. The girl, withdrawing for the night, had come but to mention that, and her mistress, supremely wide awake and with remembrance kindled, appealed to her, after a blank stare, with intensity. "What have you done with the papers?"

"The papers, ma'am?"

"All those of this morning — don't tell me you've destroyed them! Quick, quick — bring them back."

The young woman, by a rare chance, had n't destroyed the public prints; she presently reappeared with them neatly folded; and Mrs. Hope, dismissing her with benedictions, had at last in a few minutes taken the time of day. She saw her impression portentously reflected in the long grey columns. It was n't then the illusion of her jealousy — it was the triumph, unhoped for, of her justice. The reviewers observed a decorum, but frankly, when one came to look, their stupefaction matched her own. What she had taken in the morning for enthusiasm proved mere perfunctory attention, unwarned in advance and seeking an issue for its mystification. The question was, if one liked, asked civilly, yet asked none the less all round: "What *could* have made Lord Northmore's family take him for a letter-writer?" Pompous and ponderous and at the same time loose and obscure, he managed by a trick of his own to be both slipshod and stiff. Who in such a case had been primarily responsible and under what strangely belated advice had a group of persons destitute of wit themselves been thus deplorably led astray? With fewer accomplices in the preparation it might almost have been assumed that they had been designedly befooled, been elaborately trapped.

They had at all events committed an error of which the most merciful thing to say was that, as founded on loyalty, it was touching. These things, in the welcome offered, lay perhaps not quite on the face, but they peeped between the lines and would force their way through on the morrow. The long quotations given were quotations marked Why?—"Why," in other words, as interpreted by Mrs. Hope, "drag to light such helplessness of expression? why give the text of his dulness and the proof of his fatuity?" The victim of the error had certainly been, in his way and day, a useful and remarkable person, but almost any other evidence of the fact might more happily have been adduced. It rolled over her, as she paced her room in the small hours, that the wheel had come full circle. There was after all a rough justice. The monument that had overdarkened her was reared, but it would be within a week the opportunity of every humourist, the derision of intelligent London. Her husband's strange share in it continued, that night, between dreams and vigils, to puzzle her, but light broke with her final waking, which was comfortably late. She opened her eyes to it and, on its staring straight into them, greeted it with the first laugh that had for a long time passed her lips. How could she idiotically not have guessed? Warren, playing insidiously the part of a guardian, had done what he had done on purpose! He had acted to an end long foretasted, and the end — the full taste — had come.

V

IT was after this, none the less — after the other organs of criticism, including the smoking-rooms of the clubs, the lobbies of the House and the dinner-tables of everywhere, had duly embodied their reserves and vented their irreverence, and the unfortunate two volumes had ranged themselves, beyond appeal, as a novelty insufficiently curious and prematurely stale — it was when this had come to pass that she really felt how beautiful her own chance would now have been and how sweet her revenge. The success of *her* volumes, for the inevitability of which nobody had had an instinct, would have been as great as the failure of Lady Northmore's, for the inevitability of which everybody had had one. She read over and over her letters and asked herself afresh if the confidence that had preserved *them* might n't, at such a crisis, in spite of everything, justify itself. Did n't the discredit to English wit, as it were, proceeding from the uncorrected attribution to an established public character of such mediocrity of thought and form, really demand, for that matter, some such redemptive stroke as the appearance of a collection of masterpieces gathered from a similar walk? To have such a collection under one's hand and yet sit and see one's self not use it was a torment through which she might well have feared to break down.

But there was another thing she might do, not redemptive indeed, but perhaps after all, as matters were going, relevant. She fished out of their nook, after long years, the packet of John Northmore's epistles to herself and, reading them over in the light of his later style, judged them to contain to the full the promise of that inimitability; felt how they would deepen the impression and how, in the way of the *inédit*, they constituted her supreme treasure. There was accordingly a terrible week for her in which she itched to put them forth. She composed mentally the preface, brief, sweet, ironic, presenting her as prompted by an anxious sense of duty to a great reputation and acting upon the sight of laurels so lately gathered. There would naturally be difficulties; the documents were her own, but the family, bewildered, scared, suspicious, figured to her fancy as a dog with a dust-pan tied to its tail and ready for any dash to cover at the sound of the clatter of tin. They would have, she surmised, to be consulted, or, if not consulted, would put in an injunction; yet, of the two courses, that of scandal braved for the man she had rejected drew her on, while the charm of this vision worked, still further than that of delicacy over-ridden for the man she had married.

The vision closed round her and she lingered on the idea — fed, as she handled again her faded fat packet, by re-perusals more richly convinced. She even took opinions as to the interference open to her old friend's relatives; took in fact, from this time on, many opinions; went out anew, picked up old threads, repaired old ruptures, resumed, as it was

called, her place in society. She had not been for
years so seen of men as during the few weeks that
followed the abasement of the Northmores. She
called in particular on every one she had cast out
after the failure of her appeal. Many of these persons
figured as Lady Northmore's contributors, the un-
witting agents of the cruel exposure; they having,
it was sufficiently clear, acted in dense good faith.
Warren, foreseeing and calculating, might have the
benefit of such subtlety, but it was n't for any one
else. With every one else — for they did, on facing
her, as she said to herself, look like fools — she made
inordinately free; putting right and left the question
of what in the past years they or their progenitors
could have been thinking of. "What on earth had
you in mind and where among you were the rudiments of intelligence when you burnt up my husband's priceless letters and clung as for salvation to
Lord Northmore's ? You see how you 've been saved!"
The weak explanations, the imbecility, as she judged
it, of the reasons given, were so much balm to her
wound. The great balm, however, she kept to the
last: she would go to see Lady Northmore only when
she had exhausted all other comfort. That resource
would be as supreme as the treasure of the fat packet.
She finally went and, by a happy chance, if chance
could ever be happy in such a house, was received.
She remained half an hour — there were other persons present; and on rising to go knew herself satisfied. She had taken in what she desired, had sounded
to the bottom what she saw; only, unexpectedly, something had overtaken her more absolute than the

hard need she had obeyed or the vindictive advantage she had cherished. She had counted on herself
for anything rather than pity of these people, yet
it was in pity that at the end of ten minutes she felt
everything else dissolve.

They were suddenly, on the spot, transformed for
her by the depth of their misfortune, and she saw
them, the great Northmores, as — of all things —
consciously weak and flat. She neither made nor
encountered an allusion to volumes published or
frustrated; and so let her arranged enquiry die away
that when on separation she kissed her wan sister
in widowhood it was not with the kiss of Judas.
She had meant to ask lightly if she might n't have
her turn at editing; but the renunciation with which
she re-entered her house had formed itself before she
left the room. When she got home indeed she at first
only wept — wept for the commonness of failure and
the strangeness of life. Her tears perhaps brought
her a sense of philosophy; it was all so as broad as it
was long. When they were spent, at all events, she
took out for the last time the faded fat packet. Sitting
down by a receptacle daily emptied for the benefit
of the dustman, she destroyed one by one the gems
of the collection in which each piece had been a gem.
She tore up to the last scrap Lord Northmore's letters.
It would never be known now, as regards this series,
either that they had been hoarded or that they had
been sacrificed. And she was content so to let it rest.
On the following day she began another task. She
took out her husband's and attacked the business of
transcription. She copied them piously, tenderly,

and, for the purpose to which she now found herself settled, judged almost no omissions imperative. By the time they should be published — ! She shook her head, both knowingly and resignedly, as to criticism so remote. When her transcript was finished she sent it to a printer to set up, and then, after receiving and correcting proof, and with every precaution for secrecy, had a single copy struck off and the type dispersed under her eyes. Her last act but one — or rather perhaps but two — was to put these sheets, which, she was pleased to find, would form a volume of three hundred pages, carefully away. Her next was to add to her testamentary instrument a definite provision for the issue, after her death, of such a volume. Her last was to hope that death would come in time.

THE GREAT GOOD PLACE

THE GREAT GOOD PLACE

I

GEORGE DANE had opened his eyes to a bright new day, the face of nature well washed by last night's downpour and shining as with high spirits, good resolutions, lively intentions — the great glare of re-commencement in short fixed in his patch of sky. He had sat up late to finish work — arrears over-whelming, then at last had gone to bed with the pile but little reduced. He was now to return to it after the pause of the night; but he could only look at it, for the time, over the bristling hedge of letters planted by the early postman an hour before and already, on the customary table by the chimney-piece, formally rounded and squared by his systematic servant. It was something too merciless, the domestic perfection of Brown. There were newspapers on another table, ranged with the same rigour of custom, newspapers too many — what could any creature want of so much news? — and each with its hand on the neck of the other, so that the row of their bodiless heads was like a series of decapitations. Other journals, other peri-odicals of every sort, folded and in wrappers, made a huddled mound that had been growing for several days and of which he had been wearily, helplessly aware. There were new books, also in wrappers as well as disenveloped and dropped again — books from

publishers, books from authors, books from friends,
books from enemies, books from his own bookseller,
who took, it sometimes struck him, inconceivable
things for granted. He touched nothing, approached
nothing, only turned a heavy eye over the work, as
it were, of the night — the fact, in his high wide-
windowed room, where duty shed its hard light
into every corner, of the still unashamed admonitions.
It was the old rising tide, and it rose and rose
even under a minute's watching. It had been up
to his shoulders last night — it was up to his chin
now.

Nothing had *gone*, had passed on while he slept —
everything had stayed; nothing, that he could yet feel,
had died — so naturally, one would have thought;
many things on the contrary had been born. To let
them alone, these things, the new things, let them
utterly alone and see if that, by chance, would n't
somehow prove the best way to deal with them: this
fancy brushed his face for a moment as a possible
solution, just giving it, as so often before, a cool
wave of air. Then he knew again as well as ever that
leaving was difficult, leaving impossible — that the
only remedy, the true soft effacing sponge, would
be to *be* left, to be forgotten. There was no footing
on which a man who had ever liked life — liked it at
any rate as *he* had — could now escape it. He must
reap as he had sown. It was a thing of meshes; he had
simply gone to sleep under the net and had simply
waked up there. The net was too fine; the cords
crossed each other at spots too near together, making
at each a little tight hard knot that tired fingers were

this morning too limp and too tender to touch. Our poor friend's touched nothing — only stole significantly into his pockets as he wandered over to the window and faintly gasped at the energy of nature. What was most overwhelming was that she herself was so ready. She had soothed him rather, the night before, in the small hours by the lamp. From behind the drawn curtain of his study the rain had been audible and in a manner merciful; washing the window in a steady flood, it had seemed the right thing, the retarding interrupting thing, the thing that, if it would only last, might clear the ground by floating out to a boundless sea the innumerable objects among which his feet stumbled and strayed. He had positively laid down his pen as on a sense of friendly pressure from it. The kind full swish had been on the glass when he turned out his lamp; he had left his phrase unfinished and his papers lying quite as for the flood to bear them away in its rush. But there still on the table were the bare bones of the sentence — and not all of those; the single thing borne away and that he could never recover was the missing half that might have paired with it and begotten a figure.

Yet he could at last only turn back from the window; the world was everywhere, without and within, and the great staring egotism of its health and strength was n't to be trusted for tact or delicacy. He faced about precisely to meet his servant and the absurd solemnity of two telegrams on a tray. Brown ought to have kicked them into the room — then he himself might have kicked them out.

"And you told me to remind you, sir —"

George Dane was at last angry. "Remind me of nothing!"

"But you insisted, sir, that I was to insist!"

He turned away in despair, using a pathetic quaver at absurd variance with his words: "If you insist, Brown, I'll kill you!" He found himself anew at the window, whence, looking down from his fourth floor, he could see the vast neighbourhood, under the trumpet-blare of the sky, beginning to rush about. There was a silence, but he knew Brown had n't left him — knew exactly how straight and serious and stupid and faithful he stood there. After a minute he heard him again.

"It's only because, sir, you know, sir, you can't remember —"

At this Dane did flash round; it was more than at such a moment he could bear. "Can't remember, Brown? I can't forget. That's what's the matter with me."

Brown looked at him with the advantage of eighteen years of consistency. "I'm afraid you're not well, sir."

Brown's master thought. "It's a shocking thing to say, but I wish to heaven I were n't! It would be perhaps an excuse."

Brown's blankness spread like the desert. "To put them off?"

"Ah!" The sound was a groan; the plural pronoun, *any* pronoun, so mistimed. "Who is it?"

"Those ladies you spoke of — to luncheon."

"Oh!" The poor man dropped into the nearest

chair and stared a while at the carpet. It was very complicated.

"How many will there be, sir?" Brown asked.

"Fifty!"

"Fifty, sir?"

Our friend, from his chair, looked vaguely about; under his hand were the telegrams, still unopened, one of which he now tore asunder. "'Do hope you sweetly won't mind, to-day, 1.30, my bringing poor dear Lady Mullet, who's so awfully bent,'" he read to his companion.

His companion weighed it. "How many does *she* make, sir?"

"Poor dear Lady Mullet? I have n't the least idea."

"Is she — a — deformed, sir?" Brown enquired, as if in this case she might make more.

His master wondered, then saw he figured some personal curvature. "No; she's only bent on coming!" Dane opened the other telegram and again read out: "'So sorry it's at eleventh hour impossible, and count on you here, as very greatest favour, at two sharp instead.'"

"How many does *that* make?" Brown imperturbably continued.

Dane crumpled up the two missives and walked with them to the waste-paper basket, into which he thoughtfully dropped them. "I can't say. You must do it all yourself. I shan't be there."

It was only on this that Brown showed an expression. "You'll go instead —"

"I'll go instead!" Dane raved.

Brown, however, had had occasion to show before that *he* would never desert their post. "Isn't that rather sacrificing the three?" Between respect and reproach he paused.

"*Are* there three?"

"I lay for four in all."

His master had at any rate caught his thought. "Sacrificing the three to the one, you mean? Oh I'm not going to *her!*"

Brown's famous "thoroughness"—his great virtue —had never been so dreadful. "Then where *are* you going?"

Dane sat down to his table and stared at his ragged phrase. "'*There* is a happy land — far far away!'" He chanted it like a sick child and knew that for a minute Brown never moved. During this minute he felt between his shoulders the gimlet of criticism.

"Are you quite sure you're all right?"

"It's my certainty that overwhelms me, Brown. Look about you and judge. Could anything be more 'right,' in the view of the envious world, than everything that surrounds us here: that immense array of letters, notes, circulars; that pile of printers' proofs, magazines and books; these perpetual telegrams, these impending guests, this retarded, unfinished and interminable work? What could a man want more?"

"Do you mean there's too much, sir?" — Brown had sometimes these flashes.

"There's too much. There's too much. But *you* can't help it, Brown."

"No, sir," Brown assented. "Can't *you?*"

"I'm thinking — I must see. There are hours — !"
Yes, there were hours, and this was one of them: he
jerked himself up for another turn in his labyrinth,
but still not touching, not even again meeting, his
admonisher's eye. If he was a genius for any one he
was a genius for Brown; but it was terrible what that
meant, being a genius for Brown. There had been
times when he had done full justice to the way it kept
him up; now, however, it was almost the worst of the
avalanche. "Don't trouble about me," he went on
insincerely and looking askance through his window
again at the bright and beautiful world. "Perhaps
it will rain — that *may* not be over. I do love the
rain," he weakly pursued. "Perhaps, better still, it
will snow."

Brown now had indeed a perceptible expression,
and the expression was of fear. "Snow, sir — the end
of May?" Without pressing this point he looked at
his watch. "You'll feel better when you've had
breakfast."

"I dare say," said Dane, whom breakfast struck in
fact as a pleasant alternative to opening letters. "I'll
come in immediately."

"But without waiting — ?"

"Waiting for what?"

Brown at last, under his apprehension, had his
first lapse from logic, which he betrayed by hesitating
in the evident hope his companion might by a flash
of remembrance relieve him of an invidious duty.
But the only flashes now were the good man's own.
"You say you can't forget, sir; but you do forget — "

"Is it anything very horrible?" Dane broke in.

231

Brown hung fire. "Only the gentleman you told me you had asked —"

Dane again took him up; horrible or not it came back — indeed its mere coming back classed it. "To breakfast to-day? It *was* to-day; I see." It came back, yes, came back; the appointment with the young man — he supposed him young — whose letter, the letter about — what was it? — had struck him. "Yes, yes; wait, wait."

"Perhaps he'll do you good, sir," Brown suggested.

"Sure to — sure to. All right!" Whatever he might do he would at least prevent some other doing: that was present to our friend as, on the vibration of the electric bell at the door of the flat, Brown moved away. Two things in the short interval that followed were present to Dane: his having utterly forgotten the connexion, the whence, whither and why of his guest; and his continued disposition not to touch — no, not with the finger. Ah if he might *never* again touch! All the unbroken seals and neglected appeals lay there while, for a pause he could n't measure, he stood before the chimney-piece with his hands still in his pockets. He heard a brief exchange of words in the hall, but never afterwards recovered the time taken by Brown to reappear, to precede and announce another person — a person whose name somehow failed to reach Dane's ear. Brown went off again to serve breakfast, leaving host and guest confronted. The duration of this first stage also, later on, defied measurement; but that little mattered, for in the train of what happened came promptly the second, the third, the fourth, the rich succession of the others. Yet what happened was but that Dane took his hand from his pocket, held it straight out and felt it taken. Thus indeed, if he had wanted never again to touch, it was already done.

II

HE might have been a week in the place — the scene of his new consciousness — before he spoke at all. The occasion of it then was that one of the quiet figures he had been idly watching drew at last nearer and showed him a face that was the highest expression — to his pleased but as yet slightly confused perception — of the general charm. What *was* the general charm? He could n't, for that matter, easily have phrased it; it was such an abyss of negatives, such an absence of positives and of everything. The oddity was that after a minute he was struck as by the reflexion of his own very image in this first converser seated with him, on the easy bench, under the high clear portico and above the wide far-reaching garden, where the things that most showed in the greenness were the surface of still water and the white note of old statues. The absence of everything was, in the aspect of the Brother who had thus informally joined him — a man of his own age, tired distinguished modest kind — really, as he could soon see, but the absence of what he did n't want. He did n't want, for the time, anything but just to *be* there, to steep in the bath. He was in the bath yet, the broad deep bath of stillness. They sat in it together now with the water up to their chins. He had n't had to talk, he had n't had to think, he had scarce even had to feel. He had been sunk that way before, sunk — when and where? — in another flood; only a flood of rushing waters in which bumping and gasping were all. *This* was a current so slow and so tepid that one floated practically without motion and without chill. The break of silence was not immediate, though Dane seemed indeed to feel it begin before a sound passed. It could pass quite sufficiently without words that he and his mate were Brothers, and what that meant.

He wondered, but with no want of ease — for want of ease was impossible — if his friend found in *him* the same likeness, the proof of peace, the gage of what the place could do. The long afternoon crept to its end; the shadows fell further and the sky glowed deeper; but nothing changed — nothing *could* change — in the element itself. It was a conscious security. It was wonderful! Dane had lived into it, but he was still immensely aware. He would have been sorry to lose that, for just this fact as yet, the blest fact of consciousness, seemed the greatest thing of all. Its only fault was that, being in itself such an occupation, so fine an unrest in the heart of gratitude, the life of the day all went to it. But what even then was the harm? He had come only to come, to take what he found. This was the part where the great cloister, enclosed externally on three sides and probably the largest lightest fairest effect, to his charmed sense, that human hands could ever have expressed in dimensions of length and breadth, opened to the south its splendid fourth quarter, turned to the great view an outer gallery that combined with the rest of the portico to form a high dry loggia, such as he a little pretended to himself he had, in the Italy of old days, seen in old cities, old convents, old villas. This recalled disposition of some great abode of an Order, some mild Monte Cassino, some Grande Chartreuse more accessible, was his main term of comparison; but he knew he had really never anywhere beheld anything at once so calculated and so generous.

Three impressions in particular had been with him all the week, and he could but recognise in silence their happy effect on his nerves. How it was all managed he could n't have told — he had been content moreover till now with his ignorance of cause and pretext; but whenever he chose to listen with a certain intentness he made out as from a distance the sound of slow sweet bells. How could they be so far and yet so audible? How could they be so near and yet so faint? How above all could they, in such an arrest of life, be, to *time* things, so frequent? The very essence of the bliss of Dane's whole change had been precisely that there was nothing now to time. It was the same with the slow footsteps that, always within earshot to the vague attention, marked the space and the leisure, seemed, in long cool arcades, lightly to fall and perpetually to recede. This was the second impression, and it melted into the third, as, for that matter, every form of softness, in the great good place, was but a further turn, without jerk or gap, of the endless roll of serenity. The quiet footsteps were quiet figures; the quiet figures that, to the eye, kept the picture human and brought its perfection within reach. This perfection, he felt on the bench by his friend, was now more within reach than ever. His friend at last turned to him a look different from the looks of friends in London clubs.

"The thing was to find it out!"

It was extraordinary how this remark fitted into his thought. "Ah was n't it? And when I think," said Dane, "of all the people who have n't and who never will!" He sighed over these unfortunates with a tenderness that, in its degree, was practically new to him, feeling too how well his companion would know the people he meant. He only meant some, but they were all who 'd want it; though of these, no doubt — well, for reasons, for things that, in the world, he had observed — there would never be too many. Not all perhaps who wanted would really find; but none at least would find who did n't really want. And then what the need would have to have been first! What it at first had had to be for himself! He felt afresh, in the light of his companion's face, what it might still be even when deeply satisfied, as well as what communication was established by the mere common knowledge of it.

"Every man must arrive by himself and on his own feet — is n't that so? We 're Brothers here for the time, as in a great monastery, and we immediately think of each other and recognise each other as such; but we must have first got here as we can, and we meet after long journeys by complicated ways. Moreover we meet — don't we? — with closed eyes."

"Ah don't speak as if we were dead!" Dane laughed.

"I shan't mind death if it's like this," his friend replied.

THE GREAT GOOD PLACE

It was too obvious, as Dane gazed before him, that one would n't; but after a moment he asked with the first articulation as yet of his most elementary wonder: "Where is it?"

"I should n't be surprised if it were much nearer than one ever suspected."

"Nearer 'town,' do you mean?"

"Nearer everything — nearer every one."

George Dane thought. "Would it be somewhere for instance down in Surrey?"

His Brother met him on this with a shade of reluctance. "Why should we call it names? It must have a climate, you see."

"Yes," Dane happily mused; "without that —!" All it so securely did have overwhelmed him again, and he could n't help breaking out: "*What* is it?"

"Oh it's positively a part of our ease and our rest and our change, I think, that we don't at all know and that we may really call it, for that matter, anything in the world we like — the thing for instance we love it most for being."

"I know what *I* call it," said Dane after a moment. Then as his friend listened with interest: "Just simply 'The Great Good Place.'"

"I see — what can you say more? I 've put it to myself perhaps a little differently." They sat there as innocently as small boys confiding to each other the names of toy animals. "'The Great Want Met.'"

"Ah yes — that 's it!"

"Is n't it enough for us that it 's a place carried on for our benefit so admirably that we strain our ears in vain for a creak of the machinery? Is n't it enough for us that it's simply a thorough hit?"

"Ah a hit!" Dane benignantly murmured.

"It does for us what it pretends to do," his companion went on; "the mystery is n't deeper than that. The thing's probably simple enough in fact, and on a thoroughly practical basis; only it has had its origin in a splendid thought, in a real stroke of genius."

"Yes," Dane returned, "in a sense — on somebody or other's part — so exquisitely personal!"

"Precisely — it rests, like all good things, on experience. The 'great want' comes home — that's the great thing it does! On the day it came home to the right mind this dear place was constituted. It always moreover in the long run *has* been met — it always must be. How can it not require to be, more and more, as pressure of every sort grows?"

Dane, with his hands folded in his lap, took in these words of wisdom. "Pressure of every sort *is* growing!" he placidly observed.

"I see well enough what that fact has done to *you*," his Brother declared.

Dane smiled. "I could n't have borne it longer. I don't know what would have become of me."

"I know what would have become of *me*."

"Well, it's the same thing."

"Yes," said Dane's companion, "it's doubtless the same thing." On which they sat in silence a little, seeming pleasantly to follow, in the view of the green garden, the vague movements of the monster — madness, surrender, collapse — they had escaped. Their bench was like a box at the opera. "And I may perfectly, you know," the Brother pursued, "have seen you before. I may even have known you well. We don't know."

They looked at each other again serenely enough, and at last Dane said: "No, we don't know."

"That's what I meant by our coming with our eyes closed. Yes — there's something out. There's a gap, a link missing, the great hiatus!" the Brother laughed. "It's as simple a story as the old, old rupture — the break that lucky Catholics have always been able to make, that they're still, with their innumerable religious houses, able to make, by going into 'retreat.' I don't speak of the pious exercises — I speak only of the material simplification. I don't speak of the putting off of one's self; I speak only — if one has a self worth sixpence — of the getting it back. The place, the time, the way were, for those of the old persuasion, always there — are indeed practically there for them as much as ever. They can always get off — the blessed houses receive. So it was high time that we — we of the great Protestant peoples, still more, if possible, in the sensitive individual case, overscored and overwhelmed, still more congested with mere quantity and prostituted, through our 'enterprise,' to mere profanity — should learn how to get off, should find somewhere *our* retreat and remedy. There was such a huge chance for it!"

Dane laid his hand on his companion's arm. "It's charming how when we speak for ourselves we speak for each other. That was exactly what I said!" He had fallen to recalling from over the gulf the last occasion.

The Brother, as if it would do them both good, only desired to draw him out. "What you 'said' — ?"

"To *him* — that morning." Dane caught a far bell again and heard a slow footstep. A quiet presence passed somewhere — neither of them turned to look. What was little by little more present to him was the perfect taste. It was supreme — it was everywhere. "I just dropped my burden — and he received it."

"And was it very great?"

"Oh such a load!" Dane said with gaiety.

"Trouble, sorrow, doubt?"

"Oh no — worse than that!"

"Worse?"

"'Success' — the vulgarest kind!" He mentioned it now as with amusement.

"Ah I know that too! No one in future, as things are going, will be able to face success."

"Without something of this sort — never. The better it is the worse — the greater the deadlier. But my one pain here," Dane continued, "is in thinking of my poor friend."

"The person to whom you've already alluded?"

He tenderly assented. "My substitute in the world. Such an unutterable benefactor. He turned up that morning when everything had somehow got on my nerves, when the whole great globe indeed, nerves or no nerves, seemed to have appallingly squeezed itself into my study and to be bent on simply swelling there. It wasn't a question of nerves, it was a mere question of the dislodgement and derangement of everything — of a general submersion by our eternal too much.

I did n't know *où donner de la tête* — I could n't have gone a step further."

The intelligence with which the Brother listened kept them as children feeding from the same bowl. "And then you got the tip?"

"I got the tip!" Dane happily sighed.

"Well, we all get it. But I dare say differently."

"Then how did *you* — ?"

The Brother hesitated, smiling. "You tell me first."

III

"WELL," said George Dane, "it was a young man I had never seen — a man at any rate much younger than myself — who had written to me and sent me some article, some book. I read the stuff, was much struck with it, told him so and thanked him — on which of course I heard from him again. Ah *that* —!" Dane comically sighed. "He asked me things — his questions were interesting; but to save time and writing I said to him: 'Come to see me — we can talk a little; but all I can give you is half an hour at breakfast.' He arrived to the minute on a day when more than ever in my life before I seemed, as it happened, in the endless press and stress, to have lost possession of my soul and to be surrounded only with the affairs of other people, smothered in mere irrelevant importunity. It made me literally ill — made me feel as I had never felt that should I once really for an hour lose hold of the thing itself, the thing that did matter and that I was trying for, I should never recover it again. The wild waters would close over me and I should drop straight to the dark depths where the vanquished dead lie."

"I follow you every step of your way," said the friendly Brother. "The wild waters, you mean, of our horrible time."

"Of our horrible time precisely. Not of course — as we sometimes dream — of any other."

"Yes, any other's only a dream. We really know none but our own."

"No, thank God — that's enough," Dane contentedly smiled. "Well, my young man turned up, and I had n't been a minute in his presence before making out that practically it would be in him somehow or other to help me. He came to me with envy, envy extravagant — really passionate. I was, heaven save us, the great 'success' for him; he himself was starved and broken and beaten. How can I say what passed between us? — it was so strange, so swift, so much a matter, from one to the other, of instant perception and agreement. He was so clever and haggard and hungry!"

"Hungry?" the Brother asked.

"I don't mean for bread, though he had none too much, I think, even of that. I mean for — well, what *I* had and what I was a monument of to him as I stood there up to my neck in preposterous evidence. He, poor chap, had been for ten years serenading closed windows and had never yet caused a shutter to show that it stirred. *My* dim blind was the first raised to him an inch; my reading of his book, my impression of it, my note and my invitation, formed literally the only response ever dropped into his dark alley. He saw in my littered room, my shattered day, my bored face and spoiled temper — it's embarrassing, but I must tell you — the very proof of my pudding, the very blaze of my glory. And he saw in my repletion and my 'renown' — deluded innocent! — what he had yearned for in vain."

"What he had yearned for was to *be* you," said the

Brother. Then he added: "I see where you're coming out."

"At my saying to him by the end of five minutes: 'My dear fellow, I wish you'd just try it — wish you'd for a while just *be* me!' You go straight to the mark, good Brother, and that was exactly what occurred — extraordinary though it was that we should both have understood. I saw what he could give, and he did too. He saw moreover what I could take; in fact what he saw was wonderful."

"He must be very remarkable!" Dane's converser laughed.

"There's no doubt of it whatever — far more remarkable than I. That's just the reason why what I put to him in joke — with a fantastic desperate irony — became, in his hands, with his vision of his chance, the blessed means and measure of my sitting on this spot in your company. 'Oh if I could just *shift* it all — make it straight over for an hour to other shoulders! If there only *were* a pair!' — that's the way I put it to him. And then at something in his face, 'Would *you*, by a miracle, undertake it?' I asked. I let him know all it meant — how it meant that he should at that very moment step in. It meant that he should finish my work and open my letters and keep my engagements and be subject, for better or worse, to my contacts and complications. It meant that he should live with my life and think with my brain and write with my hand and speak with my voice. It meant above all that I should get off. He accepted with greatness — rose to it like a hero. Only he said: 'What will become of *you?*'"

"There was the rub!" the Brother admitted.

"Ah but only for a minute. He came to my help again," Dane pursued, "when he saw I could n't quite meet that, could at least only say that I wanted to think, wanted to cease, wanted to do the thing itself — the thing that mattered and that I was trying for, miserable me, and that thing only — and therefore wanted first of all really to *see* it again, planted out, crowded out, frozen out as it now so long had been. 'I know what you want,' he after a moment quietly remarked to me. 'Ah what I want does n't exist!' 'I know what you want,' he repeated. At that I began to believe him."

"Had you any idea yourself?" the Brother's attention breathed.

"Oh yes," said Dane, "and it was just my idea that made me despair. There it was as sharp as possible in my imagination and my longing — there it was so utterly *not* in the fact. We were sitting together on my sofa as we waited for breakfast. He presently laid his hand on my knee — showed me a face that the sudden great light in it had made, for me, indescribably beautiful. 'It exists — it exists,' he at last said. And so I remember we sat a while and looked at each other, with the final effect of my finding that I absolutely believed him. I remember we were n't at all solemn — we smiled with the joy of discoverers. He was as glad as I — he was tremendously glad. That came out in the whole manner of his reply to the appeal that broke from me: 'Where is it then in God's name? Tell me without delay where it is!'"

The Brother had bent such a sympathy! "He gave you the address?"

"He was thinking it out — feeling for it, catching it. He has a wonderful head of his own and must be making of the whole thing, while we sit here patching and gossiping, something much better than ever *I* did. The mere sight of his face, the sense of his hand on my knee, made me, after a little, feel that he not only knew what I wanted but was getting nearer to it than I could have got in ten years. He suddenly sprang up and went over to my study-table — sat straight down there as if to write me my prescription or my passport. Then it was — at the mere sight of his back, which was turned to me — that I felt the spell work. I simply sat and watched him with the queerest deepest sweetest sense in the world — the sense of an ache that had stopped. All life was lifted; I myself at least was somehow off the ground. He was already where I had been."

"And where were you?" the Brother amusedly asked.

"Just on the sofa always, leaning back on the cushion and feeling a delicious ease. He was already me."

"And who were *you*?" the Brother continued.

"Nobody. That was the fun."

"That *is* the fun," said the Brother with a sigh like soft music.

Dane echoed the sigh, and, as nobody talking with nobody, they sat there together still and watched the sweet wide picture darken into tepid night.

IV

At the end of three weeks — so far as time was distinct — Dane began to feel there was something he had recovered. It was the thing they never named — partly for want of the need and partly for lack of the word; for what indeed was the description that would cover it all? The only real need was to know it, to see it in silence. Dane had a private practical sign for it, which, however, he had appropriated by theft — "the vision and the faculty divine." That doubtless was a flattering phrase for his idea of his genius; the genius was at all events what he had been in danger of losing and had at last held by a thread that might at any moment have broken. The change was that little by little his hold had grown firmer, so that he drew in the line — more and more each day — with a pull he was delighted to find it would bear. The mere dream-sweetness of the place was superseded; it was more and more a world of reason and order, of sensible visible arrangement. It ceased to be strange — it was high triumphant clearness. He cultivated, however, but vaguely the question of where he was, finding it near enough the mark to be almost sure that if he was n't in Kent he was then probably in Hampshire. He paid for everything but that — that was n't one of the items. Payment, he had soon learned, was definite; it consisted of sovereigns and shillings — just like those of

the world he had left, only parted with more ecstat-
ically — that he committed, in his room, to a fixed
receptacle and that were removed in his absence by
one of the unobtrusive effaced agents (shadows projected on the hours like the noiseless march of the
sundial) that were always at work. The scene had
whole sides that reminded and resembled, and a
pleased resigned perception of these things was at
once the effect and the cause of its grace.

Dane picked out of his dim past a dozen halting
similes. The sacred silent convent was one; another
was the bright country-house. He did the place no
outrage to liken it to an hotel; he permitted himself
on occasion to feel .it suggest a club. Such images,
however, but flickered and went out — they lasted
only long enough to light up the difference. An hotel
without noise, a club without newspapers — when he
turned his face to what it was "without" the view
opened wide. The only approach to a real analogy
was in himself and his companions. They were
brothers, guests, members; they were even, if one
liked — and they did n't in the least mind what
they were called — "regular boarders." It was n't
they who made the conditions, it was the conditions
that made them. These conditions found themselves
accepted, clearly, with an appreciation, with a rapture, it was rather to be called, that proceeded, as the
very air that pervaded them and the force that sustained, from their quiet and noble assurance. They
combined to form the large simple idea of a general
refuge — an image of embracing arms, of liberal ac-
commodation. What was the effect really but the

249

poetisation by perfect taste of a type common enough? There was no daily miracle; the perfect taste, with the aid of space, did the trick. What underlay and overhung it all, better yet, Dane mused, was some original inspiration, but confirmed, unquenched, some happy thought of an individual breast. It had been born somehow and somewhere — it had had to insist on being — the blest conception. The author might remain in the obscure, for that was part of the perfection: personal service so hushed and regulated that you scarce caught it in the act and only knew it by its results. Yet the wise mind was everywhere — the whole thing infallibly centred at the core in a consciousness. And what a consciousness it had been, Dane thought, a consciousness how like his own! The wise mind had felt, the wise mind had suffered; then, for all the worried company of minds, the wise mind had seen a chance. Of the creation thus arrived at you could none the less never have said if it were the last echo of the old or the sharpest note of the modern.

Dane again and again, among the far bells and the soft footfalls, in cool cloister and warm garden, found himself wanting not to know more and yet liking not to know less. It was part of the high style and the grand manner that there was no personal publicity, much less any personal reference. Those things were in the world — in what he had left; there was no vulgarity here of credit or claim or fame. The real exquisite was to be without the complication of an identity, and the greatest boon of all, doubtless, the solid security, the clear confidence one could feel

in the keeping of the contract. That was what had
been most in the wise mind — the importance of the
absolute sense, on the part of its beneficiaries, that
what was offered was guaranteed. They had no
concern but to pay — the wise mind knew what they
paid for. It was present to Dane each hour that he
could never be overcharged. Oh the deep deep
bath, the soft cool plash in the stillness! — this,
time after time, as if under regular treatment, a
sublimated German "cure," was the vivid name
for his luxury. The inner life woke up again, and
it was the inner life, for people of his generation,
victims of the modern madness, mere maniacal extension and motion, that was returning health. He
had talked of independence and written of it, but
what a cold flat word it had been! This was the word-
less fact itself — the uncontested possession of the
long sweet stupid day. The fragrance of flowers just
wandered through the void, and the quiet recurrence
of delicate plain fare in a high, clean refectory where
the soundless simple service was a triumph of art.
That, as he analysed, remained the constant explanation: all the sweetness and serenity were created
calculated things. He analysed, however, but in a
desultory way and with a positive delight in the residuum of mystery that made for the great agent in
the background the innermost shrine of the idol of a
temple; there were odd moments for it, mild meditations when, in the broad cloister of peace or some
garden-nook where the air was light, a special
glimpse of beauty or reminder of felicity seemed, in
passing, to hover and linger. In the mere ecstasy of

change that had at first possessed him he had n't discriminated — had only let himself sink, as I have mentioned, down to hushed depths. Then had come the slow soft stages of intelligence and notation, more marked and more fruitful perhaps after that long talk with his mild mate in the twilight, and seeming to wind up the process by putting the key into his hand. This key, pure gold, was simply the cancelled list. Slowly and blissfully he read into the general wealth of his comfort all the particular absences of which it was composed. One by one he touched, as it were, all the things it was such rapture to be without.

It was the paradise of his own room that was most indebted to them — a great square fair chamber, all beautified with omissions, from which, high up, he looked over a long valley to a far horizon, and in which he was vaguely and pleasantly reminded of some old Italian picture, some Carpaccio or some early Tuscan, the representation of a world without newspapers and letters, without telegrams and photographs, without the dreadful fatal too much. There, for a blessing, he *could* read and write; there above all he could do nothing — he could live. And there were all sorts of freedoms — always, for the occasion, the particular right one. He could bring a book from the library — he could bring two, he could bring three. An effect produced by the charming place was that for some reason he never wanted to bring more. The library was a benediction — high and clear and plain like everything else, but with something, in all its arched amplitude, unconfused and brave and gay. He should never forget, he knew, the throb of immediate perception with which he first stood there, a single glance round sufficing so to show him that it would give him what for years he had desired. He had not had detachment, but there was detachment here — the sense of a great silver bowl from which he could ladle up the melted hours. He strolled about from wall to wall, too pleasantly in tune on that occasion to sit down punctually or to choose; only recognising from shelf to shelf every dear old book that he had had to put off or never returned to; every deep distinct voice of another time that in the hubbub of the world, he had had to take for lost and unheard. He came back of course soon, came back every day; enjoyed there, of all the rare strange moments, those that were at once most quickened and most caught — moments in which every apprehension counted double and every act of the mind was a lover's embrace. It was the quarter he perhaps, as the days went on, liked best; though indeed it only shared with the rest of the place, with every aspect to which his face happened to be turned, the power to remind him of the masterly general care.

There were times when he looked up from his book to lose himself in the mere tone of the picture that never failed at any moment or at any angle. The picture was always there, yet was made up of things common enough. It was in the way an open window in a broad recess let in the pleasant morning; in the way the dry air pricked into faint freshness the gilt of old bindings; in the way an empty chair beside a table unlittered showed a volume just laid down; in the way a happy Brother — as detached as one's self and with his innocent back presented — lingered before a shelf with the slow sound of turned pages. It was a part of the whole impression that, by some extraordinary law, one's vision seemed less from the facts than the facts from one's vision; that the elements were determined at the moment by the moment's need or the moment's sympathy. What most prompted this reflexion was the degree in which Dane had after a while a consciousness of company. After that talk with the good Brother on the bench there were other good Brothers in other places — always in cloister or garden some figure that stopped if he himself stopped and with which a greeting became, in the easiest way in the world, a sign of the diffused amenity and the consecrating ignorance. For always, always, in all contacts, was the balm of a happy blank. What he had felt the first time recurred: the friend was always new and yet at the same time — it was amusing, not disturbing — suggested the possibility that he might be but an old one altered. That was only delightful — as positively delightful in the particular, the actual conditions as it might have been the reverse in the conditions abolished. These others, the abolished, came back to Dane at last so easily that he could exactly measure each difference, but with what he had finally been hustled on to hate in them robbed of its terror in consequence of something that had happened. What had happened was that in tranquil walks and talks the deep spell had worked and he had got his soul again. He had drawn in by this time, with his lightened hand, the whole of the long line, and that fact just dangled at the end. He could put his other hand on it, he could unhook it, he was once more in possession. This, as it befell, was exactly what he supposed he must have said to a comrade beside whom, one afternoon in the cloister, he found himself measuring steps.

"Oh it comes — comes of itself, does n't it, thank goodness ? — just by the simple fact of finding room and time!"

The comrade was possibly a novice or in a different stage from his own; there was at any rate a vague envy in the recognition that shone out of the fatigued yet freshened face. "It has come to *you* then ? — you 've got what you wanted ?" That was the gossip and interchange that could pass to and fro. Dane, years before, had gone in for three months of hydropathy, and there was a droll echo, in this scene, of the old questions of the water-cure, the questions asked in the periodical pursuit of the "reaction" — the ailment, the progress of each, the action of the skin and the state of the appetite. Such memories worked in now — all familiar reference, all easy play of mind; and among them our friends, round and round, fraternised ever so softly till, suddenly stopping short, Dane, with a hand on his companion's arm, broke into the happiest laugh he had yet sounded.

V

"Why it's raining!" And he stood and looked at the splash of the shower and the shine of the wet leaves. It was one of the summer sprinkles that bring out sweet smells.

"Yes — but why not?" his mate demanded.

"Well — because it's so charming. It's so exactly right."

"But everything *is*. Isn't that just why we're here?"

"Just exactly," Dane said; "only I've been living in the beguiled supposition that we've somehow or other a climate."

"So have I, so I dare say has every one. Isn't that the blest moral? — that we live in beguiled suppositions. They come so easily here, where nothing contradicts them." The good Brother looked placidly forth — Dane could identify his phase. "A climate doesn't consist in its never raining, does it?"

"No, I dare say not. But somehow the good I've got has been half the great easy absence of all that friction of which the question of weather mostly forms a part — has been indeed largely the great easy perpetual air-bath."

"Ah yes — that's not a delusion; but perhaps the sense comes a little from our breathing an emptier medium. There are fewer things *in* it! Leave people alone, at all events, and the air's what they take to.

256

Into the closed and the stuffy they have to be driven.
I've had too — I think we must all have — a fond
sense of the south."

"But imagine it," said Dane, laughing, "in the
beloved British islands and so near as we are to Bradford!"

His friend was ready enough to imagine. "To
Bradford?" he asked, quite unperturbed. "How
near?"

Dane's gaiety grew. "Oh it does n't matter!"

His friend, quite unmystified, accepted it. "There
are things to puzzle out — otherwise it would be dull.
It seems to me one can puzzle them."

"It's because we 're so well disposed," Dane said.

"Precisely — we find good in everything."

"In everything," Dane went on. "The conditions
settle that — they determine us."

They resumed their stroll, which evidently represented on the good Brother's part infinite agreement.
"Are n't they probably in fact very simple?" he presently enquired. "Is n't simplification the secret?"

"Yes, but applied with a tact!"

"There it is. The thing's so perfect that it's open
to as many interpretations as any other great work
— a poem of Goethe, a dialogue of Plato, a symphony
of Beethoven."

"It simply stands quiet, you mean," said Dane,
"and lets us call it names?"

"Yes, but all such loving ones. We 're 'staying'
with some one — some delicious host or hostess who
never shows."

"It 's liberty-hall — absolutely," Dane assented.

"Yes — or a convalescent home."

To this, however, Dane demurred. "Ah that, it seems to me, scarcely puts it. You were n't *ill* — were you? I'm very sure *I* really was n't. I was only, as the world goes, too 'beastly well'!"

The good Brother wondered. "But if we could n't keep it up — ?"

"We could n't keep it *down* — that was all the matter!"

"I see — I see." The good Brother sighed contentedly; after which he brought out again with kindly humour: "It's a sort of kindergarten!"

"The next thing you'll be saying that we're babes at the breast!"

"Of some great mild invisible mother who stretches away into space and whose lap's the whole valley — ?"

"And her bosom" — Dane completed the figure — "the noble eminence of our hill? That will do; anything will do that covers the essential fact."

"And what do you call the essential fact?"

"Why that — as in old days on Swiss lakesides — we're *en pension*."

The good Brother took this gently up. "I remember — I remember: seven francs a day without wine! But alas it's more than seven francs here."

"Yes, it's considerably more," Dane had to confess. "Perhaps it is n't particularly cheap."

"Yet should you call it particularly dear?" his friend after a moment enquired.

George Dane had to think. "How do I know, after all? What practice has one ever had in estimating

the inestimable? Particular cheapness certainly is n't
the note we feel struck all round; but don't we fall
naturally into the view that there *must* be a price to
anything so awfully sane?"

The good Brother in his turn reflected. "We fall
into the view that it must pay — that it does pay."

"Oh yes; it does pay!" Dane eagerly echoed. "If
it did n't it would n't last. It has *got* to last of course!"
he declared.

"So that we can come back?"

"Yes — think of knowing that we shall be able to!"

They pulled up again at this and, facing each other,
thought of it, or at any rate pretended to; for what
was really in their eyes was the dread of a loss of the
clue. "Oh when we want it again we shall find it,"
said the good Brother. "If the place really pays it
will keep on."

"Yes, that's the beauty; that it is n't, thank goodness, carried on only for love."

"No doubt, no doubt; and yet, thank goodness,
there's love in it too." They had lingered as if, in the
mild moist air, they were charmed with the patter of
the rain and the way the garden drank it. After a
little, however, it did look rather as if they were trying
to talk each other out of a faint small fear. They saw
the increasing rage of life and the recurrent need, and
they wondered proportionately whether to return to
the front when their hour should sharply strike would
be the end of the dream. Was this a threshold perhaps, after all, that could only be crossed one way?
They must return to the front sooner or later — that
was certain: for each his hour would strike. The

flower would have been gathered and the trick played
— the sands would in short have run.

There, in its place, *was* life — with all its rage; the
vague unrest of the need for action knew it again,
the stir of the faculty that had been refreshed and
reconsecrated. They seemed each, thus confronted,
to close their eyes a moment for dizziness; then they
were again at peace and the Brother's confidence
rang out. "Oh we shall meet!"

"Here, do you mean?"

"Yes — and I dare say in the world too."

"But we shan't recognise or know," said Dane.

"In the world, do you mean?"

"Neither in the world nor here."

"Not a bit — not the least little bit, you think?"

Dane turned it over. "Well, so is it that it
seems to me all best to hang together. But we shall
see."

His friend happily concurred. "We shall see."
And at this, for farewell, the Brother held out his
hand.

"You're going?" Dane asked.

"No, but I thought *you* were."

It was odd, but at this Dane's hour seemed to
strike — his consciousness to crystallise. "Well, I am.
I've got it. You stay?" he went on.

"A little longer."

Dane hesitated. "You haven't yet got it?"

"Not altogether — but I think it's coming."

"Good!" Dane kept his hand, giving it a final
shake, and at that moment the sun glimmered again
through the shower, but with the rain still falling on

the hither side of it and seeming to patter even more
in the brightness. "Hallo — how charming!"

The Brother looked a moment from under the high
arch — then again turned his face to our friend. He
gave this time his longest happiest sigh. "Oh it's
all right!"

But why was it, Dane after a moment found himself wondering, that in the act of separation his own
hand was so long retained? Why but through a queer
phenomenon of change, on the spot, in his companion's face — change that gave it another, but an increasing and above all a much more familiar identity,
an identity not beautiful, but more and more distinct,
an identity with that of his servant, with the most
conspicuous, the physiognomic seat of the public
propriety of Brown? To this anomaly his eyes slowly
opened; it was not his good Brother, it was verily
Brown who possessed his hand. If his eyes had to
open it was because they had been closed and because
Brown appeared to think he had better wake up. So
much as this Dane took in, but the effect of his taking
it was a relapse into darkness, a recontraction of the
lids just prolonged enough to give Brown time, on a
second thought, to withdraw his touch and move
softly away. Dane's next consciousness was that of
the desire to make sure he *was* away, and this desire
had somehow the result of dissipating the obscurity.
The obscurity was completely gone by the time he
had made out that the back of a person writing at his
study-table was presented to him. He recognised a
portion of a figure that he had somewhere described
to somebody — the intent shoulders of the unsuccess-

ful young man who had come that bad morning to breakfast. It was strange, he at last mused, but the young man was still there. How long had he stayed — days, weeks, months? He was exactly in the position in which Dane had last seen him. Everything — stranger still — was exactly in that position; everything at least but the light of the window, which came in from another quarter and showed a different hour. It was n't after breakfast now; it was after — well, what? He suppressed a gasp — it was after everything. And yet — quite literally — there were but two other differences. One of these was that if he was still on the sofa he was now lying down; the other was the patter on the glass that showed him how the rain — the great rain of the night — had come back. It was the rain of the night, yet when had he last heard it? But two minutes before? Then how many were there before the young man at the table, who seemed intensely occupied, found a moment to look round at him and, on meeting his open eyes, get up and draw near?

"You've slept all day," said the young man.

"All day?"

The young man looked at his watch. "From ten to six. You were extraordinarily tired. I just after a bit let you alone, and you were soon off." Yes, that was it; he had been "off" — off, off, off. He began to fit it together: while he had been off the young man had been on. But there were still some few confusions; Dane lay looking up. "Everything's done," the young man continued.

"Everything?"

"Everything."

Dane tried to take it all in, but was embarrassed and could only say weakly and quite apart from the matter: "I've been so happy!"

"So have I," said the young man. He positively looked so; seeing which George Dane wondered afresh, and then in his wonder read it indeed quite as another face, quite, in a puzzling way, as another person's. Every one was a little some one else. While he asked himself who else then the young man was, this benefactor, struck by his appealing stare, broke again into perfect cheer. "It's all right!" That answered Dane's question; the face was the face turned to him by the good Brother there in the portico while they listened together to the rustle of the shower. It was all queer, but all pleasant and all distinct, so distinct that the last words in his ear — the same from both quarters — appeared the effect of a single voice. Dane rose and looked about his room, which seemed disencumbered, different, twice as large. It *was* all right.

FOUR MEETINGS

FOUR MEETINGS

I saw her but four times, though I remember them vividly; she made her impression on me. I thought her very pretty and very interesting — a touching specimen of a type with which I had had other and perhaps less charming associations. I'm sorry to hear of her death, and yet when I think of it why *should* I be? The last time I saw her she was certainly not —! But it will be of interest to take our meetings in order.

I

The first was in the country, at a small tea-party, one snowy night of some seventeen years ago. My friend Latouche, going to spend Christmas with his mother, had insisted on my company, and the good lady had given in our honour the entertainment of which I speak. To me it was really full of savour — it had all the right marks: I had never been in the depths of New England at that season. It had been snowing all day and the drifts were knee-high. I wondered how the ladies had made their way to the house; but I inferred that just those general rigours rendered any assembly offering the attraction of two gentlemen from New York worth a desperate effort.

Mrs. Latouche in the course of the evening asked me if I "did n't want to" show the photographs to some of the young ladies. The photographs were in a couple of great portfolios, and had been brought home by her son, who, like myself, was lately returned from Europe. I looked round and was struck with the fact that most of the young ladies were provided with an object of interest more absorbing than the most vivid sun-picture. But there was a person alone near the mantel-shelf who looked round the room with a small vague smile, a discreet, a disguised yearning, which seemed somehow at odds with her isolation. I looked at her a moment and then chose. "I should like to show them to that young lady."

"Oh yes," said Mrs. Latouche, "she's just the person. She does n't care for flirting — I'll speak to her." I replied that if she did n't care for flirting she was n't perhaps just the person; but Mrs. Latouche had already, with a few steps, appealed to her participation. "She's delighted," my hostess came back to report; "and she's just the person — so quiet and so bright." And she told me the young lady was by name Miss Caroline Spencer — with which she introduced me.

Miss Caroline Spencer was not quite a beauty, but was none the less, in her small odd way, formed to please. Close upon thirty, by every presumption, she was made almost like a little girl and had the complexion of a child. She had also the prettiest head, on which her hair was arranged as nearly as possible like the hair of a Greek bust, though indeed it was to be doubted if she had ever seen a Greek bust. She was "artistic," I suspected, so far as the polar influences of North Verona could allow for such yearnings or could minister to them. Her eyes were perhaps just too round and too inveterately surprised, but her lips had a certain mild decision and her teeth, when she showed them, were charming. About her neck she wore what ladies call, I believe, a "ruche" fastened with a very small pin of pink coral, and in her hand she carried a fan made of plaited straw and adorned with pink ribbon. She wore a scanty black silk dress. She spoke with slow soft neatness, even without smiles showing the prettiness of her teeth, and she seemed extremely pleased, in fact quite fluttered, at the prospect of my demonstrations. These went forward very smoothly after I had moved the portfolios out of their corner and placed a couple of chairs near a lamp. The photographs were usually things I knew — large views of Switzerland, Italy and Spain, landscapes, reproductions of famous buildings, pictures and statues. I said what I could for them, and my companion, looking at them as I held them up, sat perfectly still, her straw fan raised to her under-lip and gently, yet, as I could feel, almost excitedly, rubbing it. Occasionally, as I laid one of the pictures down, she said without confidence, which would have been too much: "Have you seen that place?" I usually answered that I had seen it several times — I had been a great traveller, though I was somehow particularly admonished not to swagger — and then I felt her look at me askance for a moment with her pretty eyes. I had asked her at the outset whether she had been to Europe; to this she had answered "No, no, no" — almost as much below her breath as if the image of such an event scarce, for solemnity, brooked phrasing. But after that, though she never took her eyes off the pictures, she said so little that I feared she was at last bored. Accordingly when we had finished one portfolio I offered, if she desired it, to desist. I rather guessed the exhibition really held her, but her reticence puzzled me and I wanted to make her speak. I turned round to judge better and then saw a faint flush in each of her cheeks. She kept waving her little fan to and fro. Instead of looking at me she fixed her eyes on the remainder of the collection, which leaned, in its receptacle, against the table.

"Won't you show me that?" she quavered, drawing the long breath of a person launched and afloat but conscious of rocking a little.

"With pleasure," I answered, "if you're really not tired."

"Oh I'm not tired a bit. I'm just fascinated." With which as I took up the other portfolio she laid her hand on it, rubbing it softly. "And have you been here too?"

On my opening the portfolio it appeared I had indeed been there. One of the first photographs was a large view of the Castle of Chillon by the Lake of Geneva. "Here," I said, "I've been many a time. Isn't it beautiful?" And I pointed to the perfect reflexion of the rugged rocks and pointed towers in the clear still water. She didn't say "Oh enchanting!" and push it away to see the next picture. She looked a while and then asked if it weren't where Bonnivard, about whom Byron wrote, had been confined. I assented, trying to quote Byron's verses, but not quite bringing it off.

She fanned herself a moment and then repeated the lines correctly, in a soft flat voice but with charming conviction. By the time she had finished, she was nevertheless blushing. I complimented her and assured her she was perfectly equipped for visiting Switzerland and Italy. She looked at me askance again, to see if I might be serious, and I added that if she wished to recognise Byron's descriptions she must go abroad speedily — Europe was getting sadly dis-Byronised. "How soon must I go?" she thereupon enquired.

"Oh I'll give you ten years."

"Well, I guess I can go in *that* time," she answered as if measuring her words.

"Then you'll enjoy it immensely," I said; "you'll find it of the highest interest." Just then I came upon a photograph of some nook in a foreign city which I had been very fond of and which recalled tender memories. I discoursed (as I suppose) with considerable spirit; my companion sat listening breathless.

"Have you been *very* long over there?" she asked some time after I had ceased.

"Well, it mounts up, put all the times together."

"And have you travelled everywhere?"

"I've travelled a good deal. I'm very fond of it and happily have been able."

Again she turned on me her slow shy scrutiny. "Do you know the foreign languages?"

"After a fashion."

"Is it hard to speak them?"

"I don't imagine you'd find it so," I gallantly answered.

"Oh I should n't want to speak — I should only want to listen." Then on a pause she added: "They say the French theatre's so beautiful."

"Ah the best in the world."

"Did you go there very often?"

"When I was first in Paris I went every night."

"Every night!" And she opened her clear eyes very wide. "That to me is" — and her expression hovered — "as if you tell me a fairy-tale." A few minutes later she put to me: "And which country do you prefer?"

"There's one I love beyond any. I think you'd do the same."

Her gaze rested as on a dim revelation and then she breathed "Italy?"

"Italy," I answered softly too; and for a moment we communed over it. She looked as pretty as if instead of showing her photographs I had been making love to her. To increase the resemblance she turned off blushing. It made a pause which she broke at last by saying: "That's the place which — in particular — I thought of going to."

"Oh that's the place — that's the place!" I laughed.

She looked at two or three more views in silence. "They say it's not very dear."

"As some other countries? Well, one gets back there one's money. That's not the least of the charms."

"But it's *all* very expensive, is n't it?"

"Europe, you mean?"

"Going there and travelling. That has been the trouble. I've very little money. I teach, you know," said Miss Caroline Spencer.

"Oh of course one must have money," I allowed; "but one can manage with a moderate amount judiciously spent."

"I think I should manage. I've saved and saved up, and I'm always adding a little to it. It's all for that." She paused a moment, and then went on with suppressed eagerness, as if telling me the story were a rare, but possibly an impure satisfaction. "You see it hasn't been only the money — it has been everything. Everything has acted against it. I've waited and waited. It has been my castle in the air. I'm almost afraid to talk about it. Two or three times it has come a little nearer, and then I've talked about it and it has melted away. I've talked about it too much," she said hypocritically — for I saw such talk was now a small tremulous ecstasy. "There's a lady who's a great friend of mine — she doesn't want to go, but I'm always at her about it. I think I must tire her dreadfully. She told me just the other day she didn't know what would become of me. She guessed I'd go crazy if I didn't sail, and yet certainly I'd go crazy if I did."

"Well," I laughed, "you haven't sailed up to now — so I suppose you *are* crazy."

She took everything with the same seriousness. "Well, I guess I must be. It seems as if I couldn't think of anything else — and I don't require photographs to work me up! I'm always right *on* it. It kills any interest in things nearer home — things I ought to attend to. That's a kind of craziness."

"Well then the cure for it's just to go," I smiled — "I mean the cure for this kind. Of course you may have the other kind worse," I added — "the kind you get over there."

"Well, I've a faith that I'll go *some* time all right!" she quite elatedly cried. "I've a relative right there on the spot," she went on, "and I guess he'll know how to control me." I expressed the hope that he would, and I forget whether we turned over more photographs; but when I asked her if she had always lived just where I found her, "Oh no sir," she quite eagerly replied; "I've spent twenty-two months and a half in Boston." I met it with the inevitable joke that in this case foreign lands might prove a disappointment to her, but I quite failed to alarm her. "I know more about them than you might think" — her earnestness resisted even that. "I mean by reading — for I've really read considerable. In fact I guess I've prepared my mind about as much as you *can* — in advance. I've not only read Byron — I've read histories and guide-books and articles and lots of things. I know I shall rave about everything."

"'Everything' is saying much, but I understand your case," I returned. "You've the great American disease, and you've got it 'bad' — the appetite, morbid and monstrous, for colour and form, for the picturesque and the romantic at any price. I don't know whether we come into the world with it — with the germs implanted and antecedent to experience; rather perhaps we catch it early, almost before developed consciousness — we *feel*, as we look about, that we're going (to save our souls, or at least our senses) to be thrown back on it hard. We're like travellers in the desert — deprived of water and subject to the terrible mirage, the torment of illusion, of the thirst-fever. They hear the plash of fountains, they see green gardens and orchards that are hundreds of miles away. So we with *our* thirst — except that with us it's *more* wonderful: we have before us the beautiful old things we've never seen at all, and when we do at last see them — if we're lucky! — we simply recognise them. What experience does is merely to confirm and consecrate our confident dream."

She listened with her rounded eyes. "The way you express it's too lovely, and I'm sure it will be just like that. I've dreamt of everything — I'll know it all!"

"I'm afraid," I pretended for harmless comedy, "that you've wasted a great deal of time."

"Oh yes, that has been my great wickedness!" The people about us had begun to scatter; they were taking their leave. She got up and put out her hand to me, timidly, but as if quite shining and throbbing.

"I'm going back there — one *has* to," I said as I shook hands with her. "I shall look out for you."

Yes, she fairly glittered with her fever of excited faith. "Well, I'll tell you if I'm disappointed." And she left me, fluttering all expressively her little straw fan.

II

A few months after this I crossed the sea eastward again and some three years elapsed. I had been living in Paris and, toward the end of October, went from that city to the Havre, to meet a pair of relatives who had written me they were about to arrive there. On reaching the Havre I found the steamer already docked — I was two or three hours late. I repaired directly to the hotel, where my travellers were duly established. My sister had gone to bed, exhausted and disabled by her voyage; she was the unsteadiest of sailors and her sufferings on this occasion had been extreme. She desired for the moment undisturbed rest and was able to see me but five minutes—long enough for us to agree to stop over, restoratively, till the morrow. My brother-in-law, anxious about his wife, was unwilling to leave her room; but she insisted on my taking him a walk for aid to recovery of his spirits and his land-legs.

The early autumn day was warm and charming, and our stroll through the bright-coloured busy streets of the old French seaport beguiling enough. We walked along the sunny noisy quays and then turned into a wide pleasant street which lay half in sun and half in shade — a French provincial street that resembled an old water-colour drawing: tall grey steep-roofed red-gabled many-storied houses; green shutters on windows and old scroll-work above them; flower-

pots in balconies and white-capped women in door-
ways. We walked in the shade; all this stretched away
on the sunny side of the vista and made a picture. We
looked at it as we passed along; then suddenly my
companion stopped — pressing my arm and staring.
I followed his gaze and saw that we had paused just
before reaching a café where, under an awning, several tables and chairs were disposed upon the pave-
ment. The windows were open behind; half a dozen
plants in tubs were ranged beside the door; the pave-
ment was besprinkled with clean bran. It was a dear
little quiet old-world café; inside, in the comparative
dusk, I saw a stout handsome woman, who had pink
ribbons in her cap, perched up with a mirror behind
her back and smiling at some one placed out of
sight. This, to be exact, I noted afterwards; what I
first observed was a lady seated alone, outside, at one
of the little marble-topped tables. My brother-in-law
had stopped to look at her. Something had been put
before her, but she only leaned back, motionless and
with her hands folded, looking down the street and
away from us. I saw her but in diminished profile;
nevertheless I was sure I knew on the spot that we
must already have met.

"The little lady of the steamer!" my companion
cried.

"Was she on your steamer?" I asked with interest.

"From morning till night. She was never sick. She
used to sit perpetually at the side of the vessel with her
hands crossed that way, looking at the eastward
horizon."

"And are you going to speak to her?"

"I don't know her. I never made acquaintance with her. I was n't in form to make up to ladies. But I used to watch her and — I don't know why — to be interested in her. She 's a dear little Yankee woman. I 've an idea she 's a school-mistress taking a holiday — for which her scholars have made up a purse."

She had now turned her face a little more into profile, looking at the steep grey house-fronts opposite. On this I decided. "I shall speak to her myself."

"I would n't — she 's very shy," said my brother-in-law.

"My dear fellow, I know her. I once showed her photographs at a tea-party." With which I went up to her, making her, as she turned to look at me, leave me in no doubt of her identity. Miss Caroline Spencer had achieved her dream. But she was less quick to recognise me and showed a slight bewilderment. I pushed a chair to the table and sat down. "Well," I said, "I hope you 're not disappointed!"

She stared, blushing a little — then gave a small jump and placed me. "It was you who showed me the photographs — at North Verona."

"Yes, it was I. This happens very charmingly, for is n't it quite for me to give you a formal reception here — the official welcome? I talked to you so much about Europe."

"You did n't say too much. I 'm so intensely happy!" she declared.

Very happy indeed she looked. There was no sign of her being older; she was as gravely, decently, demurely pretty as before. If she had struck me then as a thin-stemmed mild-hued flower of Puritanism it may be imagined whether in her present situation this clear bloom was less appealing. Beside her an old gentleman was drinking absinthe; behind her the *dame de comptoir* in the pink ribbons called "Alcibiade, Alcibiade!" to the long-aproned waiter. I explained to Miss Spencer that the gentleman with me had lately been her shipmate, and my brother-in-law came up and was introduced to her. But she looked at him as if she had never so much as seen him, and I remembered he had told me her eyes were always fixed on the eastward horizon. She had evidently not noticed him, and, still timidly smiling, made no attempt whatever to pretend the contrary. I staid with her on the little terrace of the café while he went back to the hotel and to his wife. I remarked to my friend that this meeting of ours at the first hour of her landing partook, among all chances, of the miraculous, but that I was delighted to be there and receive her first impressions.

"Oh I can't tell you," she said — "I feel so much in a dream. I 've been sitting here an hour and I don't want to move. Everything's so delicious and romantic. I don't know whether the coffee has gone to my head — it 's *so* unlike the coffee of my dead past."

"Really," I made answer, "if you 're so pleased with this poor prosaic Havre you 'll have no admiration left for better things. Don't spend your appreciation all the first day — remember it 's your intellectual letter of credit. Remember all the beautiful places and things that are waiting for you. Remember that lovely Italy we talked about."

"I'm not afraid of running short," she said gaily, still looking at the opposite houses. "I could sit here all day — just saying to myself that here I am at last. It's so dark and strange — so old and different."

"By the way then," I asked, "how come you to be encamped in this odd place? Haven't you gone to one of the inns?" For I was half-amused, half-alarmed at the good conscience with which this delicately pretty woman had stationed herself in conspicuous isolation on the edge of the sidewalk.

"My cousin brought me here and — a little while ago — left me," she returned. "You know I told you I had a relation over here. He's still here — a real cousin. Well," she pursued with unclouded candour, "he met me at the steamer this morning."

It was absurd — and the case moreover none of my business; but I felt somehow disconcerted. "It was hardly worth his while to meet you if he was to desert you so soon."

"Oh he has only left me for half an hour," said Caroline Spencer. "He has gone to get my money."

I continued to wonder. "Where *is* your money?"

She appeared seldom to laugh, but she laughed for the joy of this. "It makes me feel very fine to tell you! It's in circular notes."

"And where are your circular notes?"

"In my cousin's pocket."

This statement was uttered with such clearness of candour that — I can hardly say why — it gave me a sensible chill. I couldn't at all at the moment have justified my lapse from ease, for I knew nothing of Miss Spencer's cousin. Since he stood in that relation to her — dear respectable little person — the presumption was in his favour. But I found myself wincing at the thought that half an hour after her landing her scanty funds should have passed into his hands. "Is he to travel with you?" I asked.

"Only as far as Paris. He's an art-student in Paris — I've always thought that so splendid. I wrote to him that I was coming, but I never expected him to come off to the ship. I supposed he'd only just meet me at the train in Paris. It's very kind of him. But he *is*," said Caroline Spencer, "very kind — and very bright."

I felt at once a strange eagerness to see this bright kind cousin who was an art-student. "He's gone to the banker's?" I enquired.

"Yes, to the banker's. He took me to an hotel — such a queer quaint cunning little place, with a court in the middle and a gallery all round, and a lovely landlady in such a beautifully fluted cap and such a perfectly fitting dress! After a while we came out to walk to the banker's, for I had n't any French money. But I was very dizzy from the motion of the vessel and I thought I had better sit down. He found this place for me here — then he went off to the banker's himself. I 'm to wait here till he comes back."

Her story was wholly lucid and my impression perfectly wanton, but it passed through my mind that the gentleman would never come back. I settled myself in a chair beside my friend and determined to await the event. She was lost in the vision and the imagination of everything near us and about us — she observed, she recognised and admired, with a touching intensity. She noticed everything that was brought before us by the movement of the street — the peculiarities of costume, the shapes of vehicles, the big Norman horses, the fat priests, the shaven poodles. We talked of these things, and there was something charming in her freshness of perception and the way her book-nourished fancy sallied forth for the revel.

"And when your cousin comes back what are you going to do ?" I went on.

For this she had, a little oddly, to think. "We don't quite know."

"When do you go to Paris ? If you go by the four o'clock train I may have the pleasure of making the journey with you."

"I don't think we shall do that." So far she was prepared. "My cousin thinks I had better stay here a few days."

"Oh !" said I — and for five minutes had nothing to add. I was wondering what our absentee was, in vulgar parlance, "up to." I looked up and down the street, but saw nothing that looked like a bright and kind American art-student. At last I took the liberty of observing that the Havre was hardly a place to choose as one of the æsthetic stations of a European tour. It was a place of convenience, nothing more; a place of transit, through which transit should be rapid. I recommended her to go to Paris by the after-noon train and meanwhile to amuse herself by driving to the ancient fortress at the mouth of the harbour — that remarkable circular structure which bore the name of Francis the First and figured a sort of small

Castle of Saint Angelo. (I might really have fore-known that it was to be demolished.)

She listened with much interest — then for a moment looked grave. "My cousin told me that when he returned he should have something particular to say to me, and that we could do nothing or decide nothing till I should have heard it. But I'll make him tell me right off, and then we'll go to the ancient fortress. Francis the First, did you say? Why, that's lovely. There's no hurry to get to Paris; there's plenty of time."

She smiled with her softly severe little lips as she spoke those last words, yet, looking at her with a purpose, I made out in her eyes, I thought, a tiny gleam of apprehension. "Don't tell me," I said, "that this wretched man's going to give you bad news!"

She coloured as if convicted of a hidden perversity, but she was soaring too high to drop. "Well, I guess it's a *little* bad, but I don't believe it's *very* bad. At any rate I must listen to it."

I usurped an unscrupulous authority. "Look here; you didn't come to Europe to listen — you came to *see!*" But now I was sure her cousin would come back; since he had something disagreeable to say to her he'd infallibly turn up. We sat a while longer and I asked her about her plans of travel. She had them on her fingers' ends and told over the names as solemnly as a daughter of another faith might have told over the beads of a rosary: from Paris to Dijon and to Avignon, from Avignon to Marseilles and the Cornice road; thence to Genoa, to Spezia, to Pisa, to Florence, to Rome. It apparently had never occurred to her that there could be the least incommodity in her travelling alone; and since she was unprovided with a companion I of course civilly abstained from disturbing her sense of security.

At last her cousin came back. I saw him turn toward us out of a side-street, and from the moment my eyes rested on him I knew he could but be the bright, if not the kind, American art-student. He wore a slouch hat and a rusty black velvet jacket, such as I had often encountered in the Rue Bonaparte. His shirt-collar displayed a stretch of throat that at a distance was n't strikingly statuesque. He was tall and lean, he had red hair and freckles. These items I had time to take in while he approached the café, staring at me with natural surprise from under his romantic brim. When he came up to us I immediately introduced myself as an old acquaintance of Miss Spencer's, a character she serenely permitted me to claim. He looked at me hard with a pair of small sharp eyes, then he gave me a solemn wave, in the "European" fashion, of his rather rusty sombrero.

"You were n't on the ship?" he asked.

"No, I was n't on the ship. I 've been in Europe these several years."

He bowed once more, portentously, and motioned me to be seated again. I sat down, but only for the purpose of observing him an instant — I saw it was time I should return to my sister. Miss Spencer's European protector was, by my measure, a very queer quantity. Nature had n't shaped him for a Raphael-esque or Byronic attire, and his velvet doublet and exhibited though not columnar throat were n't in harmony with his facial attributes. His hair was cropped close to his head; his ears were large and ill-adjusted to the same. He had a lackadaisical carriage and a sentimental droop which were peculiarly at variance with his keen conscious strange-coloured eyes — of a brown that was almost red. Perhaps I was prejudiced, but I thought his eyes too shifty. He said nothing for some time; he leaned his hands on his stick and looked up and down the street. Then at last, slowly lifting the stick and pointing with it, "That's a very nice bit," he dropped with a certain flatness. He had his head to one side — he narrowed his ugly lids. I followed the direction of his stick; the object it indicated was a red cloth hung out of an old window. "Nice bit of colour," he continued; and without moving his head transferred his half-closed gaze to me. "Composes well. Fine old tone. Make a nice thing." He spoke in a charmless vulgar voice.

"I see you've a great deal of eye," I replied. "Your cousin tells me you're studying art." He looked at me in the same way, without answering, and I went on with deliberate urbanity: "I suppose you're at the studio of one of those great men." Still on this he continued to fix me, and then he named one of the greatest of that day; which led me to ask him if he liked his master.

"Do you understand French?" he returned.

"Some kinds."

He kept his little eyes on me; with which he remarked: "Je suis fou de la peinture!"

"Oh I understand that kind!" I replied. Our companion laid her hand on his arm with a small pleased and fluttered movement; it was delightful to be among people who were on such easy terms with foreign tongues. I got up to take leave and asked her where, in Paris, I might have the honour of waiting on her. To what hotel would she go?

She turned to her cousin enquiringly and he favoured me again with his little languid leer. "Do you know the Hôtel des Princes?"

"I know where it is."

"Well, that's the shop."

"I congratulate you," I said to Miss Spencer. "I believe it's the best inn in the world; but, in case I should still have a moment to call on you here, where are you lodged?"

"Oh it's such a pretty name," she returned gleefully. "A la Belle Normande."

"I guess I know my way round!" her kinsman threw in; and as I left them he gave me with his swaggering head-cover a great flourish that was like the wave of a banner over a conquered field.

III

My relative, as it proved, was not sufficiently restored to leave the place by the afternoon train; so that as the autumn dusk began to fall I found myself at liberty to call at the establishment named to me by my friends. I must confess that I had spent much of the interval in wondering what the disagreeable thing was that the less attractive of these had been telling the other. The *auberge* of the Belle Normande proved an hostelry in a shady by-street, where it gave me satisfaction to think Miss Spencer must have encountered local colour in abundance. There was a crooked little court, where much of the hospitality of the house was carried on; there was a staircase climbing to bedrooms on the outer side of the wall; there was a small trickling fountain with a stucco statuette set in the midst of it; there was a little boy in a white cap and apron cleaning copper vessels at a conspicuous kitchen door; there was a chattering landlady, neatly laced, arranging apricots and grapes into an artistic pyramid upon a pink plate. I looked about, and on a green bench outside of an open door labelled Salle-à-Manger, I distinguished Caroline Spencer. No sooner had I looked at her than I was sure something had happened since the morning. Supported by the back of her bench, with her hands clasped in her lap, she kept her eyes on the other side of the court where the landlady manipulated the apricots.

But I saw that, poor dear, she wasn't thinking of apricots or even of landladies. She was staring absently, thoughtfully; on a nearer view I could have certified she had been crying. I had seated myself beside her before she was aware; then, when she had done so, she simply turned round without surprise and showed me her sad face. Something very bad indeed had happened; she was completely changed, and I immediately charged her with it. "Your cousin has been giving you bad news. You've had a horrid time."

For a moment she said nothing, and I supposed her afraid to speak lest her tears should again rise. Then it came to me that even in the few hours since my leaving her she had shed them all — which made her now intensely, stoically composed. "My poor cousin has been having one," she replied at last. "He has had great worries. His news was bad." Then after a dismally conscious wait: "He was in dreadful want of money."

"In want of yours, you mean?"

"Of any he could get — honourably of course. Mine *is* all — well, that's available."

Ah it was as if I had been sure from the first! "And he has taken it from you?"

Again she hung fire, but her face meanwhile was pleading. "I gave him what I had."

I recall the accent of those words as the most angelic human sound I had ever listened to — which is exactly why I jumped up almost with a sense of personal outrage. "Gracious goodness, madam, do you call that his getting it 'honourably'?"

I had gone too far — she coloured to her eyes. "We won't speak of it."

"We *must* speak of it," I declared as I dropped beside her again. "I'm your friend — upon my word I'm your protector; it seems to me you need one. What's the matter with this extraordinary person?"

She was perfectly able to say. "He's just badly in debt."

"No doubt he is! But what's the special propriety of your — in such tearing haste! — paying for that?"

"Well, he has told me all his story. I *feel* for him so much."

"So do I, if you come to that! But I hope," I roundly added, "he'll give you straight back your money."

As to this she was prompt. "Certainly he will — as soon as ever he can."

"And when the deuce will that be?"

Her lucidity maintained itself. "When he has finished his great picture."

It took me full in the face. "My dear young lady, damn his great picture! Where is this voracious man?"

It was as if she must let me feel a moment that I did push her! — though indeed, as appeared, he was just where he'd naturally be. "He's having his dinner."

I turned about and looked through the open door into the salle-à-manger. There, sure enough, alone at the end of a long table, was the object of my friend's compassion — the bright, the kind young art-student. He was dining too attentively to notice me at first, but in the act of setting down a well-emptied wine-glass he caught sight of my air of observation. He paused in his repast and, with his head on one side and his meagre jaws slowly moving, fixedly returned my gaze. Then the landlady came brushing lightly by with her pyramid of apricots.

"And that nice little plate of fruit is for him?" I wailed.

Miss Spencer glanced at it tenderly. "They seem to arrange everything so nicely!" she simply sighed.

I felt helpless and irritated. "Come now, really," I said; "do you think it right, do you think it decent, that that long strong fellow should collar your funds?" She looked away from me — I was evidently giving her pain. The case was hopeless; the long strong fellow had "interested" her.

"Pardon me if I speak of him so unceremoniously," I said. "But you're really too generous, and he has n't, clearly, the rudiments of delicacy. He made his debts himself — he ought to pay them himself."

"He has been foolish," she obstinately said — "of course I know that. He has told me everything. We had a long talk this morning — the poor fellow threw himself on my charity. He has signed notes to a large amount."

"The more fool he!"

"He's in real distress — and it's not only himself. It's his poor young wife."

"Ah he has a poor young wife?"

"I did n't know — but he made a clean breast of it. He married two years since — secretly."

"Why secretly?"

My informant took precautions as if she feared

listeners. Then with low impressiveness: "She was a Countess!"

"Are you very sure of that?"

"She has written me the most beautiful letter."

"Asking you — whom she has never seen — for money?"

"Asking me for confidence and sympathy" — Miss Spencer spoke now with spirit. "She has been cruelly treated by her family — in consequence of what she has done for him. My cousin has told me every particular, and she appeals to me in her own lovely way in the letter, which I've here in my pocket. It's such a wonderful old-world romance," said my prodigious friend. "She was a beautiful young widow — her first husband was a Count, tremendously high-born, but really most wicked, with whom she had n't been happy and whose death had left her ruined after he had deceived her in all sorts of ways. My poor cousin, meeting her in that situation and perhaps a little too recklessly pitying her and charmed with her, found her, don't you see?" — Caroline's appeal on this head was amazing! — "but too ready to trust a better man after all she had been through. Only when her 'people,' as he says — and I do like the word! — understood she *would* have him, poor gifted young American art-student though he simply was, because she just adored him, her great-aunt, the old Marquise, from whom she had expectations of wealth which she could yet sacrifice for her love, utterly cast her off and would n't so much as speak to her, much less to *him*, in their dreadful haughtiness and pride. They *can* be haughty over here, it seems," she ineffably developed — "there's no mistake about that! It's like something in some famous old book. The family, my cousin's wife's," she by this time almost complacently wound up, "are of the oldest Provençal noblesse."

I listened half-bewildered. The poor woman positively found it so interesting to be swindled by a flower of that stock — if stock or flower or solitary grain of truth was really concerned in the matter — as practically to have lost the sense of what the forfeiture of her hoard meant for her. "My dear young lady," I groaned, "you don't want to be stripped of every dollar for such a rigmarole!"

She asserted, at this, her dignity — much as a small pink shorn lamb might have done. "It isn't a rigmarole, and I shan't be stripped. I shan't live any worse than I *have* lived, don't you see? And I'll come back before long to stay with them. The Countess — he still gives her, he says, her title, as they do to noble widows, that is to 'dowagers,' don't you know? in England — insists on a visit from me *some* time. So I guess for *that* I can start afresh — and meanwhile I'll have recovered my money."

It was all too heart-breaking. "You're going home then at once?"

I felt the faint tremor of voice she heroically tried to stifle. "I've nothing left for a tour."

"You gave it *all* up?"

"I've kept enough to take me back."

I uttered, I think, a positive howl, and at this juncture the hero of the situation, the happy proprietor of my little friend's sacred savings and of the infatuated *grande dame* just sketched for me, reappeared with the clear consciousness of a repast bravely earned and consistently enjoyed. He stood on the threshold an instant, extracting the stone from a plump apricot he had fondly retained; then he put the apricot into his mouth and, while he let it gratefully dissolve there, stood looking at us with his long legs apart and his hands thrust into the pockets of his velvet coat. My companion got up, giving him a thin glance that I caught in its passage and which expressed at once resignation and fascination — the last dregs of her sacrifice and with it an anguish of upliftedness. Ugly vulgar pretentious dishonest as I thought him, and destitute of every grace of plausibility, he had yet appealed successfully to her eager and tender imagination. I was deeply disgusted, but I had no warrant to interfere, and at any rate felt that it would be vain. He waved his hand meanwhile with a breadth of appreciation. "Nice old court. Nice mellow old place. Nice crooked old staircase. Several pretty things."

Decidedly I could n't stand it, and without responding I gave my hand to my friend. She looked at me an instant with her little white face and rounded eyes, and as she showed her pretty teeth I suppose she meant to smile. "Don't be sorry for me," she sublimely pleaded; "I 'm very sure I shall see something of this dear old Europe yet."

I refused however to take literal leave of her — I should find a moment to come back next morning. Her awful kinsman, who had put on his sombrero again, flourished it off at me by way of a bow — on which I hurried away.

On the morrow early I did return, and in the court of the inn met the landlady, more loosely laced than in the evening. On my asking for Miss Spencer, "*Partie*, monsieur," the good woman said. "She went away last night at ten o'clock, with her — her — not her husband, eh ? — in fine her Monsieur. They went down to the American ship." I turned off — I felt the tears in my eyes. The poor girl had been some thirteen hours in Europe.

IV

I MYSELF, more fortunate, continued to sacrifice to opportunity as I myself met it. During this period — of some five years — I lost my friend Latouche, who died of a malarious fever during a tour in the Levant. One of the first things I did on my return to America was to go up to North Verona on a consolatory visit to his poor mother. I found her in deep affliction and sat with her the whole of the morning that followed my arrival — I had come in late at night — listening to her tearful descant and singing the praises of my friend. We talked of nothing else, and our conversation ended only with the arrival of a quick little woman who drove herself up to the door in a "carry-all" and whom I saw toss the reins to the horse's back with the briskness of a startled sleeper throwing off the bedclothes. She jumped out of the carry-all and she jumped into the room. She proved to be the minister's wife and the great town-gossip, and she had evidently, in the latter capacity, a choice morsel to communicate. I was as sure of this as I was that poor Mrs. Latouche was not absolutely too bereaved to listen to her. It seemed to me discreet to retire, and I described myself as anxious for a walk before dinner.

"And by the way," I added, "if you'll tell me where my old friend Miss Spencer lives I think I'll call on her."

The minister's wife immediately responded. Miss

Spencer lived in the fourth house beyond the Baptist church; the Baptist church was the one on the right, with that queer green thing over the door; they called it a portico, but it looked more like an old-fashioned bedstead swung in the air. "Yes, do look up poor Caroline," Mrs. Latouche further enjoined. "It will refresh her to see a strange face."

"I should think she had had enough of strange faces!" cried the minister's wife.

"To see, I mean, a charming visitor" — Mrs. Latouche amended her phrase.

"I should think she had had enough of charming visitors!" her companion returned. "But *you* don't mean to stay ten years," she added with significant eyes on me.

"Has she a visitor of that sort?" I asked in my ignorance.

"You'll make out the sort!" said the minister's wife. "She's easily seen; she generally sits in the front yard. Only take care what you say to her, and be very sure you're polite."

"Ah she's so sensitive?"

The minister's wife jumped up and dropped me a curtsey — a most sarcastic curtsey. "That's what she is, if you please. 'Madame la Comtesse!'"

And pronouncing these titular words with the most scathing accent, the little woman seemed fairly to laugh in the face of the lady they designated. I stood staring, wondering, remembering.

"Oh I shall be very polite!" I cried; and, grasping my hat and stick, I went on my way.

I found Miss Spencer's residence without difficulty.

The Baptist church was easily identified, and the small dwelling near it, of a rusty white, with a large central chimney-stack and a Virginia creeper, seemed naturally and properly the abode of a withdrawn old maid with a taste for striking effects inexpensively obtained. As I approached I slackened my pace, for I had heard that some one was always sitting in the front yard, and I wished to reconnoitre. I looked cautiously over the low white fence that separated the small garden-space from the unpaved street, but I descried nothing in the shape of a Comtesse. A small straight path led up to the crooked door-step, on either side of which was a little grass-plot fringed with currant-bushes. In the middle of the grass, right and left, was a large quince-tree, full of antiquity and contortions, and beneath one of the quince-trees were placed a small table and a couple of light chairs. On the table lay a piece of unfinished embroidery and two or three books in bright-coloured paper covers. I went in at the gate and paused halfway along the path, scanning the place for some further token of its occupant, before whom — I could hardly have said why — I hesitated abruptly to present myself. Then I saw the poor little house to be of the shabbiest and felt a sudden doubt of my right to penetrate, since curiosity had been my motive and curiosity here failed of confidence. While I demurred a figure appeared in the open doorway and stood there looking at me. I immediately recognised Miss Spencer, but she faced me as if we had never met. Gently, but gravely and timidly, I advanced to the door-step, where I spoke with an attempt at friendly banter.

"I waited for you over there to come back, but you never came."

"Waited where, sir?" she quavered, her innocent eyes rounding themselves as of old. She was much older; she looked tired and wasted.

"Well," I said, "I waited at the old French port."

She stared harder, then recognised me, smiling, flushing, clasping her two hands together. "I remember you now — I remember that day." But she stood there, neither coming out nor asking me to come in. She was embarrassed.

I too felt a little awkward while I poked at the path with my stick. "I kept looking out for you year after year."

"You mean in Europe?" she ruefully breathed.

"In Europe of course! Here apparently you're easy enough to find."

She leaned her hand against the unpainted doorpost and her head fell a little to one side. She looked at me thus without speaking, and I caught the expression visible in women's eyes when tears are rising. Suddenly she stepped out on the cracked slab of stone before her threshold and closed the door. Then her strained smile prevailed and I saw her teeth were as pretty as ever. But there had been tears too. "Have you been there ever since?" she lowered her voice to ask.

"Until three weeks ago. And you — you never came back?"

Still shining at me as she could, she put her hand behind her and reopened the door. "I'm not very polite," she said. "Won't you come in?"

"I'm afraid I incommode you."

"Oh no!" — she would n't hear of it now. And she pushed back the door with a sign that I should enter.

I followed her in. She led the way to a small room on the left of the narrow hall, which I supposed to be her parlour, though it was at the back of the house, and we passed the closed door of another apartment which apparently enjoyed a view of the quince-trees. This one looked out upon a small wood-shed and two clucking hens. But I thought it pretty until I saw its elegance to be of the most frugal kind; after which, presently, I thought it prettier still, for I had never seen faded chintz and old mezzotint engravings, framed in varnished autumn leaves, disposed with so touching a grace. Miss Spencer sat down on a very small section of the sofa, her hands tightly clasped in her lap. She looked ten years older, and I need n't now have felt called to insist on the facts of her person. But I still thought them interesting, and at any rate I was moved by them. She was peculiarly agitated. I tried to appear not to notice it; but suddenly, in the most inconsequent fashion — it was an irresistible echo of our concentrated passage in the old French port — I said to her: "I do incommode you. Again you're in distress."

She raised her two hands to her face and for a moment kept it buried in them. Then taking them away, "It's because you remind me," she said.

"I remind you, you mean, of that miserable day at the Havre?"

She wonderfully shook her head. "It was n't miserable. It was delightful."

Ah was it? my manner of receiving this must have commented. "I never was so shocked as when, on going back to your inn the next morning, I found you had wretchedly retreated."

She waited an instant, after which she said: "Please let us not speak of that."

"Did you come straight back here?" I nevertheless went on.

"I was back here just thirty days after my first start."

"And here you've remained ever since?"

"Every minute of the time."

I took it in; I didn't know what to say, and what I presently said had almost the sound of mockery. "When then are you going to make that tour?" It might be practically aggressive; but there was something that irritated me in her depths of resignation, and I wished to extort from her some expression of impatience.

She attached her eyes a moment to a small sun-spot on the carpet; then she got up and lowered the window-blind a little to obliterate it. I waited, watching her with interest — as if she had still something more to give me. Well, presently, in answer to my last question, she gave it. "Never!"

"I hope at least your cousin repaid you that money," I said.

At this again she looked away from me. "I don't care for it now."

"You don't care for your money?"

"For ever going to Europe."

"Do you mean you wouldn't go if you could?"

"I can't — I can't," said Caroline Spencer. "It's all over. Everything's different. I never think of it."

"The scoundrel never repaid you then!" I cried.

"Please, please —!" she began.

But she had stopped — she was looking toward the door. There had been a rustle and a sound of steps in the hall.

I also looked toward the door, which was open and now admitted another person — a lady who paused just within the threshold. Behind her came a young man. The lady looked at me with a good deal of fixedness — long enough for me to rise to a vivid impression of herself. Then she turned to Caroline Spencer and, with a smile and a strong foreign accent, "*Pardon, ma chère!* I did n't know you had company," she said. "The gentleman came in so quietly." With which she again gave me the benefit of her attention. She was very strange, yet I was at once sure I had seen her before. Afterwards I rather put it that I had only seen ladies remarkably like her. But I had seen them very far away from North Verona, and it was the oddest of all things to meet one of them in that frame. To what quite other scene did the sight of her transport me? To some dusky landing before a shabby Parisian *quatrième* — to an open door revealing a greasy ante-chamber and to Madame leaning over the banisters while she holds a faded wrapper together and bawls down to the portress to bring up her coffee. My friend's guest was a very large lady, of middle age, with a plump dead-white face and hair drawn back *à la chinoise*. She had a small penetrating

301

eye and what is called in French *le sourire agréable*. She wore an old pink cashmere dressing-gown covered with white embroideries, and, like the figure in my momentary vision, she confined it in front with a bare and rounded arm and a plump and deeply-dimpled hand.

"It's only to spick about my café," she said to her hostess with her *sourire agréable*. "I should like it served in the garden under the leetle tree."

The young man behind her had now stepped into the room, where he also stood revealed, though with rather less of a challenge. He was a gentleman of few inches but a vague importance, perhaps the leading man of the world of North Verona. He had a small pointed nose and a small pointed chin; also, as I observed, the most diminutive feet and a manner of no point at all. He looked at me foolishly and with his mouth open.

"You shall have your coffee," said Miss Spencer as if an army of cooks had been engaged in the preparation of it.

"C'est bien!" said her massive inmate. "Find your bouk"—and this personage turned to the gaping youth.

He gaped now at each quarter of the room. "My grammar, d'ye mean?"

The large lady however could but face her friend's visitor while persistently engaged with a certain laxity in the flow of her wrapper. "Find your bouk," she more absently repeated.

"My poetry, d'ye mean?" said the young man, who also couldn't take his eyes off me.

"Never mind your bouk" — his companion reconsidered. "To-day we'll just talk. We'll make some conversation. But we mustn't interrupt Mademoiselle's. Come, come" — and she moved off a step. "Under the leetle tree," she added for the benefit of Mademoiselle. After which she gave me a thin salutation, jerked a measured "Monsieur!" and swept away again with her swain following.

I looked at Miss Spencer, whose eyes never moved from the carpet, and I spoke, I fear, without grace. "Who in the world's that?"

"The Comtesse — that *was :* my *cousine* as they call it in French."

"And who's the young man?"

"The Countess's pupil, Mr. Mixter." This description of the tie uniting the two persons who had just quitted us must certainly have upset my gravity; for I recall the marked increase of my friend's own as she continued to explain. "She gives lessons in French and music, the simpler sorts —"

"The simpler sorts of French?" I fear I broke in.

But she was still impenetrable, and in fact had now an intonation that put me vulgarly in the wrong. "She has had the worst reverses — with no one to look to. She's prepared for any exertion — and she takes her misfortunes with gaiety."

"Ah well," I returned — no doubt a little ruefully, "that's all I myself am pretending to do. If she's determined to be a burden to nobody, nothing could be more right and proper."

My hostess looked vaguely, though I thought quite wearily enough, about : she met this proposition in no

303

other way. "I must go and get the coffee," she simply said.

"Has the lady many pupils?" I none the less persisted.

"She has only Mr. Mixter. She gives him all her time." It might have set me off again, but something in my whole impression of my friend's sensibility urged me to keep strictly decent. "He pays very well," she at all events inscrutably went on. "He's not very bright — as a pupil; but he's very rich and he's very kind. He has a buggy — with a back, and he takes the Countess to drive."

"For good long spells I hope," I could n't help interjecting — even at the cost of her so taking it that she had still to avoid my eyes. "Well, the country's beautiful for miles," I went on. And then as she was turning away: "You're going for the Countess's coffee?"

"If you'll excuse me a few moments."

"Is there no one else to do it?"

She seemed to wonder who there should be. "I keep no servants."

"Then can't I help?" After which, as she but looked at me, I bettered it. "Can't she wait on herself?"

Miss Spencer had a slow headshake — as if that too had been a strange idea. "She is n't used to *manual* labour."

The discrimination was a treat, but I cultivated decorum. "I see — and you *are*." But at the same time I could n't abjure curiosity. "Before you go, at any rate, please tell me this: who *is* this wonderful lady?"

"I told you just who in France — that extraordinary day. She's the wife of my cousin, whom you saw there."

"The lady disowned by her family in consequence of her marriage?"

"Yes; they've never seen her again. They've completely broken with her."

"And where's her husband?"

"My poor cousin's dead."

I pulled up, but only a moment. "And where's your money?"

The poor thing flinched — I kept her on the rack. "I don't know," she woefully said.

I scarce know what it didn't prompt me to — but I went step by step. "On her husband's death this lady at once came to you?"

It was as if she had had too often to describe it. "Yes, she arrived one day."

"How long ago?"

"Two years and four months."

"And has been here ever since?"

"Ever since."

I took it all in. "And how does she like it?"

"Well, not *very* much," said Miss Spencer divinely.

That too I took in. "And how do *you* —?"

She laid her face in her two hands an instant as she had done ten minutes before. Then, quickly, she went to get the Countess's coffee.

Left alone in the little parlour I found myself divided between the perfection of my disgust and a contrary wish to see, to learn more. At the end of a few minutes the young man in attendance on the lady in question reappeared as for a fresh gape at me. He was inordinately grave — to be dressed in such parti-coloured flannels; and he produced with no great confidence on his own side the message with which he had been charged. "She wants to know if you won't come right out."

"Who wants to know?"

"The Countess. That French lady."

"She has asked you to bring me?"

"Yes sir," said the young man feebly — for I may claim to have surpassed him in stature and weight.

I went out with him, and we found his instructress seated under one of the small quince-trees in front of the house; where she was engaged in drawing a fine needle with a very fat hand through a piece of embroidery not remarkable for freshness. She pointed graciously to the chair beside her and I sat down. Mr. Mixter glanced about him and then accommodated himself on the grass at her feet; whence he gazed upward more gapingly than ever and as if convinced that between us something wonderful would now occur.

"I'm sure you spick French," said the Countess, whose eyes were singularly protuberant as she played over me her agreeable smile.

"I do, madam — *tant bien que mal*," I replied, I fear, more dryly.

"Ah voilà!" she cried as with delight. "I knew it as soon as I looked at you. You've been in my poor dear country."

"A considerable time."

"You love it then, mon pays de France?"

"Oh it's an old affection." But I was n't exuberant.

"And you know Paris well?"

"Yes, *sans me vanter*, madam, I think I really do." And with a certain conscious purpose I let my eyes meet her own.

She presently, hereupon, moved her own and glanced down at Mr. Mixter. "What are we talking about?" she demanded of her attentive pupil.

He pulled his knees up, plucked at the grass, stared, blushed a little. "You're talking French," said Mr. Mixter.

"*La belle découverte!*" mocked the Countess. "It's going on ten months," she explained to me, "since I took him in hand. Don't put yourself out not to say he's *la bêtise même*," she added in fine style. "He won't in the least understand you."

A moment's consideration of Mr. Mixter, awkwardly sporting at our feet, quite assured me that he would n't. "I hope your other pupils do you more honour," I then remarked to my entertainer.

"I have no others. They don't know what French — or what anything else — is in this place; they don't want to know. You may therefore imagine the pleasure it is to me to meet a person who speaks it like yourself." I could but reply that my own pleasure was n't less, and she continued to draw the stitches through her embroidery with an elegant curl of her little finger. Every few moments she put her eyes, near-sightedly, closer to her work — this as if for elegance too. She inspired me with no more confidence than her late husband, if husband he was, had done, years before, on the occasion with which this one so detestably matched: she was coarse, common, affected, dishonest — no more a Countess than I was a Caliph. She had an assurance — based clearly on experience; but this could n't have been the experience of "race." Whatever it was indeed it did now, in a yearning fashion, flare out of her. "Talk to me of Paris, *mon beau Paris* that I 'd give my eyes to see. The very name of it *me fait languir.* How long since you were there ?"

"A couple of months ago."

"*Vous avez de la chance!* Tell me something about it. What were they doing ? Oh for an hour of the Boulevard!"

"They were doing about what they 're always doing — amusing themselves a good deal."

"At the theatres, *hein?*" sighed the Countess. "At the cafés-concerts ? *sous ce beau ciel* — at the little tables before the doors ? *Quelle existence!* You know I 'm a Parisienne, monsieur," she added, "to my finger-tips."

"Miss Spencer was mistaken then," I ventured to return, "in telling me you 're a Provençale."

She stared a moment, then put her nose to her embroidery, which struck me as having acquired even while we sat a dingier and more desultory air. "Ah I 'm a Provencale by birth, but a Parisienne by — inclination." After which she pursued: "And by the saddest events of my life — as well as by some of the happiest, hélas!"

"In other words by a varied experience!" I now at last smiled.

She questioned me over it with her hard little salient eyes. "Oh experience! — I could talk of that, no doubt, if I wished. *On en a de toutes les sortes* — and I never dreamed that mine, for example, would ever have *this* in store for me." And she indicated with her large bare elbow and with a jerk of her head all surrounding objects; the little white house, the pair of quince-trees, the rickety paling, even the rapt Mr. Mixter.

I took them all bravely in. "Ah if you mean you 're decidedly in exile —!"

"You may imagine what it is. These two years of my *épreuve* — *elles m'en ont données, des heures, des heures!* One gets used to things" — and she raised her shoulders to the highest shrug ever accomplished at North Verona; "so that I sometimes think I 've got used to this. But there are some things that are always beginning again. For example my coffee."

I so far again lent myself. "Do you always have coffee at this hour?"

Her eyebrows went up as high as her shoulders had done. "At what hour would you propose to me to have it? I must have my little cup after breakfast."

"Ah you breakfast at this hour?"

"At mid-day — *comme cela se fait.* Here they breakfast at a quarter past seven. That 'quarter past' is charming!"

"But you were telling me about your coffee," I observed sympathetically.

"My *cousine* can't believe in it; she can't understand it. "C'est une fille charmante, but that little cup of black coffee with a drop of '*fine*,' served at this hour — they exceed her comprehension. So I have to break the ice each day, and it takes the coffee the time you see to arrive. And when it does arrive, monsieur —! If I don't press it on *you* — though monsieur here sometimes joins me! — it's because you've drunk it on the Boulevard."

I resented extremely so critical a view of my poor friend's exertions, but I said nothing at all — the only way to be sure of my civility. I dropped my eyes on Mr. Mixter, who, sitting cross-legged and nursing his knees, watched my companion's foreign graces with an interest that familiarity had apparently done little to restrict. She became aware, naturally, of my mystified view of him and faced the question with all her boldness. "He adores me, you know," she murmured with her nose again in her tapestry — "he dreams of becoming *mon amoureux*. Yes, *il me fait une cour acharnée*—such as you see him. That's what we've come to. He has read some French novel — it took him six months. But ever since that he has thought himself a hero and me — such as I am, monsieur — *je ne sais quelle dévergondée!*"

Mr. Mixter may have inferred that he was to that extent the object of our reference; but of the manner in which he was handled he must have had small suspicion — preoccupied as he was, as to my companion, with the ecstasy of contemplation. Our hostess moreover at this moment came out of the house, bearing a coffee-pot and three cups on a neat little tray. I took from her eyes, as she approached us, a brief but intense appeal — the mute expression, as I felt, conveyed in the hardest little look she had yet addressed me, of her longing to know what, as a man of the world in general and of the French world in particular, I thought of these allied forces now so encamped on the stricken field of her life. I could only "act" however, as they said at North Verona, quite impenetrably — only make no answering sign. I could n't intimate, much less could I frankly utter, my inward sense of the Countess's probable past, with its measure of her virtue, value and accomplishments, and of the limits of the consideration to which she could properly pretend. I could n't give my friend a hint of how I myself personally "saw" her interesting pensioner — whether as the runaway wife of a too-jealous hair-dresser or of a too-morose pastry-cook, say; whether as a very small bourgeoise, in fine, who had vitiated her case beyond patching up, or even as some character, of the nomadic sort, less edifying still. I could n't let in, by the jog of a shutter, as it were, a hard informing ray and then, washing my hands of the business, turn my back for ever. I could on the contrary but save the situation, my own at least, for the moment, by pulling myself together with a master hand and appearing to ignore everything but that the dreadful person between us *was* a "grande dame." This effort was possible indeed but as a retreat in good order and with all the forms of courtesy. If I could n't speak, still less could I stay, and I think I must, in spite of everything, have turned black with disgust to see Caroline Spencer stand there like a waiting-maid. I therefore won't answer for the shade of success that may have attended my saying to the Countess, on my feet and as to leave her: "You expect to remain some time in these *parages?*"

What passed between us, as from face to face, while she looked up at me, *that* at least our companion may have caught, that at least may have sown, for the after-time, some seed of revelation. The Countess repeated her terrible shrug. "Who knows? I don't see my way —! It is n't an existence, but when one's in misery —! *Chère belle,*" she added as an appeal to Miss Spencer, "you've gone and forgotten the '*fine*'!"

I detained that lady as, after considering a moment in silence the small array, she was about to turn off in quest of this article. I held out my hand in silence — I had to go. Her wan set little face, severely mild and with the question of a moment before now quite cold in it, spoke of extreme fatigue, but also of something else strange and conceived — whether a desperate patience still, or at last some other desperation, being more than I can say. What was clearest on the whole was that she was glad I was going. Mr. Mixter had risen to his feet and was pouring out the Countess's coffee. As I went back past the Baptist church I could feel how right my poor friend had been in her conviction at the other, the still intenser, the now historic crisis, that she should still see something of that dear old Europe.

PASTE

PASTE

"I 've found a lot more things," her cousin said to her the day after the second funeral; "they're up in her room — but they're things I wish *you 'd* look at."

The pair of mourners, sufficiently stricken, were in the garden of the vicarage together, before luncheon, waiting to be summoned to that meal, and Arthur Prime had still in his face the intention, she was moved to call it rather than the expression, of feeling something or other. Some such appearance was in itself of course natural within a week of his stepmother's death, within three of his father's; but what was most present to the girl, herself sensitive and shrewd, was that he seemed somehow to brood without sorrow, to suffer without what she in her own case would have called pain. He turned away from her after this last speech — it was a good deal his habit to drop an observation and leave her to pick it up without assistance. If the vicar's widow, now in her turn finally translated, had not really belonged to him it was not for want of her giving herself, so far as he ever would take her; and she had lain for three days all alone at the end of the passage, in the great cold chamber of hospitality, the dampish greenish room where visitors slept and where several of the ladies of the parish had, without effect, offered, in pairs and successions, piously to watch with her. His personal connexion with the parish was now slighter

315

than ever, and he had really not waited for this opportunity to show the ladies what he thought of them. She felt that she herself had, during her doleful month's leave from Bleet, where she was governess, rather taken her place in the same snubbed order; but it was presently, none the less, with a better little hope of coming in for some remembrance, some relic, that she went up to look at the things he had spoken of, the identity of which, as a confused cluster of bright objects on a table in the darkened room, shimmered at her as soon as she had opened the door.

They met her eyes for the first time, but in a moment, before touching them, she knew them as things of the theatre, as very much too fine to have been with any verisimilitude things of the vicarage. They were too dreadfully good to be true, for her aunt had had no jewels to speak of, and these were coronets and girdles, diamonds, rubies and sapphires. Flagrant tinsel and glass, they looked strangely vulgar, but if after the first queer shock of them she found herself taking them up it was for the very proof, never yet so distinct to her, of a far-off faded story. An honest widowed cleric with a small son and a large sense of Shakespeare had, on a brave latitude of habit as well as of taste — since it implied his having in very fact dropped deep into the "pit" — conceived for an obscure actress several years older than himself an admiration of which the prompt offer of his reverend name and hortatory hand was the sufficiently candid sign. The response had perhaps in those dim years, so far as eccentricity was concerned, even bettered the proposal, and Charlotte, turning the tale over, had long since drawn from it a measure of the career renounced by the undistinguished comédienne — doubtless also tragic, or perhaps pantomimic, at a pinch — of her late uncle's dreams. This career could n't have been eminent and must much more probably have been comfortless.

"You see what it is — old stuff of the time she never liked to mention."

Our young woman gave a start; her companion had after all rejoined her and had apparently watched a moment her slightly scared recognition. "So I said to myself," she replied. Then to show intelligence, yet keep clear of twaddle: "How peculiar they look!"

"They look awful," said Arthur Prime. "Cheap gilt, diamonds as big as potatoes. These are trappings of a ruder age than ours. Actors do themselves better now."

"Oh now," said Charlotte, not to be less knowing, "actresses have real diamonds."

"Some of them." Arthur spoke dryly.

"I mean the bad ones — the nobodies too."

"Oh some of the nobodies have the biggest. But mamma was n't of that sort."

"A nobody?" Charlotte risked.

"Not a nobody to whom somebody — well, not a nobody with diamonds. It is n't all worth, this trash, five pounds."

There was something in the old gewgaws that spoke to her, and she continued to turn them over. "They 're relics. I think they have their melancholy and even their dignity."

Arthur observed another pause. "Do you care

for them?" he then asked. "I mean," he promptly
added, "as a souvenir."

"Of you?" Charlotte threw off.

"Of me? What have I to do with it? Of your poor
dead aunt who was so kind to you," he said with
virtuous sternness.

"Well, I'd rather have them than nothing."

"Then please take them," he returned in a tone of
relief which expressed somehow more of the eager
than of the gracious.

"Thank you." Charlotte lifted two or three objects
up and set them down again. Though they were
lighter than the materials they imitated they were
so much more extravagant that they struck her in
truth as rather an awkward heritage, to which she
might have preferred even a matchbox or a penwiper.
They were indeed shameless pinchbeck. "Had you
any idea she had kept them?"

"I don't at all believe she *had* kept them or knew
they were there, and I'm very sure my father did n't.
They had quite equally worked off any tenderness
for the connexion. These odds and ends, which she
thought had been given away or destroyed, had simply
got thrust into a dark corner and been forgotten."

Charlotte wondered. "Where then did you find
them?"

"In that old tin box"—and the young man
pointed to the receptacle from which he had dis-
lodged them and which stood on a neighbouring chair.
"It's rather a good box still, but I'm afraid I can't
give you *that*."

The girl took no heed of the box; she continued

only to look at the trinkets. "What corner had she found?"

"She had n't 'found' it," her companion sharply insisted; "she had simply lost it. The whole thing had passed from her mind. The box was on the top shelf of the old school-room closet, which, until one put one's head into it from a step-ladder, looked, from below, quite cleared out. The door's narrow and the part of the closet to the left goes well into the wall. The box had stuck there for years."

Charlotte was conscious of a mind divided and a vision vaguely troubled, and once more she took up two or three of the subjects of this revelation; a big bracelet in the form of a gilt serpent with many twists and beady eyes, a brazen belt studded with emeralds and rubies, a chain, of flamboyant architecture, to which, at the Theatre Royal Little Peddlington, Hamlet's mother must have been concerned to attach the portrait of the successor to Hamlet's father. "Are you very sure they're not really worth something? Their mere weight alone —!" she vaguely observed, balancing a moment a royal diadem that might have crowned one of the creations of the famous Mrs. Jarley.

But Arthur Prime, it was clear, had already thought the question over and found the answer easy. "If they had been worth anything to speak of she would long ago have sold them. My father and she had unfortunately never been in a position to keep any considerable value locked up." And while his companion took in the obvious force of this he went on with a flourish just marked enough not to escape her:

"If they're worth anything at all — why you're only the more welcome to them."

Charlotte had now in her hand a small bag of faded figured silk — one of those antique conveniences that speak to us, in terms of evaporated camphor and lavender, of the part they have played in some personal history; but though she had for the first time drawn the string she looked much more at the young man than at the questionable treasure it appeared to contain. "I shall like them. They're all I have."

"All you have — ?"

"That belonged to her."

He swelled a little, then looked about him as if to appeal — as against her avidity — to the whole poor place. "Well, what else do you want?"

"Nothing. Thank you very much." With which she bent her eyes on the article wrapped, and now only exposed, in her superannuated satchel — a string of large pearls, such a shining circle as might once have graced the neck of a provincial Ophelia and borne company to a flaxen wig. "This perhaps *is* worth something. Feel it." And she passed him the necklace, the weight of which she had gathered for a moment into her hand.

He measured it in the same way with his own, but remained quite detached. "Worth at most thirty shillings."

"Not more?"

"Surely not if it's paste?"

"But *is* it paste?"

He gave a small sniff of impatience. "Pearls nearly as big as filberts?"

320

"But they're heavy," Charlotte declared.

"No heavier than anything else." And he gave them back with an allowance for her simplicity. "Do you imagine for a moment they're real?"

She studied them a little, feeling them, turning them round. "Mightn't they possibly be?"

"Of that size — stuck away with that trash?"

"I admit it isn't likely," Charlotte presently said. "And pearls are so easily imitated."

"That's just what — to a person who knows — they're not. These have no lustre, no play."

"No — they *are* dull. They're opaque."

"Besides," he lucidly enquired, "how could she ever have come by them?"

"Mightn't they have been a present?"

Arthur stared at the question as if it were almost improper. "Because actresses are exposed —?" He pulled up, however, not saying to what, and before she could supply the deficiency had, with the sharp ejaculation of "No, they mightn't!" turned his back on her and walked away. His manner made her feel she had probably been wanting in tact, and before he returned to the subject, the last thing that evening, she had satisfied herself of the ground of his resentment. They had been talking of her departure the next morning, the hour of her train and the fly that would come for her, and it was precisely these things that gave him his effective chance. "I really can't allow you to leave the house under the impression that my stepmother was at *any* time of her life the sort of person to allow herself to be approached —"

"With pearl necklaces and that sort of thing?"

Arthur had made for her somehow the difficulty that she could n't show him she understood him without seeming pert.

It at any rate only added to his own gravity. "That sort of thing, exactly."

"I did n't think when I spoke this morning — but I see what you mean."

"I mean that she was beyond reproach," said Arthur Prime.

"A hundred times yes."

"Therefore if she could n't, out of her slender gains, ever have paid for a row of pearls —"

"She could n't, in that atmosphere, ever properly have had one? Of course she could n't. I 've seen perfectly since our talk," Charlotte went on, "that that string of beads is n't even as an imitation very good. The little clasp itself does n't seem even gold. With false pearls, I suppose," the girl mused, "it naturally would n't be."

"The whole thing 's rotten paste," her companion returned as if to have done with it. "If it were *not*, and she had kept it all these years hidden —"

"Yes?" Charlotte sounded as he paused.

"Why I should n't know what to think!"

"Oh I see." She had met him with a certain blankness, but adequately enough, it seemed, for him to regard the subject as dismissed; and there was no reversion to it between them before, on the morrow, when she had with difficulty made a place for them in her trunk, she carried off these florid survivals.

At Bleet she found small occasion to revert to them

322

and, in an air charged with such quite other references, even felt, after she had laid them away, much enshrouded, beneath various piles of clothing, that they formed a collection not wholly without its note of the ridiculous. Yet she was never, for the joke, tempted to show them to her pupils, though Gwendolen and Blanche in particular always wanted, on her return, to know what she had brought back; so that without an accident by which the case was quite changed they might have appeared to enter on a new phase of interment. The essence of the accident was the sudden illness, at the last moment, of Lady Bobby, whose advent had been so much counted on to spice the five days' feast laid out for the coming of age of the eldest son of the house; and its equally marked effect was the dispatch of a pressing message, in quite another direction, to Mrs. Guy, who, could she by a miracle be secured — she was always engaged ten parties deep — might be trusted to supply, it was believed, an element of exuberance scarcely less potent. Mrs. Guy was already known to several of the visitors already on the scene, but she was n't yet known to our young lady, who found her, after many wires and counter-wires had at last determined the triumph of her arrival, a strange charming little red-haired black-dressed woman, a person with the face of a baby and the authority of a commodore. She took on the spot the discreet, the exceptional young governess into the confidence of her designs and, still more, of her doubts; intimating that it was a policy she almost always promptly pursued.

"To-morrow and Thursday are all right," she said

frankly to Charlotte on the second day, "but I'm not half-satisfied with Friday."

"What improvement then do you suggest?"

"Well, my strong point, you know, is *tableaux vivants.*"

"Charming. And what is your favourite character?"

"Boss!" said Mrs. Guy with decision; and it was very markedly under that ensign that she had, within a few hours, completely planned her campaign and recruited her troop. Every word she uttered was to the point, but none more so than, after a general survey of their equipment, her final enquiry of Charlotte. She had been looking about, but half-appeased, at the muster of decoration and drapery. "We shall be dull. We shall want more colour. You've nothing else?"

Charlotte had a thought. "No—I've *some* things."

"Then why don't you bring them?"

The girl weighed it. "Would you come to my room?"

"No," said Mrs. Guy — "bring them to-night to mine."

So Charlotte, at the evening's end, after candle-sticks had flickered through brown old passages bed-ward, arrived at her friend's door with the burden of her aunt's relics. But she promptly expressed a fear. "Are they too garish?"

When she had poured them out on the sofa Mrs. Guy was but a minute, before the glass, in clapping on the diadem. "Awfully jolly — we can do Ivanhoe!"

"But they're only glass and tin."

"Larger than life they are, *rather!* — which is

exactly what's wanted for tableaux. *Our* jewels, for historic scenes, don't tell — the real thing falls short. Rowena must have rubies as big as eggs. Leave them with me," Mrs. Guy continued — "they'll inspire me. Good-night."

The next morning she was in fact — yet very strangely — inspired. "Yes, *I'll* do Rowena. But I don't, my dear, understand."

"Understand what?"

Mrs. Guy gave a very lighted stare. "How you come to have such things."

Poor Charlotte smiled. "By inheritance."

"Family jewels?"

"They belonged to my aunt, who died some months ago. She was on the stage a few years in early life, and these are a part of her trappings."

"She left them to you?"

"No; my cousin, her stepson, who naturally has no use for them, gave them to me for remembrance of her. She was a dear kind thing, always so nice to me, and I was fond of her."

Mrs. Guy had listened with frank interest. "But it's *he* who must be a dear kind thing!"

Charlotte wondered. "You think so?"

"Is *he*," her friend went on, "also 'always so nice' to you?"

The girl, at this, face to face there with the brilliant visitor in the deserted breakfast-room, took a deeper sounding. "What is it?"

"Don't you know?"

Something came over her. "The pearls — ?" But the question fainted on her lips.

"Does n't *he* know?"

Charlotte found herself flushing. "They 're *not*
paste?"

"Have n't you looked at them?"

She was conscious of two kinds of embarrassment.
"*You* have?"

"Very carefully."

"And they 're real?"

Mrs. Guy became slightly mystifying and returned
for all answer: "Come again, when you 've done with
the children, to my room."

Our young woman found she had done with the
children that morning so promptly as to reveal to
them a new joy, and when she reappeared before
Mrs. Guy this lady had already encircled a plump
white throat with the only ornament, surely, in all
the late Mrs. Prime's — the effaced Miss Bradshaw's
— collection, in the least qualified to raise a question.
If Charlotte had never yet once, before the glass, tied
the string of pearls about her own neck, this was because she had been capable of no such stoop to approved "imitation"; but she had now only to look
at Mrs. Guy to see that, so disposed, the ambiguous
objects might have passed for frank originals. "What
in the world have you done to them?"

"Only handled them, understood them, admired
them and put them on. That 's what pearls want;
they want to be worn — it wakes them up. They 're
alive, don't you see? How *have* these been treated?
They must have been buried, ignored, despised. They
were half-dead. Don't you *know* about pearls?" Mrs.
Guy threw off as she fondly fingered the necklace.

"How *should* I? Do *you?*"

"Everything. These were simply asleep, and from the moment I really touched them — well," said their wearer lovingly, "it only took one's eye!"

"It took more than mine — though I did just wonder; and than Arthur's," Charlotte brooded. She found herself almost panting. "Then their value—?"

"Oh their value's excellent."

The girl, for a deep contemplative moment, took another plunge into the wonder, the beauty and the mystery. "Are you *sure?*"

Her companion wheeled round for impatience. "Sure? For what kind of an idiot, my dear, do you take me?"

It was beyond Charlotte Prime to say. "For the same kind as Arthur — and as myself," she could only suggest. "But my cousin did n't know. He thinks they're worthless."

"Because of the rest of the lot? Then your cousin's an ass. But what — if, as I understood you, he gave them to you — has he to do with it?"

"Why if he gave them to me as worthless and they turn out precious —!"

"You must give them back? I don't see that — if he was such a noodle. He took the risk."

Charlotte fed, in fancy, on the pearls, which decidedly were exquisite, but which at the present moment somehow presented themselves much more as Mrs. Guy's than either as Arthur's or as her own. "Yes — he did take it; even after I had distinctly hinted to him that they looked to me different from the other pieces."

"Well then!" said Mrs. Guy with something more than triumph — with a positive odd relief.

But it had the effect of making our young woman think with more intensity. "Ah you see he thought they could n't be different, because — so peculiarly — they should n't be."

"Should n't? I don't understand."

"Why how would she have got them?" — so Charlotte candidly put it.

"She? Who?" There was a capacity in Mrs. Guy's tone for a sinking of persons —!

"Why the person I told you of: his stepmother, my uncle's wife — among whose poor old things, extraordinarily thrust away and out of sight, he happened to find them."

Mrs. Guy came a step nearer to the effaced Miss Bradshaw. "Do you mean she may have stolen them?"

"No. But she had been an actress."

"Oh well then," cried Mrs. Guy, "would n't that be just how?"

. "Yes, except that she was n't at all a brilliant one, nor in receipt of large pay." The girl even threw off a nervous joke. "I'm afraid she could n't have been our Rowena."

Mrs. Guy took it up. "Was she very ugly?"

"No. She may very well, when young, have looked rather nice."

"Well then!" was Mrs. Guy's sharp comment and fresh triumph.

"You mean it was a present? That's just what he so dislikes the idea of her having received — a present from an admirer capable of going such lengths."

"Because she would n't have taken it for nothing? *Speriamo* — that she was n't a brute. The 'length' her admirer went was the length of a whole row. Let us hope she was just a little kind!"

"Well," Charlotte went on, "that she was 'kind' might seem to be shown by the fact that neither her husband, nor his son, nor I, his niece, knew or dreamed of her possessing anything so precious; by her having kept the gift all the rest of her life beyond discovery—out of sight and protected from suspicion."

"As if, you mean" — Mrs. Guy was quick — "she had been wedded to it and yet was ashamed of it? Fancy," she laughed while she manipulated the rare beads, "being ashamed of *these !*"

"But you see she had married a clergyman."

"Yes, she must have been 'rum.' But at any rate he had married *her*. What did he suppose?"

"Why that she had never been of the sort by whom such offerings are encouraged."

"Ah my dear, the sort by whom they're *not* —!" But Mrs. Guy caught herself up. "And her stepson thought the same?"

"Overwhelmingly."

"Was he then, if only her stepson —"

"So fond of her as that comes to? Yes; he had never known, consciously, his real mother, and, without children of her own, she was very patient and nice with him. And *I* liked her so," the girl pursued, "that at the end of ten years, in so strange a manner, to 'give her away' —"

"Is impossible to you? Then don't!" said Mrs. Guy with decision.

"Ah but if they're real I can't keep them!" Charlotte, with her eyes on them, moaned in her impatience. "It's too difficult."

"Where's the difficulty, if he has such sentiments that he'd rather sacrifice the necklace than admit it, with the presumption it carries with it, to be genuine? You've only to be silent."

"And keep it? How can *I* ever wear it?"

"You'd have to hide it, like your aunt?" Mrs. Guy was amused. "You can easily sell it."

Her companion walked round her for a look at the affair from behind. The clasp was certainly, doubtless intentionally, misleading, but everything else was indeed lovely. "Well, I must think. Why did n't *she* sell them?" Charlotte broke out in her trouble.

Mrs. Guy had an instant answer. "Does n't that prove what they secretly recalled to her? You've only to be silent!" she ardently repeated.

"I must think — I must think!"

Mrs. Guy stood with her hands attached but motionless. "Then you want them back?"

As if with the dread of touching them Charlotte retreated to the door. "I'll tell you to-night."

"But may I wear them?"

"Meanwhile?"

"This evening — at dinner."

It was the sharp selfish pressure of this that really, on the spot, determined the girl; but for the moment, before closing the door on the question, she only said: "As you like!"

They were busy much of the day with preparation and rehearsal, and at dinner that evening the concourse of guests was such that a place among them for Miss Prime failed to find itself marked. At the time the company rose she was therefore alone in the school-room, where, towards eleven o'clock, she received a visit from Mrs. Guy. This lady's white shoulders heaved, under the pearls, with an emotion that the very red lips which formed, as if for the full effect, the happiest opposition of colour, were not slow to translate. "My dear, you should have seen the sensation — they 've had a success!"

Charlotte, dumb a moment, took it all in. "It *is* as if they knew it — they 're more and more alive. But so much the worse for both of us! I can't," she brought out with an effort, "be silent."

"You mean to return them?"

"If I don't I 'm a thief."

Mrs. Guy gave her a long hard look: what was decidedly not of the baby in Mrs. Guy's face was a certain air of established habit in the eyes. Then, with a sharp little jerk of her head and a backward reach of her bare beautiful arms, she undid the clasp and, taking off the necklace, laid it on the table. "If you do you 're a goose."

"Well, of the two —!" said our young lady, gathering it up with a sigh. And as if to get it, for the pang it gave, out of sight as soon as possible, she shut it up, clicking the lock, in the drawer of her own little table; after which, when she turned again, her companion looked naked and plain without it. "But what will you say?" it then occurred to her to demand.

"Downstairs — to explain ?" Mrs. Guy was after all trying at least to keep her temper. "Oh I'll put on something else and say the clasp's broken. And you won't of course name *me* to him," she added.

"As having undeceived me ? No — I'll say that, looking at the thing more carefully, it's my own private idea."

"And does he know how little you really know ?"

"As an expert — surely. And he has always much the conceit of his own opinion."

"Then he won't believe you — as he so hates to. He'll stick to his judgement and maintain his gift, and we shall have the darlings back!" With which reviving assurance Mrs. Guy kissed her young friend for good-night.

She was not, however, to be gratified or justified by any prompt event, for, whether or no paste entered into the composition of the ornament in question, Charlotte shrank from the temerity of dispatching it to town by post. Mrs. Guy was thus disappointed of the hope of seeing the business settled — "by return," she had seemed to expect — before the end of the revels. The revels, moreover, rising to a frantic pitch, pressed for all her attention, and it was at last only in the general confusion of leave-taking that she made, parenthetically, a dash at the person in the whole company with whom her contact had been most interesting.

"Come, what will you take for them ?"

"The pearls ? Ah, you'll have to treat with my cousin."

Mrs. Guy, with quick intensity, lent herself. "Where then does he live?"

"In chambers in the Temple. You can find him."

"But what's the use, if *you* do neither one thing nor the other?"

"Oh I *shall* do the 'other,'" Charlotte said: "I'm only waiting till I go up. You want them so awfully?" She curiously, solemnly again, sounded her.

"I'm dying for them. There's a special charm in them — I don't know what it is: they tell so their history."

"But what do you know of that?"

"Just what they themselves say. It's all *in* them — and it comes out. They breathe a tenderness — they have the white glow of it. My dear," hissed Mrs. Guy in supreme confidence and as she buttoned her glove — "they're things of love!"

"Oh!" our young woman vaguely exclaimed.

"They're things of passion!"

"Mercy!" she gasped, turning short off. But these words remained, though indeed their help was scarce needed, Charlotte being in private face to face with a new light, as she by this time felt she must call it, on the dear dead kind colourless lady whose career had turned so sharp a corner in the middle. The pearls had quite taken their place as a revelation. She might have received them for nothing — admit that; but she couldn't have kept them so long and so unprofitably hidden, couldn't have enjoyed them only in secret, for nothing; and she had mixed them in her reliquary with false things in order to put curiosity and detection off the scent. Over this strange fact poor Charlotte interminably mused: it became more touching, more attaching for her than she could now confide to any ear. How bad or how happy — in the sophisticated sense of Mrs. Guy and the young man at the Temple — the effaced Miss Bradshaw must have been to have had to be so mute! The little governess at Bleet put on the necklace now in secret sessions; she wore it sometimes under her dress; she came to feel verily a haunting passion for it. Yet in her penniless state she would have parted with it for money; she gave herself also to dreams of what in this direction it would do for her. The sophistry of her so often saying to herself that Arthur had after all definitely pronounced her welcome to any gain from his gift that might accrue — this trick remained innocent, as she perfectly knew it for what it was. Then there was always the possibility of his — as she could only picture it — rising to the occasion. Might n't he have a grand magnanimous moment? — might n't he just say "Oh I could n't of course have afforded to let you have it if I had known; but since you *have* got it, and have made out the truth by your own wit, I really can't screw myself down to the shabbiness of taking it back"?

She had, as it proved, to wait a long time — to wait till, at the end of several months, the great house of Bleet had, with due deliberation, for the season, transferred itself to town; after which, however, she fairly snatched at her first freedom to knock, dressed in her best and armed with her disclosure, at the door of her doubting kinsman. It was still with doubt and not quite with the face she had hoped that he listened to her story. He had turned pale, she thought, as she produced the necklace, and he appeared above all disagreeably affected. Well, perhaps there was reason, she more than ever remembered; but what on earth was one, in close touch with the fact, to do? She had laid the pearls on his table, where, without his having at first put so much as a finger to them, they met his hard cold stare.

"I don't believe in them," he simply said at last.

"That's exactly then," she returned with some spirit, "what I wanted to hear!"

She fancied that at this his colour changed; it was indeed vivid to her afterwards — for she was to have a long recall of the scene — that she had made him quite angrily flush. "It's a beastly unpleasant imputation, you know!" — and he walked away from her as he had always walked at the vicarage.

"It's none of *my* making, I'm sure," said Charlotte Prime. "If you're afraid to believe they're real —"

"Well?" — and he turned, across the room, sharp round at her.

"Why it's not my fault."

He said nothing more, for a moment, on this; he only came back to the table. "They're what I originally said they were. They're rotten paste."

"Then I may keep them?"

"No. I want a better opinion."

"Than your own?"

"Than *your* own." He dropped on the pearls another queer stare; then, after a moment, bringing himself to touch them, did exactly what she had herself done in the presence of Mrs. Guy at Bleet —

gathered them together, marched off with them to a drawer, put them in and clicked the key. "You say I'm afraid," he went on as he again met her; "but I shan't be afraid to take them to Bond Street."

"And if the people say they're real — ?"

He had a pause and then his strangest manner. "They won't say it! They shan't!"

There was something in the way he brought it out that deprived poor Charlotte, as she was perfectly aware, of any manner at all. "Oh!" she simply sounded, as she had sounded for her last word to Mrs. Guy; and within a minute, without more conversation, she had taken her departure.

A fortnight later she received a communication from him, and toward the end of the season one of the entertainments in Eaton Square was graced by the presence of Mrs. Guy. Charlotte was not at dinner, but she came down afterwards, and this guest, on seeing her, abandoned a very beautiful young man on purpose to cross and speak to her. The guest displayed a lovely necklace and had apparently not lost her habit of overflowing with the pride of such ornaments.

"Do you see?" She was in high joy.

They were indeed splendid pearls — so far as poor Charlotte could feel that she knew, after what had come and gone, about such mysteries. The poor girl had a sickly smile. "They're almost as fine as Arthur's."

"Almost? Where, my dear, are your eyes? They *are* 'Arthur's'!" After which, to meet the flood of crimson that accompanied her young friend's start:

336

"I tracked them — after your folly, and, by miraculous luck, recognised them in the Bond Street window to which he had disposed of them."

"*Disposed* of them?" Charlotte gasped. "He wrote me that I had insulted his mother and that the people had shown him he was right — had pronounced them utter paste."

Mrs. Guy gave a stare. "Ah I told you he would n't bear it! No. But I had, I assure you," she wound up, "to drive my bargain!"

Charlotte scarce heard or saw; she was full of her private wrong. "He wrote me," she panted, "that he had smashed them."

Mrs. Guy could only wonder and pity. "He's really morbid!" But it was n't quite clear which of the pair she pitied; though the young person employed in Eaton Square felt really morbid too after they had separated and she found herself full of thought. She even went the length of asking herself what sort of a bargain Mrs. Guy had driven and whether the marvel of the recognition in Bond Street had been a veracious account of the matter. Had n't she perhaps in truth dealt with Arthur directly? It came back to Charlotte almost luridly that she had had his address.

EUROPE

EUROPE

I

"OUR feeling is, you know, that Becky *should* go."
That earnest little remark comes back to me, even
after long years, as the first note of something that
began, for my observation, the day I went with my
sister-in-law to take leave of her good friends. It's
a memory of the American time, which revives so at
present — under some touch that does n't signify —
that it rounds itself off as an anecdote. That walk to
say good-bye was the beginning; and the end, so far as
I enjoyed a view of it, was not till long after; yet
even the end also appears to me now as of the old
days. I went, in those days, on occasion, to see my
sister-in-law, in whose affairs, on my brother's death,
I had had to take a helpful hand. I continued to go
indeed after these little matters were straightened out,
for the pleasure, periodically, of the impression —
the change to the almost pastoral sweetness of the
good Boston suburb from the loud longitudinal
New York. It was another world, with other manners, a different tone, a different taste; a savour nowhere so mild, yet so distinct, as in the square white
house — with the pair of elms, like gigantic wheat-
sheaves, in front, the rustic orchard not far behind,
the old-fashioned door-lights, the big blue-and-white
jars in the porch, the straight bricked walk from the

high gate — that enshrined the extraordinary merit of Mrs. Rimmle and her three daughters.

These ladies were so much of the place and the place so much of themselves that from the first of their being revealed to me I felt that nothing else at Brookbridge much mattered. They were what, for me, at any rate, Brookbridge had most to give: I mean in the way of what it was naturally strongest in, the thing we called in New York the New England expression, the air of Puritanism reclaimed and refined. The Rimmles had brought this down to a wonderful delicacy. They struck me even then — all four almost equally — as very ancient and very earnest, and I think theirs must have been the house in all the world in which "culture" first came to the aid of morning calls. The head of the family was the widow of a great public character — as public characters were understood at Brookbridge — whose speeches on anniversaries formed a part of the body of national eloquence spouted in the New England schools by little boys covetous of the most marked, though perhaps the easiest, distinction. He was reported to have been celebrated, and in such fine declamatory connexions that he seemed to gesticulate even from the tomb. He was understood to have made, in his wife's company, the tour of Europe at a date not immensely removed from that of the battle of Waterloo. What was the age then of the bland firm antique Mrs. Rimmle at the period of her being first revealed to me? That's a point I'm not in a position to determine — I remember mainly that I was young enough to regard her as having reached the limit. And yet the limit for Mrs. Rimmle must have been prodigiously extended; the scale of its extension is in fact the very moral of this reminiscence. She was old, and her daughters were old, but I was destined to know them all as older. It was only by comparison and habit that — however much I recede — Rebecca, Maria and Jane were the "young ladies."

· I think it was felt that, though their mother's life, after thirty years of widowhood, had had a grand backward stretch, her blandness and firmness — and this in spite of her extreme physical frailty — would be proof against any surrender not overwhelmingly justified by time. It had appeared, years before, at a crisis of which the waves had not even yet quite subsided, a surrender not justified by anything name-able that she should go to Europe with her daughters and for her health. Her health was supposed to re-quire constant support; but when it had at that period tried conclusions with the idea of Europe it was not the idea of Europe that had been insidious enough to prevail. She had n't gone, and Becky, Maria and Jane had n't gone, and this was long ago. They still merely floated in the air of the visit achieved, with such introductions and such acclamations, in the early part of the century; they still, with fond glances at the sunny parlour-walls, only referred, in conversation, to divers pictorial and other reminders of it. The Miss Rimmles had quite been brought up on it, but Becky, as the most literary, had most mastered the subject. There were framed letters — tributes to their eminent father — suspended among the me-mentoes, and of two or three of these, the most foreign and complimentary, Becky had executed translations that figured beside the text. She knew already, through this and other illumination, so much about Europe that it was hard to believe for her in that limit of adventure which consisted only of her having been twice to Philadelphia. The others had n't been to Philadelphia, but there was a legend that Jane had been to Saratoga. Becky was a short stout fair person with round serious eyes, a high forehead, the sweetest neatest enunciation, and a miniature of her father — "done in Rome" — worn as a breastpin. She had written the life, she had edited the speeches, of the original of this ornament, and now at last, beyond the seas, she was really to tread in his footsteps.

Fine old Mrs. Rimmle, in the sunny parlour and with a certain austerity of cap and chair — though with a gay new "front" that looked like rusty brown plush — had had so unusually good a winter that the question of her sparing two members of her family for an absence had been threshed as fine, I could feel, as even under that Puritan roof any case of conscience had ever been threshed. They were to make their dash while the coast, as it were, was clear, and each of the daughters had tried — heroically, angelically and for the sake of each of her sisters — not to be one of the two. What I encountered that first time was an opportunity to concur with enthusiasm in the general idea that Becky's wonderful preparation would be wasted if she were the one to stay with their mother. Their talk of Becky's preparation (they had a sly old-maidish humour that was as mild as milk) might have been of some mixture, for application somewhere, that she kept in a precious bottle. It had been settled at all events that, armed with this concoction and borne aloft by their introductions, she and Jane were to start. They were wonderful on their introductions, which proceeded naturally from their mother and were addressed to the charming families that in vague generations had so admired vague Mr. Rimmle. Jane, I found at Brookbridge, had to be described, for want of other description, as the pretty one, but it would n't have served to identify her unless you had seen the others. *Her* preparation was only this figment of her prettiness — only, that is, unless one took into account something that, on the spot, I silently divined : the lifelong secret passionate ache of her little rebellious desire. They were all growing old in the yearning to go, but Jane's yearning was the sharpest. She struggled with it as people at Brookbridge mostly struggled with what they liked, but fate, by threatening to prevent what she *dis*liked and what was therefore duty — which was to stay at home instead of Maria — had bewildered her, I judged, not a little. It was she who, in the words I have quoted, mentioned to me Becky's case and Becky's affinity as the clearest of all. Her mother moreover had on the general subject still more to say.

"I positively desire, I really quite insist that they shall go," the old lady explained to us from her stiff chair. "We 've talked about it so often, and they 've had from me so clear an account — I 've amused them again and again with it — of what 's to be seen and enjoyed. If they 've had hitherto too many duties to leave, the time seems to have come to recognise

that there are also many duties to *seek*. Wherever
we go we find them — I always remind the girls of
that. There's a duty that calls them to those wonderful countries, just as it called, at the right time, their
father and myself — if it be only that of laying-up for
the years to come the same store of remarkable impressions, the same wealth of knowledge and food for
conversation as, since my return, I've found myself
so happy to possess." Mrs. Rimmle spoke of her
return as of something of the year before last, but the
future of her daughters was somehow, by a different
law, to be on the scale of great vistas, of endless after-
tastes. I think that, without my being quite ready to
say it, even this first impression of her was somewhat
upsetting; there was a large placid perversity, a grim
secrecy of intention, in her estimate of the ages.

"Well, I'm so glad you don't delay it longer," I
said to Miss Becky before we withdrew. "And
whoever should go," I continued in the spirit of the
sympathy with which the good sisters had already
inspired me, "I quite feel, with your family, you
know, that *you* should. But of course I hold that
every one should." I suppose I wished to attenuate
my solemnity; there was, however, something in it I
could n't help. It must have been a faint foreknow-
ledge.

"Have you been a great deal yourself?" Miss Jane,
I remembered, enquired.

"Not so much but that I hope to go a good deal
more. So perhaps we shall meet," I encouragingly
suggested.

I recall something — something in the nature of

susceptibility to encouragement — that this brought into the more expressive brown eyes to which Miss Jane mainly owed it that she was the pretty one. "Where, do you think?"

I tried to think. "Well, on the Italian lakes — Como, Bellaggio, Lugano." I liked to say the names to them.

"'Sublime, but neither bleak nor bare — nor misty are the mountains there!'" Miss Jane softly breathed, while her sister looked at her as if her acquaintance with the poetry of the subject made her the most interesting feature of the scene she evoked.

But Miss Becky presently turned to me. "Do you know everything —?"

"Everything?"

"In Europe."

"Oh yes," I laughed, "and one or two things even in America."

The sisters seemed to me furtively to look at each other. "Well, you'll have to be quick — to meet *us*," Miss Jane resumed.

"But surely when you're once there you'll stay on."

"Stay on?" — they murmured it simultaneously and with the oddest vibration of dread as well as of desire. It was as if they had been in presence of a danger and yet wished me, who "knew everything," to torment them with still more of it.

Well, I did my best. "I mean it will never do to cut it short."

"No, that's just what I keep saying," said brilliant Jane. "It would be better in that case not to go."

"Oh don't talk about not going — at this time!"

It was none of my business, but I felt shocked and impatient.

"No, not at *this* time!" broke in Miss Maria, who, very red in the face, had joined us. Poor Miss Maria was known as the flushed one; but she was not flushed — she only had an unfortunate surface. The third day after this was to see them embark.

Miss Becky, however, desired as little as any one to be in any way extravagant. "It's only the thought of our mother," she explained.

I looked a moment at the old lady, with whom my sister-in-law was engaged. "Well — your mother's magnificent."

"*Is n't* she magnificent?" — they eagerly took it up.

She *was* — I could reiterate it with sincerity, though I perhaps mentally drew the line when Miss Maria again risked, as a fresh ejaculation: "I think she's better than Europe!"

"Maria!" they both, at this, exclaimed with a strange emphasis: it was as if they feared she had suddenly turned cynical over the deep domestic drama of their casting of lots. The innocent laugh with which she answered them gave the measure of her cynicism.

We separated at last, and my eyes met Mrs. Rimmle's as I held for an instant her aged hand. It was doubtless only my fancy that her calm cold look quietly accused me of something. Of what *could* it accuse me? Only, I thought, of thinking.

II

I LEFT Brookbridge the next day, and for some time after that had no occasion to hear from my kinswoman; but when she finally wrote there was a passage in her letter that affected me more than all the rest. "Do you know the poor Rimmles never, after all, 'went'? The old lady, at the eleventh hour, broke down; everything broke down, and all of *them* on top of it, so that the dear things are with us still. Mrs. Rimmle, the night after our call, had, in the most unexpected manner, a turn for the worse — something in the nature (though they're rather mysterious about it) of a seizure; Becky and Jane felt it — dear devoted stupid angels that they are — heartless to leave her at such a moment, and Europe's indefinitely postponed. However, they think they're still going — or *think* they think it — when she's better. They also think — or think they think — that she *will* be better. I certainly pray she may." So did I — quite fervently. I was conscious of a real pang — I did n't know how much they had made me care.

Late that winter my sister-in-law spent a week in New York; when almost my first enquiry on meeting her was about the health of Mrs. Rimmle.

"Oh she's rather bad — she really is, you know. It's not surprising that at her age she should be infirm."

"Then what the deuce *is* her age?"

349

"I can't tell you to a year — but she's immensely old."

"That of course I saw," I replied — "unless you literally mean so old that the records have been lost."

My sister-in-law thought. "Well, I believe she was n't positively young when she married. She lost three or four children before these women were born."

We surveyed together a little, on this, the "dark backward." "And they were born, I gather, *after* the famous tour? Well then, as the famous tour was in a manner to celebrate — was n't it? — the restoration of the Bourbons —" I considered, I gasped. "My dear child, what on earth do you make her out?"

My relative, with her Brookbridge habit, transferred her share of the question to the moral plane — turned it forth to wander, by implication at least, in the sandy desert of responsibility. "Well, you know, we all immensely admire her."

"You can't admire her more than I do. She's awful."

My converser looked at me with a certain fear. "She's *really* ill."

"Too ill to get better?"

"Oh no — we hope not. Because then they'll be able to go."

"And *will* they go if she should?"

"Oh the moment they should be quite satisfied. I mean *really*," she added.

I'm afraid I laughed at her — the Brookbridge "really" was a thing so by itself. "But if she should n't get better?" I went on.

"Oh don't speak of it! They want so to go."

"It's a pity they're so infernally good," I mused.

"No — don't say that. It's what keeps them up."

"Yes, but is n't it what keeps *her* up too?"

My visitor looked grave. "Would you like them to kill her?"

I don't know that I was then prepared to say I should — though I believe I came very near it. But later on I burst all bounds, for the subject grew and grew. I went again before the good sisters ever did — I mean I went to Europe. I think I went twice, with a brief interval, before my fate again brought round for me a couple of days at Brookbridge. I had been there repeatedly, in the previous time, without making the acquaintance of the Rimmles; but now that I had had the revelation I could n't have it too much, and the first request I preferred was to be taken again to see them. I remember well indeed the scruple I felt — the real delicacy — about betraying that *I* had, in the pride of my power, since our other meeting, stood, as their phrase went, among romantic scenes; but they were themselves the first to speak of it, and what moreover came home to me was that the coming and going of their friends in general — Brookbridge itself having even at that period one foot in Europe — was such as to place constantly before them the pleasure that was only postponed. They were thrown back after all on what the situation, under a final analysis, had most to give — the sense that, as every one kindly said to them and they kindly said to every one, Europe would keep. Every one felt for them so deeply that their own kindness in alleviating every one's feeling was really what came out most. Mrs. Rimmle was still in her stiff chair and in the sunny parlour, but if *she* made no scruple of introducing the Italian lakes my heart sank to observe that she dealt with them, as a topic, not in the least in the leave-taking manner in which Falstaff babbled of green fields.

I'm not sure that after this my pretexts for a day or two with my sister-in-law were n't apt to be a mere cover for another glimpse of these particulars: I at any rate never went to Brookbridge without an irrepressible eagerness for our customary call. A long time seems to me thus to have passed, with glimpses and lapses, considerable impatience and still more pity. Our visits indeed grew shorter, for, as my companion said, they were more and more of a strain. It finally struck me that the good sisters even shrank from me a little as from one who penetrated their consciousness in spite of himself. It was as if they knew where I thought they ought to be, and were moved to deprecate at last, by a systematic silence on the subject of that hemisphere, the criminality I fain would fix on them. They were full instead — as with the instinct of throwing dust in my eyes — of little pathetic hypocrisies about Brookbridge interests and delights. I dare say that as time went on my deeper sense of their situation came practically to rest on my companion's report of it. I certainly think I recollect every word we ever exchanged about them, even if I've lost the thread of the special occasions. The impression they made on me after each interval always broke out with extravagance as I walked away with her.

"*She* may be as old as she likes — I don't care. It's the fearful age the 'girls' are reaching that constitutes the scandal. One should n't pry into such matters, I know; but the years and the chances are really going. They're all growing old together — it will presently be too late; and their mother meanwhile perches over them like a vulture — what shall I call it? — calculating. Is she waiting for them successively to drop off? She'll survive them each and all. There's something too remorseless in it."

"Yes, but what do you want her to do? If the poor thing *can't* die she can't. Do you want her to take poison or to open a blood-vessel? I dare say she'd prefer to go."

"I beg your pardon," I must have replied; "you dare n't say anything of the sort. If she'd prefer to go she *would* go. She'd feel the propriety, the decency, the necessity of going. She just prefers *not* to go. She prefers to stay and keep up the tension, and her calling them 'girls' and talking of the good time they'll still have is the mere conscious mischief of a subtle old witch. They won't have *any* time — there is n't any time to have! I mean there's, on her own part, no real loss of measure or of perspective in it. She *knows* she's a hundred and ten, and she takes a cruel pride in it."

My sister-in-law differed with me about this; she held that the old woman's attitude was an honest one and that her magnificent vitality, so great in spite of her infirmities, made it inevitable she should attribute youth to persons who had come into the world so much later. "Then suppose she should die?"

— so my fellow student of the case always put it to me.

"Do you mean while her daughters are away? There's not the least fear of that — not even if at the very moment of their departure she should be *in extremis*. They'd find her all right on their return."

"But think how they'd feel not to have been with her!"

"That's only, I repeat, on the unsound assumption. If they'd only go to-morrow — literally make a good rush for it — they'll be with her when they come back. That will give them plenty of time." I'm afraid I even heartlessly added that if she *should*, against every probability, pass away in their absence they wouldn't have to come back at all — which would be just the compensation proper to their long privation. And then Maria would come out to join the two others, and they would be — though but for the too scanty remnant of their career — as merry as the day is long.

I remained ready, somehow, pending the fulfilment of that vision, to sacrifice Maria; it was only over the urgency of the case for the others respectively that I found myself balancing. Sometimes it was for Becky I thought the tragedy deepest — sometimes, and in quite a different manner, I thought it most dire for Jane. It was Jane after all who had most sense of life. I seemed in fact dimly to descry in Jane a sense — as yet undescried by herself or by any one — of all sorts of queer things. Why didn't *she* go? I used desperately to ask; why didn't she make a bold personal dash for it, strike up a partnership with some one or other of the travelling spinsters in whom Brookbridge more and more abounded? Well, there came a flash for me at a particular point of the grey middle desert: my correspondent was able to let me know that poor Jane at last *had* sailed. She had gone of a sudden — I liked my sister-in-law's view of suddenness — with the kind Hathaways, who had made an irresistible grab at her and lifted her off her feet. They were going for the summer and for Mr. Hathaway's health, so that the opportunity was perfect and it was impossible not to be glad that something very like physical force had finally prevailed. This was the general feeling at Brookbridge, and I might imagine what Brookbridge had been brought to from the fact that, at the very moment she was hustled off, the doctor, called to her mother at the peep of dawn, had considered that *he* at least must stay. There had been real alarm — greater than ever before; it actually did seem as if this time the end had come. But it was Becky, strange to say, who, though fully recognising the nature of the crisis, had kept the situation in hand and insisted upon action. This, I remember, brought back to me a discomfort with which I had been familiar from the first. One of the two had sailed, and I was sorry it was n't the other. But if it had been the other I should have been equally sorry.

I saw with my eyes that very autumn what a fool Jane would have been if she had again backed out. Her mother had of course survived the peril of which I had heard, profiting by it indeed as she had profited by every other; she was sufficiently better again to have come downstairs. It was there that, as usual, I found her, but with a difference of effect produced somehow by the absence of one of the girls. It was as if, for the others, though they had n't gone to Europe, Europe had come to them: Jane's letters had been so frequent and so beyond even what could have been hoped. It was the first time, however, that I perceived on the old woman's part a certain failure of lucidity. Jane's flight was clearly the great fact with her, but she spoke of it as if the fruit had now been plucked and the parenthesis closed. I don't know what sinking sense of still further physical duration I gathered, as a menace, from this first hint of her confusion of mind.

"My daughter has been; my daughter has been —" She kept saying it, but did n't say where; that seemed unnecessary, and she only repeated the words to her visitors with a face that was all puckers and yet now, save in so far as it expressed an ineffaceable complacency, all blankness. I think she rather wanted us to know how little she had stood in the way. It added to something — I scarce knew what — that I found myself desiring to extract privately from Becky. As our visit was to be of the shortest my opportunity — for one of the young ladies always came to the door with us — was at hand. Mrs. Rimmle, as we took leave, again sounded her phrase, but she added this time: "I'm so glad she's going to have always —"

I knew so well what she meant that, as she again dropped, looking at me queerly and becoming momentarily dim, I could help her out. "Going to have what *you* have?"

"Yes, yes — my privilege. Wonderful experience," she mumbled. She bowed to me a little as if I would understand. "She has things to tell."

I turned, slightly at a loss, to Becky. "She has then already arrived?"

Becky was at that moment looking a little strangely at her mother, who answered my question. "She reached New York this morning — she comes on to-day."

"Oh then —!" But I let the matter pass as I met Becky's eye — I saw there was a hitch somewhere. It was not she but Maria who came out with us; on which I cleared up the question of their sister's re-appearance.

"Oh no, not to-night," Maria smiled; "that's only the way mother puts it. We shall see her about the end of November — the Hathaways are so indulgent. They kindly extend their tour."

"For *her* sake? How sweet of them!" my sister-in-law exclaimed.

I can see our friend's plain mild old face take on a deeper mildness, even though a higher colour, in the light of the open door. "Yes, it's for Jane they pro-long it. And do you know what they write?" She gave us time, but it was too great a responsibility to guess. "Why that it has brought her out."

"Oh, I knew it *would*!" my companion sympathetically sighed.

Maria put it more strongly still. "They say we wouldn't know her."

This sounded a little awful, but it was after all what I had expected.

III

My correspondent in Brookbridge came to me that Christmas, with my niece, to spend a week; and the arrangement had of course been prefaced by an exchange of letters, the first of which from my sister-in-law scarce took space for acceptance of my invitation before going on to say: "The Hathaways are back — but without Miss Jane!" She presented in a few words the situation thus created at Brookbridge, but was not yet, I gathered, fully in possession of the other one — the situation created in "Europe" by the presence there of that lady. The two together, however that might be, demanded, I quickly felt, all my attention, and perhaps my impatience to receive my relative was a little sharpened by my desire for the whole story. I had it at last, by the Christmas fire, and I may say without reserve that it gave me all I could have hoped for. I listened eagerly, after which I produced the comment: "Then she simply refused —"

"To budge from Florence? Simply. She had it out there with the poor Hathaways, who felt responsible for her safety, pledged to restore her to her mother's, to her sisters' hands, and showed herself in a light, they mention under their breath, that made their dear old hair stand on end. Do you know what, when they first got back, they said of her — at least it was *his* phrase — to two or three people?"

I thought a moment. "That she had 'tasted blood'?"

My visitor fairly admired me. "How clever of you to guess! It's exactly what he did say. She appeared — she continues to appear, it seems — in a new character."

I wondered a little. "But that's exactly — don't you remember? — what Miss Maria reported to us from them; that we 'would n't know her.'"

My sister-in-law perfectly remembered. "Oh yes — she broke out from the first. But when they left her she was worse."

"Worse?"

"Well, different — different from anything she ever *had* been or — for that matter — had had a chance to be." My reporter hung fire a moment, but presently faced me. "Rather strange and free and obstreperous."

"Obstreperous?" I wondered again.

"Peculiarly so, I inferred, on the question of not coming away. She would n't hear of it and, when they spoke of her mother, said she had given her mother up. She had thought she should like Europe, but did n't know she should like it so much. They had been fools to bring her if they expected to take her away. She was going to see what she could — she had n't yet seen half. The end of it at any rate was that they had to leave her alone."

I seemed to see it all — to see even the scared Hathaways. "So she *is* alone?"

"She told them, poor thing, it appears, and in a tone they'll never forget, that she was in any case quite old enough to be. She cried — she quite went on — over not having come sooner. That's why the only way for her," my companion mused, "*is*, I suppose, to stay. They wanted to put her with some people or other — to find some American family. But she says she's on her own feet."

"And she's still in Florence?"

"No — I believe she was to travel. She's bent on the East."

I burst out laughing. "Magnificent Jane! It's most interesting. Only I feel that I distinctly *should* 'know' her. To my sense, always, I must tell you, she had it in her."

My relative was silent a little. "So it now appears Becky always felt."

"And yet pushed her off? Magnificent Becky!"

My companion met my eyes a moment. "You don't know the queerest part. I mean the way it has *most* brought her out."

I turned it over; I felt I should like to know — to that degree indeed that, oddly enough, I jocosely disguised my eagerness. "You don't mean she has taken to drink?"

My visitor had a dignity — and yet had to have a freedom. "She has taken to flirting."

I expressed disappointment. "Oh she took to *that* long ago. Yes," I declared at my kinswoman's stare, "she positively flirted — with *me!*"

The stare perhaps sharpened. "Then you flirted with *her?*"

"How else could I have been as sure as I wanted to be? But has she means?"

"Means to flirt?" — my friend looked an instant as if she spoke literally. "I don't understand about the means — though of course they have something. But I have my impression," she went on. "I think that Becky —" It seemed almost too grave to say.

But *I* had no doubts. "That Becky's backing her?"

She brought it out. "Financing her."

"Stupendous Becky! So that morally then —"

"Becky's quite in sympathy. But isn't it too odd?" my sister-in-law asked.

"Not in the least. Didn't we know, as regards Jane, that Europe was to bring her out? Well, it has also brought out Rebecca."

"It has indeed!" my companion indulgently sighed. "So what would it do if she were there?"

"I should like immensely to see. And we *shall* see."

"Do you believe then she'll still go?"

"Certainly. She *must.*"

But my friend shook it off. "She won't."

"She shall!" I retorted with a laugh. But the next moment I said: "And what does the old woman say?"

"To Jane's behaviour? Not a word — never speaks of it. She talks now much less than she used — only seems to wait. But it's my belief she thinks."

"And — do you mean — knows?"

"Yes, knows she's abandoned. In her silence there she takes it in."

"It's her way of making Jane pay?" At this,

somehow, I felt more serious. "Oh dear, dear —
she'll disinherit her!"

When in the following June I went on to return
my sister-in-law's visit the first object that met my
eyes in her little white parlour was a figure that, to
my stupefaction, presented itself for the moment as
that of Mrs. Rimmle. I had gone to my room after
arriving and had come down when dressed; the apparition I speak of had arisen in the interval. Its
ambiguous character lasted, however, but a second
or two — I had taken Becky for her mother because I
knew no one but her mother of that extreme age.
Becky's age was quite startling; it had made a great
stride, though, strangely enough, irrecoverably seated
as she now was in it, she had a wizened brightness
that I had scarcely yet seen in her. I remember in-
dulging on this occasion in two silent observations:
one on the article of my not having hitherto been
conscious of her full resemblance to the old lady, and
the other to the effect that, as I had said to my sister-
in-law at Christmas, "Europe," even as reaching her
only through Jane's sensibilities, had really at last
brought her out. She was in fact "out" in a manner
of which this encounter offered to my eyes a unique
example: it was the single hour, often as I had been
at Brookbridge, of my meeting her elsewhere than in
her mother's drawing-room. I surmise that, besides
being adjusted to her more marked time of life, the
garments she wore abroad, and in particular her little
plain bonnet, presented points of resemblance to the
close sable sheath and the quaint old headgear that,
in the white house behind the elms, I had from far

back associated with the eternal image in the stiff chair. Of course I immediately spoke of Jane, showing an interest and asking for news; on which she answered me with a smile, but not at all as I had expected.

"*Those* are not really the things you want to know — where she is, whom she's with, how she manages and where she's going next — oh no!" And the admirable woman gave a laugh that was somehow both light and sad — sad, in particular, with a strange long weariness. "What you do want to know is when she's coming back."

I shook my head very kindly, but out of a wealth of experience that, I flattered myself, was equal to Miss Becky's. "I do know it. Never."

Miss Becky exchanged with me at this a long deep look. "Never."

We had, in silence, a little luminous talk about it, at the end of which she seemed to have told me the most interesting things. "And how's your mother?" I then enquired.

She hesitated, but finally spoke with the same serenity. "My mother's all right. You see she's not alive."

"Oh Becky!" my sister-in-law pleadingly interjected.

But Becky only addressed herself to me. "Come and see if she is. *I* think she is n't — but Maria perhaps is n't so clear. Come at all events and judge and tell me."

It was a new note, and I was a little bewildered. "Ah but I 'm not a doctor!"

"No, thank God — you 're not. That 's why I ask you." And now she said good-bye.

I kept her hand a moment. "*You 're* more alive than ever!"

"I 'm very tired." She took it with the same smile, but for Becky it was much to say.

IV

"Not alive," the next day, was certainly what Mrs. Rimmle looked when, arriving in pursuit of my promise, I found her, with Miss Maria, in her usual place. Though wasted and shrunken she still occupied her high-backed chair with a visible theory of erectness, and her intensely aged face — combined with something dauntless that belonged to her very presence and that was effective even in this extremity — might have been that of some immemorial sovereign, of indistinguishable sex, brought forth to be shown to the people in disproof of the rumour of extinction. Mummified and open-eyed she looked at me, but I had no impression that she made me out. I had come this time without my sister-in-law, who had frankly pleaded to me — which also, for a daughter of Brookbridge, was saying much — that the house had grown too painful. Poor Miss Maria excused Miss Becky on the score of her not being well — and that, it struck me, was saying most of all. The absence of the others gave the occasion a different note; but I talked with Miss Maria for five minutes and recognised that — save for her saying, of her own movement, anything about Jane — she now spoke as if her mother had lost hearing or sense, in fact both, alluding freely and distinctly, though indeed favourably, to her condition. "She has expected your visit and much enjoys it," my entertainer said, while the old woman, soundless and motionless, simply fixed me without expression. Of course there was little to keep me; but I became aware as I rose to go that there was more than I had supposed.

On my approaching her to take leave Mrs. Rimmle gave signs of consciousness. "Have you heard about Jane?"

I hesitated, feeling a responsibility, and appealed for direction to Maria's face. But Maria's face was troubled, was turned altogether to her mother's. "About her life in Europe?" I then rather helplessly asked.

The old lady fronted me on this in a manner that made me feel silly. "Her life?" — and her voice, with this second effort, came out stronger. "Her death, if you please."

"Her death?" I echoed, before I could stop myself, with the accent of deprecation.

Miss Maria uttered a vague sound of pain, and I felt her turn away, but the marvel of her mother's little unquenched spark still held me. "Jane's dead. We've heard," said Mrs. Rimmle. "We've heard from — where is it we've heard from?" She had quite revived — she appealed to her daughter.

The poor old girl, crimson, rallied to her duty. "From Europe."

Mrs. Rimmle made at us both a little grim inclination of the head. "From Europe." I responded, in silence, by a deflexion from every rigour, and, still holding me, she went on: "And now Rebecca's going."

She had gathered by this time such emphasis to

say it that again, before I could help myself, I vibrated in reply. "To Europe — now?" It was as if for an instant she had made me believe it.

She only stared at me, however, from her wizened mask; then her eyes followed my companion. "Has she gone?"

"Not yet, mother." Maria tried to treat it as a joke, but her smile was embarrassed and dim.

"Then where is she?"

"She's lying down."

The old woman kept up her hard queer gaze, but directing it after a minute to me. "She's going."

"Oh some day!" I foolishly laughed; and on this I got to the door, where I separated from my younger hostess, who came no further.

Only, as I held the door open, she said to me under cover of it and very quietly: "It's poor mother's idea."

I saw — it was her idea. Mine was — for some time after this, even after I had returned to New York and to my usual occupations — that I should never again see Becky. I had seen her for the last time, I believed, under my sister-in-law's roof, and in the autumn it was given to me to hear from that fellow admirer that she had succumbed at last to the situation. The day of the call I have just described had been a date in the process of her slow shrinkage — it was literally the first time she had, as they said at Brookbridge, given up. She had been ill for years, but the other state of health in the contemplation of which she had spent so much of her life had left her till too late no margin for heeding it. The power of attention came at last simply in the form of the discovery that it *was* too late; on which, naturally, she had given up more and more. I had heard indeed, for weeks before, by letter, how Brookbridge had watched her do so; in consequence of which the end found me in a manner prepared. Yet in spite of my preparation there remained with me a soreness, and when I was next — it was some six months later — on the scene of her martyrdom I fear I replied with an almost rabid negative to the question put to me in due course by my kinswoman. "Call on them? Never again!"

I went none the less the very next day. Everything was the same in the sunny parlour — everything that most mattered, I mean: the centenarian mummy in the high chair and the tributes, in the little frames on the walls, to the celebrity of its late husband. Only Maria Rimmle was different: if Becky, on my last seeing her, had looked as old as her mother, Maria — save that she moved about — looked older. I remember she moved about, but I scarce remember what she said; and indeed what was there to say? When I risked a question, however, she found a reply.

"But *now* at least —?" I tried to put it to her suggestively.

At first she was vague. "'Now'?"

"Won't Miss Jane come back?"

Oh the headshake she gave me! "Never." It positively pictured to me, for the instant, a well-preserved woman, a rich ripe *seconde jeunesse* by the Arno.

"Then that's only to make more sure of your finally joining her."

Maria Rimmle repeated her headshake. "Never."

We stood so a moment bleakly face to face; I could think of no attenuation that would be particularly happy. But while I tried I heard a hoarse gasp that fortunately relieved me — a signal strange and at first formless from the occupant of the high-backed chair. "Mother wants to speak to you," Maria then said.

So it appeared from the drop of the old woman's jaw, the expression of her mouth opened as if for the emission of sound. It was somehow difficult to me to seem to sympathise without hypocrisy, but, so far as a step nearer could do that, I invited communication. "Have you heard where Becky's gone?" the wonderful witch's white lips then extraordinarily asked.

It drew from Maria, as on my previous visit, an uncontrollable groan, and this in turn made me take time to consider. As I considered, however, I had an inspiration. "To Europe?"

I must have adorned it with a strange grimace, but my inspiration had been right. "To Europe," said Mrs. Rimmle.

MISS GUNTON OF POUGHKEEPSIE

MISS GUNTON OF POUGHKEEPSIE

"It's astonishing what you take for granted!" Lady
Champer had exclaimed to her young friend at an
early stage; and this might have served as a sign
that even then the little plot had begun to thicken.
The reflexion was uttered at the time the outlook of
the charming American girl in whom she found herself so interested was still much in the rough. They
had often met, with pleasure to each, during a winter
spent in Rome; and Lily had come to her in London
toward the end of May with further news of a situation the dawn of which, in March and April, by the
Tiber, the Arno and the Seine, had considerably
engaged her attention. The Prince had followed
Miss Gunton to Florence and then with almost
equal promptitude to Paris, where it was both clear
and comical for Lady Champer that the rigour of
his uncertainty as to parental commands and remit-
tances now detained him. This shrewd woman
promised herself not a little amusement from her
view of the possibilities of the case. Lily was, on the
whole showing, a wonder; therefore the drama would
lose nothing from her character, her temper, her
tone. She was waiting — this was the truth she had
imparted to her clever protectress — to see if her
Roman captive would find himself drawn to London.
Should he really turn up there she would the next
thing start for America, putting him to the test of

that wider range and declining to place her confidence till he should have arrived in New York at her heels. If he remained in Paris or returned to Rome she would stay in London and, as she phrased it, have a good time by herself. Did he expect her to go back to Paris for him? Why not in that case just as well go back to Rome at once? The first thing for her, Lily intimated to her London adviser, was to show what, in her position, *she* expected.

Her position meanwhile was one that Lady Champer, try as she would, had as yet succeeded neither in understanding nor in resigning herself not to understand. It was that of being extraordinarily pretty, amazingly free and perplexingly good, and of presenting these advantages in a positively golden light. How was one to estimate a girl whose nearest approach to a drawback — that is to an encumbrance — appeared to be a grandfather carrying on a business in an American city her ladyship had never otherwise heard of, with whom communication was all by cable and on the subject of "drawing"? Expression was on the old man's part moreover as concise as it was expensive, consisting as it inveterately did of but the single word "Draw." Lily drew, on every occasion in life, and it at least could n't be said of the pair — when the "family idea," as embodied in America, was under criticism — that they were not in touch. Mr. Gunton had further given her Mrs. Brine to come out with her, and, thanks to this provision and the perpetual pecuniary, he plainly figured — to Lily's own mind — as solicitous to the point of anxiety. Mrs. Brine's scheme of relations seemed in truth to be simpler still. There was a transatlantic "Mr. Brine," of whom she often spoke —and never in any other way; but she wrote for newspapers; she prowled in catacombs, visiting more than once even those of Paris; she haunted hotels; she picked up compatriots; she spoke above all a language that often baffled comprehension. She mattered, however, but little; she was mainly so occupied in having what Lily had likewise independently glanced at — a good time by herself. It was difficult enough indeed to Lady Champer to see the wonderful girl reduced to that, yet she was a little person who kept one somehow in presence of the incalculable. Old measures and familiar rules were of no use at all with her — she had so broken the moulds and so mixed the marks. What was confounding was her disparities — the juxtaposition in her of beautiful sun-flushed heights and deep dark holes. She had none of the things that the other things implied. She dangled in the air to a tune that made one dizzy; though one took comfort at the worst in feeling that one was there to catch her if she fell. Falling, at the same time, appeared scarce one of her properties, and it was positive for Lady Champer at moments that if one held out one's arms one might be after all much more likely to be pulled up. That was really a part of the excitement of the acquaintance.

"Well," said this friend and critic on one of the first of the London days, "say he does, on your return to your own country, go after you: what do you read into that occurrence as the course of events?"

"Why if he comes after me I'll have him."

"And do you think it so easy to 'have' him?"

Lily appeared, lovely and candid — and it was an air and a way she often had — to wonder what she thought. "I don't know that I think it any easier than he seems to think it to have *me*. I know moreover that, though he wants awfully to see the country, he would n't just now come to America unless to marry me; and if I take him at all," she pursued, "I want first to be able to show him to the girls."

"Why 'first'?" Lady Champer asked. "Would n't it do as well last?"

"Oh I should want them to see me in Rome too," said Lily. "But, dear me, I'm afraid I want a good many things! What I most want of course is that he should show me unmistakeably what *he* wants. Unless he wants me more than anything else in the world I don't want him. Besides, I hope he does n't think I'm going to be married anywhere but in my own place."

"I see," said Lady Champer. "It's for your wedding you want the girls. And it's for the girls you want the Prince."

"Well, we're all bound by that promise. And of course *you'll* come!"

"Ah my dear child —!" Lady Champer gasped.

"You can come with the old Princess. You'll be just the right company for her."

The elder friend considered afresh, with depth, the younger's beauty and serenity. "You *are*, love, beyond everything!"

The beauty and serenity took on for a moment a graver cast. "Why do you so often say that to me?"

"Because you so often make it the only thing to say. But you'll some day find out why," Lady Champer added with an intention of encouragement.

Lily Gunton, however, was a young person to whom encouragement looked queer; she had grown up without need of it, and it seemed indeed scarce required in her situation. "Do you mean you believe his mother won't come?"

"Over mountains and seas to see you married? — and to be seen also of the girls? If she does *I* will. But we had perhaps better," Lady Champer wound up, "not count our chickens before they're hatched." To which, with one of the easy returns of gaiety that were irresistible in her, Lily made answer that neither of the ladies in question struck her quite as a chicken.

The Prince at all events presented himself in London with a promptitude that contributed to make the warning gratuitous. Nothing could have exceeded, by this time, Lady Champer's appreciation of her young friend, whose merits "town" at the beginning of June threw into renewed relief; but she had the imagination of greatness and, though she believed she tactfully kept it to herself, she thought what the young man had thus done a great deal for a Roman prince to do. Take him as he was, with the circumstances — and they were certainly peculiar, and he was charming — it was a far cry for him from Piazza Colonna to Clarges Street. If Lady Champer had the imagination of greatness, which the Prince in all sorts of ways gratified, Miss Gunton of Poughkeepsie — it was vain to pretend the contrary — was not great in any particular save one. She was great when she "drew." It was true that at the beginning of June she did draw with unprecedented energy and in a manner that, though Mrs. Brine's remarkable nerve apparently could stand it, fairly made a poor baronet's widow, little as it was her business, hold her breath. It was none of her business at all, yet she talked of it even with the Prince himself — to whom it was indeed a favourite subject and whose greatness, oddly enough, never appeared to shrink in the effect it produced on him. The line they took together was that of wondering if the scale of Lily's drafts made really most for the presumption that the capital at her disposal was rapidly dwindling, or for that of its being practically infinite. "Many a fellow," the young man smiled, "would marry her to pull her up." He was in any case of the opinion that it was an occasion for deciding — one way or the other — quickly. Well, he did decide — so quickly that within the week Lily communicated to her friend that he had offered her his hand, his heart, his fortune and all his titles, grandeurs and appurtenances. She had given him his answer, and he was in bliss; though nothing as yet was settled but that.

Tall fair active educated amiable simple, carrying so naturally his great name and pronouncing so kindly Lily's small one, the happy youth, if he was one of the most ancient of princes, was one of the most modern of Romans. This second character it was his special aim and pride to cultivate. He would have been pained at feeling himself an hour behind his age; and he had a way — both touching and amusing to some observers — of constantly comparing his watch with the dial of the day's news. It was in fact easy to see that in deciding to ally himself with a young alien of vague origin, whose striking beauty was re-enforced only by her presumptive money, he had even put forward a little the fine hands of his timepiece. No one else, however — not even Lady Champer, and least of all Lily herself — had quite taken the measure, in this connexion, of his merit. The quick decision he had spoken of was really a flying leap. He desired incontestably to rescue Miss Gunton's remainder; but to rescue it he had to take it for granted, and taking it for granted was nothing less than — at whatever angle considered — a risk. He never, naturally, used the word to her, but he distinctly faced a peril. The sense of what he had staked on a vague return gave him, at the height of the London season, bad nights, or rather bad mornings — for he danced with his intended, as a usual thing, conspicuously, till dawn — besides obliging him to take, in the form of long explanatory argumentative and persuasive letters to his mother and sisters, his uncles, aunts, cousins and preferred confidants, large measures of justification at home. The family sense was strong in his huge old house, just as the family array was numerous; he was dutifully conscious of the trust reposed in him and moved from morning till night, he perfectly knew, as the observed of a phalanx of observers; whereby he the more admired himself for his passion, precipitation and courage. He had only a probability to go upon, but he was — and by the romantic tradition of his race — so in love that he should surely not be taken in.

His private agitation of course deepened when, to do honour to her engagement and as if she would have been ashamed to do less, Lily "drew" again most gloriously; but he managed to smile beautifully on her asking him if he did n't want her to be splendid, and at his worst hours he went no further than to wish he might be married on the morrow. Unless it were the next day, or at most the next month, it really at moments seemed best it should never be at all. On the most favourable view — with the solidity of the residuum fully assumed — there were still minor questions and dangers. A vast America, arching over his nuptials, bristling with expectant bridesmaids and underlaying their feet with expensive flowers, stared him in the face and prompted him to the reflexion that if she dipped so deep into the mere remote overflow her dive into the fount itself would verily be a header. If she drew at such a rate in London how would n't she draw at Poughkeepsie? he asked himself, and practically asked Lady Champer; yet bore the strain of the question — all without an answer — so nobly that when, with small delay, Poughkeepsie seemed simply to heave with reassurances, he regarded the ground as firm and his tact as rewarded. "And now at last, dearest," he said, "since everything's so satisfactory, you *will* write?" He put it appealingly, endearingly, yet as if he could scarce doubt.

"Write, love? Why," she replied, "I've done nothing *but* write! I've written ninety letters."

"But not to mamma," he smiled.

"Mamma?" — she stared. "My dear boy, I've not at this time of day to remind you that I've the misfortune to have no mother. I lost mamma, you know, as you lost your father, in childhood. You may be sure," said Lily Gunton, "that I would n't otherwise have waited for you to prompt me."

There came into his face a kind of amiable convulsion. "Of course, darling, I remember — your beautiful mother (she *must* have been beautiful!) whom I should have been so glad to know. I was thinking of *my* mamma — who'll be so delighted to hear from you." The Prince spoke English in perfection — had lived in it from the cradle and appeared, particularly when alluding to his home and family, to matters familiar and of fact, or to those of dress and sport, of general recreation, to draw such a comfort from it as made the girl think of him as scarce more a foreigner than a pleasant auburn slightly awkward slightly slangy and extremely well-tailored young Briton would have been. He sounded "mamma" like a rosy English school-boy; yet just then, for the first time, the things with which he was connected struck her as in a manner strange and far-off. Everything in him, none the less — face and voice and tact, above all his deep desire — laboured to bring them near and make them natural. This was intensely the case as he went on: "Such a little letter as you *might* send would really be awfully jolly."

"My dear child," Lily replied on quick reflexion, "I'll write to her with joy the minute I hear from her. Won't she write to *me?*"

381

The Prince just visibly flushed. "In a moment if you'll only —"

"Write to her first?"

"Just pay her a little — no matter how little — your respects."

His attenuation of the degree expressed perhaps a weakness of position; yet it was no perception of this that made the girl immediately say: "Oh, *caro*, I don't think I can begin. If you feel that *she* won't — as you evidently do — is it because you've asked her and she has refused?" The next moment, "I see you *have!*" she exclaimed. His rejoinder to this was to catch her in his arms, to press his cheek to hers, to murmur a flood of tender words in which contradiction, confession, supplication and remonstrance were oddly confounded; but after he had sufficiently disengaged her to allow her to speak again his effusion was checked by what came. "Do you really mean you can't induce her?" It renewed itself on the first return of ease; or it, more correctly perhaps, in order to renew itself, took this return — a trifle too soon — for granted. Singular, for the hour, was the quickness with which ease could leave them — so blissfully at one as they were; and, to be brief, it had not come back even when Lily spoke of the matter to Lady Champer. It's true she waited but little to do so. She went straight to the point. "What would you do if his mother does n't write?"

"The old Princess — to *you?*" Her ladyship had not had time to mount guard in advance over the tone of this, which was doubtless (as she instantly, for that matter, herself became aware) a little too

much that of "Have you really expected she would?"
What Lily had expected found itself therefore not
unassisted to come out — and came out indeed to
such a tune that with all kindness, but with a melancholy deeper than any she had ever yet in the general
connexion used, Lady Champer was moved to remark
that the situation might have been found more possible had a little more historic sense been brought to it.
"You're the dearest thing in the world, and I can't
imagine a girl's carrying herself in any way, in a difficult position, better than you do; only I'm bound to
say I think you ought to remember that you're entering a very great house, of tremendous antiquity,
fairly groaning under the weight of ancient honours,
the heads of which — through the tradition of the
great part they've played in the world — are accus-
tomed to a great deal of deference. The old Princess,
my dear, you see" — her ladyship gathered confidence a little as she went — "is a most prodigious
personage."

"Why, Lady Champer, of course she is, and that's
just what I liked her for!" said Lily Gunton.

"She has never in her whole life made an advance,
any more than any one has ever dreamed of expect-
ing it of her. It's a pity that while you were there
you didn't see her, for I think it would have helped
you to understand. However, as you did see his
sisters, the two Duchesses and dear little Donna
Claudia, you know how charming they all *can* be.
They only want to be nice, I know, and I dare say
that on the smallest opportunity you'll hear from
the Duchesses."

The plural had a sound of splendour, but Lily quite kept her head. "What do you call an opportunity? Am I not giving them, by accepting their son and brother, the best—and in fact the only—opportunity they could desire?"

"I like the way, darling," Lady Champer smiled, "you talk about 'accepting'!"

Lily thought of this — she thought of everything. "Well, say it would have been a better one still for them if I had refused him."

Her friend caught her up. "But you have n't."

"Then they must make the most of the occasion as it is." Lily was very sweet, but very lucid. "The Duchesses may write or not, as they like; but I 'm afraid the Princess simply *must*." She hesitated, but after a moment went on: "He ought n't to be willing moreover that I should n't expect to be welcomed."

"He is n't!" Lady Champer blurted out.

Lily jumped at it. "Then he has told you? It 's her attitude?"

She had spoken without passion, but her friend was scarce the less frightened. "My poor child, what can he do?"

Lily saw perfectly. "He can make her."

Lady Champer turned it over, but her fears were what was clearest. "And if he does n't?"

"If he 'does n't'?" The girl ambiguously echoed it. "I mean if he can't."

Well, Lily more cheerfully declined for the hour to consider this. He would certainly do for her what was right; so that after all, though she had herself put the question, she disclaimed the idea that an

answer was urgent. There was time, she conveyed
— which Lady Champer only desired to believe; a
faith moreover somewhat shaken in the latter when
the Prince entered her room the next day with the
information that there was none — none at least to
leave everything in the air. Lady Champer had n't
yet made up her mind which of these young persons
she liked most to draw into confidence, nor whether
she most inclined to take the Roman side with the
American or the American side with the Roman. But
now in truth she was settled; she gave proof of it in
the increased lucidity with which she spoke for Lily.
"Would n't the Princess depart — a — from her
usual attitude for such a great occasion?"

The difficulty was a little that the young man so
well understood his mother. "The devil of it is, you
see, that it's for Lily herself, so much more, she
thinks the occasion great."

Lady Champer mused. "If you had n't her consent I could understand it. But from the moment
she thinks the girl good enough for you to marry —"

"Ah she does n't!" the Prince gloomily interposed.
"However," he explained, "she accepts her because
there are reasons — my own feeling, now so my very
life, don't you see? But it is n't quite open arms. All
the same, as I tell Lily, the arms *would* open."

"If she'd make the first step? Hum!" said Lady
Champer, not without the note of grimness. "She'll
be obstinate."

The young man, with a melancholy eye, quite
coincided. "She'll be obstinate."

"So that I strongly recommend you to manage it,"

his friend went on after a pause. "It strikes me that
if the Princess can't do it for Lily she might at least
do it for you. Any girl you marry becomes by that
fact somebody."

"Of course — does n't she? She certainly ought to
do it for *me*. I'm after all the head of the house."

"Well then make her!" said Lady Champer a little
impatiently.

"I will. Mamma adores me, and I adore *her*."

"And you adore Lily, and Lily adores you — therefore everybody adores everybody, especially as I adore
you both. Therefore with so much adoration all
round things ought to march."

"They shall!" the young man declared with spirit.
"I adore you too — you don't mention that; for you
help me immensely. But what do you suppose she'll
do if she does n't?"

The agitation already visible in him ministered a
little to vagueness, but his friend after an instant
disembroiled it. "What do I suppose Lily will do if
your mother remains stiff?" Lady Champer faltered,
but she let him have it. "She'll break."

His wondering eyes became strange. "Just for
that?"

"You may certainly say it is n't much — when
people love as you do."

"Ah I'm afraid then Lily does n't!" — and he
turned away in his trouble.

She watched him while he moved, not speaking
for a minute. "My dear young man, are you afraid
of your mamma?"

He faced short about again. "I'm afraid of this

— that if she does do it she won't forgive her. She *will* do it — yes. But Lily will be for her in consequence, ever after, the person who has made her submit herself. She'll hate her for that — and then she'll hate me for being concerned in it." The Prince presented it all with clearness — almost with charm. "What do you say to that?"

His friend had to think. "Well, only, I fear, that we belong, Lily and I, to a race unaccustomed to counting with such passions. I think they affect us as having a taste of the wicked *cinque-cento*, of Borgia poison. Let her hate!" she, however, a trifle inconsistently wound up.

"But I love her so!"

"Which?" Lady Champer asked it almost ungraciously; in such a tone at any rate that, seated on the sofa with his elbows at his knees, his much-ringed hands nervously locked together and his eyes of distress wide open, he met her with visible surprise. What she met *him* with is perhaps best noted by the fact that after a minute of it his hands covered his bent face and she became aware she had drawn tears. This produced such regret in her that before they parted she did what she could to attenuate and explain — making a great point at all events of her rule, with Lily, of putting only his own side of the case. "I insist awfully, you know, on your greatness!"

He jumped up, wincing. "Oh that's horrid."

"I don't know. Whose fault is it then, at any rate, if trying to help you may have that side?" This was a question that, with the tangle he had already to unwind, only added a twist; yet she went on as if positively to add another. "Why on earth don't you, all of you, leave them alone?"

"Leave them — ?"

"All your Americans."

"Don't you like them then — the women?"

She debated. "No. Yes. They're an interest. But they're a nuisance. It's a question, very certainly, if they're worth the trouble they give."

This at least it seemed he could take in. "You mean one should be quite sure first what they *are* worth?"

He made her laugh now. "It would appear you never *can* be. But also really that you can't keep your hands off."

He fixed the social scene an instant with his heavy eye. "Yes. Does n't it?"

"However," she pursued as if he again a little irritated her, "Lily's position is quite simple."

"Quite. She just loves me."

"I mean simple for herself. She really makes no differences. It's only we — you and I — who make them all."

The Prince wondered. "But she tells me she delights in us; has, that is, such a sense of what we are supposed to 'represent.'"

"Oh she *thinks* she has. Americans think they have all sorts of things; but they have n't. That's just *it*" — Lady Champer was philosophic. "Nothing but their Americanism. If you marry anything you marry that; and if your mother accepts anything that's what she accepts." Then, though the young man followed the demonstration with an apprehen-

sion almost pathetic, she gave him without mercy
the whole of it. "Lily's rigidly logical. A girl — as
she knows girls — is 'welcomed,' on her engagement,
before anything else can happen, by the family of her
young man; and the motherless girl alone in the world
more punctually than any other. His mother —
if she's a 'lady' — takes it upon herself. Then the
girl goes and stays with them. But she does nothing
before. Tirez-vous de là."

The young man sought on the spot to obey this
last injunction, and his effort presently produced a
flash. "Oh if she'll come and *stay* with us" — all
would easily be well! The flash went out, however,
when Lady Champer returned: "Then let the
Princess invite her."

Lily a fortnight later simply said to her from one
hour to the other "I'm going home," and took her
breath away by sailing on the morrow with the
Bransbys. The tense cord had somehow snapped;
the proof was in the fact that the Prince, dashing
off to his good friend at this crisis an obscure, an
ambiguous note, started the same night for Rome.
Lady Champer, for the time, sat in darkness, but
during the summer many things occurred; and one
day in the autumn, quite unheralded and with the
signs of some of them in his face, the Prince appeared
again before her. He was n't long in telling her his
story, which was simply that he had come to her, all
the way from Rome, for news of Lily and to talk of
Lily. She was prepared, as it happened, to meet his
impatience; yet her preparation was but little older
than his arrival and was deficient moreover in an

important particular. She was n't prepared to knock him down, and she made him talk to gain time. She had however, to understand, put a primary question: "She never wrote then?"

"Mamma? Oh yes—when she at last got frightened at Miss Gunton's having become so silent. She wrote in August; but Lily's own decisive letter — letter to me, I mean — crossed with it. It was too late — that put an end."

"A *real* end?"

Everything in the young man showed how real. "On the ground of her being willing no longer to keep up, by the stand she had taken, such a relation between mamma and *me*. But her rupture," he wailed, "keeps it up more than anything else."

"And is it very bad?"

"Awful, I assure you. I've become for my mother a person who has made her make, all for nothing, an unprecedented advance, a humble submission; and she's so disgusted, all round, that it's no longer the same old charming thing for us to be together. It makes it worse for her that I'm still madly in love."

"Well," said Lady Champer after a moment, "if you're still madly in love I can only be sorry for you."

"You can *do* nothing for me? — don't advise me to go over?"

She had to take a longer pause. "You don't at all know then what has happened? — that old Mr. Gunton has died and left her everything?"

All his vacancy and curiosity came out in a wild echo. "'Everything'?"

"She writes me that it's a great deal of money."

"You've just heard from her then?"

"This morning. I seem to make out," said Lady Champer, "an extraordinary number of dollars."

"Oh I was sure it was!" the young man moaned.

"And she's engaged," his friend went on, "to Mr. Bransby."

He bounded, rising before her. "Mr. Bransby?"

"'Adam P.'—the gentleman with whose mother and sisters she went home. *They*, she writes, have beautifully welcomed her."

"*Dio mio!*" The Prince stared; he had flushed with the blow and the tears had come into his eyes. "And I believed she loved me!"

"*I* did n't!" said Lady Champer with some curtness.

He gazed about; he almost rocked; and, unconscious of her words, he appealed, inarticulate and stricken. At last however he found his voice. "What on earth then shall I do? I can less than ever go back to mamma!"

She got up for him, she thought for him, pushing a better chair into her circle. "Stay here with me and I'll ring for tea. Sit there nearer the fire — you're cold."

"Awfully!" he confessed as he sank. "And I believed she loved me!" he repeated as he stared at the fire.

"*I* did n't!" Lady Champer once more declared. This time, visibly, he heard her, and she immediately met his wonder. "No — it was all the rest; your great historic position, the glamour of your name and your past. Otherwise what she stood out for would n't be excusable. But she has the sense of such things, and *they* were what she loved." So, by the fire, his hostess explained it while he wondered the more.

"I thought that last summer you told me just the contrary."

It seemed, to do her justice, to strike her. "Did I? Oh well, how does one know? With Americans one's lost!"

FORDHAM CASTLE

FORDHAM CASTLE

SHARP little Madame Massin, who carried on the pleasant pension and who had her small hard eyes everywhere at once, came out to him on the terrace and held up a letter addressed in a manner that he recognised even from afar, held it up with a question in her smile, or a smile, rather a pointed one, in her question — he could scarce have said which. She was looking, while so occupied, at the German group engaged in the garden, near by, with aperitive beer and disputation — the noonday luncheon being now imminent; and the way in which she could show prompt lips while her observation searchingly ranged might have reminded him of the object placed by a spectator at the theatre in the seat he desires to keep during the entr'acte. Conscious of the cross-currents of international passion, she tried, so far as possible, not to mix her sheep and her goats. The view of the bluest end of the Lake of Geneva — she insisted in persuasive circulars that it *was* the bluest — had never, on her high-perched terrace, wanted for admirers, though thus early in the season, during the first days of May, they were not so numerous as she was apt to see them at midsummer. This precisely, Abel Taker could infer, was the reason of a remark she had made him before the claims of the letter had been settled. "I shall put you next the American lady — the one who arrived yesterday. I know you'll be kind to her; she had to go to bed, as soon as she got here, with a sick-headache brought on by her journey. But she's better. Who is n't better as soon as they get here? She's coming down, and I'm sure she'd like to know you."

Taker had now the letter in his hand — the letter intended for "Mr. C. P. Addard"; which was not the name inscribed in the two or three books he had left out in his room, any more than it matched the initials, "A. F. T." attached to the few pieces of his modest total of luggage. Moreover, since Madame Massin's establishment counted, to his still somewhat bewildered mind, so little for an hotel, as hotels were mainly known to him, he had avoided the act of "registering," and the missive with which his hostess was practically testing him represented the very first piece of postal matter taken in since his arrival that had n't been destined to some one else. He had privately blushed for the meagreness of his mail, which made him look unimportant. That however was a detail, an appearance he was used to; indeed the reasons making for such an appearance might never have been so pleasant to him as on this vision of his identity formally and legibly denied. It was denied there in his wife's large straight hand; his eyes, attached to the envelope, took in the failure of any symptom of weakness in her stroke; she at least had the courage of his passing for somebody he was n't, of his passing rather for nobody at all, and he felt the force of her character more irresistibly than ever as he thus submitted to what she was doing with him. He was n't used to lying; whatever his faults — and he was used, perfectly, to the idea of

his faults — he had n't made them worse by any perverse theory, any tortuous plea, of innocence; so that
probably, with every inch of him giving him away,
Madame Massin did n't believe him a bit when he
appropriated the letter. He was quite aware he could
have made no fight if she had challenged his right to
it. That would have come of his making no fight,
nowadays, on any ground, with any woman; he had
so lost the proper spirit, the necessary confidence. It
was true that he had had to do for a long time with
no woman in the world but Sue, and of the practice
of opposition so far as Sue was concerned the end
had been determined early in his career. His hostess
fortunately accepted his word, but the way in which
her momentary attention bored into his secret like
the turn of a gimlet gave him a sense of the quantity
of life that passed before her as a dealer with all
comers — gave him almost an awe of her power of not
wincing. She knew he was n't, he could n't be, C. P.
Addard, even though she might n't know, or still less
care, who he was; and there was therefore something
queer about him if he pretended to be. That was
what he did n't mind, there being something queer
about him; and what was further present to him was
that she would have known when to mind, when
really to be on her guard. She attached no importance to his trick; she had doubtless somewhere at
the rear, amid the responsive underlings with whom
she was sometimes heard volubly, yet so obscurely,
to chatter, her clever French amusement about it.
He could n't at all events have said if the whole passage with her most brought home to him the falsity

of his position or most glossed it over. On the whole perhaps it rather helped him, since from this moment his masquerade had actively begun.

Taking his place for luncheon, in any case, he found himself next the American lady, as he conceived, spoken of by Madame Massin — in whose appearance he was at first as disappointed as if, a little, though all unconsciously, he had been building on it. Had she loomed into view, on their hostess's hint, as one of the vague alternatives, the possible beguilements, of his leisure — presenting herself solidly where so much else had refused to crystallise? It was certain at least that she presented herself solidly, being a large mild smooth person with a distinct double chin, with grey hair arranged in small flat regular circles, figures of a geometrical perfection; with diamond earrings, with a long-handled eye-glass, with an accumulation of years and of weight and presence, in fine, beyond what his own rather melancholy consciousness acknowledged. He was forty-five, and it took every year of his life, took all he had n't done with them, to account for his present situation — since you could n't be, conclusively, of so little use, of so scant an application, to any mortal career, above all to your own, unless you had been given up and cast aside after a long succession of experiments tried with you. But the American lady with the mathematical hair which reminded him in a manner of the old-fashioned "work," the weeping willows and mortuary urns represented by the little glazed-over flaxen or auburn or sable or silvered convolutions and tendrils, the capillary flowers, that he

had admired in the days of his innocence — the
American lady had probably seen her half-century; all
the more that before luncheon was done she had
begun to strike him as having, like himself, slipped
slowly down over its stretched and shiny surface, an
expanse as insecure to fumbling feet as a great cold
curved ice-field, into the comparatively warm hollow
of resignation and obscurity. She gave him from the
first — and he was afterwards to see why — an attaching impression of being, like himself, in exile,
and of having like himself learned to butter her
bread with a certain acceptance of fate. The only
thing that puzzled him on this head was that to
parallel his own case she would have had openly to
consent to be shelved; which made the difficulty,
here, that that was exactly what, as between wife
and husband, remained unthinkable on the part of
the wife. The necessity for the shelving of one or
the other was a case that appeared often to arise,
but this was n't the way he had in general seen it
settled. She made him in short, through some influence he could n't immediately reduce to its elements,
vaguely think of her as sacrificed — without blood,
as it were; as obligingly and persuadedly passive.
Yet this effect, a reflexion of his own state, would
doubtless have been better produced for him by a
mere melancholy man. She testified unmistakeably
to the greater energy of women; for he could think
of no manifestation of spirit on his own part that
might pass for an equivalent, in the way of resistance,
of protest, to the rhythmic though rather wiggy
water-waves that broke upon her bald-looking brow

as upon a beach bared by a low tide. He had cocked
up often enough — and as with the intention of doing
it still more under Sue's nose than under his own —
the two ends of his half-"sandy" half-grizzled moustache, and he had in fact given these ornaments an
extra twist just before coming in to luncheon. That
however was but a momentary flourish; the most
marked ferocity of which had n't availed not to land
him — well, where he was landed now.

His new friend mentioned that she had come up
from Rome and that Madame Massin's establishment had been highly spoken of to her there, and this,
slight as it was, straightway contributed in its degree
for Abel Taker to the idea that they had something
in common. He was in a condition in which he could
feel the drift of vague currents, and he knew how
highly the place had been spoken of to *him*. There
was but a shade of difference in his having had his
lesson in Florence. He let his companion know,
without reserve, that he too had come up from Italy,
after spending three or four months there: though he
remembered in time that, being now C. P. Addard,
it was only as C. P. Addard he could speak. He tried
to think, in order to give himself something to say,
what C. P. Addard would have done; but he was
doomed to feel always, in the whole connexion, his
lack of imagination. He had had many days to come
to it and nothing else to do; but he had n't even yet
made up his mind who C. P. Addard was or invested
him with any distinguishing marks. He felt like a man
who, moving in this, that or the other direction, saw
each successively lead him to some danger; so that he

began to ask himself why he should n't just lie out-
right, boldly and inventively, and see what that could
do for him. There was an excitement, the excitement
of personal risk, about it — much the same as would
belong for an ordinary man to the first trial of a flying-machine; yet it was exactly such a course as Sue
had prescribed on his asking her what he should do.
"Anything in the world you like but talk about *me*:
think of some other woman, as bad and bold as you
please, and say you 're married to *her*." Those had
been literally her words, together with others, again
and again repeated, on the subject of his being free
to "kill and bury" her as often as he chose. This
was the way she had met his objection to his own
death and interment; she had asked him, in her
bright hard triumphant way, why he could n't defend
himself by shooting back. The real reason was of
course that he was nothing without her, whereas she
was everything, could be anything in the wide world
she liked, without him. That question precisely
had been a part of what was before him while he
strolled in the projected green gloom of Madame
Massin's plane-trees; he wondered what she *was*
choosing to be and how good a time it was helping
her to have. He could be sure she was rising to it,
on some line or other, and that was what secretly
made him say: "Why should n't I get something out
of it too, just for the harmless fun — ?"

It kept coming back to him, naturally, that he
had n't the breadth of fancy, that he knew himself
as he knew the taste of ill-made coffee, that he was
the same old Abel Taker he had ever been, in whose

aggregation of items it was as vain to feel about for latent heroisms as it was useless to rummage one's trunk for presentable clothes that one did n't possess. But did that absolve him (having so definitely Sue's permission) from seeing to what extent he might temporarily make believe? If he were to flap his wings very hard and crow very loud and take as long a jump as possible at the same time — if he were to do all that perhaps he should achieve for half a minute the sensation of soaring. He knew only one thing Sue could n't do, from the moment she did n't divorce him: she could n't get rid of his name, unaccountably, after all, as she hated it; she could n't get rid of it because she would have always sooner or later to come back to it. She might consider that her being a thing so dreadful as Mrs. Abel Taker was a stumbling-block in her social path that nothing but his real, his official, his advertised circulated demise (with "American papers please copy") would avail to dislodge: she would have none the less to reckon with his continued existence as the drop of bitterness in her cup that seasoned undisguiseably each draught. He might make use of his present opportunity to row out into the lake with his pockets full of stones and there quietly slip overboard; but he could think of no shorter cut for her ceasing to be what her marriage and the law of the land had made her. She was not an inch less Mrs. Abel Taker for these days of his sequestration, and the only thing she indeed claimed was that the concealment of the source of her shame, the suppression of the person who had divided with her his inherited absurdity,

made the difference of a shade or two for getting honourably, as she called it, "about." How she had originally come to incur this awful inconvenience —
that part of the matter, left to herself, she would
undertake to keep vague; and she wasn't really left to
herself so long as he too flaunted the dreadful flag.

This was why she had provided him with another
and placed him out at board, to constitute, as it were,
a permanent *alibi;* telling him she should quarrel
with no colours under which he might elect to sail, and
promising to take him back when she had got where
she wanted. She would n't mind so much then —
she only wanted a fair start. It was n't a fair start
— *was* it? she asked him frankly — so long as he was
always there, so terribly cruelly there, to speak of
what she *had* been. She had been nothing worse,
to his sense, than a very pretty girl of eighteen out
in Peoria, who had seen at that time no one else she
wanted more to marry, nor even any one who had
been so supremely struck by her. That, absolutely,
was the worst that could be said of her. It was so
bad at any rate in her own view — it had grown so
bad in the widening light of life — that it had fairly
become more than she could bear and that something,
as she said, had to be done about it. She had n't
known herself originally any more than she had
known him — had n't foreseen how much better she
was going to come out, nor how, for her individually,
as distinguished from him, there might be the possibility of a big future. He could n't be explained
away — he cried out with all his dreadful presence
that she *had* been pleased to marry him; and what

they therefore had to do must transcend explaining. It was perhaps now helping her, off there in London, and especially at Fordham Castle — she was staying last at Fordham Castle, Wilts — it was perhaps inspiring her even more than she had expected, that they were able to try together this particular substitute: news of her progress in fact — her progress on from Fordham Castle, if anything could be higher — would not improbably be contained in the unopened letter he had lately pocketed.

There was a given moment at luncheon meanwhile, in his talk with his countrywoman, when he did try that flap of the wing—did throw off, for a flight into the blue, the first falsehood he could think of. "I stopped in Italy, you see, on my way back from the East, where I had gone — to Constantinople" — he rose actually to Constantinople — "to visit Mrs. Addard's grave." And after they had all come out to coffee in the rustling shade, with the vociferous German tribe at one end of the terrace, the English family keeping silence with an English accent, as it struck him, in the middle, and his direction taken, by his new friend's side, to the other unoccupied corner, he found himself oppressed with what he had on his hands, the burden of keeping up this expensive fiction. He had never been to Constantinople — it could easily be proved against him; he ought to have thought of something better, have got his effect on easier terms. Yet a funnier thing still than this quick repentance was the quite equally fictive ground on which his companion had affected him — when he came to think of it — as meeting him.

"Why you know that's very much the same errand that took me to Rome. I visited the grave of my daughter — whom I lost there some time ago."

She had turned her face to him after making this statement, looked at him with an odd blink of her round kind plain eyes, as if to see how he took it. He had taken it on the spot, for this was the only thing to do; but he had felt how much deeper down he was himself sinking as he replied: "Ah it's a sad pleasure, is n't it? But those are places one does n't want to neglect."

"Yes — that's what I feel. I go," his neighbour had solemnly pursued, "about every two years."

With which she had looked away again, leaving him really not able to emulate her. "Well, I had n't been before. You see it's a long way."

"Yes — that's the trying part. It makes you feel you'd have done better —"

"To bring them right home and have it done over there?" he had asked as she let the sad subject go a little. He quite agreed. "Yes — that's what many do."

"But it gives of course a peculiar interest." So they had kept it up. "I mean in places that might n't have so *very* much."

"Places like Rome and Constantinople?" he had rejoined while he noticed the cautious anxious sound of her "very." The tone was to come back to him, and it had already made him feel sorry for her, with its suggestion of her being at sea like himself. Unmistakeably, poor lady, she too was trying to float — was striking out in timid convulsive movements.

Well, he would n't make it difficult for her, and immediately, so as not to appear to cast any ridicule, he observed that, wherever great bereavements might have occurred, there was no place so remarkable as not to gain an association. Such memories made at the least another object for coming. It was after this recognition, on either side, that they adjourned to the garden — Taker having in his ears again the good lady's rather troubled or muddled echo: "Oh yes, when you come to all the *objects* —!" The grave of one's wife or one's daughter was an object quite as much as all those that one looked up in Baedeker — those of the family of the Castle of Chillon and the Dent du Midi, features of the view to be enjoyed from different parts of Madame Massin's premises. It was very soon, none the less, rather as if these latter presences, diffusing their reality and majesty, had taken the colour out of all other evoked romance; and to that degree that when Abel's fellow guest happened to lay down on the parapet of the terrace three or four articles she had brought out with her, her fan, a couple of American newspapers and a letter that had obviously come to her by the same post as his own, he availed himself of the accident to jump at a further conclusion. Their coffee, which was "extra," as he knew and as, in the way of benevolence, he boldly warned her, was brought forth to them, and while she was giving her attention to her demi-tasse he let his eyes rest for three seconds on the superscription of her letter. His mind was by this time made up, and the beauty of it was that he could n't have said why: the letter was from her daughter, whom she had been burying for him in Rome, and it would be addressed in a name that was really no more hers than the name his wife had thrust upon him was his. Her daughter had put *her* out at cheap board, pending higher issues, just as Sue had put him — so that there was a logic not other than fine in his notifying her of what coffee every day might let her in for. She was addressed on her envelope as "Mrs. Vanderplank," but he had privately arrived, before she so much as put down her cup, at the conviction that this was a borrowed and lawless title, for all the world as if, poor dear innocent woman, she were a bold bad adventuress. He had acquired furthermore the moral certitude that he was on the track, as he would have said, of her true identity, such as it might be. He could n't think of it as in itself either very mysterious or very impressive; but, whatever it was, her duplicity had as yet mastered no finer art than his own, inasmuch as she had positively not escaped, at table, inadvertently dropping a name which, while it lingered on Abel's ear, gave her quite away. She had spoken, in her solemn sociability and as by the force of old habit, of "Mr. Magaw," and nothing was more to be presumed than that this gentleman was her defunct husband, not so very long defunct, who had permitted her while in life the privilege of association with him, but whose extinction had left her to be worked upon by different ideas.

These ideas would have germed, infallibly, in the brain of the young woman, her only child, under whose rigid rule she now — it was to be detected —

drew her breath in pain. Madame Massin would abysmally know, Abel reflected, for he was at the end of a few minutes more intimately satisfied that Mrs. Magaw's American newspapers, coming to her straight from the other side and not yet detached from their wrappers, would not be directed to Mrs. Vanderplank, and that, this being the case, the poor lady would have had to invent some pretext for a claim to goods likely still perhaps to be lawfully called for. And she wasn't formed for duplicity, the large simple scared foolish fond woman, the vague anxiety in whose otherwise so uninhabited and unreclaimed countenance, as void of all history as an expanse of Western prairie seen from a car-window, testified to her scant aptitude for her part. He was far from the desire to question their hostess, however — for the study of his companion's face on its mere inferred merits had begun to dawn upon him as the possible resource of his ridiculous leisure. He might verily have some fun with her — or he would so have conceived it had he not become aware before they separated, half an hour later, of a kind of fellow-feeling for her that seemed to plead for her being spared. She *wasn't* being, in some quarter still indistinct to him — and so no more was he, and these things were precisely a reason. Her sacrifice, he divined, was an act of devotion, a state not yet disciplined to the state of confidence. She had presently, as from a return of vigilance, gathered in her postal property, shuffling it together at her further side and covering it with her pocket-handkerchief — though this very betrayal indeed but quickened his temporary impulse to break out to her, sympathetically, with a "Had you the misfortune to *lose* Magaw?" or with the effective production of his own card and a smiling, an inviting, a consoling "That's who *I* am if you want to know!" He really made out, with the idle human instinct, the crude sense for other people's pains and pleasures that had, on his showing, to his so great humiliation, been found an inadequate outfit for the successful conduct of the coal, the commission, the insurance and, as a last resort, desperate and disgraceful, the book-agency business — he really made out that she did n't want to know, or would n't for some little time; that she was decidedly afraid in short, and covertly agitated, and all just because she too, with him, suspected herself dimly in presence of that mysterious "more" than, in the classic phrase, met the eye. They parted accordingly, as if to relieve, till they could recover themselves, the conscious tension of their being able neither to hang back with grace nor to advance with glory; but flagrantly full, at the same time, both of the recognition that they could n't in such a place avoid each other even if they had desired it, and of the suggestion that they would n't desire it, after such subtlety of communion, even were it to be thought of.

Abel Taker, till dinner-time, turned over his little adventure and extracted, while he hovered and smoked and mused, some refreshment from the impression the subtlety of communion had left with him. Mrs. Vanderplank was his senior by several years, and was neither fair nor slim nor "bright" nor truly, nor

even falsely, elegant, nor anything that Sue had
taught him, in her wonderful way, to associate with
the American woman at the American woman's best
— that best than which there was nothing better, as
he had so often heard her say, on God's great earth.
Sue would have banished her to the wildest waste of
the unknowable, would have looked over her head
in the manner he had often seen her use — as if she
were in an exhibition of pictures, were in front of
something bad and negligible that had got itself
placed on the line, but that had the real thing, the
thing of interest for those who *knew* (and when did n't
Sue know?) hung above it. In Mrs. Magaw's presence everything would have been of more interest
to Sue than Mrs. Magaw; but that consciousness
failed to prevent his feeling the appeal of this inmate
much rather confirmed than weakened when she reappeared for dinner. It was impressed upon him,
after they had again seated themselves side by side,
that she was reaching out to him indirectly, guardedly,
even as he was to her; so that later on, in the garden,
where they once more had their coffee together — it
might have been so free and easy, so wildly foreign,
so almost Bohemian — he lost all doubt of the wisdom of his taking his plunge. This act of resolution
was not, like the other he had risked in the morning,
an upward flutter into fiction, but a straight and
possibly dangerous dive into the very depths of truth.
Their instinct was unmistakeably to cling to each
other, but it was as if they would n't know where to
take hold till the air had really been cleared. Actually, in fact, they required a light — the aid prepared

by him in the shape of a fresh match for his cigarette after he had extracted, under cover of the scented dusk, one of his cards from his pocket-book.

"There I honestly am, you see — Abel F. Taker; which I think you ought to know." It was relevant to nothing, relevant only to the grope of their talk, broken with sudden silences where they stopped short for fear of mistakes; but as he put the card before her he held out to it the little momentary flame. And this was the way that, after a while and from one thing to another, he himself, in exchange for what he had to give and what he gave freely, heard all about "Mattie" — Mattie Magaw, Mrs. Vanderplank's beautiful and high-spirited daughter, who, as he learned, found her two names, so dreadful even singly, a combination not to be borne, and carried on a quarrel with them no less desperate than Sue's quarrel with — well, with everything. She had, quite as Sue had done, declared her need of a free hand to fight them, and she was, for all the world like Sue again, now fighting them to the death. This similarity of situation was wondrously completed by the fact that the scene of Miss Magaw's struggle was, as her mother explained, none other than that uppermost walk of "high" English life which formed the present field of Mrs. Taker's operations; a circumstance on which Abel presently produced his comment. "Why if they're after the same thing in the same place, I wonder if we shan't hear of their meeting."

Mrs. Magaw appeared for a moment to wonder too. "Well, if they do meet I guess we'll hear. I will say for Mattie that she writes me pretty fully. And I presume," she went on, "Mrs. Taker keeps *you* posted?"

"No," he had to confess — "I don't hear from her in much detail. She knows I back her," Abel smiled, "and that's enough for her. 'You be quiet and I'll let you know when you're wanted' — that's her motto; I'm to wait, wherever I am, till I'm called for. But I guess she won't be in a hurry to call for me" — this reflexion he showed he was familiar with. "I've stood in her light so long — her 'social' light, outside of which everything is for Sue black darkness — that I don't really see the reason she should ever want me back. That at any rate is what I'm doing — I'm just waiting. And I did n't expect the luck of being able to wait in your company. I could n't suppose — that's the truth," he added — "that there was another, anywhere about, with the same ideas or the same strong character. It had never seemed to be possible," he ruminated, "that there could be any one like Mrs. Taker."

He was to remember afterwards how his companion had appeared to consider this approximation. "Another, you mean, like my Mattie?"

"Yes — like my Sue. Any one that really comes up to her. It will be," he declared, "the first one I've struck."

"Well," said Mrs. Vanderplank, "my Mattie's remarkably handsome."

"I'm sure —! But Mrs. Taker's remarkably handsome too. Oh," he added, both with humour and with earnestness, "if it was n't for that I would n't trust her so! Because, for what she wants," he developed, "it's a great help to be fine-looking."

"Ah it's always a help for a lady!" — and Mrs. Magaw's sigh fluttered vaguely between the expert and the rueful. "But what is it," she asked, "that Mrs. Taker wants?"

"Well, she could tell you herself. I don't think she'd trust me to give an account of it. Still," he went on, "she *has* stated it more than once for my benefit, and perhaps that's what it all finally comes to. She wants to get where she truly belongs."

Mrs. Magaw had listened with interest. "That's just where Mattie wants to get! And she seems to know just where it is."

"Oh Mrs. Taker knows — you can bet your life," he laughed, "on that. It seems to be somewhere in London or in the country round, and I dare say it's the same place as your daughter's. Once she's there, as I understand it, she'll be all right; but she has got to get there — that is to be seen there thoroughly fixed and photographed, and have it in all the papers — first. After she's fixed, she says, we'll talk. We *have* talked a good deal: when Mrs. Taker says 'We'll talk' I know what she means. But this time we'll have it out."

There were communities in their fate that made his friend turn pale. "Do you mean she won't want you to come?"

"Well, for me to 'come,' don't you see? will be for me to come to life. How can I ccme to life when I've been as dead as I am now?"

Mrs. Vanderplank looked at him with a dim delicacy. "But surely, sir, I'm not conversing with the remains —!"

"You're conversing with C. P. Addard. *He* may be alive — but even this I don't know yet; I'm just trying him," he said: "I'm trying him, Mrs. Magaw, on you. Abel Taker's in his grave, but does it strike you that Mr. Addard is at all above ground?"

He had smiled for the slightly gruesome joke of it, but she looked away as if it made her uneasy. Then, however, as she came back to him, "Are you going to wait here?" she asked.

He held her, with some gallantry, in suspense. "Are you?"

She postponed her answer, visibly not quite comfortable now; but they were inevitably the next day up to their necks again in the question; and then it was that she expressed more of her sense of her situation. "Certainly I feel as if I must wait — as long as I *have* to wait. Mattie likes this place — I mean she likes it for *me*. It seems the right *sort* of place," she opined with her perpetual earnest emphasis.

But it made him sound again the note. "The right sort to pass for dead in?"

"Oh she doesn't want me to pass for *dead*."

"Then what does she want you to pass for?"

The poor lady cast about. "Well, only for Mrs. Vanderplank."

"And who or what is Mrs. Vanderplank?"

Mrs. Magaw considered this personage, but didn't get far. "She isn't any one in particular, I guess."

"That means," Abel returned, "that she isn't alive."

"She is n't more than *half* alive," Mrs. Magaw conceded. "But it is n't what I *am* — it 's what I 'm passing for. Or rather" — she worked it out — "what I 'm just not. I 'm not passing — I don't, can't here, where it does n't matter, you see — for her mother."

Abel quite fell in. "Certainly — she does n't want to have any mother."

"She does n't want to have *me*. She wants me to lay low. If I lay low, she says —"

"Oh I know what she says" — Abel took it straight up. "It 's the very same as what Mrs. Taker says. If you lie low she can fly high."

It kept disconcerting her in a manner, as well as steadying, his free possession of their case. "I don't feel as if I *was* lying — I mean as low as she wants — when I talk to you so." She broke it off thus, and again and again, anxiously, responsibly; her sense of responsibility making Taker feel, with his braver projection of humour, quite ironic and sardonic; but as for a week, for a fortnight, for many days more, they kept frequently and intimately meeting, it was natural that the so extraordinary fact of their being, as he put it, in the same sort of box, and of their boxes having so even more remarkably bumped together under Madame Massin's *tilleuls*, should n't only make them reach out to each other across their queer coil of communications, cut so sharp off in other quarters, but should prevent their pretending to any real consciousness but that of their ordeal. It was Abel's idea, promptly enough expressed to Mrs. Magaw, that they ought to get something out of it; but when he had said that a few times over (the first time she had met it in silence), she finally replied, and in a manner that he thought quite sublime: "Well, we *shall* — if they do all they want. We shall feel we've helped. And it is n't so *very* much to do."

"You think it is n't so very much to do — to lie down and die for them?"

"Well, if I don't hate it any worse when I'm really dead —!" She took herself up, however, as if she had skirted the profane. "I don't say that if I did n't *believe* in Mat—! But I do believe, you see. That's where she *has* me."

"Oh I see more or less. That's where Sue has *me.*"

Mrs. Magaw fixed him with a milder solemnity. "But what has Mrs. Taker against you?"

"It's sweet of you to ask," he smiled; while it really came to him that he was living with her under ever so much less strain than what he had been feeling for ever so long before from Sue. Would n't he have liked it to go on and on — would n't that have suited C. P. Addard? He seemed to be finding out who C. P. Addard was — so that it came back again to the way Sue fixed things. She had fixed them so that C. P. Addard could become quite interested in Mrs. Vanderplank and quite soothed by her — and so that Mrs. Vanderplank as well, wonderful to say, had lost her impatience for Mattie's summons a good deal more, he was sure, than she confessed. It was from this moment none the less that he began, with a strange but distinct little pang, to see that he could n't be sure of her. Her question had produced in him a vibration of the sensibility that even the long series of mortifications, of publicly proved inaptitudes, springing originally from his lack of business talent, but owing an aggravation of aspect to an absence of nameable "type" of which he had n't been left unaware, was n't to have wholly toughened. Yet it struck him positively as the prettiest word ever spoken to him, so straight a surprise at his wife's dissatisfaction; and he was verily so unused to tributes to his adequacy that this one lingered in the air a moment and seemed almost to create a possibility. He wondered, honestly, what she could see in him, in whom Sue now at last saw really less than nothing; and his fingers instinctively moved to his moustache, a corner of which he twiddled up again, also wondering if it were perhaps only *that* — though Sue had as good as told him that the undue flourish of this feature but brought out to her view the insignificance of all the rest of him. Just to hang in the iridescent ether with Mrs. Vanderplank, to whom he was n't insignificant, just for them to sit on there together, protected, indeed positively ennobled, by their loss of identity, struck him as the foretaste of a kind of felicity that he had n't in the past known enough about really to miss it. He appeared to have become aware that he should miss it quite sharply, that he would find how he had already learned to, if she should go; and the very sadness of his apprehension quickened his vision of what would work with her. She would want, with all the roundness of her kind, plain eyes, to see Mattie fixed — whereas he 'd be hanged if he was n't willing, on his side, to take Sue's elevation quite on trust. For the instant, however, he said nothing of that; he only followed up a little his acknowledgement of her having touched him. "What you ask me, you know, is just what I myself was going to ask. What has Miss Magaw got against *you?*"

"Well, if you were to see her I guess you'd know."

"Why I should think she'd like to show you," said Abel Taker.

"She doesn't so much mind their *seeing* me — when once she has had a look at me first. But she doesn't like them to hear me — though I don't talk so very much. Mattie speaks in the real English style," Mrs. Magaw explained.

"But ain't the real English style not to speak at all?"

"Well, she's having the best kind of time, she writes me — so I presume there must be some talk in which she can shine."

"Oh I've no doubt at all Miss Magaw *talks!*" — and Abel, in his contemplative way, seemed to have it before him.

"Well, don't you go and believe she talks too much," his companion rejoined with spirit; and this it was that brought to a head his prevision of his own fate.

"I see what's going to happen. You only want to go to her. You want to get your share, after all. You'll leave me without a pang."

Mrs. Magaw stared. "But won't you be going too? When Mrs. Taker sends for you?"

He shook, as by a rare chance, a competent head. "Mrs. Taker won't send for me. I don't make out the use Mrs. Taker can ever have for me again."

Mrs. Magaw looked grave. "But not to enjoy your seeing — ?"

"My seeing where she has come out? Oh that won't be necessary to *her* enjoyment of it. It would be well enough perhaps if I could see without being seen; but the trouble with me — for I'm worse than you," Abel said — "is that it does n't do for me either to be heard *or* seen. I have n't got *any* side — !" But it dropped; it was too old a story.

"Not any possible side at all?" his friend, in her candour, doubtingly echoed. "Why what do they want over there?"

It made him give a comic pathetic wail. "Ah to know a person who says such things as that to me, and to have to give her up — !"

She appeared to consider with a certain alarm what this might portend, and she really fell back before it. "Would you think I'd be able to give up Mattie?"

"Why not — if she's successful? The thing you would n't like — *you* would n't, I'm sure — would be to give her up if she should find, or if you should find, she was n't."

"Well, I guess Mattie will be successful," said Mrs. Magaw.

"Ah you're a worshipper of success!" he groaned. "I'd give Mrs. Taker up, definitely, just to remain C. P. Addard with you."

She allowed it her thought; but, as he felt, superficially. "She's your wife, sir, you know, whatever you do."

"'Mine'? Ah but whose? She is n't C. P. Add-ard's."

She rose at this as if they were going too far; yet she showed him, he seemed to see, the first little concession — which was indeed to be the only one — of her inner timidity; something that suggested how she must have preserved as a token, laid away among spotless properties, the visiting-card he had originally handed her. "Well, I guess the one I feel for is Abel F. Taker!"

This, in the end, however, made no difference; since one of the things that inevitably came up between them was that if Mattie had a quarrel with her name her most workable idea would be to get somebody to give her a better. That, he easily made out, was fundamentally what she was after, and, though, delicately and discreetly, as he felt, he did n't reduce Mrs. Vanderplank to so stating the case, he finally found himself believing in Miss Magaw with just as few reserves as those with which he believed in Sue. If it was a question of her "shining" she would indubitably shine; she was evidently, like the wife by whom he had been, in the early time, too provincially, too primitively accepted, of the great radiating substance, and there were times, here at Madame Massin's, while he strolled to and fro and smoked, when Mrs. Taker's distant lustre fairly peeped at him over the opposite mountain-tops, fringing their silhouettes as with the little hard bright rim of a coming day. It was clear that Mattie's mother could n't be expected not to want to see her married; the shade of doubt bore only on the stage of the business at which Mrs. Magaw might safely be let out of the box. Was she to emerge abruptly *as* Mrs. Magaw?—or was the lid simply to be tipped back so that, for a good look, she might sit up a little straighter? She had got news at any rate, he inferred, which suggested to her that the term of her suppression was in sight; and she even let it out to him that, yes, certainly, for Mattie to be ready for her — and she did look as if she were going to be ready — she must be right down sure. They had had further lights by this time moreover, lights much more vivid always in Mattie's bulletins than in Sue's; which latter, as Abel insistently imaged it, were really each time, on Mrs. Taker's part, as limited as a peep into a death-chamber. The death-chamber was Madame Massin's terrace; and — he completed the image — how could Sue *not* want to know how things were looking for the funeral, which was in any case to be thoroughly "quiet"? *The* vivid thing seemed to pass before Abel's eyes the day he heard of the bright compatriot, just the person to go round with, a charming handsome witty widow, whom Miss Magaw had met at Fordham Castle, whose ideas were, on all important points, just the same as her own, whose means also (so that they could join forces on an equality) matched beautifully, and whose name in fine was Mrs. Sherrington Reeve. "Mattie has felt the want," Mrs. Magaw explained, "of some lady, some real lady like that, to go round with: she says she sometimes does n't find it very pleasant going round alone."

Abel Taker had listened with interest — this information left him staring. "By Gosh then, she has struck Sue!"

"'Struck' Mrs. Taker —?"

"She is n't Mrs. Taker now — she's Mrs. Sherrington Reeve." It had come to him with all its force — as if the glare of her genius were, at a bound, high over the summits. "Mrs. Taker's dead: I thought, you know, all the while, she must be, and this makes me sure. She died at Fordham Castle. So we're both dead."

His friend, however, with her large blank face, lagged behind. "At Fordham Castle too — died there?"

"Why she has been as good as *living* there!" Abel Taker emphasised. "'Address Fordham Castle' — that's about all she has written me. But perhaps she died before she went" — he had it before him, he made it out. "Yes, she must have gone as Mrs. Sherrington Reeve. She had to die to go — as it would be for her like going to heaven. Marriages, sometimes, they say, are made up there; and so, sometimes then, apparently, are friendships — that, you see, for instance, of our two shining ones."

Mrs. Magaw's understanding was still in the shade. "But are you sure —?"

"Why Fordham Castle settles it. If she wanted to get where she truly belongs she has got *there*. She belongs at Fordham Castle."

The noble mass of this structure seemed to rise at his words, and his companion's grave eyes, he could see, to rest on its towers. "But how has she become Mrs. Sherrington Reeve?"

"By my death. And also after that by her own. I had to die first, you see, for *her* to be able to — that is for her to be sure. It's what she has been looking for, as I told you — to *be* sure. But oh — she was sure from the first. She knew I'd die off, when she had made it all right for me — so she felt no risk. She simply became, the day I became C. P. Addard, something as different as possible from the thing she had always so hated to be. She's what she always would have liked to be — so why should n't we rejoice for her? Her baser part, her vulgar part, has ceased to be, and she lives only as an angel."

It affected his friend, this elucidation, almost with awe; she took it at least, as she took everything, stolidly. "Do you call Mrs. Taker an angel?"

Abel had turned about, as he rose to the high vision, moving, with his hands in his pockets, to and fro. But at Mrs. Magaw's question he stopped short — he considered with his head in the air. "Yes — now!"

"But do you mean it's her idea to marry?"

He thought again. "Why for all I know she is married."

"With you, Abel Taker, living?"

"But I ain't living. That's just the point."

"Oh you're too dreadful" — and she gathered herself up. "And I won't," she said as she broke off, "help to bury you!"

This office, none the less, as she practically had herself to acknowledge, was in a manner, and before many days, forced upon her by further important information from her daughter, in the light of the true inevitability of which they had, for that matter, been living. She was there before him with her telegram, which she simply held out to him as from a heart too full for words. "Am engaged to Lord Dunderton, and Sue thinks you can come."

Deep emotion sometimes confounds the mind — and Mrs. Magaw quite flamed with excitement. But on the other hand it sometimes illumines, and she could see, it appeared, what Sue meant. "It's because he's so much in love."

"So far gone that she's safe?" Abel frankly asked.

"So far gone that she's safe."

"Well," he said, "if Sue feels it —!" He had so much, he showed, to go by. "Sue *knows*."

Mrs. Magaw visibly yearned, but she could look at all sides. "I'm bound to say, since you speak of it, that I've an idea Sue has helped. She'll like to have her there."

"Mattie will like to have Sue?"

"No, Sue will like to have Mattie." Elation raised to such a point was in fact already so clarifying that Mrs. Magaw could come all the way. "As Lady Dunderton."

"Well," Abel smiled, "one good turn deserves another!" If he meant it, however, in any such sense as that Mattie might be able in due course to render an equivalent of aid, this notion clearly had to reckon with his companion's sense of its strangeness, exhibited in her now at last upheaved countenance. "Yes," he accordingly insisted, "it will work round to that — you see if it does n't. If that's where they were to come out, and they *have* come — by which I mean if Sue has realised it for Mattie and acted as she acts when she does realise, then she can't neglect it in her own case: she 'll just *have* to realise it for herself. And, for that matter, you 'll help her too. You 'll be able to tell her, you know, that you 've seen the last of me." And on the morrow, when, starting for London, she had taken her place in the train, to which he had accompanied her, he stood by the door of her compartment and repeated this idea. "Remember, for Mrs. Taker, that you 've seen the last —!"

"Oh but I hope I have n't, sir."

"Then you 'll come back to me? If you only will, you know, Sue will be delighted to fix it."

"To fix it — how?"

"Well, she 'll tell you how. You 've seen how she can fix things, and that will be the way, as I say, you 'll help her."

She stared at him from her corner, and he could see she was sorry for him; but it was as if she had taken refuge behind her large high-shouldered reticule, which she held in her lap, presenting it almost as a bulwark. "Mr. Taker," she launched at him over it, "I 'm afraid of you."

"Because I 'm dead?"

"Oh sir!" she pleaded, hugging her morocco defence. But even through this alarm her finer thought came out. "Do you suppose I shall go to Fordham Castle?"

"Well, I guess that 's what they 're discussing now. You 'll know soon enough."

"If I write you from there," she asked, "won't you come?"

425

"I'll come as the ghost. Don't old castles always have one?"

She looked at him darkly; the train had begun to move. "I *shall* fear you!" she said.

"Then there you are." And he moved an instant beside the door. "You'll be glad, when you get there, to be able to say —" But she got out of hearing, and, turning away, he felt as abandoned as he had known he should — felt left, in his solitude, to the sense of his extinction. He faced it completely now, and to himself at least could express it without fear of protest. "Why certainly I'm dead."

The Riverside Press
PRINTED BY H. O. HOUGHTON & CO.
CAMBRIDGE, MASS.
U. S. A.